**Also available from Paris Wynters**

*Hearts Unleashed*
*Issued*
*Matched*
*Love on the Winter Steppes*

**Coming soon from Paris Wynters**

*Assigned*

# CALLED INTO ACTION

PARIS WYNTERS

Recycling programs for this product may not exist in your area.

ISBN-13: 978-1-335-60084-4

Called into Action



This edition published by arrangement with Harlequin Books S.A.

For questions and comments about the quality of this book, please contact us at CustomerService@Harlequin.com.

Carina Press
22 Adelaide St. West, 40th Floor
Toronto, Ontario M5H 4E3, Canada
www.CarinaPress.com

**Printed in U.S.A.**

# CALLED INTO ACTION

# *Chapter One*

*Penelope*

A whiff of damp leaves filled Penelope's nose as she inhaled and sank back, exhausted, against a thick elm trunk. The air was crisp and invigorating with the recent rain, the pale sunshine adding freshness as it reflected off the wet leaves. The weather was so perfect. Unlike her life, which was currently in a state of upheaval thanks to her ex.

*Damn you, Trevor.*

It was tough enough working for Tío Enrique's construction company. People assumed she'd been promoted because she was family. But she'd put in the time and done the work because she wanted to get the promotion on merit, or else she didn't want it at all. Only her pendejo ex-boyfriend stole the promotion right out from under her.

A muscle in her jaw ticked.

On top of everything else, having to see his smug face at work right now was too much, so Penelope decided to take a break to clear her head and do something just for herself. Which had led her to this idyllic state park in Vermont.

Penelope pushed off the elm, glanced at her Audi, and groaned. Her dog was perched in the backseat, slobbering all over the window. The usual. Havoc always had to keep an eye on her, even when sleeping. There was nothing creepier than waking up to the serious stare of a large male German shepherd mere inches from her face. And right now, she could have sworn her exuberant dog was smiling at her, his long tongue dangling out the side of his mouth.

She'd worked so hard for little perks, like being able to afford leasing this car, and had hoped that her dedication would pay off. She closed her eyes and took a long centering breath.

*Focus on the positives.*

At least she had leather seats. And Havoc. She rolled her shoulders, knowing she couldn't have asked for a better partner for her search and rescue plans.

Somehow, her ex had hated Havoc. Enough so that the total annihilation of their relationship had nothing to do with jobs or sex or money. Rather, it had to do with the dog and a pair of shoes. Almighty Ferragamo shoes to be exact.

Honestly, unwanted dog behavior was almost always the human's fault. A dog couldn't chew what he couldn't find. Penelope had imparted that particular bit of wisdom every time she found one of her ex's stupid loafers in the middle of the floor. He couldn't blame a dog for being a dog. But he had, giving her the ultimatum of him or Havoc.

She chose Havoc.

He was not only her partner, but her best friend. Okay, so Havoc actually tied for the role with her father. Even when in grade school, she'd always considered

Papá her confidant. And that relationship continued through adulthood and only got stronger when her mother died.

A sharp bark from the backseat caught her attention. The Havoc-needs-to-use-the-bathroom-now bark that meant if she didn't let him out fast, those leather seats were going to require more than a slobber wipe-down.

The moment she opened the door, Havoc bounded out, racing into the field like a bullet. At two years old, he still bounced with puppy exuberance and was stubborn as hell. But he was exactly what she always wanted. A true working dog.

She pulled out her phone to check the time as Havoc burned off some energy. Another two and a half hours to kill.

When Penelope had pulled into the driveway at the duplex in town where she'd be staying, Mrs. Dubczek, the stout and rosy-cheeked housekeeper, was still in the middle of scouring already-clean floors, fitting the bed and bathroom with fresh sheets and towels, vacuuming, and generally applying her personal brand of spit and polish to the already immaculate unit. The gray-haired woman had cast her most powerful malocchio at Havoc, but the dog seemed impervious to her evil eye curse and promptly licked her face.

So, Penelope had dropped off one suitcase and escaped the bustling—and exceedingly chatty—Mrs. Dubczek to take Havoc to the state park.

And what a slice of paradise it turned out to be.

Penelope was familiar with autumn colors, but this park was beautiful. Too bad in her rush to beat traffic, she'd forgotten to pack her DSLR camera. Havoc's sable coat against the red, yellow, and brown leaves would've made for some stunning pictures.

At least she had her phone. It just wasn't the same. Lighting is a critical aspect of photography, and like most smartphones, hers had an LED flash instead of the preferred Xenon the digital camera had. The phone's flash just wasn't bright enough, nor could it cover large areas, which was important for when it came to taking photos of wildlife.

But she hadn't driven to Vermont for vacation, nor was it her first choice for her Search and Rescue K-9 Air Scent handler evaluation. She wasn't used to the landscape, but it was the only place she could find someone to evaluate her this month since she refused to wait any longer. So, she took some time off work and drove up to Maple Falls a couple of days early to get a feel for the topography without needing to rely on her GPS. Part of the evaluation would require her to explain her location on a map based on identifying at least three landmarks by sight. Etching landmarks into her mind would be vital. Just like it had been to pass her basic land searcher certification.

Only where she tested in New York was basically flat, so there wasn't much to memorize.

She'd white-knuckled the steering wheel until the moment she'd arrived in the southern Vermont town. The place was gorgeous, full of charming local businesses with old-fashioned Victorian architecture set against a beautiful backdrop of brown, gold, orange, and red. The townspeople had already started decorating for the holidays with pumpkins, hay bales, and mums. Not to mention the vastly forested landscape. The aura of the town relaxed her instantly.

She giggled as Havoc attempted to chase a chipmunk up a tree and stretched her arms over her head, taking in more of her surroundings. In contrast to the careful landscaping of the picnic area, to her left sat a dilapidated building, barely hanging on, close to the main trail leading off into the forest. The roof shingles were worn and missing in a couple of places, and the siding appeared to suffer from some wood rot, visible in the many bare areas where the decades-old paint had peeled away. Cardboard and packing tape held one of the broken windowpanes together. Penelope inched closer to read the "closed" sign on the door, which included an opening date about a month away. Penelope shook and waved her arms. Damned cobwebs were everywhere. Hopefully, the poor sucker who had to sit in this thing would at least get some hazard pay. A strong gust of wind would bring the whole place down.

She turned away from the building. If she wanted to see urban decay, she could head back to New York where even the garden view outside her office was tainted by reflective metallic structures. Hell, it wouldn't take much to get used to seeing only trees and colorful flowers.

Penelope walked a couple of feet toward the trail and knelt in the grass to take a photo of freshly bloomed stonecrop flowers. The tiny maroon blossoms grouped together to form clouds of sweet-smelling blooms. Breathing in their fragrance, she recalled the roof garden of an office building in New York she'd visited once during a work conference. She'd found the same flowers there.

A big-bellied thrush landed a few feet away and posed, proudly sticking out his chest. She laughed and snapped a few pictures, a rush of warmth filling her chest. She hadn't spent much time solely on photography in more than a year, her time mostly devoted to attempting to balance work, SAR, and a relationship. Boy, did she miss it, and kicked herself harder for not bringing the professional camera.

The thrush, who now perched on a log, cocked its head, staring at her with wide jeweled eyes, then puffed its chest out again. Penelope laughed. "Yes, I can take more pictures of you, gorgeous."

She looked up and glanced around to find Havoc sniffing around the check station. He paced back and forth, the distance he traveled gradually shortening before his spine curled. Penelope stood and headed back toward the car to grab a poop bag. As she reached over the console, she grimaced. Sitting on the floor behind the passenger seat was the damn box of ex-boyfriend crap she'd forgotten to throw out in her haste to beat city traffic.

Her fingers dug into the console. Just the sight of the box made her mad. Her dog! He'd demanded that she get rid of Havoc! Like, what, she should just dump Havoc at the shelter, over a stupid shoe? To think, all of the time she'd wasted on someone like that. Her temples pounded, and her blood pressure rose. And yeah, maybe her chest ached a little too at seeing the physical reminders of her failed relationship. All of those knickknacks, snapshots, and mushy, cornball cards, from an ass who never appreciated or understood her. She glared through a watery gaze at the ratty teddy bear with the bright pink and black button eyes that he won for her on a carnival date. With an eye on Havoc, she picked up the box—pink bear and all—and carried it to a painted red picnic table close to the old building.

Havoc chased a less savvy thrush and barked when it took flight.

"Havoc, no."

He stopped and turned to face her, cocking one forepaw and holding it up—the way he always did when he wasn't sure. His dark ears twitched as he turned his head in the direction where the bird disappeared. But he looked back and slowly took a few steps toward her, paws crunching the leaves.

"Good boy."

The fading late afternoon sunlight reflected off a piece of green plastic in the grass. The tiny object blended in so well she wouldn't have noticed it if the shiny surface and little silver cap wouldn't have caught the light at just the right angle.

It was a sign, one she wasn't about to ignore.

She stood and walked over to pick up the discarded cigarette lighter. As her hand closed around it, she took a quick second to thank God no one was around to read her mind.

Some things didn't need an audience—and cleansing herself of Trevor once and for all was one of them. She picked up the box and walked over to one of the park's steel grills, emptying the contents of the box into it. She held the lighter, arm halfcocked with indecision. Just like Havoc. *If the lighter ignites, this is the right thing.* If not, she'd find a dumpster and dispose of her ex the old-fashioned way.

Moment of truth. With a single flick of her thumb, a small flame danced to life. Penelope bent down and held the flame against the corner of a playbill until it blackened and caught. A breeze rolled through, and the flame burned across the items.

"Adiós, old life." Penelope took a step back and shoved her hands into her pockets. As she stared, she could have sworn the bear smiled as its plastic-fur face melted away.

Havoc barked, startling her. She turned in time to see him bounding toward her. She sidestepped and placed herself in the dog's path, trying to grab his collar, but he was too quick and cut to the side. "Havoc! Down!"

He dropped to the ground, his eyes locking on the bright flames and the steadily disintegrating pink bear. "No!" Penelope latched onto his collar as he lunged, but she lost her balance and knocked into the grill.

Penelope cringed and Havoc whimpered at the split-second high-pitched grinding sound that cut through the air. Her gaze jerked to the side only to watch as the top of the grill snapped off its rusted post and fell to the ground. A strong gust of wind swirled, sending burning ticket stubs and flaming embers across the roof and front elevation of the wooden shed. Within seconds, the fire burned like a temper, as if the leaping inferno was fueled by a terrible anger toward the world—the same fury that had churned inside her.

"No!"

Her fingers curled tighter around Havoc's collar as terror swelled throughout every cell in her body. Her mouth hung open, her throat so dry she couldn't scream. When Havoc barked, she blinked as if coming to from a trance. Her head jerked from side to side as she took in the scene. "No, no, no!"

She snatched her phone from her pocket, thumb

trembling as she punched in the unlock code. One bar of service! But it was enough.

"911, what's your emergency?"

"My name is Penelope Ramos, and there's a fire! I'm at some state park. I don't know which one. It's about, uh, I don't know, maybe twenty minutes west of Maple Falls. The building here is on fire, and it's going up so fast, I don't know what to do!"

*And I set it, but you can arrest me later.*

The dispatcher asked a series of questions, probably to help keep her calm, but not being able to answer most of them only amplified her anxiety. As they continued their backward game of testing what Penelope didn't know, she put Havoc in the car. He whimpered, doggy-smile gone, ears flattened sideways.

Penelope paced as she waited for help to come, her fingers curling and uncurling against the seams running down the outside of her jeans.

Carajo.

This was bad. Epically stupid, even. A fire. In a state park. With trees. And wind. She forced back tears, but her throat tightened, and she leaned against the car for support.

Minutes that felt like hours later, sirens blared in the distance. The first responders pulled up on the grass, hopped out, and started working to contain the blaze. Penelope watched in horror as the firefighters sprayed water onto the burning building, but the flames prevailed. She'd started a forest fire all because she'd wanted to burn everything her ex-boyfriend had ever given her. Penelope fell to her knees, sobs shaking her shoulders.

She was completely alone, and an arsonist. She'd never pass the search and rescue evaluation now.

# *Chapter Two*

*Jay*

In all the days of his life, Jay had always become uneasy around crying women. At even the hint of a sniffle, his body seized, rendering him unable to provide anything remotely resembling comfort. Maybe it was due to his grandmother never shedding a tear—none that he ever saw at least. Or maybe it was because the first time he'd seen a girl cry was when he bumped into Jenna Smith and caused her to drop her ice cream cone at the first-grade picnic. Man, so many of his classmates had been angry at him for such an innocent accident. Either way, it was one of the many things his ex-wife, Karen, told him to work on. Apparently, he hadn't made much progress because the woman clinging to him while sobbing right now was making him all kinds of uncomfortable.

He shot another longing look at where his buddies wrestled with hoses to get the flames under control. Black smoke billowed up into the sky. The heat of the flames wiped out the cool breeze and warmed his skin uncomfortably while an acrid, burning aroma tingled his nose and throat. He itched to help fight the fire, something that was impossible given the brunette currently latched to his side.

Jay frowned down at the top of her shaking head. Did he pat her head? Her shoulder? Detach himself and hide? Since none of those seemed appropriate, he continued to stand stiffly and scanned the otherwise deserted stretch of park in search of clues. How could this have happened? Yeah, the day was windy and the building was old, but it had rained recently and there were no campers in this part of the park.

Maybe the woman saw something or someone? Not to mention asking her a few questions might snap her out of drenching the entire front of his ranger uniform.

"Did you see anyone else around?" he asked, but she was crying too hard to even hear him. He repeated himself to no avail. Time for a new tactic.

He rubbed her shoulder, consciously making sure he wasn't crossing a boundary even if she was burrowing against his chest crying. Crazy how perfectly she fit against him, like two matching puzzle pieces. He tensed at the thought and refocused on calming her down. "Shhh, you're gonna be okay." He pitched his usual baritone several octaves higher than normal, like his grandma used to do to calm his nerves during severe thunderstorms. But, Christ, he sounded like a tool instead of a sympathetic individual. He cleared his throat and tried again. "What's your name?"

"P-P-Penelope," the woman choked out.

Jay sighed, softening a little. She was probably in shock. "I bet that must have been real scary, going for a stroll in the park and then coming across a fire. It's going to be okay, though. The flames were contained to the building."

He glanced back over at the building in question, except there was nothing left beyond dark smoke, a few dying flames, and the gunshot pops of crackling wood. He struggled to keep his growing despair in check. The fire didn't make it to the trees, but it had destroyed the check station, burning the structure and everything inside like a bonfire set with gasoline. The check station where he'd stored the GPS watches, laptops, and software for his Stay Safe program, all the expensive technology he meant to use to keep the hunters safe this season.

Everything. Gone. A total loss.

He'd worked so hard on his plan to implement the Stay Safe program, in hopes that its success would lead to government approval for expansion to benefit other residents in need. Like people with Alzheimer's and autism.

And Parkinson's, like his grandfather.

Now what the hell were they going to do?

His jaw clenched and he dropped his head, visualizing his breaths coming in calmer, steadier inhales. His gaze connected with a pair of wide green eyes framed with spiky eyelashes. The woman's sobs had subsided, and this was the first time her face had appeared from behind her hands. Despite his worry, despite everything going on around them, he felt the impact like a punch in the gut. Because even tear-streaked and sniffling, she took his breath away.

"I'm so sorry," she said between sniffles. "I didn't think…didn't mean to…the embers just…"

Jay didn't register her words right away, too caught up in studying her face up close. In the slight upturn of her nose, to her full lips, and high cheekbones. But when he did, adrenaline flooded him anew. He separated their bodies with surgical precision as he stepped back in horror, his jaw going slack. No way he'd heard her right. No way had she just admitted what he thought she did. "Wait. *You* started the fire? You did this?"

What kind of a cosmic joke was this? That this same woman he'd been feeling sorry for had destroyed his entire project? Had burned everything he'd worked so hard to implement these past two years to the ground, and then had the nerve to cry about it and use him as her sobbing post? And yeah, maybe it was neither here nor there because arsonists came in all varieties, but damned if it didn't upset him even more that he'd never even suspected her.

A sour taste filled his mouth. Sure, it had felt good to hold her, and a part of him still wanted to comfort her. But at the end of the day she destroyed state property and a project that was important to him and the community. He ground his molars. Just like him to take interest in someone who'd destroy his world.

Karen was enough for one lifetime. Taught him a valuable lesson.

Jay pulled out his handcuffs, and her green eyes widened to an anime kind of degree as she stepped back, her gaze bouncing between her car and the handcuffs. "What are you doing?"

"Arresting you for arson."

Defying the laws of nature, her eyes somehow managed to get even bigger. "It was an accident. Not arson."

His jaw ticked, unsure if he believed her or not. But at this precise moment, he didn't much care. "You set a fire in a state park."

Jay reached for her wrist to snap the cuffs on, but she

yanked away before he could touch her. She scrambled back a step, shaking her head back and forth. "In one of the grills!" she yelled on the edge of hysteria. "I started a fire in one of the grills! That's what they're there for, right? And then I tripped and bumped it, and the st-stupid thing," she hiccupped, "broke apart and fell."

A yip cut through the air, and he turned, spotting the large, perky ears of a German shepherd. Of course there was a dog. Because his day didn't suck enough. "Is he yours?"

The woman—Penelope, he mentally corrected—wiped her eyes and nodded.

All he had was her word right now. She could be lying about how the fire started, or she could be telling the truth. He wouldn't know until the report came in. His throat tightened when he thought about the people who would be in more danger than necessary without his safety program in effect. Maybe Penelope, with the fancy Audi, had the funds to pay for everything she'd destroyed. God, he hoped that were the case. "Get your dog."

"Thank you."

Her subdued voice soothed some of his residual anger. At least she was cooperative. For now, he'd take whatever small favors he could get. He trailed closely behind her as they walked to her fancy SUV. *City folk.* Anyone up in these parts wouldn't have used the grill. They would've known how dry the past summer had been. But city folk only visited his town as if to show off to their friends a new place they *found.* As if Maple Falls was some hidden, undiscovered place. He ran his fingers through his hair as he waited, trying not to worry about Gramps's fall this morning.

Was his Parkinson's progressing?

Of course it was. There was no cure. But how much longer would Gramps be able to live independently? Jay groaned inwardly. That was a conversation he dreaded even more than having to comfort a sobbing woman.

But in time Gramps would develop dementia. Maybe sooner than later since Jay already started noticing Gramps's memory loss. Which was why the Stay Safe program was so personal to him. The GPS trackers would help keep Gramps safe if he wandered off into the forest that surrounded their small town.

Now this *Penelope* had destroyed that option.

Speaking of, how long did it take to snap a leash on a dog?

"Easy, boy," Penelope said when the dog barked as she let him out, her voice surprisingly calm. She opened the front side door and grabbed her bag before closing all doors and locking the car. She returned, shoulders sagging, with the dog at her side. "Ready."

Jay grunted and turned on his heels, leading the way to his truck. "Why are you up this way?"

"Weekend getaway," she said quietly. "I'm staying at a duplex in town."

Jay snorted. "Yeah. Not anymore."

He looked over his shoulder to find the woman evaluating him, as if judging him then finding him lacking. He bristled. Ridiculous! He cracked his knuckles, muscles quivering. This woman put so many people at risk, yet she was acting like *she* had a right to feel put upon because it was his job—and, okay, right now, his pleasure—to arrest the seemingly entitled woman for dangerous and illegal behavior. "What's your full name?" he asked, not because he cared, but because he'd need it for the arrest report.

"Penelope Ramos." She paused as if debating something before lifting her chin. "And I get that I did something wrong, but shouldn't you be a little bit more professional?"

Jay could hardly believe his ears. *Professional?* Oh, forget *seemingly*. This woman definitely thought she was entitled, even after burning down part of a state park. His pulse rate jacked up to the point he could feel each thump in his neck.

Not good. Some stranger shouldn't get the best of him.

Jay counted to ten silently before replying, and was pleasantly surprised at how steady his voice came out. "You could have burned this whole place to the ground. It was irresponsible, illegal, and stupid."

That took the wind out of her sails. Penelope's elfin chin wobbled, almost making him feel bad. Almost. She cleared her throat and spoke softly again. "I just meant you shouldn't make fun. That's all."

He chuckled, but the raspy sound held more angst than humor. Stupid knot in his throat. "I wasn't making fun. I was simply pointing out that your weekend getaway is gonna be spent inside county lockup instead of some cushy duplex."

With a huff, she rolled her eyes and increased her gait. "Whatever, Mr. Personality."

Jay blinked, shocked by her attitude once again. People in Maple Falls never acted this way. The community always looked out for one another, helped whenever there was need. He dug his nails into his scalp, scratching.

Penelope wasn't from Maple Falls. She was a visitor. A tourist. And that meant, like many others who came to the small town, they really didn't care about how their actions affected the place.

Jay widened his stride to catch up to her. Hell, the woman could walk fast. When they got to the government-issued green truck, he paused and glanced back at the building one last time. Black smoke mingled with steam from the fire hoses, making one indistinguishable from the other. A fall breeze carried them up, and a gritty mist of soot hung in the air. One of the firefighters held up what looked like a small teddy bear, mostly black but one leg still a bright pink. Jay's muscles tensed. She'd burned a teddy bear. A goddamned teddy bear.

Shaking his head, he turned back toward Penelope Ramos and wrenched the door open. It creaked, groaned, and popped. New truck. Bad roads. Unparalleled wear and tear. The dog jumped into the vehicle without prompting and settled into the middle seat like he'd found his spot and planned on staying. Penelope climbed in, too, but much less gracefully. Jay stifled a laugh when he closed the door, but he could hear Gramps's voice in his head. *Boy, you know better. When it comes to helping a lady, you put your crap aside and you do it because it's the right thing.* He could almost feel the slap to the back of his head.

He was failing on all levels today.

The short drive to the park's main office was silent. Jay snuck a peek at Penelope, resting her head against the window as they passed the station. Her dark brown curls were unruly, and her eyes bloodshot and drifting shut.

Since it would be a twenty-minute ride into town, he flipped on the radio in an attempt to ease the tension in the cab and Creedence Clearwater Revival blasted through in Dolby sound. His fingers tapped along with the drumbeat. But even with John Fogerty's guttural wail and the dog's occasional snores, Penelope continued to stare out the window.

Maybe she regretted her actions. Or was whatever caused her to burn the teddy bear the reason for her melancholy? Jay didn't know, and why he was curious boggled his mind. He sniffed hard to chase the lingering tickle in his nose and focused on the road instead of the woman to his right.

By the time the song ended, they'd pulled in front of the white stone building that acted as the small town's jail and police department. Since most of the crime in Maple Falls was petty, requiring nothing more than an overnight stay, the building only had four cells, two offices, an evidence locker, and a booking area where photos and fingerprints were taken.

Everyone exited the truck and entered the building. Deputy Mason, who looked like late-era Elvis after too many fried peanut butter and banana sandwiches, had his legs up on the front desk when they walked in. He sat up to greet them as if he'd just been caught sleeping on the job.

Jay led Penelope closer to the desk and nodded at the deputy. "Scottie, Ms. Ramos here needs to be processed and sent to lockup overnight."

Scottie raised a confused brow. "DUI?"

"I caused the ranger station to catch fire," Penelope volunteered, surprising him and also Scottie, based on the way the deputy's eyebrows shot up. "Accidentally. But it was still my fault."

Jay felt a flicker of reluctant admiration at her ownership of the blame. Not everyone would be so forthcoming in her situation.

"How did you accidentally start a fire?" Scottie's mouth twisted to one side and Jay bit back a smile. Disbelief definitely didn't make his ugly mug any prettier.

"Well, the fire was on purpose, but the spreading wasn't." She used her thumbs to crack the knuckles of her index fingers and must've found the move interesting since her brows scrunched together when the bones popped in response to the pressure.

"Can you get me the booking paperwork?" Jay was anxious to head back to the park and sign off on reports, as well as see if there was anything he could salvage from inside the check station. His gut told him it wouldn't be much.

"Sure thing, Ranger Gosling." Scottie rummaged through some file folders before handing a stack of papers to Jay. "Now, Ms. Ramos, I'll take your fingerprints and then another officer will take your official statement and bring you to your cell."

"My cell." Penelope blew a stray brown curl of hair out of her face. "I never thought I'd hear those words."

"Shouldn't have started the fire, then." Jay might have sounded as if he was having a lot of fun at her expense, but the truth was, he was devastated. Everything he'd worked for to protect those he cared about had just gone up in smoke.

Penelope breathed out a loud whoosh of breath, not quite a sigh, not quite a gasp, then turned to Scottie, all business. "Do I at least get a phone call? Or is that only in movies?"

"You can call as many people as you want, Ms. Ramos." Scottie glanced from the woman to the dog. "What about that thing?"

"What about him?" Jay jutted his chin at the dog. "Call animal control."

"No!" Penelope wailed—an out-loud, heart-wrenching sound worse than a thousand tears. "Please. Don't put him in a cage."

The dog laid his head on the ground and groaned.

"Aww. Look at him. How can you resist?" Scottie puckered his lips and the baby talk that came out of his mouth wasn't fit for a grown man's voice. "He's so cute. Aren't you, boy? Yes, you are. Yes, you are."

"You like him so much, you take him home." Jay had let the dog ride in the cab of the truck. That was just about all the goodwill he had left in him.

"You know my mom's rules. Nothing comes home that drools more than Dad." Scottie shook his head and shrugged. "Wish I could help."

Jay took another quick look at the woman, then her dog, who gazed up at him with big brown eyes. Ah, damn. It wasn't the dog's fault his owner started a fire. Also not the dog's fault he'd adopted a no-pets-especially-dogs rule. Jay straightened his spine. This wasn't his responsibility. The sheriff could decide the dog's fate, and he could walk away absolved. Yeah. He liked that idea. "Let Charlie decide."

"You know Charlie's going to call animal control," Scottie said.

Jay glanced from the dog to Penelope, indecision tugging at him. Two sets of big hopeful eyes pleaded with him and he blew out an audible breath. She had been through enough stress today, like he had. "Fine. I'll take him to the office. I'm sure Nick will watch him."

Penelope's eyes narrowed as her gaze bounced between him and Scottie. "Who's Nick?"

"My boss. He loves pets." Jay was done answering questions, and he was sure Nick wouldn't mind a dog for a night or two until the judge decided what to do with the firebug. He clicked his tongue against his teeth, and the dog's ears perked. Jay handed the booking forms back to Scottie. "Take care of this for me?"

Scottie nodded and stood, papers in hand. "Miss, you need to come with me. We need to get your statement on record." He walked around the desk and waited, squinting to read Jay's handwriting—and a big fat good luck with that—while Penelope dried her eyes with her thumbs in that sleek way girls who cared about their makeup did.

"Thank you," she said softly, before straightening her shoulders. "But also—know that if anything happens to my dog, I'm going to post your name and face all over social media. You know animal abuse is a federal crime now, right?"

Jay was so offended, he didn't even bother to reply beyond a grunt. What kind of lowlife scum abused dogs? Not him, that was for sure. He just preferred not to have a canine around because it just hurt too much to have one. As if he would be replacing his beloved Zip.

Penelope knelt on the floor in front of the shepherd. The dog whined, big brown eyes closing as Penelope scratched his ears. "Be a good boy. I'll see you tomorrow, buddy."

And despite how turbulent his day had been so far,

Jay found himself struggling not to smile. No matter what he thought of Penelope, her dog really loved her. And he'd always believed dogs had better instincts about people than people had about dogs.

When Penelope finally stood, her eyes glittered with—yep—more tears. Had she not ruined his work and forced a dog on him, Jay would have felt bad for her. Penelope stared at her just-scuffed-enough sneakers, color coming into her cheeks. "His name is Havoc, and please give your boss my thanks for taking him."

Jay took Havoc's leash. "We'll be back first thing in the morning with the judge."

"Back with the judge?" She blinked. "Does that mean I won't go to court?"

"Don't worry. It'll all be on the record. We just don't generally open the courtroom unless we have a regular court day. Tomorrow isn't one of those."

Penelope nodded, biting her lip. He'd find out soon if the fire was truly accidental, but her wide eyes pulled at his heart. And her ferocity in making sure her dog would be safe made him admire her. Jay shook his head, scowling. The last thing he needed was to add Penelope Ramos to his already heaping plate of life challenges. He'd had enough loss in his life, and with his grandfather's declining health, it was only a matter of time before he'd lose another person.

No, he didn't have enough strength to care for someone else. Or their pet.

# *Chapter Three*

*Penelope*

Deputy Scottie Mason took her statement, then brought her to the back of the office. The metal-barred door to a cell straight out of the *Andy Griffith Show*, an old black-and-white comedy her grandma had loved to watch, stood open as if awaiting her grand entrance. The smell of body odor and stale cigarette smoke from years gone by permeated the chilly air. There was nothing redeeming about the place, and Penelope's stomach quivered at the thought of spending the night there.

And some grand entrance it would be. She'd washed off the soot and ash from her face, neck, and arms using a washrag and sink water, but her hair hadn't fared as well and had managed to soak up the smell of smoke as it turned to a frizzy ball on top of her head. Under normal circumstances, she would have consoled herself with a long training session with Havoc, maybe a run, but she sighed. Nowhere to run. And the ranger who'd arrested her had her dog.

She stepped inside the cell, and the metal clank of door against frame thudded through her head. Loud. Obnoxious. Shameful. It mocked her. She hadn't meant to start a fire or burn down the check station. Foolish, yes. Intentional, no. And that was what she would tell the judge. Hopefully, he would listen, unlike the jerk who'd consoled her at first only to slap handcuffs on her as if she'd thrown a box of kittens out the window of a moving car.

Yes, there were some crimes where the reason behind the action didn't matter. But this wasn't the case. And the ranger with the chiseled jaw that looked like it was created by Michelangelo himself should have taken the time to hear her out.

She clutched her stomach, her body beginning to shake. The gray stone walls, barred windows that looked like they hadn't ever opened, and lighting that did nothing more than buzz overhead allowed a darkness to envelop her. Suffocating and heavy. Not that she expected this to be a walk in the park full of sunlight and warmth.

When she was alone, just her, a pillow, and a mattress, she sat on the edge of the bed, bounced once to test it. A plume of dust shot out, and Penelope wafted her hand about as she coughed and smacked her lips to chase the dry particles from her mouth.

Fabu-fucking-losa.

She scooted until her back rested against the wall and pulled her knees to her chest. Her stomach grumbled, and her eyes watered—maybe from the dust, maybe because she was all alone in a jail cell without so much as a blanket. She hadn't eaten since she couldn't remember when and her dog was in the care of un estupido park ranger who had taken a bit too much pleasure in bringing her to jail.

Trevor.

Really, this was all his fault. If he hadn't been such a pendejo in the first place, she never would have felt compelled to burn everything he'd given her. Heck, she wouldn't even have been in that park—or this tiny little town—in the first place.

Thinking of him just made her all kinds of upset and mad again, so she shifted her thoughts to Ranger Gosling.

Tall. Dark. Handsome. Six foot plus of lean muscle, eyes like the most decadent dark chocolate, and the hint of a beard that made her palm itch to touch it. Also, he was surly, grumpy, cranky, crotchety, prickly, sulky, and moody. His personality read like an ill-tempered version of the seven dwarves. But he had taken pity on Havoc and kept him out of animal control, so he couldn't be all bad. Not to mention, those eyes.

She huffed. A book or magazine would have been nice because there was no way she'd be able to fall asleep tonight. Of course, thanks to Mr. Personality, they probably thought she'd light anything in arm's reach on fire, too. Not like she had a match, and they'd taken the lighter for evidence. She rested her forehead against her knees and went over what she could remember from her training manuals.

"The signs for canine bloat include a distended abdomen, dry heaves, and restlessness." Reciting the facts helped her remember, so using this time to talk to herself made sense. "The femoral artery is the best location to take a canine's pulse. Lethargy, labored breathing, pale gums, and elevated heart rate are signs of shock. Agility practice works on canine control." She tried to visualize her flash cards. "Terrain and man-made obstacles affect how scent is carried and distributed by the wind."

Because of the fire, she hadn't managed to scout much of the terrain on the trail. So far, all she'd really managed to see was the inside of the ranger's truck and the inside of the jail. Neither would help on her examination.

Her body grew heavy. So much for achieving her dream, the goal she'd spent the last couple of years working toward. Right now, she needed her phone to email the evaluator or call the office number and let the man know she wouldn't be able to make it. She also needed to use the bathroom.

"Deputy?" When he didn't answer, she tried again. "Deputy Mason?" Mierda. What if he'd gone home, left her till the morning? A second ago, literally, one second, she'd had a mild urge, and now her bladder threatened to burst. "Deputy Mason! Por favor!"

The reassuring jangle of keys as he came down the hall said the man didn't have a speed faster than turtle-slow. Her heart pounded and her bladder demanded attention that required a shuffling dance of one-foot hops and short sidesteps. He stood on the outside of the cell, watching her for a moment before he cocked an eyebrow. "Can I help you?"

"I have to pee."

He nodded and took the ring from his belt. When he swung the door open, he waved her out. "Come on."

The hall, ill-lit and narrow, didn't let her walk beside him, rather a step behind. "Do I get a phone call still?" she spoke to his back.

"You can call." He stopped in front of the bathroom

door. "Don't try crawling out the window. If I have to chase you down, it won't be good for either of us."

She nodded, not really seeing a great escape in her future. "Just have to pee."

Once inside, she glanced up at the window, neither desperate enough nor athletic enough to scale a wall to reach and fit through a window scarcely big enough to let a sliver of light through. All she wanted was her phone and her dog. Since she would only get one of those and it was at the mercy of the deputy waiting outside, she took care of her business, washed her hands, and walked out. "Now, about that phone call…"

Instead of a detour to his desk to retrieve her phone, he led her back to her cell, stopping short so she bumped into him. He smoothed his shirt, hiked up his pants. "Sheriff Hart."

The sheriff, who couldn't have been more than five foot four and maybe a hundred twenty pounds, had an air to the way she held her head. Thumbs tucked into her pockets of her jacket, the sheriff shot a smirk for Mason that made Penelope fold in on herself. This was a woman who knew her power and how to wield it.

"Deputy Mason." The sheriff nodded once. "You're wasting all of our renovation dollars." She pushed off the edge of the cell and crossed her arms. "Didn't spend a lot of money on those new cells for you to keep using this one."

"Just thought I could see her better." Color bled into his cheeks. "In case she needed anything." He lacked conviction and the words ended softer than they began. This was not a man who challenged his boss. Likely not anyone else either.

"Did you offer her food? A clean blanket or pillow?"

She spoke as if her deputy should have offered concierge service. Not that it would have been unappreciated, but jail was hardly a place Penelope would expect pillow fluffing or turndown service.

He could have made her stay much worse, but he'd been polite, kind, even respectful. "He offered me food and drink. And my phone call." Where her loyalty to Deputy Mason came from, she couldn't say, but the words were out so she let them stand.

"Good." The sheriff held up a white bag grease-stained at the side, and it smelled like someone had deep-fried heaven. Penelope's mouth watered. "Come with me."

Sheriff Hart led her to the same room where Deputy Mason had taken her statement. She opened the door and motioned Penelope inside. "Best table in the house." She left the door open and pulled out a chair across from Penelope, then set a burger and an order of fries on the table. "It's not Michelin rated, but"—she shrugged—" you're in jail." Her smile at the end was friendly rather than smug. "Tell me how you managed to burn down our check station. I hear the story's a pretty good one."

Boy, was she going to be disappointed. "Not really."

The sheriff bit into her own burger and wiped her mouth with a napkin. "Gosling was all fired up." She chuckled. "Pardon the pun."

Penelope was tempted to ask if he was always such a colossal grump, but she didn't. She also tried to wipe the memory of how he'd held and attempted to soothe her. How his hand brushed against her arm, the contact creating a different kind of tension within her body. And those muscles hidden under the unflattering tan uniform shirt she'd blubbered into. No point pondering on those memories, not after the way he'd flipped a switch when he found out she'd started the fire. He probably wouldn't bother touching her with a snare pole.

"So, what happened?"

Penelope sighed. "I had a box of my ex's stuff. Found a lighter. Saw a way to exorcize a demon or two. Bumped into the grill, and the wind, burning papers—you can do the math."

Sheriff Hart frowned. "I wouldn't be so flippant about it with the judge. There was a lot of equipment being stored in that check station. Safety equipment that Gosling worked his ass off to get. He's not exactly a social butterfly, and to get the funding, he had to make calls, rub elbows, be human." She took another bite as Penelope let all that sink in.

No wonder he hated her. She closed her eyes, stomach no longer grumbling in hunger. Now it rolled with shame. Having worked with park rangers in New York, she understood how difficult it was to get funding. Sure, the state allocated money, but sometimes it wasn't enough. Even her search and rescue group had to fundraise or pay for their own equipment. The reality was, getting donations was damn near impossible most days.

She narrowed her eyes. Was she making excuses, trying to sympathize with the cute ranger? Even if she could understand why he'd gotten so grumpy, he still should've been more open-minded to the option that the fire could've been an accident. She sat back and crossed her arms. "Who expects a grill to snap off its stand? The thing is supposed to be solid. Made of steel."

"Hate to break it to you but steel rusts, even galvanized steel. Just takes longer and those grills are not brand-new. Look, just state the facts during your hearing. Don't be defensive. Judge Carter likes a good apology. Could save you jail time." Hart finished her burger.

Penelope swallowed hard. "How much jail time?"

"Two years, if he's in a bad mood." She shrugged. "Or a fine. Or some community service. Never really know with Carter. But he's fishing buddies with Jay."

Oh, great. Just great. She was going to the big house. Orange was so not the new black. It would clash with her hair.

Hart nibbled a French fry and nodded at Penelope. "Jay's grandpa and Carter have been best friends since, you know, I doubt anyone in this town really knows."

What had been a low rumble in her stomach morphed into a full-on barrel roll. "You've got to be kidding me."

"Little bit. They do fish together, though." She winked, as if it was of no consequence whether Penelope got the jail time or not.

Penelope was glad she'd given the people of Maple Falls bits for their comedy sketches. A nice story they could tell at parties and those social engagements Jay dreaded and would have to give another go because of her. "What if I pay for the damages?"

"You have a spare hundred grand lying around? And that's just equipment costs. God knows what it'll cost to rebuild the check station." Everything the sheriff said seemed to be matter-of-fact, as if Penelope's future wasn't riding on a judge's good or bad mood and his friendship with a park ranger.

Penelope wanted to roll into a ball the way Havoc did when he was in trouble. She wanted to pretend this day never happened. "I'm screwed."

"Don't be a pessimist. Could be worse."

"How could it possibly be worse?"

The sheriff chuckled. "Jay could be the one handing down your punishment. But you got lucky. Jay isn't a judge, so you get Carter. And if you play your cards close, he won't put it on your record."

Her head reeled. Damn. She hadn't even thought about her record. They wouldn't let her take the test if this put a permanent mark in her file. All the studying, the training, the travel to get here, and everything that happened over the last weeks—everything she'd survived to be here—would all have been for nothing. Her breath came in short gasps, heart pounding in her ears. Was this what a panic attack felt like, or was she in the throes of an honest-to-goodness heart attack?

Sheriff Hart stood and came around the table. She took the bag the food had come in and held it up to Penelope's mouth. "Breathe. In and out." Her voice soothed, along with the hand at Penelope's back keeping time with the number of breaths she wanted Penelope to take.

There were a hundred reasons Penelope couldn't go to jail. Not the least of which was Havoc. He'd come so far from the abandoned and abused pup she'd rescued. No way could he go back to a shelter.

She considered—because she needed a plan B, just in case—everyone she knew as a possible caregiver for her dog. There was certainly no one who would continue his training, so all his hard work would be lost, forgotten. And if that was the only issue, she might have been okay. But everyone she knew was either too old for a dog like him, lived in a no-animals-allowed apartment, or didn't like or want pets.

Maybe she should've spent more time with the search and rescue group back home outside of training. Created friendships with them instead of sharing friends with Trevor. Maybe then she would have had some options.

Her eyes misted as she pulled the bag away from her face and looked up at Sheriff Hart. "What do I do? I can't go to jail. I have a dog dependent on me."

The sheriff walked around to her side of the table and sat, leaned forward on her arms, and folded her hands. "Be honest. Admit what you did and beg for mercy."

Beg? She could do that. In fact, she would damned well get on her hands and knees if that was what it took. Pride, even dignity, had no place in her life after today. Not if it would save Havoc from a barred cage. "Okay."

"And no matter what Jay says, don't react. He's rightfully pissed off, and he isn't the kind of guy who's going to be quiet about it. So, don't lose it in there. And don't cry. Carter will think you're being manipulative to gain sympathy. Keep it together."

Penelope nodded, making a mental checklist.

The sheriff stood and pushed back her chair. "I have to get going, but I'll bring you to the cell you should be in. It has a nicer bed, a sink, and a toilet. You won't need Scott to take you when you have to go." She waited for Penelope to stand, then opened the door. "I put a couple of books in there along with your cell phone."

Penelope nodded, feeling a swell of unexpected gratitude. For being the third person today to want her locked in a cell, Sheriff Hart was much nicer than the others.

She followed behind to a plain wooden door with a small window and a slot where Penelope assumed they would slide a tray of food through to her. "Thank you."

"We just renovated, so the bed is new. No TV, but there's a button on the wall you can push if you need anything. Scott leaves in a few hours, but the night dispatch will answer."

Penelope stepped inside. It smelled like fresh paint and newly sawn lumber. "I should be fine." The concrete floor was newly painted and smooth under her feet.

"I'll be back in the morning with some clothes for you. Get some rest."

Sheriff Hart left and Penelope grabbed her cell. The first email in her inbox was a notification stating her exam had been cancelled. Her heart sank. Of course the evaluator would've found out what she did. Especially in such a small town.

She tossed the phone onto the mattress and glanced around the new cell. Her accommodations were certainly better than she'd expected, but rest might have been optimistic. Or that was what she thought until she lay back on the bed and closed her eyes.

# *Chapter Four*

*Jay*

Jay glanced sideways at the dog as the truck bounced over the gravel road. His markings were beautiful, and if it was possible, the damned thing had soulful eyes full of blame Jay couldn't bear to look at. "Face the front."

If the dog would have howled or yipped in reply, Jay would have been impressed. As it was, Havoc only drooled in response. On the seat. Of his personal truck. Jay winced and sighed. Cleaning the car was one more thing to add to his day. His mood matched the impending rainstorm about to break overhead. It had been a long time since he'd had a canine companion. A companion of any kind, if he was honest.

For a minute today, when he'd first put his arms around Penelope, he'd felt something. A shock. A vibration. A tingling, at least. It had been a while. Too long since he'd had such close contact with another woman. Try as he might, he couldn't help but notice how soft she'd felt, or the way she molded into him. Like God had created her just for him.

He rolled his eyes at such romantic notions.

Okay, maybe he needed a night out. Some female

attention. He went through his mental contact list and came up bone-dry. There was a joke in there somewhere, but after the day he'd had, he didn't have the heart to look for it.

"Dick move to put your owner in jail. On the bright side, you're not going to have to put up with me much longer." The German shepherd looked at Jay before dropping to his belly, head lying on Jay's lap. He gave Havoc a rub between his ears, running his fingers through a well-groomed coat. A couple of shed strands floated on the air in front of him. Remarkably, Havoc didn't smell much like smoke, but more the clean, fresh scent of some shampoo. He was one of the most beautiful creatures Jay had ever seen with his exquisite markings—reddish brown and black and tan that blended to create a stunning fur.

He checked the dog again, only to find those sad eyes staring up at him. "Dude, she burnt down the check station. I had to learn to waltz to get some of that equipment. Do you have any idea how ridiculous I looked suited up, waltzing old Mrs. Kerrigan around a banquet room lit by candles and scented with roses?" Tuxedo. Waltz. Banquet room. Each bullet point hit another note of humiliation. Not to mention he was talking to a dog. "I mean, you don't know me, but I can tell you I was not meant to dance. No Magic Mike money for me. That's why I'm a park ranger."

Not solely true, but Havoc didn't seem to be much of a fact checker. He did have a judgmental look on his face, though. "You would have sold yourself for a check that big, too. Don't think you're better than me. That equipment was going to save lives."

Jay pulled the truck into the parking lot at the office,

his frustration growing again at all that time and money wasted. He was going to push for formal charges against Penelope Ramos. No way should she get to walk away with just a slap on the wrist because the fire was an *accident.* If she was telling the truth, she'd still been negligent. And there had to be consequences. When they brought her in front of Carter in the morning, he would have plenty to say. He wasn't going to allow the judge to be lenient, like everyone from Maple Falls knew Carter could be. Not when Penelope wasn't from the area and therefore would go home without a second thought as to the damage she'd caused.

Jay slid out of the truck and patted his leg. Havoc came to stand beside him. He took two steps. The dog took two steps. He moved to the side, the dog sidestepped, leaving one hand length between their bodies. Jay walked to the stairs and stopped. The dog matched his moves.

He could add well-trained to well-cared-for.

He scolded his heart when, once again, it threatened to soften. So what if she trained her dog? That alone didn't make her a good person. Hell, he'd cared about a dog once, more than he cared for the people in his life. And look where it got him. A wave of nausea washed over him as he clenched his teeth. Besides, a trained dog didn't get him any closer to his goal of helping the local community, especially those who were at risk of getting lost in the woods.

Like Gramps.

*Neither did sending Penelope to jail,* a little voice in his head whispered. He scowled. Maybe not, but damned if a little justice wouldn't at least be satisfying. It was just one night in jail, and in one of the newly renovated cells.

He took a deep breath and strode into the office to find Nick behind a small desk, muttering in Greek, papers spread from one corner of the room to the other. Or maybe the desk just looked small because Nick wasn't. Behind the desk, the state flag stood on a pole next to a picture of the president and the American flag on the other side. Typical government office. The air was dry and chilly since Nick loved his air-conditioning, and when Havoc strolled in, each dirty paw sent paper fluttering. The wag of his tail disrupted more. Nick stood, his muttering now a shout.

Nickos Karalis, Jay's boss, had a temper, and by the strain around his eyes and downturn of his mouth, he'd already run the numbers for today's losses. When Jay grabbed a sheet of paper from beneath Havoc's paw, he found the evidence.

"Why is all of this on the floor?"

"Because the fire marshal has the conference room on lockdown to prepare his report," Nick barked back.

*Conference room* was a generous description for one white folding table and three chairs in a room that used to be the break room before the fridge went out. The great state of Vermont decided picnic tables outside were a more cost-effective option than a new refrigerator.

"Prepare his report? Doesn't get much more arson than having a woman admit she set a fire."

Havoc turned in a circle, seeming to chase his tail, and Nick shouted again as the dog's paws tore holes in his valuable information. Valuable enough he'd left it on the floor, anyway. It took a minute, but Nick snatched up every piece of paper to take back to his desk. "Damnit, Gosling. It took me all day to get this together, and in one minute, you and your mutt destroyed it all." He growled a few more Greek words at the dog, who lay on the now-open carpet space, head up, tongue out, drool falling.

"Not my mutt."

"Don't care."

But he would care when Jay walked out without him. Instead of asking just yet—Nick needed a few cooling-off minutes—Jay picked up another sheet of paper. "What's this for?"

"Judge Carter. He's gonna need to know the extent of the damage." Fire lit Nick's brown eyes. Hell, even his blacker-than-Elvis hair had a spontaneous-combustion glow. "When I think of all the hours I spent signing letters, begging the state and the feds for money, it burns my ass."

Jay could relate. He'd been chafing for a few hours now. "Yeah, well, I had to dance with LuAlice Kerrigan. I have the permanent imprint of her hand on my ass."

Nick glared. "I'm not gonna stand here and compare buttock injuries with you. I'm the boss, and this is all going to blow back on me when I have to go beg for more money."

Nick held up Penelope's background check that he must have fast-tracked. Jay took it and read. Okay credit. Pretty decent income. Savings by no means enough to pay for the lost equipment. And not enough to rebuild the shack. "Damn. Figured her for a trust fund baby. Or someone who had a big fancy job. You know, the type of person who could drop a six-hundred-dollar tip just because."

"Anyone can buy a fancy car. And not everyone from a big city is wealthy." Nick stood and walked around the desk. "I have to drive to Montpelier tomorrow to pick up the hunting permits. Don't know if I'll be here for court. You're gonna have to attend the hearing. And while I need you fired up, I don't need your past working against us."

Jay suppressed an eye roll behind closed lids. If only his boss had witnessed the entitled behavior the woman displayed. But instead of filling Nick in, he had other matters that needed tending to. "I need you to do something for me. Remember those Red Sox tickets I got you for your birthday? You took your dad? Great time was had by all. Remember that?"

Nick cocked his head and twisted his mouth to one side. "Vaguely."

"Well, I did that out of friendship, so you could show your pop a good time on his vacation."

Nick sighed. "Get to what you wanna ask. I don't have time for you to remind me of every single thing you've ever done." He shook his head. "And if I would've known you were holding all this shit back to redeem at a later time, I would have told you to shove your damned Red Sox tickets."

"Playoff Red Sox tickets."

"Uh-huh. Ask."

Jay nodded to the dog. "He needs a place to stay tonight. Naturally, I thought of you and your nurturing spirit, your kinship with all living things, your—"

Nick held up his hand. "Hauling out the big guns." He clicked his tongue against his teeth. "And nice try, but I can't help you." Jay stared, waiting for the excuse. Rebuttal ready. Nick didn't offer one.

"Why not?"

"Lady friend staying at my place. And the way things

are going, I'm not going to want to stop to take out the dog." The eyebrow wiggle was implied.

Oh, come on. He was already taking Nick's place with the judge. The very least his friend could do was take the dog. Especially since Nick was there for everything Jay went through when he lost his partner. "I would do it for you."

Nick chuckled. "Yeah, maybe, but what my date can do for me trumps anything you might do. Just call animal control. The dog isn't our problem."

Jay grunted, raking his hands through his hair. Fuck his life right now. "I already told the woman I would take care of the dog."

Nick continued trying to smooth the papers as he looked up at Jay. "Don't think the dog is going to look very good in lingerie. Sheila, on the other hand, is a masterpiece."

"Come on, Nick. You know what I went through with Zip." Not a story he could think of without losing his breath, without his stomach clenching into a tight fist, without rethinking every single thing about that day. That week.

Nick wavered, his expression softening, but just as quickly, his mouth formed a straight line. "No."

*"Nick."*

Nick held up both hands. "Sorry, Jay. I can't help you. If you don't want the dog to go to animal control, you're going to have to keep it yourself."

A certain amount of pity was expected. Jay had come to understand that mentioning Zip brought it on, and for a while, he'd stopped talking about his former canine partner. But he'd never tried to use it for gain before, and a bolt of shame pumped through his veins.

"Fine." Jay ground his teeth. It was just one night, and the dog could sleep on the porch. "I'll be back in the morning to pick up whatever you want me to take to the judge."

Jay snatched the leash from the floor and immediately Havoc stood, walked beside him to the truck, and climbed into the passenger seat as if they'd been best friends all their lives. As soon as Jay started the car, the dog scooted across to lay his head on Jay's lap.

One night. He could get through one night. And however long it took to get the smell of dog out of his truck. And off his hands. And out of his mind.

"You get that I'm not a dog person anymore, right? So, we need to get the rules straight." Havoc lifted his head as if he understood, and Jay stroked the dog's ear. "Stay off the furniture. My house isn't your bathroom. And you're sleeping on the screen porch."

But after three hours, the damned genius dog had somehow managed to whimper, cry, and pace enough to yank Jay's heartstrings. And the damned thing snored. Jay shoved the dog away and flopped back against the pillow. "Jesus. Get on your own damned pillow."

Since only one of them would be getting any sleep, Jay went over what he would say to the judge. His mind whipped with words like *careless disregard* and *financial devastation to the safety program*. When he closed his eyes, he could smell the fire, see the flames licking the side of the building.

The fire Penelope had started.

What if his grandfather had been in the building, waiting for him as he'd done in the past when Jay had to go check on a hiker or hunter? And if Gramps had one of his memory lapses that prevented him from getting out of the building, like how he'd forgotten how to unlock the bathroom door last week, the old man might've died in the fire.

The dog laid its head on his chest and Jay was grateful for the momentary distraction. "Seriously. You need a breath mint." But the familiar weight and the paw over his gut was too much. He threw the blanket back and shifted from beneath the dog.

As the coffee brewed, he leaned against the counter and peered out the window. Gramps's house was still dark. At least the old man was asleep. Jay snorted, hoping Penelope lay awake. Would be penance for making a mess of everything he worked for. Not to mention how unfair it would be if he was the only one who remained awake most of the night because of the incident.

But damned if he could concentrate on anything other the memory of those pleading emerald eyes.

# *Chapter Five*

## *Penelope*

Despite being in a strange town in a strange bed while Havoc stayed God only knew where, Penelope had slept as if she didn't have a care in the world. That peace was over now. From the narrow window above her bed, sunlight streamed in, and by the direction of the rays, it was long past dawn. Even if she'd been in a windowless room, her bladder would have let her know how late in the morning it was. Or her growling stomach. And only one of those things required immediate attention because if she ate anything right now, it'd probably come right back up.

She might be going to jail. All over an impulsive exorcism by lighter and a decrepit old grill.

After using the bathroom, she sat on the bed thinking. About everything. Havoc, the fire, the sullen park ranger, and her breakup. Her nostrils flared. If Trevor had been supportive and tried to understand how important search and rescue was, she might not be in this mess. "Like that was the only thing wrong with our relationship." Why was she continuing to fool herself? Trevor's acceptance of Havoc and her volunteer activities only touched the surface of their relationship issues. But if he could have just accepted those two parts of her, she would've tried harder to change to make them work as a couple. Hell, she'd given up creating her own friendships outside of the one with Lori because they were always hanging out with his friends.

And where were those people now? MIA, obviously having either chosen loyalty to Trevor or remained distant because of the awkwardness. Either way, no one appeared to care about her except her family and Lori.

Her stomach twisted. Speaking of family, what would Papá and Tio Enrique say when they found out she'd been arrested? What would Lori say? Her friend-slash-coworker loved this town. It's where the woman came for vacation numerous times a year. Lori even owned the duplex Penelope was staying in.

"Guess I'll be losing another friend."

Penelope shook herself as if covered in cobwebs. She didn't have time to spend being dejected. It wouldn't help her with the judge. She needed to focus on what the sheriff said, on acting remorseful and apologetic. Which shouldn't be too hard, considering she was both. No, her anxiety came more from what that grump Ranger Gosling might say and the wrench he could throw into things. She pushed off the mattress and paced the length of her cell. Nine steps to the door, nine back to the wall.

The sheriff approached, bag in one hand, pile of clothes in the other, face stern, eyes narrow. She shifted the bag to sit atop the clothes and slipped a key into the cell lock. She swung the door open. "Good morning, Penelope."

Not much good about it now that Penelope's stomach twisted and her brain couldn't form words. Plus, she would've killed for a toothbrush to get rid of the nasty morning-mouth taste. She took the pile of clothes and sat hard on the bed.

Jeans and a shirt.

"Judge Carter will be here in a few minutes. Better get changed while we set up."

There was almost nothing Penelope wouldn't have done for a shower, but she didn't really want to push her luck by asking. The sheriff pulled a brush and small makeup bag from beneath the T-shirt and turned. "Good luck today."

"Thanks."

As soon as she changed, Penelope made the bed and folded the clothes she'd taken off. She couldn't look at the food. Maybe after she knew whether or not she'd be coming back to this cell, or whether or not she was going to have to get a second and third job to pay for the damages, or after…nope. That was it. Once she knew what the future held, she'd eat.

For the hundredth time, she went over what happened. And while she wanted to blame the broken grill, the fire had been wholly her fault. Her ex hadn't been at the state park. He hadn't struck up the lighter. Her bad choices had done that.

She scratched her arm, nails digging into the skin and leaving red tracks. She'd come out here to prepare, to learn, to take one of the most important tests of her life, and in a few minutes, she'd be begging for her freedom in front of a judge.

Sherriff Hart opened the door again. "Ready?"

No. She wasn't ready. Not for this. She was ready to go home. To find somewhere else to get her certification. To see Havoc. But she nodded and walked beside the sheriff down the hall through a couple of doorways and into a room that looked suspiciously like a courtroom.

"I thought Jay said—"

The sheriff held up a hand, palm facing forward. "The judge wanted to open the courtroom. He said this was bigger than we could handle in the break room." She tilted her head and shrugged. "I think he wanted to intimidate you a little."

The courtroom was smaller than the ones she'd seen on TV, but most of the furniture was the same. A raised oak bench for the judge with a wing on one side for the witness box and a desk on the other where a court reporter had taken up residence. It smelled like history and old paper in here, and the reporter didn't so much as glance at Penelope as she walked in and sat at the table across from a man in a zip-up hoodie and jeans—apparently prosecutors dressed down in this court—and Ranger Gosling, who wore a scowl with his olive-green park ranger uniform that matched well with his tanned skin, no doubt from working outdoors. A slight groan caught in Penelope's throat as her gaze traveled lower. Michelangelo didn't just create Jay's gorgeous chiseled jaw, but his nice, round ass as well.

A man strolled in and plopped a briefcase on the table in front of her, pulling her attention away from Jay. Her lawyer couldn't have been more than thirty, if that. His hair was a mess, flopping over his eyes and around his ears. His black tie hung at an angle from a Fred Flintstone knot, and he had one brown shoe and one black. Penelope hoped he was a better lawyer than dresser. Maybe she should have asked to meet with her lawyer before the trial when Deputy Mason had made the offer for a court-appointed legal counsel. "Jackson Unger." He held out a hand.

"Penelope Ramos."

"All right, Miss Ramos." He had a swaggery Southern twang to go with his smile, and a sudden calm washed over Penelope. "My aunt told me about your case, and I'm here to help you." He pulled out a copy of her statement. "You signed this willingly. Is it a true and accurate representation of what happened at the park?" When she nodded, he frowned. "Okay." His lips twitched before he glanced over at the other table, then back to her. "I guess we'll hope the judge is in a good mood." He pulled her up with him as a side door opened, and the judge—also in a hoodie, also scowling—walked to his chair and sat down.

"Good morning." Judge Carter—not at all what Penelope expected—nodded to her, then smiled at Jay. He had to be in his sixties, dressed like he was thirty, and glanced at her like she was ten. A naughty ten. "Mornin', Jay. Heard you had some problems out at the park."

Jay nodded. "Yes, sir."

"Nothing that's going to upset our fishing trip this weekend, right? Marylou has her sister coming to stay and if I get stuck at home with them I might end up presiding over my own divorce."

So much for formal. And impartial.

Jay stood. "I don't know yet. We haven't assessed what to do about rebuilding yet. The funding just isn't there right now to rebuild and buy new equipment for the safety program. I'll probably have to work this weekend to see what we can shuffle around."

Penelope watched their interaction with an open

mouth even when Ranger Gosling shot a smug smile to her. Bastard had already tainted the judge.

The judge nodded, then turned to look at her, lips pursed, eyes narrowed. "You're the defendant?" Wasn't like it took the Hulk to light a lighter, but his eyebrow cocked as if he couldn't quite believe what he was seeing.

"Yes, sir." Penelope had never sounded so small. Nerves did that to her.

"Good morning, Your Honor. Jackson Unger for the defense."

The judge nodded. "Jack, you've been in my courtroom about a thousand times. You don't have to introduce yourself. This is just an informal hearing to see if we can come to some kind of resolution."

If it was so informal, why had he opened the courtroom? Penelope kept the question to herself.

Her lawyer's face turned a pleasant shade of scarlet, but he grinned. "All right."

The judge opened the folder he'd walked in carrying. He read for a minute. "Old boyfriend, huh?"

Penelope nodded as slightly as she could manage. How could she have been so stupid to let her emotions ruin her life? To let a relationship cause such damage that she could lose everything she cared about? If she got out of this, no one would distract her, hurt her again. No mas amor. No mas novios. Nada. Passing her evaluation and doing the job that would come with it would be her only focus.

The judge looked at Ranger Gosling. "Total loss?"

"Ranger Karalis sent over the pictures of the scene," the prosecutor said.

The judge nodded. “Received them when I came in. Miss Ramos, could you approach the bench?”

Penelope held her head high as she followed her lawyer until the judge’s bench towered over her. Her throat constricted when the judge handed Mr. Unger a picture, who then handed it to her. The photo was of the burned building’s interior, its focal point a table with charred remains of what had once been electronics. As she handed it back, the lawyer gave her another. This one showed damage to the land around the building, charred grass, murky puddles from the fire hoses, and debris from the building.

He handed down picture after picture, and the evidence of her destruction made her eyes water and her heart ache. She loved nature. Should have known better. Did she burn the thrush’s home? Poor bird. Hopefully, it was okay.

“I’m sorry,” she whispered.

The judge slapped the file closed. “Well, that’s good enough for me. Let’s all go home.”

Even with her heart heavy and her ears ringing from shame, she could hear the sarcasm.

“Your Honor, my client”—the attorney might have taken a step away from her—” is a first-time offender with no history of criminal behavior.”

“Oh, yeah. Since it was just this once, let’s all just forgive and forget the thousands of dollars she’s cost this county.” Ranger Gosling’s tone had a bite to it that made her wince.

Unger turned to stare at him. “Come on, Jay. It was an accident. Not her fault the grill broke. Shit happens.”

The scrape of a wooden chair on hardwood echoed through the room as Ranger Gosling shot up out of his chair despite the prosecutor urging him to calm down. "Shit happens doesn't rebuild the check station or replace the GPS locators, the computers, or the beacons Princess Penelope burned up because some guy broke her poor pampered heart. Hell, I'm sure even New York City has rules about setting fires in local parks. Why would it be okay to do it in our parks?"

Penelope's nostrils flared at the nickname. Who the hell was this man to make such assumptions about her? Did he assume that because she lived in the city, she was rich? Joke was on him though, because she was anything but pampered. And she fought hard to earn what she had—even if she worked for family.

But the judge banged his gavel before she could respond. "Jay, I suggest you take a seat."

Then he waved Penelope and her lawyer back to their chairs. When she was seated, the judge walked around the court reporter to pace in front of the tables before he turned to address her. "The way I see it, we have two choices. We can schedule a hearing, let you plead guilty or not, go through the whole process. Or, you can haul out a checkbook and pay for the entirety of the damages and everybody walks away happy."

Oh, how she wished she could. And while she made a great salary, New York wasn't a cheap place to live. "I don't have that kind of money."

When Park Ranger Gosling scoffed, the judge turned to him. "Something you want to contribute, Jay?"

He stood. "I'm not a big car guy, but even I know an Audi SUV like the one she's driving—shiny, new, bells and whistles out the tailpipe—starts at fifty grand."

He had to be joking. He was judging her based on the car she drove. Her fingers wrung around the armrests of her chair as if strangling the life out of them. "Have you not heard of leasing? I didn't buy it outright."

The judge paced back and forth, his footsteps the only sound in the room except a few not-so-subtle sighs from the park ranger. After a few minutes, he stopped and turned to the prosecutor. "What is the Parks Department asking for?"

"A new check station and replacing all the equipment that was destroyed, especially the GPS items for the Stay Safe program."

The judge stared at Penelope, his eyes narrow. "And you can't afford to pay what it would cost."

She shook her head.

"Putting you in jail would serve no earthly purpose except to cost the county for your room and board." He pursed his lips and clicked his tongue. "All right, here's what's going to happen. I'm going to offer you a deal. Counsel, you should advise your client to take it." Beside her, Jackson Unger nodded, and the judge looked at Ranger Gosling. "And you, my friend, are going to have all the help you can handle."

Judge Carter smiled and turned back to Penelope. "I find there is reason to hold you over for trial. You acted with a reckless disregard for this community and for government property. And that's by your own admission. I, however, am a judge who knows that people make mistakes." He looked at the park ranger again. "Remember your senior year, Jay? And the spray paint? Remember how we all sat down in this very courtroom and decided you and Unger would clean the mess you made? And look at you both now. Your second chance worked out pretty well. So, I will allow you this chance, Miss Ramos, to keep this indiscretion off your record."

"Thank you!" Penelope said in a gush.

Judge Carter chuckled. "After I finish, you might want to reconsider and take a few months or years in jail." Gosling groaned as if he knew what was coming, and the judge held up his hand. "Miss Ramos, I will allow you to make restitution, keep your record unblemished, and learn your lesson. And all you have to do is help rebuild the check station and help the park service raise the money to replace the equipment they need."

Her heart sank. While the deal was definitely better than jail, which would affect her dog and her life, and strip her of the chance to reach her goals, she couldn't stay that long. "But I have a job."

"Which you'll lose anyway if I keep you in custody until trial."

Could he do that? She turned to the lawyer, who nodded as if she'd asked the question aloud. "I don't know how to do manual construction. I've never operated machinery or tools before."

"Well, you're in luck because Ranger Gosling happens to be an expert." If she hadn't set the fire and hadn't just seen picture proof of the damages, she would have glanced around for a hidden camera. This was too insane to be real life and not someone's idea of a joke. "I'm releasing you to Jay's supervision if you accept. Otherwise, we'll remand you into custody and set a hearing date. Your choice."

He shrugged as if he didn't give a damn one way or the other that he'd only left her one viable choice. A choice that was about to change her life one way or another.

# *Chapter Six*

## *Jay*

This was not the day Jay wanted to have. Not after a sleepless night with a dog in his home. A dog that wasn't his beloved Zip. Not after Gramps questioned why he was in the kitchen because the old man had momentarily forgotten who his grandson was. No, adding someone else for him to be responsible for was not the intended outcome Jay had expected. At least if Penelope was put away until trial, she wouldn't have been his concern.

But Carter, self-proclaimed patron saint of second chances, erred in judgment. The woman should have been held over for trial, not assigned to him like he was some sort of warden or babysitter, neither of which had been listed in his job description. How the hell had Carter came up with that idea? Maybe the old man was losing his faculties. Just like his grandfather.

Jay grimaced and mentally kicked himself for that last thought, even though it was because he secretly hoped that what Gramps was going through had more to do with age than the progression of his disease.

"You look like you sucked a lemon dipped in pickle

juice." Gramps leaned his cane against the table and lowered himself to his seat, left leg held straight by a brace. The kitchen was remodeled sometime in the late fifties and still sported a white table with a metal edge and old-time metal chairs with red vinyl seats. In the eighties Gramps updated and purchase a yellow fridge and white stove. And the place always smelled like pot roast.

"And you look like you should be in bed."

Gramps nodded to the coffee maker. The coffee was hours old and probably as thick as tar, but Gramps could drink it day or night. "Pour me a cup of that and keep your opinions quiet." When Jay handed him a mug of sludge, he took a sip. "Why is it that your coffee always tastes like you mixed it with gasoline and manure?" Gramps shrugged and took another sip, hand that held the cup shaking slightly. Neither of them made mention of it, or the increasing frequency of it. The cup came down hard on the tabletop. "Now, tell me what has your britches tangled."

His britches were just fine, but he sat across from his grandfather and looked down into his own cup. Muddy and so brown it looked almost black, like his mood. "Your buddy Carter making deals and passing sentences that..." He could tell Gramps all of it or he could sulk. Right now, he wanted to sulk.

"That what, boy? You can't take so long with your stories. I could keel over and miss the end." His grandfather toyed with his cup but stared at Jay so hard his skin burned. "Spit it out. Passing sentences that...?"

"That mean I'm stuck working with the woman who burned down the check station."

Gramps raised his eyebrows. "What's wrong with

that? Is she stupid? Does she wear her shoes on the wrong feet or pick her nose? What's the problem with her? Just don't leave the matches lying around, and you should be safe."

Jay had no idea about her intellect. So far all he knew about Penelope was her common sense wasn't a strong suit, she owned up to her actions, and she cared about her dog in such a way that she threatened to blast him all over social media for animal cruelty if any harm had come to Havoc. The corners of his mouth began to tug upward. While at first he'd been offended by the comment, now the idea of how protective she was became endearing. He'd do the same to anyone who would've harmed Zip. Actually, he would've done worse.

He groaned and lowered his head. There was also the fact the broken grill was cited in the report from the fire chief. And as much as he wanted to blame Penelope for ruining everything he'd been working on, not everything was truly her fault. She'd been telling the truth and he'd been a jerk for not listening.

But that wasn't the only problem. Penelope had some similarities to his ex-wife, mostly on how she spent her money. As if to show those around her how much more important she was. "She's some city princess. Manicured and styled. Shoes that cost more than a week's salary. And a vehicle that costs more than this house."

"Reminds you of Karen." Gramps pointed at him and shot a wink. Either the man had instincts or Jay wasn't hiding his feelings.

Jay sighed. There was an even bigger problem. One he definitely wanted to avoid discussing. But his mouth didn't get the message. "She has a dog."

Gramps feigned shock with wide eyes and a hand

over his heart. "Oh, God. A dog. What is she thinking? The nerve." He pulled himself straighter in the chair so he could lean on his elbows and point his gaze into Jay's eyes. "Boy, what happened to Zip wasn't your fault. I know you're carrying around that grief, made some silly promises to yourself to never get close again, but if you ask me, what you need is to get yourself another dog." He leaned back and grinned. "Or a princess with a dog. Can't make assumptions everyone is going to be like Karen."

Jay shook his head, the disgust inside him brimming. Gramps couldn't have been further off the bag. Getting another dog was out of the question. Losing Zip had taken the soul right out of him. Reminded him that nothing remained in his life forever. Except for Gramps, and even that… Bile crept up Jay's throat. No, he wasn't going there.

"I don't have time for pets. I have to rebuild the check station, figure out how to make enough money to buy new equipment, and supervise this woman until Carter thinks she's served her penance. And somehow in all of that, I have to find the time to come by here and take your abuse so you don't wither away from boredom." Jay smiled at his grandfather as he stood to place his half empty cup in the sink. He'd spent more time fundraising than walking the trails and setting the beacon sensors. And now he'd have to do it all over again. No point in sitting here and wallowing. He could just as well do it at home. "You need anything before I head home?"

Gramps stared up at him. "Do I look like I need to be tucked in?"

"Suppose not."

Gramps stood to walk Jay to the door. He'd always

done that. Now he was slower. Less steady on his feet. Jay held out his arm for assistance, but Gramps pooh-poohed him.

"Bah, be gone, would ya? Go take a shower. Sleep on it. Tomorrow, it won't be so bleak."

Jay hugged his grandfather and walked across the field with the crickets chirping and the moon shining over him. He needed to make a plan, but first, Gramps was right. He needed a shower, needed to think logically.

When he opened the door to his house, Jay kicked off his boots and headed up to the bathroom. He undressed and stepped into the shower, toes flinching as they touched the chilled ceramic floor. He turned the dial, old and metallic, releasing thousands of lukewarm drops that dripped down his hair onto his body. But even the water couldn't chase away his foul mood.

After he toweled off, pulled on a pair of flannel pajama bottoms, and climbed between the sheets, he pulled his laptop off the table. The only damned idea he'd been able to come up with—and he'd let the water run cold because he'd been too engrossed with finding a solution to notice—was using his own money.

But his savings wouldn't be enough. Not by tens of thousands of dollars. And it didn't matter how many times he looked or how many different ways he tried to figure it. It wouldn't make a dent in what he needed to start the safety program. And what if he needed to help fund Gramps's care? Could be next month or next year. The doctors said dementia was an eventual part of the disease.

He flicked the laptop shut and scrubbed his hands over his face. Moonlight glimmered through the window, and Jay kicked off the blanket. Even his damned bed wasn't comfortable tonight. He blamed Penelope Ramos. If not for her, he would be sleeping like a baby, knowing his work was secure and people would be rescued if they got lost or injured.

For years, they'd done it the old-fashioned way. Trucks circled the park, checking campsites, watching out for dangers and victims of those dangers. But budget cuts took half their force. Put a cap on fuel expenditures. Made safety a lesser concern than expenses.

Then, after a day of hunting, Nick and Jay had brainstormed this idea. Technology was taking over the rest of the world, why not use it to pitch in where the government had left them short. They'd spent weeks researching and product testing for range and sensory compatibility with the elements, the elevations in the park, and the terrain. Found a similar program that was being used for autistic children down in Virginia.

If Penelope Ramos had waited one more day, just one, the sensors would have been on the trees, the power boosters attached to the already set posts, and the GPS monitors would have been back at the office waiting to be sent out with the first wave of hunters. One more damned day and the check station and a computer would have been the only loss.

He cursed her again. And her dog. And the fire. And the grill. And the equipment. And damn him for leaving it there, unprotected in the check station. Murphy's Law. Karma. Something had it out for him. Or someone. Besides Judge Carter, though he had a part in this farce. Since when did park ranger duties include babysitting would-be felons? A would-be felon, that is, if Carter would have thought to look at what she'd destroyed. If he'd done that, Penelope would be sitting in a jail cell right now instead of some cushy duplex cuddling her drooling mutt.

He knew he wasn't being completely fair, but he didn't have to be. Not to her or her dog. Maybe the dog. Havoc hadn't been so bad. Of course, he was no Zip. But not so bad.

Penelope Ramos was another story. With the glossy brown curls and emerald green eyes. And her soft, sweet smell and equally soft and curvy body that looked amazingly sexy even in a pair of baggy jeans and a plain T-shirt that was a tad too large. Charlie, being the perfect sheriff, must've grabbed Penelope some clothes for the trial. He shifted. Damn. And no. Hell, no. He wasn't going to spend another minute recalling anything about how good the little pyro felt all pressed up against him. Because something like that would never happen again.

He opened his computer once again and typed her name into the search engine, clicking on the link to her Instagram profile. This was stupid. He didn't need to know. But then he found out she took pictures. Good ones. Mostly of birds and her dog, but wow, the clarity, the contrast to lighting and color. He didn't know much about photography, but these were good. Not surprisingly, she had a lot of followers. He clicked back to the search results and checked the next link. Her professional profile, complete with a headshot.

His lips pursed and a low growl rumbled in his chest.

She minced her words at the hearing. Or at least made a very conscious choice about what to say because she made a living in construction. The website read, "For your custom construction bid, contact Penelope Ramos." So maybe she hadn't operated machinery but that didn't mean she was green at the whole concept of rebuilding a structure.

But did it really matter? Carter had made sure Jay was stuck with Penelope. And the judge wasn't one to listen to any rebuttals after a sentence was handed down. But Jay was certain about one thing. With all he had going on, he wouldn't become endeared to the city girl, no matter how hard she worked. Once the job was done and her sentence was complete, he'd send Penelope and the dog packing without a second thought.

# *Chapter Seven*

*Penelope*

Penelope lugged her other suitcase up the front steps to the duplex, cursing under her breath. She would have used the garage, but the opener was inside the house. Damnit. She could've gone in first, opened the garage, pulled the car in, and then wrestled with her suitcase. With a growl she yanked the suitcase up another step. She was too far in to go back now. And all she wanted was to get inside and shower the jail grime off.

"Need some help?"

Penelope recognized that voice. She turned, using her knee to steady the suitcase to keep it from toppling over and down the steps. "Sheriff Hart. Are you following me?"

The woman laughed. Instead of a police uniform, Hart wore a pair of leggings and a hoodie as if she'd been or was heading out for a run. A headband held her short hair back from her face. "You can call me Charlene or Charlie. I'm not at work right now. And no, not following you. I live in the other side of the duplex." She made a sweeping gesture to the other half of the brick-and-stone house.

"Oh."

Charlie crossed her arms and glanced at Havoc, whose head was wedged out the space left by the open window. "Was your dog happy to see you?"

"Oh, yeah." Penelope laughed and glanced down at her shirt. The way Havoc had nuzzled and jumped on her, she probably had enough fur on her clothes to build a new dog. "He was excited. I think he wants to get back to working." Not that Penelope would mind, but it was late, she was hungry, and she wanted a shower before she did anything else.

There wasn't a lot they could do anyway since Penelope would need another person to help with Havoc's training. And with the waning sunlight, she didn't want to risk injury to herself or her dog by hiking in unfamiliar territory.

"I'm going to grill some steaks if you want to join me. The diner closed about an hour ago and unless you want to drive for it, there isn't much else to eat here in town."

Penelope grimaced. She hadn't even thought to stop at the grocery store to pick up food. "I hate to impose."

"Oh, please. I'd like the company, to be honest. Unless Lori's in town, the only one who ever gets to see my social graces is my sister."

After her breakup, Penelope's ever-understanding uncle—and boss—gave her a couple of days off to get her head on straight so she wouldn't fail her evaluation. And Lori offered up the vacation duplex she owned in Maple Falls. Guess she was lucky Lori rented the other half of the duplex to Charlie, because she could use a friend. Even if it was temporary.

If only some of her friends back home didn't distance

themselves after the breakup. What she wouldn't give to have had a sister right now. Penelope wouldn't even care if said sibling made fun of her current predicament. At least then she'd have someone to console her, to vent to before having to inform Papá, Tío Enrique, and Lori about what just happened. They were going to be very disappointed.

"What's that look?"

Of course Charlie would notice her scowl. But she wasn't ready to have a conversation about how the only friends she'd had were her father, uncle, and coworker. All much older than she. Or how she allowed Trevor to influence her time to the point he chose their friends. So, she waved a dismissive hand in the air. "Nothing. Just had a random thought."

"Must not have been a good one." Charlie hefted the suitcase so Penelope could open the door, then carry it inside.

Penelope blew a huff of breath from her puffed-up cheeks. "Just that you'd be the only friend I have while I'm up here. Everyone else hates me." She dropped her luggage on the floor. "Why did I bring so much stuff?"

"How long are you staying?"

That had become a lot more complicated. "I had planned to only stay a couple of days. I was supposed to take my search and rescue evaluation and then maybe stay a few extra days to relax, but the judge sentenced me to hard labor."

"I heard." Charlie stared at her. "With Jay spearheading the project, it shouldn't take more than a month or so."

A month? A freaking *month*. She had a job to get

back to. A life to get back to. "That's longer than I hoped."

Charlie chuckled. "Don't tell Jay I said so, but you probably did them a favor. That old check station should have been rebuilt years ago. It was falling down."

The equipment, though. Penelope shifted her weight. How passionate Jay had been, the same way she was about search and rescue. And she destroyed that for him. She literally burned his passion to the ground. Guilt flicked through every one of her cells. "Maybe, but I don't think Ranger Gosling is going to see it that way."

"Probably not." Charlie nodded to the door. "Why don't I take your dog with me. The backyard is fenced, and you can get cleaned up and head over when you're done."

"That sounds fabulous." A peaceful shower without a four-legged stalker was a luxury she hadn't had in over a year, and a steak would certainly cure her grumbling stomach. After she closed the door, Penelope bounced up the stairs and into the bathroom.

Once she was done, she searched through her bag for comfortable clothes, got dressed, then headed over to her neighbor's. Charlie's backyard had it all. A deck. Room for Havoc. Landscaping the likes of which big chain hotels used in their brochures. Plants and flowers grew along the deck, lined the fence on one side, and circled the two large trees. "This is amazing."

Havoc whined and before she could stop him, he began digging a hole next to the tree, upsetting two of the flowering plants. Penelope ran over and grabbed Havoc's collar. "*Lo siento!* I'll pay to have it replaced or replanted or—"

Charlie waved her off with a laugh. "He's feisty."

Feisty was a nice way of saying naughty. She held the plant up for a careful inspection with her free hand. So far, this trip had cost her pride, dignity, reputation, and now, cold hard cash.

Charlie shook her head and gazed at the withering plant, then took it to the trash can at the edge of the deck. "No worries. I was going to put some lavender there for the mosquitoes, anyway."

Penelope released Havoc, who was apparently worn out from his escapade, and they walked up the steps to the deck. Penelope sat down, Havoc at her feet. "How long have you lived here?"

Charlie set a plate in front of her. "Since my divorce. My husband was a good man and good father, but not a great husband. Not for someone who spent half her marriage deployed anyway. Our daughter is away at college, but she grew up here." As if captured in a fond memory, Charlie looked out at the yard, a smile brightening her face. "She helped with the gardening."

"A military woman. Impressive." And admirable. Courageous. From articles Penelope read on the internet, being a woman in the military still came with a lot of obstacles, adversity. Even while equality was expressed publicly, many servicewomen spoke out about inequalities and harassment they suffered. Yet they didn't allow it to deter them, instead pushing through adversity to achieve great things.

Charlie snorted. "You'd think other people would see it that way. But nope. Put up with a lot of shit, from family and those I served with."

"I can't even pretend to relate. Some women I follow online talk about the struggles they encountered from their own superiors even because of their gender."

"Ugh. Don't get me started. Toughened me up, though. And the friendships and bonds I made with those who supported me are sacred."

Penelope hoped maybe she could build a sacred bond with a woman like Charlie. There was so much she respected about the sheriff already, including how Charlie took care of her, offering food and bringing spare clothes for the trial.

Penelope cleared her throat, chasing away the longing bubbling up. "Do people here give you a hard time?"

"Not at all. Except Nick. But it's no different than the way he treats anyone else in town. Plus, he's a badass, so I tend to listen when he has something to say. Even if he doesn't always communicate properly."

Nick? Penelope's brows pinched together. "I haven't met him, but I think he's the one who watched Havoc. Or at least Ranger Gosling said he was supposed to."

"Nick's the head park ranger. Just as grumpy as Jay. Passionate. Cusses in Greek." She rolled her eyes. "Some might call him handsome."

"Some? As in who—the elderly crowd, millennials, Gen X?" Penelope cut into her steak, which was perfectly seasoned, juicy, and seared brown on the outside. Just the way she liked it. She scooped a bite into her mouth and quirked a brow at Charlie as she chewed.

"All of the above. Every woman drools over the man."

Penelope giggled.

"Oh, you have no idea. Not that I don't have my own fan club made up of some of the rangers and firefighters." Charlie raised her fork in the air. "Though, come to think of it, maybe they're scared of me considering how some squirm and speak so fast when I'm around."

"If Nick is so grouchy maybe people aren't drooling over him but it's more of a keep-your-enemy-close kind of deal."

Charlie shook her fork sideways. "Oh, no. At scenes I have to push my way through women who stare daggers at me as if I'm flirting with their husbands. Like they lose all common sense that I'm the sheriff, not a groupie."

Since they were on the topic of park rangers and she had to work with one for the next month or so, she needed to know about Ranger Gosling. Like what made him into such an unspeakable jackass. She swallowed her food and took a sip of water before turning her attention back to Charlie. "What do you know about Jay?"

"He's been through a lot." Charlie shoved a heap of mashed potatoes into her mouth, placed her fork down, and wiped her lips with a napkin. She grabbed her beer and leaned back in her chair. "In a small town, a teenage pregnancy could be considered scandalous. His mother didn't want a baby, and after Jay was born the family moved away. Before he even turned one, his dad went off and joined the military or went to college first, can't remember. Jay ended up living with his grandparents his whole life. He still would be if Gramps hadn't told him to get his own life." Charlie smiled and took a swig of beer. "Gramps is something else. That man speaks his mind, but everybody loves him."

Penelope bit into another piece of steak and chewed viciously. She couldn't imagine being ripped away from her mother. Her mother died a couple of years ago, and the sting of that loss still haunted her at times. Even the memories of how her mother walked her to the bus every year on the first day of school to take a picture caused her to choke up. When she'd gotten older and graduated from middle school, their ritual had changed to going for weekly pedicures together. She still went to the same nail salon every week.

And she certainly could never imagine her father not wanting her.

Charlie chuckled. "Don't overthink it. Jay has had a good life. And he's normally a nice guy. Would give you the shirt off his back if you needed it. Thing is, I was really surprised to hear he kept your dog last night after what happened to Zip."

"I thought Nick kept Havoc? And who's Zip?"

"Not sure what happened, but Jay watched Havoc. As for Zip…prettiest German shorthaired pointer I've ever seen." She bent over to rub Havoc's sable coat. "Jay did search and rescue with Zip. Jay and Zip went to help out after some recent floods in West Virginia almost a year ago. They worked it. Hard. While they were down there the dog ended up dying."

Penelope coughed. The food she just swallowed had gotten temporarily stuck when her throat knotted at Charlie's words. God, losing Havoc would be like losing a part of herself. She reached down to pet the dog snoozing now at her feet. No wonder Jay had been so against watching her dog for the night. Losing a pet, especially a working partner, took a while to get over, if a person ever got over it. She knew handlers who had quit after the loss of a canine partner. And there she was, sticking Havoc with him overnight. If only she would've known.

Seems all she'd done so far was cause Jay pain in one form or another. No wonder the man hated her. Penelope hated her own self right now.

"He took it bad." Charlie's frown turned to a scowl. "Didn't help his wife filed for divorce a couple of months afterward. She couldn't handle his grief. The only thing she did like was money until that wasn't enough."

Penelope swallowed a piece of bread, but it grated against the lump in her throat. Seemed like something Trevor would do. People could be so shallow and self-absorbed. And some had no idea what a loss of a pet could mean, how it could hurt just as much as a loss of a parent. "He must really hate me."

"He might be angry, but I've never known Jay to hate anyone. Not even his ex-wife. Working with him shouldn't be too bad. He's professional, plays by the rules." Charlie pointed a fork in her direction and licked a small glob of mashed potatoes from the side of her lips. "If there's one thing I can say and know it in the bottom of my heart, that man walks a straight line." Charlie said it as if there might be some sort of flaw to Jay's way of thinking, but Penelope only saw the advantages. No surprises. No hard decisions. "What about you? What do you do when you're not burning down buildings and spending nights in jail?"

Penelope groaned. She wasn't ready to laugh about the incident yet. "I'm a project planner for a construction company. I do the bids and arrange delivery of products. I schedule crews and equipment." Compared to being a sheriff, Penelope's job description made her want to fall asleep.

"Well, that could be useful."

If only. "My connections are all in New York. Along with my list of suppliers." And getting Tío Enrique to turn it over once she told him about her extended absence from work would be impossible. She sighed. That wasn't going to be a fun phone call.

"You can only do the best you can." Charlie stood and walked over to the cooler by the grill and grabbed two beers, handing one to Penelope when she returned to the table. "No one expects a miracle. You hammer a few boards, sand some walls, and call it a day. I would bet, if you work hard and find a way to stay on Jay's good side, he'll go to Carter and you'll get to go home sooner than you think."

"You think so?" While logical, it sounded a bit optimistic.

"It could go either way. Just don't be extra or a diva when working with Jay. Keep your head down. Do whatever stupid job he needs done. And whatever you do, don't try to suck up."

They finished dinner and cleaned up—easy enough with paper plates—then Penelope went back to her own place to call her tío. She filled him in, then sat back as he complained.

"I know, but there's really nothing I can do about it." She hadn't quite explained all the details. Just told him there'd been an accident and she was going to be in Vermont longer—much longer—than expected.

"What did you do? Burn down the courthouse?"

She couldn't help but smile. "Not the courthouse."

The line went silent before he murmured, "Are you kidding me? What did you do?"

A throb at the back of her skull moved its way to the front. "It was an old shack at the park, and it was an accident. But now I can't leave until it's rebuilt."

Tío Enrique huffed. "You need a crew?"

Oh, that would be a lifesaver. But nothing that came

from her tío came without a price. Her uncle never gave anything for free, even to family. Sort of like how Havoc never got a treat for free. He had to work for it one way or another, even if just a simple action as giving his paw when asked. Tío Enrique felt it built character, responsibility. "You have one to spare that won't break the bank?"

"Are you paying for the rebuild?"

As far as she knew, the government would be financing the work she was supposed to do. "I better check with the guy in charge. I'll let you know."

"I suppose you can work remotely while you're there. I'll send you some proposals that need the bid attached. One for a shopping center, one to redo Artie's Butcher Shop, and the golf course wants to add a couple thousand square feet to the clubhouse, so that one needs an overhaul. Did you bring your laptop?"

Penelope's shoulders relaxed. At least he wasn't firing her, and she would need money for dog food and necessities. "Yeah. Can you send me the list of suppliers we used for the bank in Williamstown? I might be able to get some good prices for lumber and supplies since I used them before."

Tío Enrique grumbled. "I guess. Let them know this isn't one of your regular contracts in case the state forgets to sign the check or something."

"Got it." She told him how to access the files on her computer and hung up.

There was one more call she needed to make. Her fingers tapped at the screen and her teeth sank into her bottom lip as the phone rang.

"Hello?"

"Hola, Papá." Penelope wrapped a strand of hair

around one of her fingers. "Hope I didn't wake you, but I wanted to talk to you before Tío got ahold of you."

Her father sighed. "He told me about the blowout with that jerk. Pen, I told you months ago to get rid of him."

Her father wasn't the only one. Lori wasn't a Trevor supporter, either. After her coworker offered the beautiful little duplex to Penelope and Trevor to use one summer, he vetoed the idea, preferring suites at the Plaza, Broadway shows, and fancy meals at the latest-trending wine bars for vacations. Lori hated how condescending he'd been at the mere mention of staying in a small town. And she did as well, since most places that would be great for wildlife photography had only small towns nearby. Then again, photography was just a hobby and wasn't worth having a fight over.

But while she'd been out with Havoc taking photos that first day in the state park, it was like a breath of life had revived a dormant part of her.

"It's not about that, Papá. Unfortunately, I have to stay up here a bit longer than planned. I, um, accidentally burned down a building and now I have to help fix it."

"Dios mío! Mi hija, are you all right? Did you get hurt or anything?"

Tears welled in the corner of her eyes. Her father was the only one who'd asked if she'd gotten hurt. "I'm okay. But I need you to go to my apartment and ship me some clothes. I'll text you the address."

"Okay, sweetheart. Go get some rest. Love you."

"Love you, too." Penelope hung up and texted her father the address of the duplex. Then she tossed her phone on the bed and lay back. Exhausted. Nervous.

Too wired to sleep. Her mind full. Charlie's words floated to the front of her mind, including that Jay was the one to watch Havoc.

She couldn't imagine how he must've felt. Was Havoc the first dog he had in his home since Zip had died? Penelope's chest hitched. It hurt deep in her soul to try to even relate. Jay had gone above and beyond by the simple action, especially after learning about his past. Not only was he ho—*cute*, but deep down he had a heart of gold. Even if it might only be reserved for dogs.

So, she would be nice. Play by his rules. Get her certification and start her life over. This was a blip on her plan. A stopover. But nothing—or no one—would derail all she and Havoc had worked for. And if in the future she ever met a man she wanted to date, she'd make sure that he was a little bit like Jay.

# *Chapter Eight*

*Jay*

Oh, perfect. Instead of meeting him at the site, Penelope pulled her fancy SUV into the lot outside the office. He stared out the window from her vehicle to his, noting how the rays of sunshine bounced off the hood of her shiny vehicle. Of course, Jay hadn't told her to meet him anywhere. He'd assumed. And Gramps always said… *When you assume, you make an ass out of you* and…nope. Jay had only made an ass out of himself. No doubt Penelope would happily tell him about it, too. And Gramps's wisdom didn't stop the sight of her in her skinny jeans and hiking boots from knocking the wind out of him. He took some shallow breaths and attempted to keep his tongue from hanging out of his mouth as he stared out the window.

Nick watched her from beside Jay at the window. "That's her?"

"Yup."

Nick laughed as his palm slapped Jay's shoulder. "Well, this should be fun."

Jay grunted, then met his boss's gaze. "What should be fun?"

"Watching you handle all that." He whirled his finger in a circle toward the woman walking up the steps to the door. And if the bastard didn't stop laughing—boss or not—Jay was going to deck him.

The moment she stepped inside, Nick—ever social—walked over to her, hand extended, a smile cracking his face. "You must be Penelope."

"Yes." She extended her hand as she blinked rapidly, a rosy color extending from her cheeks to her neck. "I just wanted to say, I am so sorry. I am normally very conscious of the environment, and I never burn anything…the ozone… I was even taking pictures before… because I love…birds."

Jay groaned, clenching his jaw. Penelope managed to stumble upon the one topic Nick could jabber about for days. Jay tried to tune them out as Nick gave Penelope the vital statistics of the hermit thrush—the Vermont state bird, chosen in 1941, home in Vermont in the summer, the beauty of the woeful song the birds sang. Nick's bird-watching addiction might have required a twelve-step program of some sort to cure him, but Jay didn't have time to counsel him. He had a meeting with the fire marshal and the building inspector. Though he couldn't help but notice the way she earnestly listened to Nick, as if respecting his friend's fascination with birds.

Maybe she wasn't *so* bad.

"Jay mentioned you're a photographer," Nick said.

Great. Now she would know he'd stalked her social media footprint. When she turned to smile at him, Jay shrugged. "I stumbled upon your profile last night when I was online."

She turned back to Nick. "I dabble when I'm not working."

"Working construction?" He just wanted to hear her admit she'd perjured herself.

Penelope swiveled her head and narrowed her eyes at him. "Not really. My part is mostly on the computer side. I make arrangements for construction. I don't actually hold the hammer or anything."

He would bet this woman had skills enough to sidestep land mines. And she would do it with that smile on her face. Nick and Penelope moved on to talking about dogs. And if Nick liked talking about birds, he loved chatting about dogs. At this rate, they would never get out of there.

"I was scheduled to be your evaluator." Nick clucked his tongue against his teeth. "Have you rescheduled yet?"

Penelope's cheeks heated, and she shook her head, her smile fading. "I don't know when I'll have time. And I wasn't sure if I'd get a fair shake up here with what happened."

The hopelessness in her tone didn't sway Jay at all. This wasn't supposed to be easy. Not her punishment and certainly not getting certified with a dog to save lives. His neck corded, bile creeping up his throat. The pain in his chest intensified as if his heart was being squeezed to death. If he could find a way, he would happily blame Penelope for the renewed ache over his beloved canine partner.

Instead, he grunted. Loudly. Penelope and Nick went silent and turned to stare at him. He cleared his throat. "We'd better go. Fire marshal is probably waiting for us."

Nick shook Penelope's hand again. "I'll check out your Instagram. I would love to see your pictures." Of course he would. By day's end, his boss would probably have ten of them framed and hanging on the wall in the office. After all, Jay had noticed Penelope would occasionally sell prints of some of the photographs.

Nick glanced at him. "Keep me posted on what Ken says. I have some of the rangers coming in to start hauling away the debris, so they should be out there this afternoon."

"Will do." Jay looked Penelope up and down and his heart stuttered. He cleared his throat and pointed at her boots. "Are those steel-toe?"

She held up her leg as if she expected him to bend down and inspect for himself. "Yeah."

"Let's go." He had a long day planned for Princess Penelope. There was a site to be cleared so they could start building. Pieces of wall still needed to be knocked down. Every nail, bolt, screw, and fixture would need to be picked up. Assorted equipment—a sledgehammer, a floor magnet, various saws, and power tools to finish the building destruction she'd started—sat in a heap in his truck bed. He also had empty buckets and a cooler of bottled water. No way would he let the princess use dehydration as an excuse to get out of her community service.

She waited until they were almost at the site before she turned her head away from the window to look at him. Not that he'd been checking. His peripheral vision was just that good.

"I'm really sorry for the trouble I've caused. And I know what it cost you to watch Havoc the other night."

If she'd left it at the apology, he might not have responded at all. "What are you talking about?"

"Charlie told me about how your dog died."

Oh, fuck. He whipped his head sideways to meet her gaze and saw nothing but pity in her eyes. Damn Charlie. If he'd wanted every Tom, Dick, Harry, and Penelope to know his business, he would have advertised in the local newspaper. "It's none of your concern."

Gramps would maim him if he ever heard him talking to anyone—much less a woman—that way. He sighed. "It's touchy for me. Still."

She turned and gazed out the window in front of her. "I can't imagine what I would do if something happened to Havoc. Did you have him long?"

"Adopted him from a breed rescue when he was a pup." And that was all he wanted to say about it.

"I got Havoc from a shelter. He was just a little scrap of a thing. Malnourished. Patches of fur missing." She spoke with such adoration for her dog. "But he came around. Now, he's vibrant and full of spirit." She twisted her lips to one side. "Sometimes a little too much."

Another reason to like Penelope. He groaned inwardly. Why did she have to rescue a shelter dog to be her partner? Only those who believed in second chances, saw past the surface to find potential, did things like that. Good, caring people did that.

Jay scrubbed a hand over his face. He didn't have the time nor the extra emotional energy to care for another person, even if they possessed the qualities he valued in life. Plus, Penelope lived in New York City while his home was in Maple Falls.

She was just a visitor. A tourist.

Temporary.

"Charlie said you're a SAR instructor?"

Charlie was in for it when he got ahold of her. "Got some credentials. Taught some classes." In truth, it had been a lot more than that, but it wasn't worth mentioning since he had no intention of ever using the information. Not anymore.

"Do you ever think about getting back into it?"

"No." He pulled the truck into a space in the parking lot, not bothering to further expand because that would mean brushing across the idea of getting another dog, which meant replacing Zip. And no one would ever replace Zip.

A couple meters away the broken grill still lay on the ground. "Could we just meet the fire marshal and concentrate on that instead of playing twenty none-of-your-business questions?"

He didn't miss the hurt that flashed in her eyes or the frown she tried to wipe away. "You bet."

Smoke still faintly wafted through the air. The normal sounds one took for granted in the woods were gone. No birds chirping. No buzzing insects. Instead, his boots crunched over the burnt grass as he walked over to the other ranger truck where Brent and Eric walked around the front to stand behind him.

Eric nodded at Penelope before addressing Jay. "Nick sent us out here to clean up, but McKinney said we have to wait a while."

Ken McKinney, the building inspector who had the distinct mad scientist hairdo and horn-rimmed-glasses look, stood at the edge of what remained of the check station. He waved at Jay.

"He mention when he'd be done?"

"No. Just told us to wait."

Jay tromped through the grass with the other rangers and Penelope behind him. McKinney and Greg Davies each had a clipboard and scribbled notes as they checked various parts of the building. "What's the good word?"

McKinney shook his hand while Davies continued picking up pieces of sooty wood to examine and make note of. "Total loss, obviously. But the foundation looks good." He glanced at Penelope and stepped around Jay to offer his hand. "Hi. I'm Jude McKinney. Building inspector." As he took his hand away, he held out a badge attached to a lanyard around his neck. "I don't think we've met."

Her face went crimson. "I'm, um, Penelope Ramos."

"You're Penelope Ramos?" He flipped to a second page on his clipboard. "The firebug?"

She nodded and stared at her shoes.

"Building should have been rebuilt a decade ago." McKinney shook his head. "I don't know how many times I told Nick it was an eyesore and a fire hazard. Not that I think starting a fire so near a tinderbox like this one is a good idea."

Penelope bit her bottom lip and dug the tip of her boot into the dirt. "I should have known better."

McKinney stuck his pencil behind his ear and glanced at the remains of the check station. "What's done is done. It can be rebuilt. But now the park service is gonna come up short budget-wise."

And for once, Jay wasn't the one who had to remind everyone of the expense she'd burdened the state with.

Brent stepped around Jay to shake Penelope's hand. "I'm Bent." He shook his head and his face went ruddy. "I'm Brent. Not bent."

Eric chuckled. "No. He's definitely bent."

"Shut up."

"You know it's true."

As the tiff between them raged on for a minute, Jay stepped around to talk to Davies. “Hey, Greg. You guys be done here soon?”

“I’m about finished.” The man nodded to Penelope. “That’s her? Was she out here alone?”

Jay shoved his hands into his pockets and followed the man’s gaze back to Penelope. “She was cleansing herself of a bad-boyfriend experience, from what I heard.” Must’ve been some kind of asshole.

“Guess the common-sense gene skipped her.”

He’d thought the same thing. But looking at Davies, maybe there was something to bad breakups disrupting common sense. Maybe he was being too hard on Penelope. Jay chuckled and clapped his friend on the shoulder. “Seems I remember you jumping naked into Lake Bomoseen because that fortune teller told you Gwen cursed you with some bad juju.”

“So?”

“It was January and you spent three days in the hospital with hypothermia. Anyway, McKinney said the foundation is sound. You agree?”

Davies nodded. From the back of his clipboard, he pulled another paper. Building codes and specs. “You’re going to need this.”

Jay read the paper. He could handle this one of three ways: Ask Penelope for help. Wing it and build a crooked building not up to code. Or ask Google for help and hope he could decipher the information to prevent option two. He folded the paper into a neat square and tucked it into his pocket.

Brent and the other young ranger still stood with Penelope. And Davies was still talking. “The whole town is talking about Carter letting the girl off without any jail time."

"Carter has always been unorthodox," Jay said, a little uneasy that the town might harbor more than a little ill will toward the firebug in their midst. Especially since she didn't seem to have a mean-spirited bone in her lithe body. And no matter how he tried to dismiss the thought, he wanted to feel her warmth against his chest again. Without the snot.

Davies shrugged. "Maybe, but after he sentenced those boys last year to juvie for setting fire to the football field at the high school, townspeople are questioning his judgment."

"That was a completely different situation." Those boys had poured gasoline on the freshly laid sod and lit it up so that it spelled out their school's—a rival to the Maple Falls Minutemen—mascot's name. Malicious intent versus accidental flying embers. "Carter knows what he's doing," Jay finished, then frowned.

Had he been defending the judge or Penelope? She was definitely getting under his skin. But defending her from other's misconceptions was different from caring for her in a way that took more emotion. He could clear up people's perceptions. That didn't require much effort.

Davies stepped over a pile of burned wood that had once been a table. "Didn't find much to salvage. I gotta get back and file my report so you guys can start construction. Let's have a few beers this weekend. Wife's away at a girls' weekend in Vegas."

"Sounds good." Jay waved as Greg joined McKinney and the Penelope fan club. He waited as long as he could, information in hand, before he headed back to her, and motioned for her to join him at the truck.

They hopped in and drove in silence all the way back to the office. He'd tried to think of something to say, but every time he snuck a glance in her direction, she looked so lost in thought he didn't want to disturb her. Besides, he couldn't say what he really wanted to ask—*what did your ex do that made you want to incinerate everything that reminds you of him?*

*None of your goddamn business, Jay.* He needed to get this job done for both of their sakes. Then life could go on as it always had.

He frowned. Not that life was so great right now, but it was the devil he knew.

When they arrived back at the office, he parked, they exited, and Penelope came around the truck to stand in front of him. Waiting for him to say something. There had to be some wisdom to be gained for both of them. But of course, there was no answer. So, he said, "You're done for the day. We'll start at six tomorrow. You can meet me at the site. Don't be late."

Her shoulders dipped slightly as she nodded, then headed off to her own vehicle.

He stared after her a moment, feeling as though he'd lost a moment he'd never get back. Why hadn't she said anything? What was on her mind? He hadn't been quite as gruff with her today.

Had he?

He grunted and shoved his hands into his pockets. Standing here wasn't going to get him anywhere, unlike the coming hours he'd spend hunched over at his computer. He had building codes to decipher and a project to plan.

Jay trudged up the steps to the office, knowing he'd need a full pot of coffee and a handful of prayers to keep his mind off the Latina with the face of an angel and the body of a goddess.

# *Chapter Nine*

## *Penelope*

The next day, Penelope didn't do her hair because she wanted to look nice. And she didn't put on mascara because she cared if her eyes popped. Today was about righting her wrongs, repairing the damage she'd done, making amends. But it also didn't mean she had to look like a dishrag while working her butt off.

After one last check in Lori's antique mirror, she let Havoc outside, then poured a thermos of water and added some ice. While standing at the back door waiting for the dog, she stuffed half of a bland, lukewarm waffle in her mouth, inhaling the sweet aroma of all-natural maple syrup. A cool breeze whipped around her, birds chirping in the trees surrounding the yard.

Maybe she could stay home today. After all, she hated leaving Havoc alone, but taking him along might not be the best idea considering what Ranger Gosling was going through. So, she let the dog back inside and chuckled when he padded across the room to the cool tile in front of the dormant fireplace. He lay down and stared at her as if she'd said aloud he couldn't go.

"Oh, come on. You know I can't take you." He tilted

his head and if he had the comprehension to glare, he did. "When I get home, we'll go on a long walk." There were miles of sidewalks and countless species of trees and plants, plus a fair number of trails for them to explore. His baleful gaze made her heart ache. "Come on. I have to go. Be good, and I'll bring you some treats." Although they wouldn't be the homemade ones she'd found in New York. He turned his head to face the fireplace. "Fine. Pout if you must. But don't tear anything up, or tomorrow, you're outside the whole day."

Not that he would mind. He loved the outdoors, and it was probably a good idea, but the temperature was supposed to skyrocket today, and she didn't want to take a chance on the heat affecting his health. Bad enough she had to be out in it.

She sighed and went out.

Charlie waved and walked toward her. She wore a pair of black cargo pants and a black T-shirt with the word POLICE stamped across the back. Somehow, she managed to make the whole getup look stylish. "Good mornin'."

Penelope groaned as she came to a stop. "Is it?"

Charlie laughed. "First day?"

"Yeah." Her stomach hadn't stopped grumbling since she woke.

"Don't worry yourself too much. Everyone will get over the accident. Just give them time." Charlie walked to her sheriff's SUV and waved again before she climbed inside.

Penelope hopped into her own vehicle and drove to the work site, trying to figure out how to make things less awkward between her and Ranger Gosling. It wouldn't do any good to try to be his friend since he was probably still angry about what happened, so maybe silence would work. Speak when spoken to. It seemed to work okay yesterday.

Until she went to say goodbye to him. Her heart began to race and her brain went fuzzy. And when he became awkward, she'd been embarrassed. So, besides being quiet, her plan for today also included not looking at the ranger close up.

And the plan worked for the better part of the day since she hadn't seen hide nor hair of the tall, dark, and grumpy ranger, until several hours later when he called her name.

"Can I talk to you for a second?" Jay held out a bottle of water as if he'd have to bribe her into it.

Penelope stood knee-deep in a debris pile, soot on her forehead mingled with sweat that ran underneath her sunglasses to her eyes. She'd broken the laces on one of her boots so now her foot rubbed against the back and a blister had started to form. But sure. Ranger Gosling wanted to talk, in the thousand-and-a-half-degree heat. She took the bottle and drank in quick, small sips.

But she defaulted on her plan, staring at his chiseled jaw, and his almond-shaped eyes that were framed by thick brows, until he coughed, and she realized he was waiting for her answer. "What do you need?"

He looked at the ground, then the sky, then over her left shoulder. Finally, he held out a piece of paper that had been folded, crumpled, and torn, judging by the wrinkles, creases, and tape holding it together. "I don't understand building codes. Can you explain this to me?"

She bit her lip to keep from smiling. Last thing she wanted was him thinking she was making fun of him. But there was something endearing about how Jay had almost looked around to see who might be listening. As if asking her for help was some kind of secret. She took the paper and read it. "A building code is a set of standards for construction and remodeling. There are federal and state standards. This paper just tells you the code numbers and stuff."

"Which ones apply here?" He made a sweeping gesture toward the slightly smaller pile of rubble.

She shook her head, handing the paper back to him. "All of them. You can't just build something, particularly for public use, without making sure the electrical, plumbing, fire safety, and so many more codes are up to state and federal standards. There are entire crews that'll be needed. Inspections have to be done every step of the way."

His face contorted. "So, more money?"

"Unfortunately."

He stalked away without another word. So much for a moment of possibly getting along. Of him possibly forgiving her. Penelope sighed and adjusted her gloves, tugged her boot gingerly back into place, and tried not to limp back to her debris pile next to the young park rangers who hadn't made much of a dent in cleaning up.

"Gosling used to date my older sister, way back in the day. High school." Brent, the older of the two young rangers, smiled at her and threw another charred board onto the trailer they were using to haul the mess away. "They were always in trouble for spray-painting and breaking curfew. Kids had to be safely inside and tucked into bed by eleven back then. My mom and my dad were always in court with them."

So, Gosling had a past. And while she remembered Judge Carter mentioning the incident, Brent divulged it was over a girl. Looked like Ranger Gosling also acted without common sense when it came to relationships. Maybe they had more in common than either of them realized. At least enough for an understanding to be built that could replace some of the anger.

Brent continued. "Then, they gave him a choice. If he didn't get his act together and graduate high school, he had to join the military. If he graduated, he could go to college and choose what he wanted to be."

Another ranger stopped mid-shovel. "He took college?"

"Wouldn't you?" Brent stood and swiped his wrist over his forehead, leaving a black streak of ash from eyebrow to hairline. "I should've worn a hat, too. I'm dying."

She smiled. These guys—and really, they couldn't have been much older than boys—had been working steadily since they'd all arrived at six. "Take a break. Get some water."

"No way. Can't have Jay going back to Nick complaining about us. This fire brought us out of a layoff." He leaned closer and lowered his voice. "Money's always tight, mid-summer. And the senior rangers like Jay can handle the crowds when the weather's too hot for many people to come out. I'm kind of glad this whole place burned with all the equipment. I mean, you know, it costs a lot to replace, but those machines were going to replace us."

She didn't know much about the program, but from what Charlie had explained, the GPS was to help rangers locate hunters if they needed help, got lost, faced a danger they couldn't get past, or any of the hundred other things that could go wrong when men with guns and arrows were set free in a wooded environment. The beacons were to guide the rangers to the hunter in the event the GPS failed. “Wouldn’t you guys still be needed to go get the hunter?”

Brent nodded. “But the patrols will be cut in half, so fewer patrols mean less manpower. We’ll be the first to go.” He grinned. “But not this fall.”

Now it all made sense, but she went back to work without comment because Ranger Gosling stood scowling at the edge of the parking lot.

She had blisters on top of her blisters—hands and feet. It’d probably be a year before she could make a fist. Her muscles ached, and the back of her neck had never been so sunburned. But still, she worked. By the end of the day, the site was mostly ready. There were nails to be picked up and the charred bits and pieces of the building still littered the ground, but they had made good progress.

She walked beside her new ranger friends, Brent and Eric, to her car. Jay approached, a rare smile on his face that made her heart skip a beat even as tired as she was. He was ridiculously handsome when his lips curled like that.

“You guys worked really hard today. Thank you,” he said.

Ranger Gosling had taken the trailer to remove the debris whenever the rangers and Penelope filled it. Then he brought it back for another go-round. She had no idea who helped him unload it because there was no one else around, but neither did she really care. Exhaustion, pain, the fact her hair was plastered to her cheeks and neck, all made it impossible to care about Jay Gosling's thoughts on her work ethic.

But damn him, that smile.

While he spoke to Brent, she began to ease her hand out of her gloves. She held her breath, a sick feeling rushing through her gut. Would've opened her mouth and yelped had there not been three people around. And even though one of them couldn't possibly think less of her, she held her head up and tried to exhale slowly. Slowly to rise above the fire in her hand.

"What are you doing?" Jay glanced at her, eyes narrow, brows drawn together.

Her glove slipped free, and she couldn't help the gasp that slipped out. "Nothing."

At her tone—an octave higher than usual—Ranger Gosling took her wrist in his hand to examine her blistered skin. His touch burned in a way she hadn't expected, one which she found pleasurable. Until he cursed creatively. "Why didn't you say something?"

Because he called her Princess Penelope. Because she didn't want him to think she couldn't handle it. Because this was her fault to begin with. She looked down at her palm and fingertips. Even the inside of her wrist where the fabric rubbed against her skin had blistered.

"It's not that bad." And still, she sounded like a member of cartoon land.

*"Penelope."* It was a growl, but somehow soft. A wounded rebuke like he was feeling her pain. He pulled her hand close to his lips and blew on each blister.

Her pulse began to race, an electrical jolt firing through her body. "I—I'm fine. I'll wrap them for tomorrow."

Ranger Gosling scoffed and shook his head. "You're

not working out here tomorrow. You can work in the office with Nick. You can help him choose the construction crew or whatever. But you're not coming out here. Clear?"

"Okay." She would have agreed to anything with him blowing on her hand like that. It was so sweet and disorienting after he'd been so cold and remote. Now it was like he wanted to heal her with his very breath.

This protective side came at her like a wrecking ball. She didn't know which way was up.

Until she looked back at her hand and the sting returned to her consciousness full force. Oh, to be able to leave this damn work site, put cream on her hands, and sleep until next week.

He gently lowered her hand. "You want me to drive you to the clinic to have that looked at? There's risk of infection if those blister pop open, you know."

She stared at his mouth, the white of his teeth so stark against his pink lips. Her face heated. Her pulse pounded so hard and fast that her entire body felt as if it was thumping. She swallowed hard and instinctively pressed her thighs together, an anticipating quiver in her lower belly.

When she felt the warm arousal between her legs, she forced her gaze from his eyes. "Lori has a first aid kit at the duplex. I can fix myself up."

He gave her a hard stare for a moment like he wasn't sure she was being truthful. Then, "Okay, but make sure you do. Now, off with you."

But she couldn't use her hands to open the car door, and the long and winding road would make driving a dangerous proposition since she wouldn't be able to grip the steering wheel with any kind of control. If not for

Havoc, she would have crawled into the hatchback and slept. But the dog had already been cooped up all day.

Brent and Eric had wasted no time climbing into their truck to leave, so Ranger Gosling was her only option. She dropped her hands to her sides since she couldn't bear to remove the other glove yet. "Ranger Gosling, can I get a ride home?"

He looked at her car and wrinkled his forehead, but nodded. "You can call me Jay."

He helped her climb in the truck and shut the door behind her. If she had one muscle that didn't ache or burn or feel like it had been twisted into a knot, she couldn't imagine where it was.

"Did you eat today?"

"Yeah." If an apple and a bag of dried banana chips could be called a meal. Not that she was dieting or on a health food kick, she just hadn't managed to pick up any real food.

He checked his watch. "I'll take you home and you can get comfortable, then I'll bring you something."

She wanted a bed and a pillow. And the last thing she wanted was to be a burden. Plus, she wanted to be able to have the ugly cries if she felt like it. Pity party for one tonight. That was totally on the menu. "I'll be fine. I'm sure there's something you'd rather be doing."

His sigh whooshed out as he started the engine before he squeezed his eyes shut and pinched the bridge of his nose. "This is my fault. I should've checked on you more often."

His words sounded choked out. For a moment she was too stunned to say anything.

"Are you saying I'm too delicate to clean up the mess I made?"

Jay shook his head. "Not at all. You did twice the work of those kids today, but your hands." He glanced at the hand still gloved on her lap. He shook his head. "You can't take that glove off, can you?"

No damned way would she complain and reinforce the Princess Penelope moniker. She'd been in worse shape.

Okay, not that she could remember.

Jay's fingers curled around the steering wheel. "Here's what we're going to do. I'm going to take you home and a friend of mine is going to come and take care of your hands while I get food, then you're going to bed. And you're not going to worry about working anywhere tomorrow."

His voice, forceful and direct, allowed no room for refusal or argument. She nodded, mostly because of the last part. And also because his commanding tone had reignited the flutter in her lower belly. If she tried to speak, her voice might give away her arousal.

Jay pulled into the street and headed toward town. "Where do you live?"

"I'm staying in the duplex on Sleigh Bell, the one with the cobalt blue siding."

"You live by Charlie?"

Penelope nodded and smiled despite the throbbing in her hands. She enjoyed having Charlie as a neighbor more than she ever imagined. And especially as a friend. Back in Manhattan, she hardly interacted with the people who lived in her apartment building, let alone barbecued with them. Work, Havoc, and her relationship had been her life.

Jay hung his head and sighed. Long. Deep. Loud. "She's going to kill me."

She glanced at his profile. "It isn't your fault."

"That's nice of you to say, but you were my responsibility, and I let you get injured."

Penelope shook her head. "I should've taken a break. I know better. If you can just get me home, I can handle everything else. I promise."

He pulled into her driveway, killed the engine, and turned in his seat to face her. "Unbutton your pants."

Her eyes widened and a giggle slipped out before she could stop it. She knew what he meant. Knew the exact point he was trying to make. But still, after his initial gruffness the first day, a little payback was deserved. So, she bit her lower lip and lowered her voice to be more sultry. "Ranger Gosling, are you getting fresh with me?"

He yanked at his collar, his cheeks turning red as he squirmed in the seat. "I'd like to see if you have the ability to use your hands to work a simple button. If that's being fresh, then yes."

She clicked her tongue three times and batted her lashes. "Well, I would love to show you, but I don't feel like our relationship has reached that point yet."

Plus, there was no way she could.

He squirmed again as if trying to shift to be more comfortable and she forced herself not to look down, to the area below his waist. He let out an audible breath. "Penelope, we're going back to the original plan. Food, doctor friend, bed, day off." When she opened her mouth to protest, he held up a finger. "No."

"But—"

"No."

"Jay—"

"*Penelope*, I'm going to take care of you, and if you

raise a fuss, you're going to have to call Charlie in her official capacity to get me out of there. Understood?"

Her little seductive payback appeared to have more of an effect on her than on Jay because the idea of him in her home, taking care of her, had her head spinning. Okay, and at the mention of Charlie in her official capacity, the image of handcuffs may have flashed in her mind.

But when she placed a hand on the door handle, the instant sharp pain chased away every thought and she nodded. "Can I just say one thing?"

His eyes narrowed as he considered her. "Not if it has anything to do with telling me you'll be fine, you can handle this yourself, or anything of that nature." He held up a finger for each of his conditions.

In the time it took him to lay out his conditions, she developed a sudden and powerful urge to use the bathroom. Which posed a whole new set of problems. But no damned way was he going to be in the bathroom helping her pee. "Counteroffer. You get Charlie and food and your doctor friend—in that order—then you are absolved from your obligations to me. Deal?" She would have held out a hand to shake, but the thought of anyone or anything touching her hands ever again made her cringe.

Jay nodded. "Fine."

Her bladder insisted she move. She powered through the pain of pushing the door open and slid out of the car. That was going to hurt like hell later on, probably as soon as her mind wasn't so entirely focused on getting to the bathroom. And, of course, her keys were tucked securely in her pants pocket.

Jay jogged to Charlie's side of the duplex and

knocked. After a minute with no answer, he stood and looked in the window of the garage door. "She's not home yet," he yelled over as Penelope was ready to cry in frustration before her front door.

In order, she mentally recounted her problems. Hands useless. Keys in pocket. Need to pee. Glove still snug on one hand. Sucking up her embarrassment seemed the most viable and expedient option before she ended up leaving a puddle on the sidewalk.

She exhaled in a burst. "You're right! I can't get the keys out of my pocket. I can't undo my pants, and I *really* have to pee. Please get over here now!"

Humiliating. Embarrassing. Worst day of her life. And considering her last couple of months, that said something.

Until he slid one arm around her waist to steady her and pushed his hand into her pocket. It took maybe a second, second and a half tops, before every nerve ending in her skin fired off. His body pressed against hers, ignited her blood. Caused her heart to race, her nipples to pebble, and when she felt his arousal against her, a small moan escaped her lips. She'd all but forgotten why she'd been in such a rush to get inside until his arm around her waist tightened.

"Jay..."

# *Chapter Ten*

### *Jay*

His dick twitched against his zipper, the little metal teeth ready to latch onto his wayward erection. Like he was some goddamned high school kid. The only way he wasn't going to embarrass himself was to move away before she felt the evidence of what simply touching her did to him. His mind went blank as he inhaled her floral coconut scent, strong even through the soot, ash, and sweat that encased her body. His nerves were shooting off sparks, like it was the Fourth of July and he was the show finale.

"Jay, the door," she choked out.

He blinked hard, stepped around her, and unlocked the duplex. In all the fuss about her hands, he'd forgotten about the dog, who barreled out to welcome Penelope home. Even she took a moment too long to brace herself and ended up on her butt with an eighty-pound dog's tongue bathing her face as she fought between laughter, swearing, and gasps of pain.

He wrestled the dog off her so she could scramble to her feet and speed walk to the bathroom. And damnit, she still needed help. He hauled the dog back inside and kicked the door shut. “Penelope?”

“In here. Hurry!”

He followed her voice down the hall and knocked on a door, his stomach hitting his feet. “Okay for me to come in?” This was way too weird and personal and awkward.

Her voice came an octave higher than normal, followed by a sniffle. “You’ll have to.”

His fault. Every bit of this. Her hands. The dog knocking her down. The fact he was going to spend all night—probably the rest of the year—remembering how soft, how perfect her body felt against his.

*“Jay.”*

“Okay. I’m coming in.” *Don’t make this weirder than it has to be.* He pushed open the door, then closed his eyes and stood to wait for direction.

Her pained chuckle floated over his skin. “Uh, how the hell are you going to see the button with your eyes closed?”

“I don’t need to see it.” He didn’t. Buttons on pants were all located in basically the same spot. She was roughly six inches shorter than him, which would put her button about six inches lower. Simple math. He reached down to where her button should have been.

And wasn’t.

He’d misjudged their height difference and grabbed a bit lower than her waistband. Nothing in the danger zone, thank God. His eyelids snapped open and heat flooded his cheeks. “Penelope, I’m so sorry.”

She danced from one foot to the other. “Really don’t have time for this.”

More of an idiot had never lived. He unbuttoned her pants and turned. "You need anything else?"

"No. Nope. I can take it from here." She shooed him away with her raw hands.

He left before he could do anything else that would haunt him for the rest of his life. Guilt ate at him. The dog stared at him. And Penelope was injured. All his fault. He should've been more careful. Should have spent more time making sure everyone took breaks and stayed hydrated instead of assuming everyone was as much of a workhorse as he was.

"Stop looking at me like that." Havoc put his head down as Jay pulled out his phone and called Doc Baker. Jay'd spent a whole day helping Doc and his wife, Angela, move into their new place a couple months ago. A house call would be repayment for services rendered.

Just as he ended the call, Penelope walked out in a pair of sweats nearly as enticing as her jeans. Loose strands of brown hair framed her oval face as her emerald green eyes focused on him. "Who were you talking to?"

"Johnny, erm, Doc Baker, should be here soon. Is there anything I can get you?"

"Nope. I'm good." But the lines around her narrowed lips and the squint of her eyes said otherwise.

Jay paced back and forth before sitting on the chair across from her, scratching behind his ear. He wanted to rewind the day and keep her from getting hurt. Every time his gaze fell to her hands, his chest tightened. When he looked into her eyes, his heart stuttered.

Where was all this coming from? If it was another member of the work crew, he'd be just as concerned, right?

Well, no. The rest of the crew were guys. Or mostly anyway. Maybe that was it. She was a woman, and Gramps had always taught him to treat them with care and consideration.

But care and consideration didn't make your guts somersault and your pulse rip through your veins. Huh. He'd have to be careful around this female all right. Keep his feelings in check.

He looked at Havoc as the German shepherd crawled onto the sofa beside Penelope, leaving him to his fractured thoughts and haphazard topics of conversation as they waited for the doctor.

Two hours later, with the doctor gone, her hands medicated and wrapped in white gauze, food from Clover's in her belly and her eyes drooping in response to both the oral painkillers and the long day of work, Jay *could* have left. Charlie had come bearing dog treats, but she'd long ago left to get some sleep before her morning shift. A shift he'd have to get up for also.

"You doing okay?"

Penelope nodded, drowsily, invoking all manner of inappropriate thoughts involving bedsheets and tangled brown hair. Whatever Doc Baker had given her to ease the pain had obviously started working. Before he could force himself to leave, she smiled. Really smiled.

His stomach clenched, his gaze moving from that sexy smile to her eyes. *Exquisite.*

Havoc sat between them with his head in her lap, his tail slapping Jay's leg. That tail never seemed to stop. Jay placed a hand on Penelope's forearm. "You should probably go to bed. Those pills seem to be doing their job."

"Yeah." She leaned her head back for a moment, then scooted toward him, pushing Havoc off the sofa. There were about a thousand reasons he should get up and go home. But he remained glued in place as she inched closer.

"Why don't you like me? I mean other than the fire, why don't you like me?" With her eyes half-lidded, determination still shone through bright enough to take his breath. She closed the gap between them and slipped her gauzed hand up his chest to his throat. Her unwrapped thumb stroked the line of his jaw, making his insides heat and his dick throb.

He gripped her wrist firmly. "Penelope…"

She countered by leaning in closer with that sultry smile, and that damned stroking thumb. "I tried to work hard today, to show you how sorry I am."

"I know." His voice was tight and strained, like his body. Their lips were a hair apart. God, he wanted to kiss her, to explore her mouth. He didn't move, thought about closing the last distance to find out what she tasted like.

His eyes started to flutter closed, his breaths growing shallow. But instead of moving forward, Jay scooted away from her hand. She wasn't in charge of her own mind. She was high on painkillers. And he wasn't the type of guy to take advantage.

She snorted and quirked a brow. "Good to know you're a man of honor. Anyway I have something for you, a quote. For the rebuild. And suppliers who will give you the deals I based those prices on. Not my body." She jerked her head to the left, her voice slightly slurred from the meds. "It's on the desk by the laptop. Red folder. I put a list of contractors who could do the work you need done. They're all good. I've worked with them before on jobs. The quote includes a high ballpark estimate of what it would cost for labor."

He stood, walked to the desk, and picked up the folder. This would determine how much money they would have left over or have to raise to implement the safety program. With a quiet deep breath, he opened the folder and flipped through—as if he had any idea what he was reading, because all he could focus on was Penelope and how much he wanted to feel her in his arms, feel her lips against his.

Until his eyes fell on the bottom line, the all-important dollar amount. His heart sank. Plummeted, actually, straight to his shoes. The number couldn't be right.

Fuck.

He'd hoped they could rebuild and have enough money left over for the equipment he needed to replace. So much for anything going his way lately. He closed the folder and his eyes.

"What about insurance?" She mumbled the question as she slumped farther down on the sofa.

"Insurance?"

She sighed, the soft, quiet sound almost content. It settled somewhere inside him, warm and peaceful. "Shouldn't the park service have its building and equipment insured? Wouldn't that help with the repairs?"

Insurance. *Of course.* There'd be coverage in case of fire. There was the bright light he'd been looking for at the end of the tunnel. And thanks to Penelope Ramos, it would light his way through this wreck.

"That's…yeah. Insurance. I'll look into that." God, she looked beautiful, her eyelashes lying against her cheeks, her feet tucked up underneath her as she snuggled into the sofa, ready to sleep.

*Get. The fuck. Out. Now.*

He stumbled around the couch and grabbed his keys before he was tempted to stay and curl up beside her. "I'll check on you later, but if you need something sooner, call me." He jotted his number on the message pad on the desk, then walked back to her, leaned down, and pressed his lips against the top of her head before he even knew what he was doing. Her eyes fluttered open, but before she could say anything, he left, locking the door behind him, and drove first to the office to grab the insurance file, then to Gramps's house.

The drive wasn't far and while he should be focused on the road, especially for deer that might pop out, his attention roamed back to Penelope. On how she got hurt under his watch. See, this was why he couldn't be responsible for someone else. But it wasn't just that. His attraction to her was becoming a problem. At first it was about the parts of her being he admired. Now his body was responding, craving to be close to her.

And having sex with the person he was supervising for the court was out of the question. Conflict of interest. No, he followed the rules. And sleeping with Penelope would break all sorts of rules.

But she just had to keep clawing her way under his skin, this time with the damn quote. How would he be able to continue resisting her? He gripped the steering wheel. He had to find a way.

He climbed out of his truck, clutching the papers detailing the quotes Penelope had gotten tightly in his fist. The lights were still on at Gramps's. Jay hurried up the porch stairs, his hand pounding a bit too hard against the wooden door.

Several moments later his grandfather swung open the door, his brows furrowed. “Jay, everything okay?”

“Maybe.” Jay walked past his grandfather and straight into the kitchen, placing the papers on the table as he dropped into one of the chairs.

Gramps sat across from him. After putting on his reading glasses, Gramps looked over the paperwork. Jay sat barely resisting the urge to bite his nails while his grandfather read every letter on every page, sometimes nodding, sometimes shaking his head.

“I don’t know. Without building plans, a diagram, something more than a material list and numbers on a page, I can’t tell if she knows her business or if she’s putting words in a file.”

Jay frowned. “She said she went with a simple square building, front and back door, a couple windows in front, and a bathroom. She has fixtures listed for the bathroom and measurements for the foundation. I would assume she went with that.”

“Metal roofing. An option for vinyl siding or wood. That’s good.” Gramps nodded again. “Was the equipment inside the building added to the insurance before it burned?”

“I don’t know. I’ll find out from Nick tomorrow morning. I submitted all the paperwork when we bought it, but it could be sitting on someone’s desk at the capital for all I know.” And wouldn’t that be just his luck?

Gramps flipped to another page. “Langdon Construction. I know old Cal Langdon. Good guy. Left the company to his idiot son.” He ran his finger down the page. “Monroe Building and Design is also a good operation. They work around the state." Gramps had been a painter for most of his life and had worked on large and small jobs with a variety of contractors, so Jay trusted his judgment. "If I had to pick who to work with, based on reputation and quality, you want Monroe. They'll stand by their bid. Some of the others lowball and then put you through eighty paces to keep the prices low, or they 'find' things they didn't 'account for.'" Gramps used his air quotes to emphasize his distaste for the shadiness in the business.

"I think it'll come down to the bids. I don't know that I'll have much input."

Gramps shook his head. "Take some initiative. Tell Nick that a bid that's a lot lower is going to be one that ends up costing more with add-ons and short shipments. Trust me. Monroe is your guy." He set the folder down and picked up his coffee shakily, blowing into the mug before taking a sip, though it had been poured more than an hour ago. Gramps didn't drink iced coffee, but he certainly didn't mind letting his cup of joe cool to room temperature.

"There are some cuts you could make if you have the manpower to do it yourselves." Gramps twisted his lips to the side. "She has a line item for painting labor. That's a place where your crew could do the work and save right around a thousand smackers. And you cut a lot of hours off the drywall crew if you do the sanding. But the material looks about right, assuming you build a straight square with nothing fancy."

"What do you think the chances are?"

Gramps shook his head. "Carter said the governor is planning a visit with the election year coming up. He won't want to look like he's cheaping out. Could work in your favor if you pitch him the safety program. But if he's working the budget side, it's not going to be pretty. Think you can fox-trot your way into another fundraiser?"

"Very funny."

"I'm not laughing."

And if it was what Jay had to do to put his safety program into action, he'd waltz until his legs fell off.

# *Chapter Eleven*

*Penelope*

The next morning, Governor Sam Felton stood, hard hat on his head, shovel in his hand, at the edge of the work site while about ten photographers snapped their shutters and shouted questions. The governor wouldn't likely use the shovel or need the hard hat, but it sure made for good press. Penelope chuckled when Jay—who stood beside Nick on stage—rolled his dark eyes and clenched his chiseled jaw.

Penelope's neck and cheeks heated when her gaze focused on the angry set of Jay's lips. The full, luscious, begged-to-be-kissed kind. And oh, how she'd wanted him to kiss her last night. Their lips had been so close his breath tickled her skin. Sure, she'd been dazed because of the meds. But once the pain in her hands subsided she couldn't concentrate on anything but Jay's hard body. All of it. She swallowed and returned her focus to the governor before she ended up soaking her underwear from fantasizing about the hot ranger.

"A bigger, better check station, full service, manned by the best rangers this fine state has to offer." Bigger?

Better? To Penelope, it sounded like money. A lot of money.

One of the reporters stepped forward, hand raised. "Jim Duquette. *Vermont Voice.* Last year, you pitched a safety program with GPS location services and emergency beacons that would reduce the number of personnel staffed during hunting seasons and, therefore, decrease the budget. Now we've been told the equipment burned up inside the check station. Will it be replaced and ready for this year?"

The governor turned his chin down. "Sadly, this year the budget isn't going to allow us to replace the equipment, but the state and forest service will be best served by spending the funds to rebuild the check station. We have the staff in place to ensure another completely safe hunting season without having to rely on the new equipment."

Damn.

"Was the equipment covered on the state's insurance policy?" Thank God for Jim Duquette.

"Unfortunately, since it was purchased in the early summer, the paperwork didn't go through with Vermont State Insurance."

"Shouldn't it have been covered at the federal level?"

Good point.

"All we know so far is that due to a clerical error, the equipment wasn't covered." The governor smiled, nodded, removed the hard hat, and waved to the reporters as he walked back to his black SUV.

Penelope turned on her heels and hurried back to her own vehicle before any of the reporters noticed her. She'd hid at the back of the crowd, baseball cap pulled down to cover her face. When she was about ten feet from the SUV, Havoc bounded out the window.

*Mierda.*

She'd left the window too low and in his excitement at seeing her, he must have realized freedom was within reach. He ran right to Jay, who cringed as the dog slipped his wet snout against his left hand. Her hands were still bandaged, thick with white gauze that left only her thumbs visible. Penelope was about to run toward them when Jay stopped her and pointed to one of the young rangers speaking to a reporter. The young ranger then pointed at Penelope.

"Miss Ramos! Jim Duquette from the *Vermont Voice*. Do you have a minute for an interview?"

Jay beelined toward her and took her by the arm, Havoc at his heels. He shielded her with his body as Penelope loaded Havoc back into the vehicle. "Miss Ramos has no comment."

Duquette shoved his voice recorder in Penelope's direction. "Do you plan to pay any restitution for the money you've cost the state of Vermont, and can you explain why Judge Carter sentenced you so lightly?"

"No comment."

"Do you have a special arrangement with the governor?"

Her breath stopped, then restarted on a furious inhale. There was no mistaking the innuendo in the question. Before she could give the reporter a piece of her mind, Jay shoved Duquette hard. And when the reporter stepped toward her once more, Jay swung and caught the reporter in the jaw, dropping him to the asphalt beside her SUV.

Jay shook his hand at his side as Nick rushed over.

Duquette promised to have Jay's job. Penelope gritted her teeth to keep from making the situation worse. God, she wanted to spit in Duquette's face. No, more like plant a foot in the jerk's face. But molten red crawled up Nick's neck, and when his narrow eyes fell on her, she backed up.

"The two of you get out of here now." Nick spoke from between clenched teeth and turned to Jay, shoving him toward the parking lot. Penelope climbed into her Audi and Jay walked—head down, eyes on his feet—to his own truck.

Penelope's hands trembled as she drove into town. Why had Jay punched the guy? Not that the reporter didn't deserve it, but *whoa*. No man had ever stood up for her like that. But Jay didn't care for her very much. Though after last night *and* the way he took care of her *and* the way he'd been shielding her from the reporter, maybe that was changing.

Either way, his action was exhilarating. Everyone always talked about finding a partner who would stand up for them when it counted. Just the way Jay had. It made her like him even more. Not to mention jumped her attraction to the ranger from off the chart, due to his honorability last night in not taking advantage of her, to damn near infinite.

She kept watch in her rearview mirror as Jay followed her all the way back into town. She blew out a breath and pulled up to Clover's. As she got out of her car, Jay pulled in next to her.

He exited his truck and shoved his hands into his pockets, flinching when his knuckles rubbed against the fabric. Penelope bit her bottom lip and dragged her feet as she walked over to him. *What do I say?* Why would he have put himself—his job—on the line for her like that? She suddenly found herself strangely shy. "Is your hand okay?"

He nodded. "Want to get something to eat?"

This time she nodded.

They walked into the diner, taking a booth toward the back of the room. People stared. It was what they did, but damn, that didn't make it easier to sit without fidgeting. She considered hiding behind her menu, but instead, pretended she didn't notice. *Fake it, 'til you make it.*

The TV played in one corner of the diner, a local news program, but she didn't listen. Didn't care. That same program had detailed the fire, her part in it complete with her booking photo, and what the fire had and would cost the government.

"Ready to order?" The waitress—Marly, according to her name tag—came to the edge of the table bringing two cups of coffee. She aimed a bright smile at Jay as she took out her pen and pad. "Hi, Ranger Gosling. Special today is roast beef on a hoagie with au jus, mashed potatoes with a savory brown gravy, and fresh steamed green beans." She popped a hip and cocked her head. "Interested?"

No way was the woman talking about the food. Penelope didn't know if she should laugh or stare her down. This was the man who'd just slugged a reporter on her behalf; no one else should dare flirt with him for at least the rest of the day.

Maybe all week.

Jay nodded and awarded the waitress a smile with maybe even a glint of humor in his eyes. "Sounds great to me."

"Yeah, me, too." Penelope closed her menu and

handed it back to perky Marly, who made a point of taking the unlit candle off the table. Penelope rolled her eyes. "The people here just love me."

Jay set his coffee down with a clank of restaurant china against the Formica tabletop. "Does it matter?"

The staring bothered her. The whispers annoyed her. Apparently, yeah. It mattered. She took a sip of her coffee and stared out the window. "Not to me."

He chuckled. "Looks like it matters."

Once upon a time, before burnt-down buildings and swollen hands, she hadn't really cared what people thought. Now, her head ached with how much it mattered. Especially to Jay. "Let's just talk about something else."

She glanced back at the TV, listened as a picture of the proposed design for the new check station flashed up onto the screen. Not the design she'd seen in Nick's office. This one had more windows, a second floor, twice the size of the original. The screen flashed back to a shot of the governor next to one of the news anchors who looked like the live-action version of a Barbie doll.

Anchorwoman Susan Doyle smiled at the mayor, her powder blue suit the perfect contrast to his navy pinstriped pants and crisp white button-down. They could have been Barbie and her much older boyfriend, Ken.

Because of the silverware clanking, china plates thwacking, coffee maker brewing, and murmuring of conversations, Penelope couldn't hear the news broadcast. But then her picture flashed onto the screen next to a photo of Judge Carter. She should've stopped watching, but she couldn't. And when a graphic—cost to the county $430,000—flashed onto the lower half of the picture, an ache rushed through her. When several heads turned in her direction, she wanted to shrink, to curl into herself and disappear. Oh, where was a magician to Houdini her out of there when she needed one?

"Want to get out of here?"

Apparently, Jay was her defender and Houdini rolled into one delicious, brooding package. She wanted to say yes—*really* wanted to—but shook her head. If she left now, she would look so weak to everyone. It would be another level of shame. Like she didn't deserve to be among them. Not to mention, she felt safe in Jay's presence. "No. I'm hungry. You're hungry. Plus, we already ordered."

Honestly, with so much happening in the world, how long could the news spend on a local story? Not to mention, four hundred and thirty grand was a substantially larger number than she'd proposed for the new building. Her eyes narrowed. "So, they changed the building plans?"

"*Changed.* Nice way to put it." His dry tone said he didn't approve. So did the glare up at the TV and the clenching of his fists until his knuckles turned white. "State of the art. Governor wants to move the offices to the check station instead of having a separate building. It's a bad idea."

"Outside of the cost, why is it a bad idea?" Penelope took another sip of coffee. There would be more room for him and his crew to work, to spread out, to really utilize the features of the safety equipment.

"Even if the state could afford it, we'll have to borrow from federal funds, which is allowed, but then there will be loan fees from the feds we hadn't counted on before. Then there's the fact the check station is in a secluded area for a reason. Hunting areas that are full of people don't have much to hunt. The animals spook and find new places to bed down and to live. So, not only will the environment be trampled, first during construction, then again when the general public has to come out here to get their permits and their hunting licenses, it's going to be changed when the animals migrate to a different area." He shook his head, drumming his fingers against the Formica tabletop. "And let's not forget the rentals that draw people out here—kayaks, bikes for the trails, climbing equipment. Right now, it all comes from the office, which is close to the lake, close to the bike trails. The check station site is too far away for those rentals to be convenient. And they're taking another acre of ground to enlarge the parking lot. One acre doesn't sound like a lot, but it's an entire ecosystem out there that will be disrupted. The environmental ramifications are endless."

"And the safety program?"

"There's no money this year to replace the equipment." He nodded to the waitress as she set his plate in front of him and smiled like she'd just won the Miss America pageant. She gave Penelope her plate sans smile, but courteously anyway.

She kinda liked that Jay didn't understand the effect he had on women. When they'd walked in earlier, people stared at her, but women fawned over him. Marly was only one of his admirers. Not that Penelope didn't understand. Jay had plenty of likable and admirable attributes. All that wavy, satin, black hair that begged to be touched, eyes so expressive with a gaze so intense she'd spent a night dreaming about him just staring at her, a body built by hard work, a mind always working, spinning on invisible wheels that connected one thought to the next. A working mind was damned attractive. And the way he cared for her, protected her.

Yeah, he was attractive beyond his physicality.

Not that she'd ever share any of that with him.

"Hey." He snapped his fingers twice in front of her face. "Where'd you go?"

She straightened her spine, brushing her hands over her thighs, chasing off invisible crumbs. She sank an end of her roast beef sandwich in the au jus sauce and took a bite. A bit of the juice dribbled down her chin, and she raised her napkin to catch it. "Just thinking. I destroyed your program. It was important and I need to do something more than what Judge Carter has me doing. I don't have money, but I have skills." She glanced away from him and lined up the green beans next to one another, as if they were cord wood.

"Skills?" He quirked an eyebrow at her and plowed his fork into the mound of mashed potatoes.

"You've seen my pictures." She placed her forearms on the table and leaned back. "Maybe we could find a way to get people out here, get their pictures taken and charge a couple bucks each." She'd never done that before, but grasping at straws previously had produced some of her best ideas.

He chuckled. "You're not at all like I suspected." He forked in a bite of his green beans, which were dripping with savory bacon grease, and chewed thoughtfully. "You're remorseful and working so hard to try to fix this. Even after I've been…" He looked down at his plate.

"A little less than nice." She softened the words with her tone.

He nodded.

"You're not all bad. You didn't have to stay with me yesterday or call your doctor friend. And you certainly didn't have to punch the reporter, not that I'm complaining." She winked at him and noticed the way color began to blossom on his cheeks. Penelope fiddled with the fork in her hand, wanting to know more about the blushing ranger who sat across from her. "What do you do when you aren't working?"

"These days all I do is work."

So, Jay didn't like talking about himself. She wasn't surprised based on the few details Charlie had mentioned about him. She'd dated several guys who hadn't minded talking about themselves. In fact, they'd talked themselves right out of a relationship with her. Selfishness was definitely in the non-attractive column for dating.

She'd learned her lesson. No more selfish pricks. Not that she was planning on dating Jay, either. But he was certainly setting a bar for any future dates she may go on.

Penelope sipped her water, her gazed focused on unselfish, protective, brooding Jay. She smiled to herself, wondering how many adjectives she'd pile on him before the night was over. "Come on. There has to be some pastime you enjoy."

He stared at her for a long few seconds then set his fork down and leaned in. He waited for her to move forward as if he didn't want anyone else to hear his top-secret hobby. "I sculpt."

"Sculpt? Like statues?"

"Some. Other pieces are more obscure."

Penelope leaned back into her seat. Creative. Huh. She bit her bottom lip to stop a smile from tilting her lips and fiddled with a piece of roast beef. Exactly how creative could her ranger get? Like Swayze in *Ghost* level? She cleared her throat when her cheeks started to heat, then looked up at him. “Can I see?”

He didn’t waver, didn’t look away or flinch. “Why?”

Now it was her turn to stare, to try to read the studied stillness behind his eyes, to figure if her answer was important. She only had one answer to give. “I’m interested.”

“In what?”

“You.” The answer came automatically. No sensor. No filter for content.

Jay cleared his throat as if he’d choked on his potatoes just as his phone pinged. When he checked the message, his shoulders slumped forward while his mouth downturned. “We have to get back to the office. Nick wants to meet with both of us.”

Penelope reached across the table and laid her hand on top of Jay’s forearm. “Look at it this way, if you get fired, more time in the studio, right?” Not her best comforting words, but he had punched a guy. While in uniform. On government property. Fired was probably one of the better outcomes he could hope for.

# *Chapter Twelve*

## *Jay*

Penelope sat in a chair across the desk from Nick while Jay paced behind her in the small office, definitely not thinking about the scent of gardenia emanating from her hair, about the way the sun streaming through the window made her hair glow like the fire she'd started, nor about the fire she stirred in his belly, especially when she flirted with him at the diner.

Jay's neck corded. He was about to be fired because of some misogynist asshole. "He implied—"

"That's what reporters do. They imply and infer, and we, employees of the state, take what they say and disregard it. Ignore it. We, sure as hell, do not go Muhammad Ali on them and try to take them down." Nick tapped his pen against the desk at a fast pace. "The governor is going to be on my ass because instead of his photo op on the front page of the paper, it's going to be you throwing down with a reporter to save Penelope's reputation. You're goddamned lucky I could smooth this over with the reporter and your ass isn't sitting in jail."

Nick turned his attention to Penelope. "And you! Hope you're happy."

Penelope threw both hands up in the air. "What did I do?"

"Leave her out of this. I hit the…guy." His nostrils flared. Not the word he wanted to use, but considering Nick's current state of anger, anything else would have only further incited his boss.

Nick threw the pen onto the desk. "Didn't you tell her to stay home?"

"He actually told me to work with you today, which is why I came out there. One of the rangers in your office told me where you'd be." She met Nick's glower with one of her own, and Jay couldn't help but be proud. A woman who wasn't afraid to stand up to Nick. Kinda like Charlie.

"The point is, if you hadn't burned down my building, the governor would never have come, the reporters would have found something more interesting to report, and I wouldn't have to spend my afternoon writing up my chief of rangers and fielding phone calls from an angry governor."

"That's enough, Nick." Boss or not, Jay needed to squash Nick's tantrum before it got worse. After all, Jay'd experienced Nick at his worst, when stress got the best of him, and that would be too much to take out on Penelope. "I acted without her permission, knowledge, or any sign she wanted me to take a swing at the guy. Hell, I don't even know if she'd heard what that jackass said. I'm the one who hit him. Not her."

"Oh, I heard, and trust me when I say I held back from kicking him when he was down." Her glower dropped, and she smiled at Nick. "And you're right, everything since the fire has been my fault, but I'm here now, trying to make it right in the best ways that I can. And I take full responsibility for this latest fiasco, too."

Jay walked until he was standing right next to Penelope. She wasn't going to take full blame for everything that happened. He wouldn't let her be a martyr. "Anyone who read the fire report would know it wasn't entirely your fault. More like Murphy's Law. If the building was up to date, if the grills were replaced, maybe this whole fiasco wouldn't have happened." He placed a hand on her shoulder. "And no way in hell was anything that jerk said your fault."

Nick rolled his eyes. "Hey, Romeo, get Juliet out of my office before I fire you and call Carter and have her sent to jail."

Without a word, Jay placed his hand on Penelope's shoulder and led her out of the building to where she'd tied Havoc to the porch rail outside. Even being in the chilled air was a lot better than standing in the office a second longer. Besides, his damned hand still ached.

But he wasn't ready to part ways. Not from someone who was strong, someone who stood by his side when Nick scolded him. "Still want to see my sculptures?"

Penelope's eyes widened while her mouth opened and closed a couple of times, yet no words came out. Eventually, she just nodded and followed him to the parking lot. They climbed into his truck. She wanted to see the part of him no one else knew about, the part that had saved him from himself, and for some reason he wanted to show her.

He drove quietly, blowing out a breath every once in a while, trying to calm his racing heart, trying not to lean over and inhale the floral coconut scent emanating from her skin. He'd been hurt enough to last a lifetime, and giving Penelope the chance to judge him and his creations was a big step.

He pulled up at the farm and bypassed the house to park in front of the barn. It didn't look like much from the outside, certainly not a place that had saved his life. The hayloft door had long ago been replaced with a plain, discolored grouping of boards that either looked too new or too old to match the rest. Jay could never decide. And the wooden doors had been weatherproofed to protect his work so the grinding noise as he slid them open always grated on his ears.

Today he didn't notice them so much, and that alone said a lot.

Penelope was here because he'd asked her, and as much as he was having second thoughts and wanted to steer her back to the truck, he didn't. He let her walk in before him, let her breathe in the smell of hay and freshly chipped wood, the scent of clay that had been fired in the oven. He flicked on the overhead lights and stood against the doorframe, not quite ready to bare his soul through his work. These sculptures were pieces of himself, parts he'd opened up and wrestled with in the work.

Penelope now stood where he'd spent so much time converting the barn into his studio. The big windows had been added so he could have adequate daylight, the high ceiling that allowed his creativity to soar, the kiln oven that transformed his work from blobs of clay into lasting pieces, and sculptures of wood, clay, and metal, some finished, but many in various stages of production.

She wandered from one piece of artwork to another, her small hand reaching out and touching his work. Jay thought it would be agony to have someone, anyone, in his studio, a place where he created light from his darkness, where he worked on exorcizing his demons. To his surprise, he enjoyed watching her weave her way through the room. Though, she hadn't said anything about the quality of his workmanship, or if she understood his vision.

He found himself holding his breath, unsure if he truly wanted her to understand, to see his pain. Maybe it would change the way she viewed him. Maybe instead of someone strong enough to protect her, she'd see him as less than. The same way Karen did. As if there was a limit to what he could offer.

Finally, Penelope turned to him. "Have you ever thought of selling your work?"

Jay expelled his breath and cleared his throat. She thought his work had merit? It shouldn't have meant as much as his heart was making it out to be. He tried to control his galloping pulse as he gazed at her. He had no clue whether she understood anything about sculpting, but hopefully she could tell how deeply he cared for the subjects of the clay statues—an old man, a beautiful German pointer, and a woman whom he'd fashioned after his grandmother. Was Penelope able to see the love that went into each piece? And the carved wooden pieces—the same German pointer, his beloved Zip in motion, a ship that could have belonged to a pirate or a Viking king, and a half-finished replica of the house they'd passed as he drove them in—could she tell he'd created them with care and a firm, but delicate touch? Suddenly, he was dying to know which she considered worthy of trying to sell.

He glanced around at the various pieces dotting the

floor of the barn. It would be hard to let go of the things he'd created. They were all personal, created in times of despair as a way to remember those he'd lost. A physical representation of happier times, life, and joy he held in his heart. "Do you honestly think someone other than myself would appreciate my art?"

She ran her fingers over the wood carving of the German pointer. "I took an art appraisal class in college, and I know work like this could bring a substantial payday."

The thought was so unexpected he didn't know what to say. *Again.*

This was becoming a common occurrence around her.

He dug the toe of his boot into the dirt and chewed on the inside of his cheek, trying to find a way to calm all the fluttering occurring in his chest.

"The world needs to see your talent, Jay. This work needs to be in people's homes. I know a few galleries in town that we visited during my art class. I can help you with some introductions, if you'd like. I could take some pictures of your work, see if there's any interest." She shifted her gaze from the art to him. "That is, if you're willing to let some of these go. I know artists can fall in love with their work and don't want to relinquish it, regardless of the price tag someone's willing to meet."

She ran her hand along the carved wood dog's coat, over the curve of its back. The wood had been sanded to a smooth, splinter-free shine. "How did you learn to do all this?"

Jay followed the sensual movement of her fingers, swallowing past the lump in his throat. The statue wasn't the real Zip, but he used to pet his partner in the same way, with the same care. "Gramps taught me the wood-carving."

Her smile warmed him to his core. "Did Gramps ever sell any of his work?"

He shrugged. "It was always just a hobby with him. He'd whittle little pieces while he was teaching me how to be a man, and I finally got him to stop giving me life lessons and instead give me wood-carving lessons." His face heated even more with the admission. Something about Penelope flayed him open. Made him vulnerable.

He hoped it wouldn't come back to bite him.

"Every strand of hair has its own identity on the wooden dog. The sails on the boat are held by slivers of wood so thin and delicate it's a wonder you didn't break them while you were carving them. Gramps knows his stuff." Penelope's gaze shifted from the wood sculptures to the other mediums. "And the rest?"

"I learned to sculpt clay in high school. I took art as one of those easy classes, just to get the letter grade. I figured how hard could it be to draw some lines, make some ashtrays. But I ended up liking it." He found working with clay soothing. And art class was a way to get out of chorus. No matter how hard he tried, Jay couldn't hold a tune. "Now, I come out here when I can't sleep, when my mind won't quiet." More self-disclosure. Jesus.

"You live in the house?"

"No, the house belongs to Gramps." He jerked his head toward the road they'd come in on. "I live at the edge of the property. Gramps didn't like having me under his feet and telling him what to do, so I'm close enough to watch out for him, but far enough away we both get some privacy."

Penelope spun around to meet his gaze. "Is Gramps okay?"

Jay rubbed the back of his neck, his body growing cold as if someone shoved him into a meat locker. "He has Parkinson's and sometimes...it's rough. Sometimes he needs help."

Penelope placed her gauzed-wrapped hand gently on his upper arm. "I understand. Since my mom died a couple of years ago, I've been having dinner with my father every other week. A way to check in and see how he is. Guess it's our turn to start worrying about the people who raised us."

His breath caught in his throat as he stared at her, warmth enveloping his body. The loss of a caretaker was personal, so personal, and Penelope had allowed herself to be vulnerable with him. He appreciated it more than he could even articulate to himself. When he brought his hand up to her cheek, her olive skin tinted pink. "I'm sorry for your loss, Penelope."

They stared into one another's eyes for a long moment, a quiet communication that knocked down another layer of his defenses. His pulse sped up, a lightheadedness rising into the silence that alarmed him.

*Easy does it.*

Penelope was only here temporarily. She lived in New York City. Her life was there. Her job was there. And as she just mentioned, so was her father, whom she needed to check up on. Just like Gramps was here in Maple Falls for him to take care of.

Which was why there was no possible future for them as anything more than coworkers, because she would eventually leave him. Just like everyone else.

Jay's heart hammered at his ribs like it wanted to

tear right out of his chest. He grabbed the front of his shirt, stepping back to create distance between them. The warmth in Penelope's eyes morphed into hurt and confusion, and that made it worse.

What the hell was he doing opening himself up to someone like this again? Especially when the writing was on the wall that it would never work. And not because she was some awful person.

He needed to get her home. Get her. Out. Of. Here. Even with a hot clay oven, wood-carving knives, and a torch for his metalwork, Penelope was the most dangerous thing in the room.

Because he didn't have the first clue how to shut down all the unwanted emotions stirring in his heart for her.

# *Chapter Thirteen*

*Penelope*

After the most awkward ride home ever, Jay roared off in his truck and Penelope breathed a sigh of relief as she unlocked the door of her duplex. Yes, relief. It was totally relief. Not disappointment. Nope, no letdown after that uber-vulnerable shared moment in the barn.

What had happened? One minute it had felt like he was baring his soul, and the next…the castle drawbridge had snapped up, dropping her into the moat.

She was still floundering for something to say, some way to reach him, when he hurried out of the barn to check on his grandfather. Desperate to ignore all these messy feelings, she decided to take action instead of brood. He'd left her alone with just a germ of an idea and the camera on her phone. So, she snapped pictures of a couple of her favorite art pieces.

But now, after a decent night's sleep and an excellent brunch, she had to get serious about the real reason she was still here in Vermont. She moved through the duplex's living room and grabbed her gear. This was going to be tough with her hands wrapped, but they needed as much practice as possible. Her GPS needed charging, so she plugged it into the outlet and got the rest of her supplies ready. She popped open her laptop in order to print out the topo map of the park. Today was a good day to improve her land navigation skills.

She pulled her phone from her pocket to get the local weather for the afternoon, but ended up looking at one of the pictures of Jay's sculptures again. While he hadn't said as much, Penelope could only guess the GPS program was personal to Jay because of his grandfather. She didn't know too much about Parkinson's, except that it was progressive. No doubt her moment of stupidity with the lighter could one day lead to Jay's grandfather being in harm's way.

No, that wouldn't happen. Because she had an idea.

While it may not bring in a lot of money, selling some of her pictures would sure help. Especially if she mentioned why she was selling them. And she already had some customers who'd bought prints in the past. This time she'd even offer up selling the rights to them if it meant bringing in a couple of extra dollars.

Penelope scrolled through the camera reel on her phone. None of the newer pictures really popped in a way that would be attention grabbing. Until the next image loaded up. "This could work."

The photo she took of the dog sculpture at Jay's hit all the right checkboxes. The lighting was phenomenal, the angle really caught the craftsmanship, and who didn't love dogs. Tapping on the photo, she uploaded it to her social media account. She added a message about selling her photographs to help raise funds for the Stay Safe program, along with a description about the initiative and whom it helped.

Her finger hovered over the delete key for several

drawn-out moments. Selling the rights to her photos would mean they no longer belonged to her. Could she do that? Penelope shook herself. She had to do this.

Penelope closed her laptop, turned from her kitchen table, and grabbed her gear. "Come on, Havoc. Let's go."

An afternoon without any responsibility meant time to train Havoc. She drove to the park and pulled into the exact location where her adventure had begun. Only instead of a run-down cabin, she now parked in front of an active construction site. Heavy equipment—a front-end loader, an earth-moving machine, a backhoe—sat blocking the parking spaces at the front and middle. She pulled in behind, attached Havoc's leash, and led him around the danger zone, where a *hard hat required* sign hung. They'd hired Monroe Building and Design, a company Tío Enrique did a lot of business with.

Daniel, the crew boss, shouted direction to a crane operator lifting a piece of prefab floor into place. Eight or ten of his men stood on the ground helping guide the massive section. She'd met him two years ago at one of her tío's business parties. He was young, strong, and handsome with a killer smile and twinkling blue eyes that made even little old ladies flustered.

He was also hopelessly enamored with his young, beautiful wife and their gorgeous, three-month-old baby.

*Life goals, that's for sure.* She smiled and waved as she walked toward him. "Hey, Daniel."

His eyes went blank first, then sparked with recognition. "Penelope Ramos. I should have known this was one of yours. Fast hire and all. Thanks for the business."

She shook her head, not interested in sharing her

connection to the project. Didn't need one more person thinking she was a superlative idiot. Especially someone who could take that knowledge back to her hometown. "Just here on vacation. Training with my dog."

"Oh, I see. This is a great place." Daniel's blue eyes filled with concern as they took in her gauzed hands. "What happened to you?"

Penelope chewed the inside of her cheek. Her blisters and scratches had almost healed, but she still needed to keep the wraps on for protection. "Pushed too hard and blistered the crap out of them."

Daniel grimaced. "Ouch. Well, be careful. Lots of equipment and materials moving around here." He leaned down to pet Havoc and was rewarded with a slobbery kiss. He grouched good-naturedly, pushing Havoc back down onto all fours. "Down, ya brute." Daniel's gaze was warm when he brought it back to Penelope's face. "He's a beauty. Make sure you say hi to your uncle, yeah?"

"You know I will."

The gravel crunched behind her, and she turned to find Jay walking up to them. Jay stopped at her side opposite to Havoc and stared at Daniel. "You need something?"

She winced at his brusque question. Apparently, Jay was in full-blown grumpy mode today. "I just came out to do some map and compass training. Ran into an old friend who did some work for us in New York," she said, gesturing at Daniel.

When her phone pinged in her pocket three times in rapid succession, she pulled it out, checked the notifications, and slid it away before anyone could look over her shoulder. She wanted to squeal. People had started to message her. One notification mentioned purchasing rights. Another made an offer worth more than selling a hundred prints. She couldn't wait to find out what photo it was for.

Jay nodded and she turned toward Daniel, extending her hand to shake his before she left.

Instead of reciprocating, Daniel turned and glared at Jay. "Are you just going to let her go into the woods unattended?"

Jay straightened to his full height. "She's here to train for her K-9 Air Scent handler evaluation, so she needs to practice. Are you qualified to help train her?" Jay paused and waited for Daniel to shake his head no before he continued. "Then maybe just stick to what you know."

Penelope glanced between the two men, her fingers nearly strangling the strap of her backpack, but she managed a smile for Daniel. "I'm not Dorothy. I don't need a pair of ruby slippers to find my way home. Nor an escort. I have all my equipment and my dog."

She turned *without* saying another word to either man—for which she should receive a freakin' medal thankyouverymuch—and headed into the forest.

She'd been hiking and taking notes while trying to memorize the landscape for about an hour, compass in one hand and map in the other. Havoc ran circles, but never ventured too far that he wouldn't return when she whistled.

"Hey."

Penelope jolted and glanced up to find Jay standing to her right. She walked a few steps as Havoc trotted past them sniffing the ground. "What are you doing way out here?"

He shoved his hands into his pockets and rocked back onto his heels. His gaze softened as it landed on her face. "Thought you might like some help. I know this country like the back of my hand."

Penelope bit the inside of her cheek. She was still irritated by his obvious jealousy over Daniel. It was one thing to punch a reporter spewing insulting innuendos, but it was another to proverbially piss on her as if marking his territory. However, the terrain up here was different than what she was used to training in, even when she traveled to Virginia. She sighed. A blow to her pride wouldn't be as bad as having to bivouac with the ticks and mosquitoes. "I would appreciate it."

He pointed northwest with one hand. "There's a creek about one hundred and fifty meters away. The drainage you passed about seventy-five meters back empties into it. The terrain can be especially hazardous in the rainy season." He moved alongside her and pointed to the map in her hands. "Can you find where we are, based on those cues from the topography?"

Penelope inhaled. The mix of his shampoo, a fresh soap smell, and the damp bark of the trees tickled her nose. She wanted to step in closer. But she was here for a purpose, and kissing Jay in the middle of the forest was not it.

"Let me try to get my bearings. Give me a minute." She glanced at the map and her forehead furrowed as she concentrated on the features he'd pointed out. They were also currently standing in the middle of a saddle, which happened to be one of the easiest features to identify. Finally, she found the spot and pointed to it on the map. "Are we right here?"

Jay leaned over and studied where she was pointing

on the map. She waited for the verdict and inhaled his outdoorsy scent mixed with clean sweat once again. God, he was making it difficult for her to concentrate.

Finally, he glanced at her and grinned. “You got it.”

Penelope pumped her fist and giggled with glee. Havoc yipped his enjoyment as well. She ran over and hugged him before scratching his head. Then she stopped and stood up while still on the side of the hill, putting her at eye level with Jay.

“Understanding your bearings isn’t just about finding the subject, but about keeping yourself and your team safe. I want you to be safe.” His gaze dropped to the ground as he stuck his hands in his front pants pockets. “Can I tell you something?”

Before she could respond, Jay blew out a breath and he walked closer. He reached up and tucked a loose tendril of her hair behind her ear, then cupped her chin, drawing her closer to him.

Her breath hitched and butterflies fluttered in her belly. Penelope closed her eyes, breathless, and remained still, hoping he wouldn’t run off the way he did back at the barn. Hoping he would finally kiss her.

Except Havoc barked and her eyes flew open just in time to spot her dog tearing after a squirrel, bounding between her and Jay, and knocking Penelope on her ass, completely destroying the moment. *God damnit, Havoc.*

The squirrel scaled a tree and Havoc stopped, his front legs pawing the bark as if he could make that climb. Penelope muttered a string of curses under her breath, her hands stinging from catching her fall.

Jay helped her to her feet, his voice gruff when she gripped his arm and winced in pain. “You better get his crittering under control, because if he pulls that during the test both of you will fail. Not to mention your situational awareness is weak. You shouldn't have stopped and stood on that slope but moved a couple of feet north to flatter terrain."

The tender moment with the unsure park ranger vanished, destroyed by a flash of dog fur. Penelope would decide later how to *thank* Havoc because at the moment, the skin from her chest to the top of her head was burning from embarrassment. And maybe residual arousal.

Not that Jay's comment on her dog's shortcoming helped the matter. Why couldn't he have just laughed? Then again, she'd probably feel even more embarrassed if he did.

For whatever reason, the universe appeared to be running interference whenever Penelope and Jay were about to kiss. Maybe they weren't meant to be together.

Her shoulders slumped. If only the universe had a map she could read, the same way terrain did. Then at least she could understand what path to take. She turned to Jay. "Would you take me to my car? I'm really tired."

He forced a grin and turned toward the trail heading to the parking lot. While he made an effort to engage her in conversation on their way back, she was beat and didn't have much to say. Eventually, he gave up, and they walked in silence. The surge of relief she felt when she was back at her SUV would have been comical if she didn't feel so close to crying. Vermont was meant to be an escape from the crap she'd went through back home. It was meant to bring back hope and success.

So far, this trip just kicked Penelope while she was down. Maybe it was time to give up and go home.

# *Chapter Fourteen*

## *Jay*

Jay drove his truck, following Penelope to her duplex even though her silence on the way back to her Audi all but screamed that she wanted him to bug off. Maybe that's why he was following her? She was by nature social and optimistic, so seeing the other side of that—her exhaustion and dejection—bothered him on a level he hadn't expected.

He didn't want to leave her like that—even if he was part of the reason why.

Okay, more like *most* of the reason why.

He shook his head, disgusted with himself. He hadn't ever considered himself a killjoy, but she seemed to bring out the mother hen in him. A worried streak that came out in gruff barks and raw edges.

What was it about her? And why now?

Sure, she was beautiful, had a smile that made his heart palpitate and his hands become clammy. He also liked the initiative she took with the quote, the hard work she put in at the construction site, the attention to detail that showed she cared. And the way she could relate to what he was going through with Gramps helped.

Her concern wasn't phony or done to be polite. She could really understand.

She was also smart, kind, and generous in so many ways.

It wouldn't be difficult to fall for a woman like that.

The last time his skin caught fire when a woman brushed against him was during the early years of his marriage—when he and Karen got along. And therein lay the problem because sooner or later Penelope was going back to New York.

He sighed heavily. What the hell was he thinking?

He *wasn't* thinking, and that was the problem. Where Penelope was concerned, he just reacted.

She pulled into the driveway, and he turned in behind her. The dog jumped out of the car behind her and ran to the porch, then sat like an angel while Penelope turned a suspiciously watery and confused look at Jay. "You didn't need to see me home. I know the way by now."

He had to come up with an excuse. And fast. "You asked to pick my brain sometime about Havoc's training. Figured this was a good enough time."

She raised an eyebrow, but didn't say anything. He shifted on his feet like a truant schoolboy. Cleared his throat. "I've got some time right now. How about it?"

"It can wait," she said.

He looked at the ground, trying to understand why his gut was so unsettled. A part of him was disappointed, while the other part was relieved. He wasn't ready for a relationship, for something serious. He had a lot on his plate, a lot he needed to take care of, but he could at least answer her questions. He glanced back up at her. "You sure? I don't mind."

"Not now, Jay."

His name on her lips—the way she said it like she wanted to cry—wedged a sliver in his heart. He walked over to her and brushed his thumb across her cheek. "I'm sorry I acted so surly with Daniel. I don't know what came over me." Well, actually he did. He'd been worrying about her training in addition to fretting over her effect on him, and then having someone who knew nothing about search and rescue question his judgment had pushed him over the edge. "Can I start over?"

One side of her lips tilted up as she nodded.

He became almost light-headed in relief. "Great." He held out his arm for her to grasp it and steered them toward her front porch. "So… Havoc's training. Ask away."

He felt her slight form inhale all along his side where they touched. The contact was comforting and electric all at once.

"Havoc doesn't critter when he's got his gear on. But I'm worried since it's a new area he might act up."

When they reached the landing, Penelope pulled away to grope clumsily in her bag for her keys while Jay leaned against the railing. "You've never trained in different areas?"

"Oh, I have. And when he's geared up, he's good."

"So, why are you worried?"

"I don't want to fail. Not after all the work I put in. I just want something to go right." Penelope's shoulders sagged, and she turned to face him, fussing at the gauze that wasn't so tight around her fingers anymore. "Also, picking your brain wasn't…the only reason I asked you here."

While he waited because he didn't know what to say, she twisted her hands in front of her. But when she remained quiet, he stepped closer, heart knocking against his ribs. Hope a fission of energy zipping through him. "Why else did you ask me here?"

She stared at him like she expected him to say something else. When he didn't, she said, "Forget it, it's really not important."

But the *way* she said it told him she was lying. He really had no idea what was going on. "Penelope, I'm not leaving until you tell me why you want me here."

She made a rude noise and threw up her hands. "Guys can be so dense sometimes!"

That made him smile. "Sometimes," he said, agreeably. Anything to make her tell him what was the matter. Because he hadn't been lying. He was absolutely not leaving until he slayed whatever demon she was dreaming up now. "Pen? Let me help you. I owe you that much because of your hands."

She shook her head and began unwrapping the gauze. "They're getting better."

He stepped closer to stop her. "Keep them covered." His hands wrapped around hers, and somehow they wound up pressed against his chest where his heart felt like it was beating twice its usual rate. "Wouldn't want to get them infected."

"I guess you're right," she murmured, one hand slipping free of his, sliding up his chest to the back of his head, the exposed tips of her fingers curling against his scalp. Her other hand remained over his heart.

But it was her eyes that got him. Wide, trusting eyes. A smoky gaze clouded by desire.

He lowered his head at the same moment she urged him toward her. He brushed his lips over hers, and his body ignited. One kiss wouldn't be enough. Or two. Or three. He teased her with his tongue, sliding it over her lower lip. He had to taste her. Had to explore her mouth.

She grasped a handful of his shirt and used her other hand to push the front door open. Havoc ran in first, then Jay guided Penelope, mouths still fused together. She backed them toward the sofa, and he helped her down without ever letting go of the kiss.

This was better than anything he could have imagined. Her lips were as soft as the petals on his grandmother's roses. The floral coconut scent emanating from her skin was stronger between her breasts. He sighed audibly as he buried his nose into the cleft, then panted while she fumbled with the buttons of his uniform shirt. When she pushed it off his shoulders, he let go of her long enough to yank his hands out of the cuffs and toss it aside as she threw her own shirt onto the floor.

Jay didn't know the proper names for women's lingerie or much about the fabrics, but he knew that a bra made of lace and little strips of silk wasn't one bit about form or function and wasn't made for much more than show. And he'd appreciated no garment in his life more than he appreciated this one. She pulled him down so that they were skin to skin.

When he'd accepted her invitation, he would have never guessed they'd end up tumbling onto her sofa while their clothes huddled in a corner. He slid his hand up her rib cage, her satin skin as beautiful and soft as the rest of her. His thumb brushed over her nipple, still encased in the scrap of a bra, which peaked at his touch, then his palm as he moved his hand to cup her face and guide her back for another kiss.

She moaned and pushed his hand around to her back. “Unhook it.” Her two-word command was probably the sexiest utterance he’d ever heard. As soon as it was loose, she tugged his hand back to her breast, vocalizing beautifully when he dragged his mouth away from hers to run his tongue over her sensitive nipple.

The erotic sound went through him and his cock strained against his pants, ready to explode. He wanted her. Now. Naked and writhing, calling out his name, matching him move for move. He continued to lave her breast with his tongue and slid his hand down her belly to the waistband of her jeans.

He shifted, moved his mouth to the other breast, and unbuttoned her pants, let his fingertips brush over her underwear. His hands and mouth were everywhere, trying to map the contours of her body. She whimpered and reached to help him shove her jeans down. As she kicked her legs trying to remove the pants completely, Jay let his knuckles drag over her, then he brought his fingertips up and teased her clit through the transparent underwear that matched her bra. How had he gotten so lucky?

His mouth watered and his dick throbbed. He hadn’t thought his dick could get any harder, but he’d been wrong. Just seeing her made his erection stand tall in anticipation. He grimaced, praying for control over the primal impulse to speed things up, to plunge inside of her and feel her wet heat wrap around him. No, first he needed to taste her, touch her in a way that made her quiver with need. With each stroke of her soft skin, his need built, the pressure in his dick and balls exquisite torture.

He slammed his eyes closed. *Can't look at her.* What kind of thirty-seven-year-old guy comes in his fucking pants? He needed to get control of himself, so he let his mind pore over things unrelated to Penelope—baseball statistics, the elements on the periodic table, the names of trees and plants he'd studied in a botany class in college.

Gauze on his cheek. "W-what's wrong?"

He opened his eyes. The concern plastered on Penelope's face snuffed out his desire. He blinked rapidly and pushed away from her to stand. How was he supposed to explain that he almost came? This never happened to him before. Ever. And what would she say if she found out? Wasn't it a joke women laughed about among friends? No, he didn't want Penelope laughing at him.

Mortified, he shook his head and grabbed his shirt from the floor. "I'm sorry. I have to go."

And before she could respond, he raced out the door, climbed into his truck, and drove the hell away.

Once he pulled onto the road, he adjusted himself. Though his own hand felt both good and painful considering how sensitive his dick was. He grabbed a baseball cap from the passenger seat and put it on, pulling the bill low, hoping to hide from any passersby. No need for anyone in town asking why he'd been driving shirtless. A bit of relief washed over Jay when he pulled into the driveway. He walked into his house, not bothering to flip on a light. Should he pass a mirror, he didn't want to see himself. The shame. The longing to go back and be with Penelope the way he wanted to would be written all over his face.

He was still hard enough to cut glass. God. She was beautiful. And sensual. Sexy in ways he couldn't wrap his head around.

He tossed and turned the entire night, and morning brought no clarity on how to handle the situation with Penelope. Facing her, after she'd seen him panting and begging, after she'd almost made him come in his pants, would be damned near the most embarrassing thing he'd ever had to do. When he tried to convince himself not to worry because she'd be leaving soon, his stomach twisted.

He didn't want to think about what that meant.

Maybe he should call in. He glanced at the cell in his hand. Nick would question him since he never called out of work, never took vacation or personal time. Not to mention the construction guys needed someone there to handle the busywork, and that someone was him.

He shoved the phone into his pocket, tucked in his shirt, and strode out the front door. It was a normal day. Nothing more. If he had any luck, maybe Penelope would be the one to take the day off. Or maybe she would skip out on her sentence, and he'd never have to see her again.

His lips pressed into a thin line. Penelope going back home definitely wasn't what he wanted. But she would leave soon enough. Maple Falls wasn't her home. Jay jumped in his truck, turned the key, and drove. When Penelope infiltrated his brain again, he turned the radio up and sang along to an old country song about a redhead trying to steal Dolly Parton's man, which brought about thoughts of Gramps—he'd always said he would marry Dolly Parton if she ever got divorced—which led back to thoughts of Penelope.

Well, there was only one thing to do. Avoid her. At all costs.

And he would have, had she not been sitting on the front steps of the office with her dog at her side. She'd removed the gauze from her hands, the little stinker. Had it not made him look like a jerk, he would have stayed in the truck, maybe backed out and driven away, but he didn't. He opened the door and slid out.

She rubbed her dog's head and didn't speak as her skin turned a vibrant shade of red. Oh, yeah. She was furious, but he certainly deserved it. He'd left her high and dry when she'd been so gloriously aroused. My God, he was an idiot. He leaned against the porch rail feeling two inches tall. "Hey."

She looked up, gave one of those cool-kid nods, then went back to ignoring him, stroking Havoc's ears. The dog lifted his head to sniff Jay, then stood and nuzzled his head against Jay's leg. Penelope clasped her hands and exhaled through her nose.

There had to be a way to fix this. He hated that she wouldn't look at him. "About last night…"

She stood and met him on the bottom step. "No big deal. Once you left, I sat down and thought about it. It's not your fault if you don't find me attractive."

Jay jerked his head so his gaze fell directly in line with Penelope's. What the hell? She was *embarrassed*? He had to fix this. "Wait, I didn't leave because—" He snapped his mouth shut as Nick walked out of the office.

"Are you two going sit out here all day while I do all

the work?" Nick tromped down the steps and handed Jay a clipboard. "The park is low staff today and rain showers are movin' in, so you can work on the donations. Here's a list of last year's donors. Penelope made a list of new businesses we can hit up, and she'll be calling them. Figured you could head into town and call on some of these folks in person."

Not that he didn't want to go. But he wanted to set things straight with Penelope first. She thought he wasn't into her. He felt more like an asshole than before. "Maybe you should do the visits. Might look better if the man in charge is the one doing the asking."

Nick cocked his head and narrowed his eyes, tapping his chin with his forefinger. "I am better with people. Okay. You two can hold down the fort here, and I'll go out and schmooze the people."

The color drained from Penelope's face, and she ducked into the office as Nick went over some last-minute updates with him. When Jay finally entered, she was already with the phone to her ear and the dog at her feet, sipping coffee. He stood at the front of her desk, waiting. And waiting. And waiting before she spun her chair to face the wall.

Jay sighed and walked resignedly to his desk to start his day. The hours dragged by until finally the workday was over. Maybe an offer to buy Penelope dinner since they'd worked through lunch might give them time to talk. Before he could offer, she jumped out of the chair and headed toward the door with Havoc. She stopped before exiting and turned to Jay. "Would you mind helping me with a quick runaway? Havoc needs the practice."

Jay almost fell off his chair in a massive rush of light-headed relief. As he rose to stand, he fumbled to put his pen in the cup holder, upending the entire thing, spilling pens all across the damn desk. As he lunged to grab one before it launched to the floor, his chair shot out and slammed against the wall. *Egit!* His face was hot and itchy. *Be cool.* He swallowed hard before bringing his gaze to hers. "Sure."

They headed over to Penelope's SUV, where she gave him Havoc's coveted tug toy. "I'd say run about fifty feet and tuck in behind a tree. Crouch down because Charlie's been mostly standing when she helps out, and I want him to remember that he might find people in different positions."

Jay nodded, then took off across the parking lot and into the group of trees behind the building. Once he was about fifty feet away, he hid behind a tree and lay down, tucking the juke under his body.

Moments later the jingle of a bear bell filled his ears. Seconds after that Havoc's slobber landed on his face as the dog continuously barked until Penelope arrived and instructed Jay to reward Havoc. Jay pulled out the toy, allowed Havoc to bite on it, and an intense game of tug began. "Good boy. Such a good boy."

After two minutes of play and praise, Jay released the toy, allowing Havoc to win. The dog trotted off intensely proud of himself. Jay got to his feet. "He did very well."

"We've been working on his focus and control, adding in a lot more of the basic foundational work. I'm waiting for the new test dates to be posted online so I can sign up, but I think he's more prepared than when we first got here."

She'd taken his advice. A little bubble of hope

swelled in his chest. This was his chance to set things right about last night. Jay raked his fingers through his hair. “Can we talk for a minute?”

She turned and walked over to where Havoc lay on the ground a couple of feet away, attempting to shred his toy. She bent down and removed the dog’s harness, avoiding Jay’s gaze. “I actually have to head out. I’m busy tonight.”

Jay shoved his hands into his pockets, dying to know with whom. But after the way he’d left her yesterday, he knew he didn’t have the right to ask.

She looked at him for a moment more like she expected him to say something. But when he didn’t, she compressed her lips, got in her car, and drove off.

Jay swore and kicked a rock down the street. Shoulda just told her he was the one who’d almost blown his load last night. That he hadn’t wanted to unman himself with how goddamn gorgeous she was. But more than that, he should’ve told her how much he admired her as a person. How much it meant to him that she stood up for him against Nick that one day. How brave he considered her to come up to Vermont on her own to train.

Now he’d lost his chance. Again.

He was really making a shit show of things considering how much he didn’t want to eff things up with her. She was the first person he’d opened up to in a long time. He cared about what Penelope thought of him. And he cared about her. Maybe he wished she also cared about him. But how could she, considering the way he constantly screwed up.

Jay headed back to the building to lock up for the night, trying not to think about how Penelope was probably getting dolled up to go on a date with someone who'd make her feel desirable. Someone who would support her courageous spirit.

Someone who would taste her kisses.

Jay curled his fists and chewed his cheeks so hard he tasted blood.

This was not fine. Not fine at all.

He just needed to decide what he was willing to do about it, and not fuck up in the process.

# *Chapter Fifteen*

## *Penelope*

He'd been about to tell her. She just knew he had. She should've given him just a few more moments to gather his gumption because part of her needed to know why the big, surly creep left her. But part of her didn't want to know. Didn't want to hear that he just wasn't into her. It's not like she hadn't been rejected before.

Penelope let out a growl, swung her arm, and punched the sofa pillow before picking up her book—her convenient "date" tonight. She'd purposely let Jay think she was going out with someone else to see how he would react.

*Childish!*

She growled as she viciously thumbed through the pages. She shouldn't be concerned with men right now. No, she should be concerned with fixing the problem she'd caused, signing up for a new handler evaluation, and going home.

Her heart sank at the last thought. Not because she'd be going back to an empty apartment. But she'd miss Vermont. And Charlie. And the people she'd met in Maple Falls. Even Jay because as much as she didn't want to admit it, but she'd think about his soul-searing kisses and his mind-bending touches. The way the sun made his coal-black hair shine. The glints of amber in his chocolate eyes. And she'd especially miss those rare glimpses of his vulnerability, when he showed her his tender side.

She laid her head against the arm of the sofa, checking her social media. Her inbox had over one hundred messages. Looked like she was going to do something right after all. Until she began to read them.

Oh. Shit.

She clicked on the next one. Then the next one.

After about twenty messages, she dropped the phone onto the kitchen counter. Only five of them were about her photographs. The rest were all offers to buy Jay's sculpture. The one of the dog she posted. How could this have happened? When she scrolled back to the description, she figured it out. She never made it clear the sculpture wasn't for sale.

But the amount people were offering would cover a majority of the costs for the equipment. This could work. But what if Jay didn't want to sell? Well, she'd just have to explain her mistake to the bidders.

Her eyes fell back to the description and one phrase in particular.

*The Stay Safe program.*

*Gramps.*

"Oh, my God." Did Jay run out because he had to take care of his grandfather? He mentioned how they lived on the same property so he could be there for the elder man. Penelope winced. She should have let him explain. Now he probably thought she was a selfish brat.

Tomorrow she definitely needed to take Havoc out

to the park for another training session, but she'd also make sure to apologize to Jay. And as much as she wanted to call him now and do so, she wasn't exactly sure what to say.

Plus, she was exhausted, both physically and emotionally.

She needed to sleep.

And sleep she did. So much and so heavily that she was late getting to the office the next morning. Nick grumbled at her a bit on his way out the door to a meeting, and unfortunately Jay was already at the construction site, so she ended up with the office to herself all morning, making calls and following up with subcontractors. It was after noon when her stomach rumbled for food. She decided to grab Havoc, brave the locals, and head to Clover's Kitchen for lunch.

Penelope opened the car windows on the drive to the restaurant, and when she pulled into a parking spot right outside Clover's Kitchen, which sat between the Happy Time Drycleaners and Mel's Barber and Wax Hut, the scent of fries, pies, and coffee wafted into the car.

She walked inside and stepped into a different world. The black-and-white-checkered floor gleamed, and the booths alternated in color from black to white in a line along the windowed walls. The long counter in polished black marble was poised along the backside with white leather-padded barstools, a donut case on one end and a pie pantry on the other. Tables with white tops and black chairs broke the center of the room into sections. Very aesthetically pleasing. But the joy came when she found silver dog bowls beneath the edge of some of the booths. She loved that the staff thought about the needs of service and working dogs who may visit.

Havoc, the perfect date for this place, led her to the booth nearest the door, and lay at her feet when she sat. An older couple sat across from her and smiled down at Havoc. The man took a treat from a canister in the center of his table and handed it to Havoc.

"Thank you." Although she usually preferred that Havoc get his treats from her as part of his training, once wouldn't hurt.

"You must be new in town." The woman looked Penelope over. "I would remember such beautiful curls."

Penelope bit into her bottom lip and smiled, happy to meet someone who hadn't seen her face on the local news or read about her in the *Vermont Voice*. "I'm here for a little while. For work."

The woman stood and walked over to her table. She reached down to pet Havoc, then stood, and as if by magic, held a pad and a pen. "What can I get you?"

"You work here?" She had to be at least seventy. Her white hair had been pulled back into a bun. She had orthopedic shoes and a black-and-white gingham apron over her white uniform dress.

"Lurlene Clover. My great-grandpa opened this place, left it to my granddad, who left it to my dad, who didn't have any sons, so he left it to me." She jerked a thumb over her shoulder at the man still seated at the table. "That's my husband, Fred. He helps out every once in a while, but not so much these days. What with the gout keeping him down."

Well, that was a lot of information, but Penelope liked her, and she liked the atmosphere. Lurlene put a hand on Fred's shoulder, gave a squeeze and a wink, then turned back to Penelope. The affection between

Lurlene and Fred made her smile. "Now what can I get you?"

Penelope hadn't even looked at the menu. "A burger?"

"No." The woman shook her head. "You look thin. I think you need a nice big plate of roast beef and potatoes." She scuttled around the counter and through a door painted in the same black-and-white subway tile as the wall. She returned with a heaping plate of food and a small basket of bread.

Penelope could eat for a week on this amount of food. But she accepted the plate and picked up her fork. Before she'd taken her first bite, a tall glass of iced tea with a lemon wedge hanging off the rim appeared in front of her.

Mrs. Clover seated herself across from Penelope. "Tell me, dear. What brings you to Maple Falls?"

Penelope moaned at the first bite of her food. It was heaven in her mouth, and she wanted to savor the flavor, but the woman cocked her head to the side as if waiting for an answer. "I came to test for Search and Rescue K-9 Air Scent certification, but it was cancelled. And now I'm working out at the state park with the rebuild of the check station and raising money for the safety program."

Fred shook his head. "Crying shame about that check station. All that money. And the way they crucified that poor girl." His eyes sparked with recognition. He cocked his head. "You didn't get a fair shake in the press."

If only he knew how fair they'd been, considering how much she'd cost the state and the hunting program.

"That snooty TV anchor made it sound like you were out there having yourself a tantrum over a man and set the place on fire." He clucked his teeth. "Irresponsible reporting if you ask me. Could've started a riot with all those hunters."

In a nutshell, there wasn't a lot about the story she could deny. Lurlene patted his shoulder. "Fred's a vegetarian. He hates the hunting seasons. God's creatures and all that." She leaned in close and waved Penelope in. "He doesn't hear good so I can tell you that sometimes I catch him in the kitchen eating sliced ham right out of the package. He can't help it. His body craves it." She shielded her mouth from Fred's view with her hand. "I think it's the Viagra."

Penelope had just taken a drink and almost choked trying to keep it down. She swallowed but hacked and coughed until Mrs. Clover stood and came around to pat her back. "I'm fine." Shocked but fine.

Lurlene moved back to her side of the table. "Are you working with that handsome Ranger Gosling?" She shook her head. "That man is lady Viagra, I am telling you. Great shoulders, great ass, great hands. And when he walks in here in that uniform." Now she started fanning herself with a menu. "Temperature in here goes up by at least ten degrees."

Penelope stifled a slightly confused grin. She couldn't disagree with the assessment. "We're working together."

"Did you know he's an artist? His grandfather always talks about his work. But the boy never lets anyone see it. Such a shame."

"He mentioned he did some sculpting." Penelope bit the inside of her cheek, hoping the woman didn't probe further. Jay was guarded about his art and his life outside of work. She didn't want to offer up that she'd actually seen it and have him be mad. Not after they'd been getting along.

"He dances like a young Fred Astaire, too. I think he could lead a broomstick in a waltz and make it look elegant." She patted Penelope's hand. "I paid four hundred dollars for a night out on the town with Ranger Gosling at the auction last summer. After LuAlice Kerrigan hogged the handsome ranger's time during the Valentine's Day ball fundraiser, I sure wasn't going to let her monopolize all his time again. He took me to the cutest dance club in Rutland. It closed down this year…no call for ballroom since that dancing show went off the TV, but I haven't danced like that since I was twenty-five and I met my first husband, Mountain Joe."

"Mountain Joe?" Oh, there had to be a story there.

Lurlene shook her head and slanted her eyes toward Fred. She whispered, "Fred doesn't like when I reminisce about my old loves. But you come in on a Tuesday while Fred's over at Mel's getting his weekly hot shave and haircut. I'll tell you all about it."

The bell above the door jingled and Lurlene had to move away to take care of three other customers. Penelope finished her plate of food and drank another glass of iced tea before she paid and left.

"You come back on Tuesday," Lurlene said with a wink. "And I'll tell you about Mountain Joe and the hay fluffer." Penelope wasn't sure if it was a euphemism—for what she couldn't have begun to guess—or what it meant, but it was definitely a story she wanted to hear.

As she stood to leave, her phone beeped with a text.

*Charlie:* Want to go out later?

Her fingers plucked at the screen. A night out would be good.

*Penelope:* Sure. Send me the details.

Penelope turned back to Mrs. Clover and smiled. "I will definitely visit again."

Later, she was still thinking of Lurlene—her sass, her charm, her willingness to love and love again—when she pulled up to the bar where Charlie asked to meet. There weren't too many people in her life whom she considered a mentor. And wasn't that sad? Everyone needed mentors in their life. Lurlene could be one of those for her.

But of course, that would mean Penelope would have to stay.

She sighed as she locked her car, then walked into the bar.

"I'm so glad you came out tonight." Charlie set a drink with mint leaves, a slice of lime, a sparkly clear liquid, and four cubes of ice in front of Penelope. The place was packed with people for a Sunday night. Apparently, karaoke in Maple Falls brought out the singing sensations in the entire town. Charlie had been lucky to score them a table. "It's a Mojito."

Penelope was glad she'd come out, too. An afternoon nap, a hike with Havoc, and watching TV had not cured her of obsessing over Ranger Jay Gosling. Hopefully, adult beverages in a bar with loud music and dim lighting would pick up the slack. But before she could take a sip—and as if her mind had conjured him—Jay walked up to their table.

*Holy crap.* Penelope's palms began to sweat. This

was the first time she'd seen him not in his uniform, and damn, he looked good. But she'd always been a sucker for black button-downs and dark jeans. His cologne, woodsy with a hint of citrus, made her want to breathe him in, and he'd even shaved.

"Hey, Charlie. Penelope." Jay's gaze met hers and held.

"I'm just gonna..." Charlie pointed to the bar and left the table.

Jay continued to stare at Penelope and damn if she could look away. He sat beside her, brushed her hair off her forehead and tucked a few strands behind her ear. "You look amazing tonight."

"You, too."

His lips turned up into a smile that wrinkled the corner of his eyes, and her heart stuttered. He twisted the glass on the table a few times as if contemplating something. Then took a visible deep breath. "Can we dance?"

When he held out his hand, she took it and stood. Every muscle and bone in her body tingled. Every cell came alive. Again. And when he slid his arm around her waist and drew her closer, so close she had to bend backward a fraction to look up at his face, her heart beat erratically in her chest so hard she thought it might fly out.

"They built this place sometime around the Boston Tea Party. It survived prohibition. They remodeled a couple years ago." He spun them toward the scarred wood dance floor. The music, not really her taste, was some country ballad that made swaying in his arms easy. Or maybe he made it easy.

She looked up at him. "I didn't think you went out much?"

Her heart did its own dance when he smiled, and his gaze held hers. “Nick claims it’s good when we’re asking for money from the town to be seen spending money *in* the town.”

She continued to nod as he discussed the importance of supporting local businesses, But her mind remained focused on the warmth of his hand against her back through her silk blouse, the way his touch burned, and the scent of his cologne.

“I was hoping when I mentioned to Charlie that Nick and I were heading here tonight, she would think to bring you with her.” Jay ducked his chin, his cheeks turning a light shade of pink. “About the other night. I haven’t…it’s just been a while. And it was a little overwhelming for me. It had nothing to do with you.”

Penelope sucked in a sharp breath, her mouth hanging open. Not what she’d been expecting to hear. Hell, she’d been ready to apologize to him. Was going to ask and make sure Gramps was okay. While her brain tried to define *overwhelming*, Jay began to tense up. *No, no, no. Okay, what would Lurlene do?* She tilted her head and ran her thumb across his cheek. “I like you, Jay.”

He blushed. Then gave her one of those looks—the one with soft eyes and slightly upturned lips. “I like you, too, Penelope.”

The tempo of the music changed, but Jay continued to hold her close, kept their moves slow, sexy, pulse-pounding. Halfway through the second song, he pulled her tighter into his body and lowered his head. All light and sound died away, and his lips caressed hers, lingering for a second before he pulled away. When her eyes opened, he shot her a sultry smile. “I could hold you like this all night.”

*All night?*

The noise in the room returned along with the smell of French fries and alcohol. She stepped back and tilted her head to the door. She needed the space to catch her breath. Would have worked, too, but he slid his arm around her waist and moved closer to her side, matched his step with hers. "Want to get some air?"

He nodded and guided her through the crowd as the karaoke DJ called out to Charlie and Nick to come to the stage. They stopped to listen, and Jay moved to stand behind her, clasping his hands at her belly button. Her pulse beat in her temples, every nerve in her body firing off at once. She couldn't remember the last man who made her feel this alive. Jay swayed, his hips guiding hers this time along with his hand splayed on her stomach, igniting a slow burn in her belly that curled down into the cradle of her hips. And it felt *right.*

Jay's hard, lean body pressed into hers had her picturing them in ways he'd already rejected—correction, was overwhelmed by. If she had any hope of keeping her sanity, she had to slow things down. Create some physical space. As luck would have it, the song ended, and Charlie rushed off the stage heading toward the bathroom. *Here's my break.* Penelope pulled away from Jay. "I should see if she's okay."

Jay nodded thoughtfully and released his grip.

Penelope cut through the crowd and pushed open the bathroom door only to find Charlie leaning against the sink, breathing deep and staring at herself. She put her hand on Charlie's shoulder, finding it rigid. "That was great. I had no idea you could sing. You okay?"

Charlie grimaced. "I don't know how I let him talk me into it." She shook her head. "I don't know what the hell happened. I just started sweating and my heart started to race."

Penelope offered a wry smile. "Public speaking is one of humanity's biggest fears. I'd imagine public singing is even a level above that. I probably would've wet myself up there. You were fabulous!"

Charlie laughed. A full belly laugh. She turned to Penelope and leaned her hip against the counter, the frown suddenly back in full force. "Sweet Jesus. What if it's menopause?"

Penelope pursed her lips and wiggled her finger back and forth. "We are both too young for that. But tell me, how was it up there with Nick?"

Charlie smirked. "You should've seen the glares I got from the women in the audience. I get it, though. All that wavy, midnight hair, and that dark-eyed, passionate Greek thing he has going on. Not to mention the way he walks that has every woman in the room watching him."

Penelope nudged her friend. "And you aren't interested?"

"A couple of months ago we went out on a date. It was fine. Conversation was great. But when he kissed me, it was like kissing a fish. No tingle. No spark. Nada. Zilch. Nothing. Not even a flutter." Charlie groaned and wiped her forehead with a paper towel. "Maybe that was the first sign of menopause."

Penelope laughed. "Come on. No need to go all biological. Nick just isn't the water that floats your boat."

Charlie popped a hand on her hip. "This is stupid. The lights probably got to me. And I'm sure the alcohol didn't help."

"There you go. Mystery solved." Penelope smiled.

Charlie turned to the mirror and checked her hair. "Ugh, do you think the guys are going to ask what happened? I'm really not up for the next-stage-of-life talk."

"I'm sure they will, but we can just steer the conversation to something else. What you can't do is hide out in the bathroom all night. For sure those two will end up charging in here." Penelope giggled, imagining the two rangers bursting through the door only to find them having a casual conversation.

Charlie rolled her eyes with lips tight and pinched. "The mark of a true genius is how much time she can spend in the bathroom before slinking out of the window unseen. If this was a rom-com movie, my tall blond hero would raze that door right now and would end up comforting my insane thoughts."

"I think in the movie the heroine would try to sneak out of the bathroom and end up falling at the feet of the tall blond hero, and then stand up to make some embarrassing confession. After that, she'd run out to hole up in her apartment with a few quarts of Ben & Jerry's while the new hero sulks around because he can't get her out of his head." Penelope snorted. What did it say about her that she knew the tropes so well? She leaned her hip against the sink and tried not to think about romance.

Or Jay.

Charlie sighed and ran her hands down the front of her jeans. "You ready to go before I do something stupid like grab a microphone and hold my own pretty-boy contest so I can feel young again?"

Penelope raised an eyebrow. Pretty-boy contest? That might get her mind off Jay because he sure as hell didn't qualify. Too brooding, too tall, and definitely too rugged.

Too much of what she was realizing she liked. A lot, damnit.

She sighed. This not-think-about-Jay business was not going well. Not when he looked sexy as hell tonight. But her friend needed her right now. "Sure, just let me tell the guys we're leav—"

Charlie slapped her forehead. "Wait! Don't do that. You need to stay here. Have fun. With Jay." She wiggled her eyebrows. "My bits of insanity shouldn't ruin your night."

Penelope shook her head. "No big deal. I'll see him tomorrow." She threw an arm around Charlie. This was the kind of thing friends did for each other. Support. Leaving the bar early when one friend had a sudden bathroom revelation.

But it didn't mean she was without regret. Jay had admitted he liked her. She wanted to explore that. Wanted to dance with him and see where the night went. But she also wanted true friendship. She'd been missing it in her life for far too long.

# *Chapter Sixteen*

## *Jay*

Jay couldn't take his eyes off Penelope. He watched her eat. Watched her walk. Watched her train Havoc. And when he wasn't watching her, he imagined holding her. Kissing her. Touching her. And that led him down the dark road of wanting a woman who would only end up hurting him. Because for better or worse, he just couldn't forget how Karen had hurt him.

He'd done all he could to try to keep her happy. But it was never enough.

He leaned his shoulder against a four-hundred-year-old oak tree and watched Penelope some more. Havoc sniffed the ground around another tree about a hundred feet north of where he stood. The dog's tail rose and wagged as he shuffled from side to side, pawing at the dirt.

Penelope clapped a hand against her leg. "Havoc. No. Get back to work."

Jay shook his head. She should have checked to see what the dog had found, investigated if there was something to find. Jay knew the terrain, he knew that just over the crest on the opposite side of the tree, there was a ditch, and that's where he'd instructed Brent to hide when he found out the man would be helping Penelope train.

"Hey." Jay pushed off the tree and walked toward her when Havoc trotted off to another area.

She jumped and clutched her chest. "Are you just lurking in the woods trying to scare the crap out of me?"

Jay chuckled. "Nick told me to find you. He has some questions about the contractor's bid. But I actually came to help."

"I don't need help."

"Yeah, you do." He stuck his fingers in his mouth and whistled. Havoc stood, ears pointed, tail at attention.

Brent came over the crest dusting old leaves and dirt from his arms and pant legs. "Hey, Pen." He gave a little wave. "I was in the ditch."

Penelope pursed her lips and blew a loud breath out her nose as the dog walked toward Brent and barked. She shot Havoc a narrow-eyed look, then turned to Brent. "Thanks anyway."

"We can try again tomorrow." The young ranger smiled at her as if he'd been more than her search dummy. "I can stay late, and we can do some night searches, too, if you want."

Jay rolled his eyes before turning his focus back on Penelope. The potential harm she could do by ignoring the dog's alerts was as great as the potential to save if she paid attention. "You shouldn't have called him off."

Penelope frowned. "I thought he was crittering."

Jay raked his hands through his hair. "You have to trust his training. And you have to investigate before you call him off. He could have stumbled onto a scent left by an article of clothing hidden in the brush, or maybe scent was climbing from a hidden sinkhole invisible from this far back."

"You're right." She kicked a stone and sent it flying into a nearby bush. "You must have been great at this."

Jay's muscles tensed. People used to say he was one of the best. Incident commanders from across the United States would call him to come help with large disasters. Some would even call for advice on smaller cases. But that wasn't his life now. "I trained hard. I didn't stop until I got it right."

Her head jerked as if he'd slapped her. "*Cabron*, I train hard."

He scrubbed his hands over his face and grimaced as a knot formed in his stomach. He'd always been a hard trainer and an equally hard evaluator. But those who had worked with him ended up being some of the strongest canine teams around. "Human error can cost a life just as much as canine error."

"I made a mistake." She clamped her lips together and glared before she turned away.

So this was one of the pitfalls he heard about when it came to having a relationship with a teammate. Or a coworker. "You asked for my help and I'm helping. You made a mistake. Own it."

"Making insinuations I don't train hard isn't instructing me."

Jay shoved his hands into his pockets, eyes narrowing, and lowering his tone to one close to that of a drill sergeant. "Penelope, good handlers train more than forty hours a week. In all types of weather. In all terrain. They take criticism and learn from it. Not get all defensive."

"God, you must've been one of those asshole instructors." Penelope wheeled around. She patted her leg and Havoc returned to her side before the two turned to the trail. Brent followed her, leaving Jay alone in a copse of trees on a hill above a ditch.

Indeed, he had been called as such. But his approach was also how he'd been invited, hell, sought after, by many search and rescue groups. Including some government groups. If Penelope truly wanted his help, truly wanted to be the best she could be, then she'd have to get used to it.

And if she couldn't take criticism, then maybe she shouldn't be out here because human error cost more lives than K-9 errors ever did.

Including possibly her own.

His insides went cold. The thought of Penelope getting injured or even dying was not an option. He wouldn't let that happen, would protect her even if it meant from herself. Even if it meant preventing her from testing.

Jay walked into the office. Havoc sat at Penelope's feet while Nick stood over her desk, as angry as Jay had ever seen him. He slammed the *Vermont Voice* down onto her desk. "Fucking governor."

After a moment, she looked up. "What does this mean?"

"It means he's sticking the money he promised to allocate for the safety program into a game-tracking program that will supposedly help increase the population of animals and allow the state to draw more hunters. He's promised increased revenues from the sale of additional licenses and longer hunting seasons."

"Fuck!" Not a word he said often at work, but the

situation earned it. "Longer hunting seasons? Increased animal population? It's an environmental disaster created by humans who won't have the added protection of the safety program."

Penelope stood. "I'm so sorry, you guys."

The governor of the great state of Vermont had probably never hunted a day in his life, didn't know the dangers of animal overpopulation or of inviting nonresidents into the area to hunt unfamiliar terrain. The whole thing stank of politics. Jay grimaced. Now, more than ever, the safety program was important. More than important. Vital. A necessity.

"Raising all the money is going to be up to us since the program was never a government initiative. And if he's going to throw people out there longer, we need that program up and running. The moron probably didn't take into account weather shifts and the dangers they cause." Nick paced a line in front of Penelope's desk before looking Jay up and down. "Better dust off your dancing shoes, Gene Kelly."

No way he wanted to spend the next month working his schedule around foxtrots and tangos. There had to be another way. Some big-ticket fundraiser they could hold. He needed to think. And not about Penelope.

Nick glanced at her and chuckled. "And you'd better find yourself a genie with the lottery numbers etched into his lamp."

He turned on his heel and walked into his office, probably to slam drawers shut and curse at the picture of the governor hanging next to the one of the president.

Jay shoved his hands in his pockets. "Any ideas?"

The look in her eyes said, oh, hell yeah, but then she

compressed her lips and shook her head. Now, what was that about?

"How much do we have in the donation fund?" she asked, her voice slightly higher than normal.

He narrowed his eyes. She was hiding something. "Two grand."

She nodded, dropping her gaze to her desk. Now he was really getting concerned.

"And we need?" she squeaked.

"About ninety-eight more. And why don't you tell me what's on your pretty little mind?"

This time she pursed her lips and blew little bursts of air through from her puffy cheeks. The pencil tapping between her fingers shouldn't have had him mesmerized, but he found the way it lolled as it smacked against the desk blotter next to her keyboard sexy because it showed her focused determination. "What about contacting some companies that do guided hunts? If you contract with them, they might be convinced to put some dollars into the fund."

Nice idea, but guided hunts invited the random novice armed and dangerous out into their park, which presented a whole other set of dangers. Of course, if they were guided, the ranger responsibility would decrease, and they could work fewer rangers on the schedule.

It could work. Maybe. Depended on if the park would have to be reclassified to accommodate the commercial businesses operating the program. "I would have to check into the logistics. And the companies providing the guides would have to be found and vetted, then trained and instructed on what is and isn't allowed." Penelope scribbled notes onto a yellow legal pad while he spoke aloud the list forming in his head. "We would need to write up a plan, make some projections based on the projections from the company or companies we contract." He glanced up at her. "It's a lot of legwork. And you didn't answer my question."

"Legwork is my specialty." She smiled innocently, further avoiding his question. "Maybe you should talk it out with Nick?"

Jay snorted. "Maybe *you* should talk it out with Nick."

She sat back and tossed her pencil on the desk in front of her as she blew a strand of hair from the front of her face. "I don't think Nick wants to talk to me right now since this is all my mess."

Jay leaned back and crossed his arms in front of his chest. "Look, we know you didn't do it on purpose, and you're working to make it right. This is your idea, and it's a good one. Take it to Nick."

Between the way she found a quote and a decent crew to help out with the building, to tackling the fund-raising, Jay couldn't have been more amazed by how she was throwing herself into a career she knew very little about. And she was learning fast. Color him impressed.

"Come with me?" She cocked one eyebrow and stared, a lopsided grin on her perfectly pink lips. "I only have an idea. But the three of us could devise a plan to make it work. And if this one won't, we can all work together to find one that will." When he didn't answer immediately, she batted her eyelashes. "Come on. I can't do it alone."

"Let's take today and see what we can figure out without him. We can work out an actual proposal and present it to him tomorrow or Wednesday." They would need information that might not be immediately available on a Monday afternoon.

"You're right. We should get everything together first." Her demeanor changed from excited to hand-wringing nervous. "Might take a while—like all evening. We could have dinner at my house and work?"

Jay rubbed a hand over his chest where his heart started thumping at just the mention of time alone with her again. "You going to work with me or fight with me if I don't agree?"

Her hands flew to her hips and her eyes narrowed. "Depends on *how* you say things. Anyway, I'll pick up some takeout so don't worry about dinner."

A few hours later, he pulled up to Penelope's duplex.

This was a bad idea. Especially since his gut was certain there was something she wasn't telling him. When she opened the front door, Jay handed her the bottle of wine he'd picked up on the way over and walked into a cloud of her perfume as she shut the door behind him. He'd changed from his uniform to a pair of jeans and a T-shirt. Underdressed compared with her.

She'd changed out of her jeans into a loose sundress with tiny little shoulder straps and a heart-shaped neckline, exchanged her work boots for sandals that showed off her painted toenails, and taken down the ponytail in favor of loose brown curls that hung over her shoulders.

He wanted to devour her.

The table, a small, round two-seater, wasn't set for an intimate dinner for two, but the energy charging the air more than made up for a lack of flickering candles and the presence of foam to-go boxes from Clover's. She could have had live snails in the box, and he wouldn't have cared one damned bit. Probably would have eaten them anyway and never known since he couldn't stop looking at her long enough to focus on much else.

"You look pretty."

"Thanks." Her skin flushed from forehead to chin and down her throat. She held up the bottle of wine. "Can I get you a glass?"

He nodded because the sultry rasp of her voice rendered him speechless, stole his breath. Didn't stop his legs from working, though, and he followed her into the kitchen. She opened a couple drawers before she found the wine opener and struggled with the top.

He moved behind her, laid his hand over hers, and twisted the corkscrew with her. But only because of his ever-helpful nature. The cork popped and her hands trembled as she set it on the counter, then turned in his arms. Her tongue slid over her lower lip, leaving a glistening trail he ached to taste. Desire burned through him. He began to lower his head, but Havoc barked and barreled into the kitchen, launching himself at Jay.

"Havoc, down."

As if she'd raised her voice to shout the command rather than spoken it in her usual soft tone, the dog heeled beside her. Penelope ran a hand over Havoc's head while Jay stood back, wondering if he'd ever experience a normal heartbeat again. She pointed to the hallway and the dog walked away and climbed the steps.

"Nice work. He's doing much better with commands than when I first saw him."

Penelope smiled as if he'd just crowned her Queen of America. "We've been working on it."

"I can see."

She walked around him to the wineglasses. Her

hands didn't shake when she poured, nor did her smile falter as she handed him his wine. "Would you rather eat first and then work?"

He cleared his throat. The things he'd rather do weren't appropriate for a business dinner. "Uh, yeah. That sounds good."

She gestured to the table with a sweep of her arm. He could sit and have a quiet dinner alone with a beautiful woman. Of course he could.

She opened the foam boxes and tilted her head as her lips pursed. "Okay, we have meat loaf with mashed potatoes and steamed broccoli, or we have meat loaf with mashed potatoes and green beans."

He chuckled and rubbed the back of his neck. "What did you actually order?"

"Burgers with fries, but Mrs. Clover must've thought we needed something more substantial." Penelope handed him a fork. "If we eat all of this, I'll be too full to work. I'll need a nap."

"We could work first and warm these up later." He reached to close the lid to the container in front of her at the same time she did and their fingers brushed. Such an innocent touch, but a jolt of electricity shot up his spine. More so when she turned her hand so their palms touched.

"Counteroffer." She came around the table to angle her body between him and the edge. Not touching. Staring. Gazing. At him. With her clear, wide eyes.

"I don't have much to offer."

"I didn't ask for anything." She raised her hands and slid them around his neck, then put one against his scalp and urged him down. "Yet."

"And what will you ask for later?"

"Just tonight." She pressed a hot kiss against the pulse point in his throat. "Tomorrow will work itself out."

Not that he could walk away if he wanted to, but in his experience tomorrow never just worked itself out. "Penelope—"

She placed a finger over his lips to silence him before replacing it with her mouth over his, not tentative but sure; not asking, telling. When she had him completely pliant under her magic, she angled her head and whimpered, the sound sweeter than any song he'd ever heard. He opened his mouth and lifted her so her legs wrapped around his waist. He needed to feel more of her, all of her. And if he had to open every door to find a room with a bed, he would do it with his mouth melded to hers, his tongue tasting her sweetness.

She clung to him until he found the master suite, then slid her down his body. They both groaned at the friction. *"Penelope."* More groan than whisper, more sigh than breath. They didn't bother with the light. The triangle of moonlight through the split in the curtains provided enough to see the bed and its twenty pillows, ruffled quilt, and carved wood headboard.

Her kisses sparked fire in his blood. He pulled away and smoothed her hair back over her shoulders. She deserved candles and soft music, a man who would worship her body long into the night until the sun peeked through the curtains.

"What's wrong?"

The uncertain catch in her voice went straight to his heart. "You deserve candles and music," he whispered, feeling out of his element. Unmoored. But after what he'd done to her last time, he wanted to make sure she knew he wasn't leaving her in the lurch again.

Candles and music would have to wait because he wasn't going anywhere right now.

"I already hear music when we're together like this," she murmured back. And it was all he needed to know.

He kissed her again, hard, demanding, meeting her intensity with his own as she shoved her hands under his shirt and pushed it up. He sucked her lower lip, soothing it with his tongue as she moaned, pushing against him to break the kiss and yank his shirt over his head, throwing it somewhere they'd discover later. All that mattered was feeling her skin against his, tasting and touching.

When she lowered her hands to his belt and slipped it free, he waited until she unfastened the button of his jeans, then pulled her hands away. "You have far too many clothes on."

He unfastened the top button of her dress, then worked his way down to her waist, letting his fingers dip through the opening in the fabric to stroke the swell of her breast. When he pushed the light cotton off her shoulders, she lowered one strap of her bra, then the other. She pulled the corner of her lower lip into her mouth and reached around to unfasten the lace.

The bra fell away, and sweet Jesus. "You're perfect," he growled.

He wrapped an arm around her waist to walk her one step backward and gently ease her down onto the bed. She felt soft, right, pressed against him, and as soon as he released her, he missed her touch.

She scooted backward until only her feet dangled off the bed, and she kicked off her shoes. He crawled up her body, and her eyes sparkled as he moved to lie beside her. When he lowered his head to take her nipple into his mouth, she arched her back and shoved her hand through his hair, holding him to her. "Oh." The word shuddered out of her, erotic, sexy, straight to his dick.

He drew his finger down her stomach, circled her belly button, slow, a feather of a touch, as he lifted his head to blow a slow burst of cool air on her nipple. Need pulsed through him but he tamped it down. Her first.

When he moved his trail of kisses down her rib cage to her stomach, she curled her fingers into the comforter, wild and wanton, every moan more guttural. And when he moved to stand and tugged her floral satin panties down, slipping them over her feet and dropping them onto the floor, she panted and reached for him, clawing the air.

He spread her legs apart, kissing the inside of each thigh before drawing his tongue in a swirl over her clit, hot, hungry, on fire. She cried out and leaned up for a quick second onto her elbows before throwing herself back against the mattress. Oh, God. She was wet heat and writhing muscle, and every part of him wanted every part of her. He pushed a finger inside of her. She tightened around him, crying out, bucking her hips until her body shuddered and she went pliant. To watch her come like that had him breathing like he'd run a marathon, his cock stiff and aching for her. Penelope smiled lazily, her arm reaching for him languidly.

He moved to lie down beside her. The look in her eyes was pure satisfaction. He wanted to beat his chest like a goddamn gorilla. He smiled, feeling lighter than he had in years.

"I want you."

The three sexiest words he'd ever heard, ones he would hear in his dreams every night for the rest of his life.

His heart stuttered. Whoa. Rest of his life? Where the hell had that come from?

Unnerved, but desperate to chase the thought away, he rolled away to stand and pull a condom out of his pocket. Then toed his shoes off and pushed his jeans aside. She sat up, smiling as she took him first into her hand, stroking from the base to the tip of his dick. His knees went weak and his eyes closed.

Then she took him into her mouth. His eyes slammed open at the exquisite contact. "Oh, fuck, Pen," he gritted out. The sensation of her tongue teasing the tip while her hand pumped the base made his head spin as if he'd finished the wine he'd brought.

"Oh, God." The pressure built, and he pulled away, too close, too desperate to slide inside her.

He tore open the condom and rolled it on, then eased on top of her, sliding in slow and deep. They both gasped. She cupped his face and pulled him into a kiss long and deep, her tongue thrusting in and out of his mouth matching the rhythm he'd set with his cock.

This woman had moves. She sucked his tongue into her mouth and used her body to roll them toward the end of the bed. When she was securely on top of him, she tucked her legs and lifted until only the tip of him remained inside her. Then in a slow, almost agonizing slide, she lowered her hips and took all of him. His breath hitched and he could only see her, her eyes hazed with passion, her hands, braced on his chest for leverage, her breasts, pert and round.

His body tightened, and he couldn't think, couldn't

do more than feel, and it was a sweet relief. She lifted her hips, then brought them down as he rose to meet her, hard, hot, so fucking hot. She threw her head back and he sat up to hold her, to press wet kisses against her nipples before he turned them and slammed into her as she wrapped her legs around him, used them to pull herself up to take every plunge and roll of his hips.

He was so close and when she dug her nails into his shoulder and cried out his name, he couldn't hold back any longer.

There were many reasons why this was wrong, why things between them couldn't work. The biggest being she would leave soon. But his heart wasn't listening to any of those reasons. All he wanted was more of Penelope. More of being with her sexually, working with her physically, opening up to her. Even if deep down he knew the pain that would eventually come.

Why was he such a glutton for punishment?

# *Chapter Seventeen*

## *Penelope*

Penelope squealed in delight and bounced around clutching her phone to her chest. Best news she'd had in weeks, and it completely exonerated her for that damned fire. She held the phone out and stared at the subject line that seemed to glow in iridescent letters rather than the simple black on white. Her mind toyed with ideas on how to share the news with Jay until she came up with a surprise of epic proportions.

She dialed Nick and told him she would be late, then showered with Guinness World Record speed before rushing out the door to load Havoc into the Audi. Before she made her first foot off the step, Charlie opened her door—the telltale squeal of her hinges always announced her comings and goings—and strolled across their shared yard.

"I was going to stop over last night, but I saw Jay's truck in the driveway. Didn't want to interrupt." Charlie quirked an eyebrow at her.

Penelope couldn't help the huge smile that slipped out. God, what a night. Her body still tingled from Jay's immersive lovemaking. She cleared her throat, trying for nonchalance. "We had dinner."

"*Dinner.* Uh-huh." Charlie folded her arms in front of her chest, smirking. "We share a common wall, girlfriend. Our *bedroom* wall."

Penelope bit her lower lip, but lost the battle with her urge to smile again. "I promise we'll meet up later and talk about last night with the naughty reverence and umbrella drinks it deserves, but right now, I'm in a big hurry." She needed to get going on Jay's surprise.

The previously nonexistent lines in Charlie's face dug deep. "You better not be rushing off to see Jay. You need a grace period. A cooldown to process."

"It's not about last night." Penelope clutched the strap of her purse, her pulse racing as she bounced on her toes. "It's something work related. Something that will erase the bad reputation I have with the residents of Maple Falls."

"Uh-huh?"

*Screw it.*

Penelope pulled out her phone, called up her email, and handed it over to Charlie. She expected a few kudos. A celebration even. Instead, Charlie frowned, handed the phone back, and wiped her hand down her sheriff's uniform—today, black cargos and a black T-shirt with the word POLICE emblazoned in white on the back—as if the phone had infected her with a flesh-eating disease. "Well, good luck with that."

Penelope's eyebrows squished together and her mouth opened but nothing came out. What the hell? She tucked the phone back into her purse and stared at her friend. "I didn't purposely put it up there to sell. My photos were what people could buy."

Charlie arched a brow. "Yet, you didn't correct them or the message. Did you mention it to Jay at all?"

Penelope chewed the bottom of her lip. She hadn't, wanting to surprise him and explain the misunderstanding at the same time. The program was so important to him, he'd share in her enthusiasm. Wouldn't he?

Charlie strode past toward the police cruiser and paused before closing the door. "Have to get to work, but I'll be home later if you need to talk."

"Wait!" Penelope blinked rapidly as her friend drove off. Penelope's heart throbbed. Why did her friend seem to be warning her? People would understand if Jay didn't want to sell. And if they didn't, she'd just block them. No harm, no foul.

She rolled her tight shoulders, but it didn't help her climbing anxiety. Or was Charlie implying she came off as if she was some sort of savior instead of having found a way to correct her mistake?

Please no. That would be *awful.*

She hopped into her Audi and drove to the hobby store, printed the email, then had it matted and framed along with the picture of Jay's sculpture that started it all. A very precise customer service woman wrapped it in gold-and-black wrapping paper, then tied it with a bow. After Penelope finished paying, she placed the gift into the car, mindful of Havoc, who settled into his harness in the front seat. "It's going to be a great day, buddy."

Moments later she pulled up to the office, pulse racing to see Jay again after last night. She hoped she wouldn't blush if Nick was in the office. She'd have trouble concealing her happiness today. She unhooked her seat belt, vacillating between wanting to give Jay the gift now and waiting until they were alone. "Nah, let's do it tonight since we have plans later," she told Havoc, then got out of the SUV along with Havoc and bounded up the stairs. She'd forgotten how energizing an active sex life could be.

Well, maybe not active yet, but last night was a really great start.

When she pushed the door open, she was greeted by two grumpy-faced men, but neither of them would put a damper on her mood.

"Morning." Her voice was full of cheer as she leveled a hot look at Jay since Nick was behind her.

Jay's eyes flickered with low-level danger, a dead-sexy smile teasing the edges of his lips as he continued speaking on the phone. And just like that, her engine was revved.

Tonight couldn't get here soon enough.

*Sit your ass down and get to work.*

Nick grunted as he nodded and walked over to the copy machine. Havoc made his way over to Penelope's desk and plopped down next to the chair as she sat.

Penelope flung her bag onto the desk, wide smile plastered on her face, and started on the to-do list Nick had left her. For the next couple of hours, she bounced back and forth between fighting to concentrate on the tasks she needed to complete, remembering Jay's eyes boring into hers as he'd come, and imagining his surprise when he opened the gift.

"Stop it," Jay whispered as Nick droned on about his early morning call with Governor Spends-A-Lot—his new pet name for the man who'd "absconded" with the safety program's money.

"Stop what?"

"Grinning like that."

She cast a glance at Nick, whose pitch had grown to a slight warbling rant, the kind that would only get louder and gain strength as he went on. "Grinning like what?"

"Like someone who spent the night with someone else."

His words made her blood hot. Coupled with the memory of last night, the heat spread through her and settled low in her hips. But it wasn't the whole of the reason she couldn't wipe the smile from her face. She just wasn't about to tell him that yet.

"Am I disturbing you two?" Nick glared at Penelope, then at Jay. "Do you not understand the gravity of what that damned fool is doing?"

"What can we do?" Penelope kept her gaze off Jay because she had loads of ideas she wanted to test-drive on his body tonight.

"Get out there and raise some money. Money he can't touch. Money that doesn't have a damned thing to do with his reelection." Nick growled and stomped to his office.

Penelope stared at Jay, his smile, the shirt that buttoned over what she knew was a broad and well-defined chest, pants that zipped over his thick—

"Stop it." Jay looked over his shoulder toward Nick's office, then back at her. "Now you're looking at me like I'm lunch."

"I was thinking more of dessert, but now that you mention it, you're more of a main course." She punctuated with an eyebrow wiggle, then cleared her throat. Even tried to sober her expression, but her lips twitched back to a smile.

"Get out of here and raise some money." Nick's gruff voice boomed from his office.

"Yes, sir!" Penelope singsonged, absolutely absurd in her good mood, but too far gone to be embarrassed by it.

Jay followed her into the lobby area. When they cleared the door and he shut it behind them, he used his free hand to pull her into the hallway and wrapped her in his arms until her chest bumped his. "You are a devil, woman."

She cocked an eyebrow, giddy to be in full-frontal contact with him again. "You're the one who came in here looking like *that*."

"It's just a uniform."

She ran her fingers across the back of his neck, stopping to massage the hollow just under his skull. When he furrowed his brows, she pulled him down until her breath warmed his ear. "I have a very specific fantasy about taking that thing off of you." He tilted his head and she flicked his earlobe with her tongue. "With my teeth."

His hand at the small of her back pushed her closer so she could feel his very strong reaction. "Maybe we can give that a go." He turned his head into her kiss, a slow, soft kiss full of promise and desire. When he lifted his head, his dark eyes told her he was as affected as she was. "I want you. I didn't want to. God, but I do."

She didn't respond. Better to show him. She pulled him down again, kissed him with all the pent-up lust he'd just inspired. Right up to the minute the door to the inner offices swung open. Jay pushed her away—shoved, really—then turned to walk down the hall, his broad back and finely sculpted ass almost as nice to watch as the front of him.

* * *

Penelope stared across the kitchen at Jay. Her foot bounced against the tile floor, stomach twisting with nerves. The creaks of the house settling and clattering of pipes were louder than they should be. The dinner she'd hoped would include candlelight, some flirting, and a few smoldering gazes before she surprised him with news about the offer on his sculpture had become a dinner for three. Which was really okay, because Jay had introduced her to his grandfather.

That had to mean something, right?

Her gift, still in the backseat of her SUV, called out to her as she stared at the back door to the farmhouse. It would only take a second to get it. Another few for him to open it. And while she wanted to wait until they were alone, she'd held on as long as she could. "I'll be right back. I have to get something out of the car."

Jay looked up from the salad he was crafting at the island counter. "You want me to come with you? It's kind of dark."

Time alone with Jay in the dark or in the light or wherever they could manage would be great since Nick had accompanied them to lunch, then did progress checks every few minutes throughout the day. Penelope shook her head. "I'll be okay. I parked close."

Jay wiped his hands on a dish towel, then took a quick look into the living room, where Gramps sat watching a game show and shouting out the answers. "I'll just come along." He waited until they were outside before he spun her against him. "Sorry about tonight. Gramps seemed a little off today, but backing out of our plans for tonight was unacceptable."

His fingers slipped along her cheek into her hair.

This was a man who knew how to use touch to entice, to tempt, to make her skin come alive. She brushed her thumb across his cheek. “It’s okay. I like getting to know more about your life.”

Crickets chirped, leaves beat against their branches, and the moon shined, but when Jay kissed her the world went quiet and still. Only he existed. His mouth. His tongue. The crush of his body against hers as he moved in closer and held her hip to hip against a tree.

Her hands slid down his chest, and she held one over his heart, and slipped the thumb of her opposite hand into his belt loop, her fingers curling into a fist at his hip. Of all the things in this world, his kissing skills ranked high on her top-ten favorites.

“Jay!” Gramps called out from the back door. He had one hand shielding his eyes as if the moon was too bright. “Jay! Are you out here?”

Jay leaned his head against Penelope’s forehead and closed his eyes before he turned his head. “You okay, Gramps?”

Penelope saw his shoulders relax. “Ah, yeah. I just didn’t know where you went.”

Jay’s hands massaged her hips. It was just as comforting as it was arousing.

“Penelope needed something in her car is all,” Jay called out. “We’ll be back inside in a sec.”

She went up on her tiptoes to give Jay a peck on his stubbly chin. “You go ahead. Not much chance I’ll get lost before I make it back inside.”

“Thank you.” He kissed her quickly and turned while she hustled to the SUV.

Nervous anticipation tingled through her like electrical sparks on the way to the ground, gathering at her toes. She'd waited all day for this moment.

Jay's art gave him an opportunity to save the things he cared about, and she really wanted to help him do that. For a second, she stood, holding the gift, imagining how happy he would be.

Hurrying back inside, she let the screen slam shut behind her. Gramps jumped, grabbing onto the counter for support as he listed heavily to the left.

Jay was at his side in a flash, grabbing him before he could go down. "Whoa, easy does it, old geezer."

Gramps cursed and grumbled as he found his feet. "These damned legs. Don't know what's got into them these days." Jay released his grandfather when he seemed steady. Then Gramps held out his hand as he grinned at Penelope. "Forgive my clumsiness. I'm a sucker for a woman with hair the brown of aged mahogany, deep and rich. Pretty girls like you make me go weak in the knees, I guess. Now, tell me your name again?"

Penelope took Larry Gosling's hand and smiled her brightest. "Penelope Ramos. And aren't you just a charmer?"

Gramps ran a trembling hand across the front of his shirt. "Look here, boy. She brought a present."

Penelope stared at the small wrapped box, then held it out to Jay. "It's for you."

"It's not his birthday."

Penelope chuckled, so nervous the box shook in her hands. "I know. I, um, that is…we work together, and he's been helping me with my search and rescue training, so…" Oh, God. She'd become a bumbling idiot. "Anyway. Here."

She shook the box and the frame inside hit against the edge. Jay cocked an eyebrow but took the package, then sat at the table with the box in front of him. "I don't understand. I didn't get you anything."

"No need. Just open it." She clasped her hands to her chest.

He did, carefully, though, as if he didn't enjoy it and probably had never experienced the satisfaction of the paper tearing to reveal the big surprise of a present. Gramps watched, patting Penelope's shoulder and rolling his eyes when Jay loosened the tape on one end, then flipped the box over to slide his finger under the bottom flap.

"Get on with it, boy!"

Penelope shifted her weight from one foot to the other as she wrung her fingers together. Never before had she cared so much about the way one of her gifts was received. Jay finished unwrapping the box, then ever so slowly lifted the lid and turned back the tissue paper. He read the words on the framed paper—an email that offered a tremendous price for the dog carving, one that would cover the entire cost of the equipment that was destroyed in the fire.

Why wasn't he saying anything? She watched his face anxiously.

A deep frown settled on his features, his jaw ticking with each passing second. "What is this?"

She cleared her throat, every instinct telling her to run. Fast. Far. "I, um, snapped a picture of the dog sculpture and posted it on my social media page, the one with all my photos. I explained the program and offered to sell my pictures as a fundraiser. Offers have been pouring in, but not for my pictures. People wanted to buy your sculpture. This particular offer beat the rest by miles."

"You did what?" He shoved his chair back and walked to the edge of the sink to brace his hands. When he turned, his eyes flashed fire, his face completely red, the vein next to his left temple throbbing visibly. "You had no right to take a picture of anything."

Gramps slid the frame his way and read.

Her cheeks burned like a thousand suns and she crumpled under his scrutiny. "It was beautiful. All I did was take a picture. I didn't even mention it was for sale. I just used the image because it was new and would pop up on everyone's newsfeed. People starting sharing it, and offers came in. I didn't read the messages at first because I thought they were for my photos. Either way, this could be a solution to raising the funds for your program."

Jay banged his fist against the countertop. "Who the hell do you think you are? It wasn't your business to post anything online."

Remorseful. Guilty.

That was how she felt at that very moment, wishing for a time machine to go back and rectify the mistake.

Jay was a private person, didn't share a lot and she certainly overstepped. But as she told him, it wasn't like she went online purposely trying to sell something that was his. Wasn't the photo the equivalent of her taking a picture of the check station she burnt down and posting it? By the fury in his eyes, the answer was no. And there was nothing she could do now except live with her actions.

She clasped her hands in her lap and remained silent, staring at the table as she awaited the rest of Jay's wrath. But it never came. Instead, he stalked out of the kitchen and seconds later a door slammed somewhere else in the house.

Gramps shook his head. "Well, that didn't go over too good, now, did it? Don't feel bad. You probably don't know that the dog in the carving was Zip, who meant the world to Jay. Got the dog after my wife passed on. And when that dog died, I thought I was going to lose Jay. He mourned so deep in his soul. Every night he'd disappear out to the shed. Stayed out there until dawn most times. I think creating that carving healed him."

Penelope wanted to curl into a ball and bawl. "I'd heard about what happened. I just thought the sculpture was of a pointer, not Zip specifically. But it's all just a misunderstanding. I could email the person and just let them know that the sculpture isn't for sale, only my pictures are." Penelope slid her chair back. "I should go talk to him. Clear this whole mess up."

Gramps gently grabbed her forearm. "Not unless you want more arguing. Let him cool off. Might take him a minute but he'll see you meant well." He nodded to the counter. "Help me finish this dinner, then we can eat while he pouts."

Penelope looked from the older man next to her to the door. "Maybe I should just go."

Gramps snorted, stood, and handed her an apron. "You should sit here and make sure an old man eats since my grandson isn't in a kind mood. Hell, I'd rather eat with a beautiful woman than with an old grouch like him anyway."

Penelope took the apron and walked over to the countertop, where she diced a tomato for the sauce to top the Tuscan chicken Jay had in the oven. The least she could do was help complete dinner. Once or twice Gramps reached over to give her one of those sympathetic pats of her shoulder or back. Not that she deserved them. She'd hurt Jay on a level he didn't deserve. All she'd wanted to do was help make his dream become a reality. And not because she'd been the one to destroy the dream in the first place, but because Jay meant something to her. She liked him, cared about him. She was falling for him.

Hard.

Once or twice she checked the stairs and the hallway for some sign of Jay. But she caught neither sight nor sound. Her heart plummeted each time to her stomach. Maybe the door slamming had been the front door. God only knew after everything she'd done, accidental or not, she didn't deserve Jay.

"Don't mind him. Sometimes it takes a fat second for him to get his head wrapped around things and make sense of them."

Penelope nodded, not quite sure how long a fat second lasted. She swallowed past the giant lump in her throat. What had seemed like a good idea earlier, a fabulous idea, now held center stage in the moments of her life that made her want to kick her own ass.

# *Chapter Eighteen*

## *Jay*

Jay glared at his alarm clock. Six a.m. The hours between supper and now had done little to unclench his stomach. And he only had one woman to blame. Penelope Ramos. Firebug. Busybody. Practically a thief to his way of thinking. Honestly. How else could she have sold his sculpture except by sneaking in to steal it? He was damn sure he never gave her permission to post his artwork online, even if it had resulted in that outrageous offer.

He rolled over, leg hanging off the bed, and rubbed the small of his back. The mattress in his old room offered no lumbar support and now his lower back ached. Penelope's fault, too. Why the hell hadn't she gone home instead of sleeping on the couch? Probably Gramps's idea. The same Gramps who'd come into his room and called him a stubborn fool before the man went to bed.

He put on his work uniform and walked out to the kitchen and flipped on the light. Where the hell had the coffee maker gone? He clicked off the light, then turned it on again as if that would make the appliance magically appear. His mood darkened in direct proportion to his growing need for caffeine as he hunted through cabinets, the pantry, and the buffet hutch.

"You're making enough racket to wake your grandmother, God rest her soul." Gramps stood in the doorway, bathrobe open, chest and feet bare and tighty-whities in place, thank heavens. "What in the Sam Hill are you looking for?"

"Coffee."

Gramps closed his robe and stomped to the cabinet, slung the door open, and pulled out a jar of instant decaf. "You made me promise to give my coffee maker away, remember?"

Jay recalled the time he'd lectured his grandfather after reading the article about the correlation between excessive caffeine consumption and rising blood pressure. But no way would the old man give in that easy. He crossed his arms and stared at his grandfather. "Where's the leaded stuff?"

Gramps scowled, narrowed eyes and a slight twist to his mouth, but stomped over to the buffet and pulled out an old vase—might've been an urn since it had a lid—and handed it to Jay. "I bought it at the flea market. Used to hide money in it 'til I had to find a place to keep my Folgers."

Jay opened the lid and took a desperate sniff like a junkie hitting his low.

"Percolator is in the laundry room at the bottom of the clothes hamper. I always put it there when I know you're coming."

Jay barked out a laugh in spite of his raging need for caffeine. "You are one sneaky old man." When he returned from the laundry room, Penelope sat at the table, adorably mussed and disheveled.

As soon as Jay stepped into the room, she stood and tucked a strand of hair behind her ear. “I thought you left already. I’m sorry. I’ll just get my bag and—”

“Sit yourself down, young lady. We do not do the walk of shame out of this house. Especially when we haven’t gotten around to earning the shame.” Gramps cleared his throat. “Well, you haven’t anyway.”

“Gramps.”

“Don’t you ‘Gramps’ me, boy. This young lady brought you a gift and you were less than gracious.”

He didn’t have to defend himself. Penelope had gone behind his back. Not the other way around. Invaded his privacy. But the way she glanced around the kitchen, the paleness of her skin tone, made his chest constrict.

She’d also been helpful, gracious, charming, kind, and so sexy it made him forget how to breathe. He had been falling for her, but what she did, going behind his back to take photos of his private life, then posting them, betrayed his trust. He hadn’t let anyone in, hadn’t shown anyone he’d been hurting. And now God only knew how many people saw it. People he didn’t even know. Or worse, people he did know.

She looked up at him from beneath lashes wet with tears. “I’m really sorry. I didn’t mean to hurt or offend you.”

He took a step closer to her but left enough distance as to not invade her space. “I know.”

“When the bids came in and they started outdoing each other, I thought I’d found a way to make the safety program work. My own pictures came nowhere close.” She rubbed her hands down her pant legs, pupils dilated. “I guess I didn’t realize how attached you were to your work.”

He swallowed past the lump in his throat. God, all he wanted to do was hold her and smooth her hair. Instead, he stood cradling the coffee maker. "I overreacted."

Gramps scoffed. "Piss-poor apology, if you ask me."

Because the man had raised him, taken care of him when no one else would, and showed him how to be a man—not to mention the murderous expression plastered on his grandfather's face—Jay didn't respond. Instead, he dipped his chin toward his chest, allowing his gaze to fall to the ground. "I'm sorry, Penelope."

"You should tell her why you're sorry. Carries more weight that way."

Jay's head jerked up and he leveled a glare at his grandfather. "Aren't you just full of advice for a guy who hides his coffee in an urn and his percolator in a laundry hamper?" But Gramps was right. "Penelope, I'm sorry for overreacting to your gift."

"And I'm sorry for not checking with you before I posted the sculpture. I honestly didn't know it was a sculpture of Zip." Penelope grabbed her purse and keys from the table. "I need to get going. Havoc had a sleepover with Charlie last night, and he probably misses me."

Jay set the percolator on the counter and followed her out. There were a hundred better things to say than asking her to take the picture down, but he couldn't think of any. Not after the wounds that were ripped open last night. "I'd like you to take the picture down."

"Okay." She continued to walk straight for her SUV without turning around. She climbed in and shut the door without so much as a goodbye.

Jay caught up and knocked on the window, which she lowered as she pulled her seat belt across her body.

He leaned his forearms against the car. "I'll see you at the office?"

She nodded and drove away, leaving him to stand in the driveway until her taillights disappeared.

An hour later, after a good bit of cursing and slamming cupboard doors and stomping out to his truck, Jay drove into the office to find her already there with her hair curled, makeup on and an outfit—jeans and a plain white T-shirt—that no woman on earth could wear as well or make look so good. And she had nothing to say to him.

But damned if she didn't use that sugar-and-honey voice on the phone and with Nick and with the hunters who'd come in and try to by their seasonal license from her. He couldn't blame them. What guy wouldn't want to talk to her? He sure as hell did. Even as mad as he was.

And that pissed him off even more.

He really needed to get his emotions in order, damnit all.

After lunch, he walked to her desk, where she studiously ignored him as he leaned down to pet Havoc. What should he say? *Did you have a good lunch?* What kind of idiot was he?

He stood abruptly to return to his desk, but then his cell rang. He checked the screen. Not a number he recognized, but since it could have been one of the donors he'd given his personal number to, he answered. "Hello."

"I need to speak to Jay Gosling. This is Dr. Morgan from Maple Falls Memorial."

His hand gripped his phone tighter as his throat began to constrict. "This is Jay."

"Your grandfather was admitted this morning. Someone found him walking along the highway in his bathrobe with a head injury."

The air rushed from Jay's lungs with Dr. Morgan's news. When he saw Penelope staring at him, concern etched in her features, he marched out the door for privacy. "Is he okay?"

"He's resting now, but he's been asking for you. He says he remembers falling because his legs gave out. He must have hit his head pretty hard on the way down. We see this a lot in Parkinson's patients, unfortunately. You should probably consider a nursing home, or at the very least, assisted living or in-home care for him at this stage. He's not safe at home alone anymore."

"I'm on my way." He clicked the phone off knowing he should have at least found out who brought Gramps in and if he'd sustained any lasting brain injury, but he couldn't think in terms of more than getting to his grandfather. He started the truck and gunned the engine.

Nursing home. Jay couldn't quite digest the concept. When he tried to say it, his breath caught in his throat. There had to be another way. *Still, though.* He'd already lost his grandmother and Zip. He couldn't bear to lose his last family member—or at least the last family member who cared enough not to abandon him—to a disease that was making it dangerous for him to keep living in his own home.

"Parkinson's is a progressive disease. I'm sorry, but he's just not going to get any better," Dr. Morgan continued. "Things will only continue to deteriorate. Including his mind."

Jay clenched and unclenched his fists. Gramps had been on medicine for a while now, hoping to slow down the degeneration, but it wasn't working. A nursing home? God damnit. He should've been researching this more instead of refusing to admit his grandfather was getting worse. "Are there any other options?"

"His insurance along with a bit of government assistance would pay almost completely for a skilled nursing facility. But if you can afford the out-of-pocket costs, we have an in-home program that I can refer you to. Assisted living might be a good option, too, if he passes their requirements."

Dr. Morgan had come to town only a couple years ago when Doc Farley retired, so she had no idea how adamantly Gramps had refused help in the past. "What if I move back in with him?"

"Can you stay with him all the time? He's going to need constant supervision."

Jay groaned and rubbed his palms down the side of his thighs. Not working wasn't an option. "Ballpark, what's the in-home care cost?"

"Round-the-clock care is about fifteen hundred a week. But if you only need someone during the day while you work, at least until he's in need of more skilled care, you could probably count on it being about five hundred a week. Give or take. There might be some wiggle room if you check with his insurance."

Five hundred extra a week? Jay clenched his jaw. Maybe if he sold his place, he could make enough to pay off the mortgage and give himself enough for a year of home care. Jay pulled out his phone and dialed the one person who might just be able to help him.

After Jay had said goodbye, since Gramps had to remain in the hospital another day before being released, he headed home to meet the Realtor. Betsy Privu had always been optimistic. And upbeat. A cheerleader in their high school days, she'd gone from a perky pep squad captain to a peppy mother of five who sold real estate when she wasn't baking for the PTA, chaperoning class trips, and being the eye candy at her husband's—Mayor Donald Privu—golf outings and election rallies. She also had a foot in every gossip pot in town. Gramps wouldn't like Betsy knowing his business and spreading it for everyone else to know, but there wasn't much Jay could do about it. He needed money, and Betsy had a proven track record for sales.

She held a clipboard in one hand and a digital camera in the other. Occasionally, she snapped pictures or made notes, sometimes nodding, sometimes widening her eyes, and smiling sideways at him like she'd shared some secret. But she didn't really say much until she'd photographed every room from two or three angles.

"Good news. Real estate in this area is up." He expected nothing less from her, but then she frowned. "Bad news. You need to throw some fresh paint up and fix that squeaking front door. Also, there's a tick to the furnace and you have a water stain on the ceiling in the downstairs bathroom. So you'll need to get a plumber to sign off on the pipes."

Nothing too drastic so far. "Okay."

"Aesthetically, you could use some landscaping in front. Those old bushes are a relic these days. People want some nice lava rock, maybe some stonework and flowers." She pointed to the front porch. "And for goodness' sake, take down that rusty porch swing and put some hanging plants up. Otherwise, I'd say we can get your money back and maybe a little left over."

"Sounds good." It sounded like work he didn't have time for and no money to hire someone else to complete.

It took another hour and a half of her taking notes on the property and gossiping before she pulled a contract from her bag for him to sign. "This gives me the permission to come and go while you're gone and show the place to buyers."

"How long do you think it'll take to sell?" Not that he wanted to be pushy, but the sooner, the better.

"I have a couple who might be interested. They're looking for something with a nice big yard away from town. Let me give them a call, but like I said, if you want top dollar, you need to fix a few things up."

He led her to the door. "Thanks, Betsy."

She placed a hand on his shoulder. "And so sorry to hear about Gramps. I always liked him."

Well, he wasn't dead yet, for God's sake. "Thanks."

"And if you need anything, please, don't hesitate to give me or Donnie a call."

Well, now that she mentioned it. Jay rubbed the back of his neck. "Have you heard about the GPS safety program for the park?"

"Oh, sure. After those kids got lost a couple years ago in Donnie's town, we were so glad you came up with that idea."

"We are still in need of donations. If you and Donnie could help at all, I'd appreciate it." Nothing like dropping a reminder the mayor didn't follow through on his campaign promise to help start up the program. The man hadn't even donated a dollar to the cause yet.

Betsy clutched the diamond-and-pearl necklace she

wore and twirled it around her finger until Jay thought she might actually choke herself. “Of course we will help.”

After he secured a donation from Betsy, he got to work fixing the house until he could barely keep his eyes open. He’d oiled all the hinges, painted most of the trim on the second floor, called Paul Perkins to check the plumbing, and taken down the porch swing, although the front of the house looked naked without it. And now, anyone who pulled up could see into the living room through the picture window. After work tomorrow—correction, today—he would stop and get some plants and landscape rocks. And he supposed he would have to arrange for the in-home counselor to meet Gramps. Then he’d have to find time to paint the living room a shade of white with just a tinge of gray, then clean and polish the downstairs trim, the stair rail, and every door in the house.

Jay stared at his feet, chin tucked to his chest. He didn’t want to sell his house. Nor move in with Gramps, and not because he didn’t love the man, but moving back into his childhood home felt like he failed. A lump formed in the back of his throat the more he thought about it, his hand rubbing the center of his chest as he tried to chase the pain away. If only he’d never married his ex, Karen wouldn’t have buried him in a mountain of debt. Hell, if only he’d chosen a career that paid him more.

Jay gritted his teeth as he fought back the tears forming in his eyes, shame washing over him. Now, more than ever, the safety program was a necessity, not only for hunters and hikers, but also for situations like this morning. Gramps had been wandering aimlessly. Lost.

He didn't have dementia yet, but how many others did? How many other families worried about their loved ones leaving the house unattended?

And Gramps would get there if he lived long enough. Dr. Morgan said dementia was just another devolution of a person with Parkinson's.

Not that he could force a GPS sensor on Gramps, but if he explained it was this or a nursing home, Gramps would comply. Jay was sure of it.

# *Chapter Nineteen*

*Penelope*

Havoc stared at the ravine, inching closer to where the rocks and land were unsteady, some tumbling away with each step he took closer to the edge. The dog paced back and forth, looking from Penelope to the area down the cliff. Then he barked. And barked. And barked again until saliva flew from his mouth.

"Havoc, down."

The dog lay down as Penelope approached, her grip tightening around a skinny tree trunk for support. Brent, who had chosen to hide at the bottom of a small cliff, waved up at her. She gave him a thumbs-up and returned the gesture, grabbed his gear, and took off down a narrow path.

Penelope turned to Havoc. "Good boy. Good job."

She pulled her dog's reward from her pocket and Havoc clamped onto his favorite toy as they both moved away from the edge of the cliff to safer ground. Once they were on flatter terrain, Penelope tugged and whipped the toy and Havoc around with as much gusto as she could muster.

Behind her, Nick was talking to someone, but Penelope focused all her energy and attention on Havoc. She trained him to respond to both her silent and spoken commands, to save lives, to be an extension of herself. And he'd done it!

"Good boy. Yay! What a good dog." She continued the celebratory party until her arms couldn't hold the tug toy any longer. And when Havoc gave her one final tug, she released the toy, allowing him to win his payday.

"That was amazing. You should reschedule your test, Pen." Nick hugged her.

"I've been looking online but no new test dates in the Northeast have been listed as of yet. In the meantime, we'll keep practicing. You have any pointers?"

He clicked his tongue and shook his head from side to side. "Wish I could help you, but it would be unethical since I'll be the one running the evaluation."

Penelope's mouth gaped. "You're kidding me."

Nick shook his head. "Pen, you should have told me sooner you wanted to test. I'll call the organization and give them a new date so they can get it up on the schedule. I'll check that your paperwork is still on file with them since we had to cancel the original date."

"Awesome! Thank you!" The day was improving by the minute, so she was absolutely *not* going to ask about Jay. So what if he hadn't called. Hadn't been at work. Of course, Nick would know where Jay was. But no way could she ask. "So, um, everything at work is going according to schedule?"

He nodded. "Yeah, those guys you recommended are just about done, so we'll be open by hunting season."

"They didn't slow down since Jay's been gone and

not supervising?" She cringed hearing the desperation in her voice. She didn't do apathy well.

"Not at all. If anything, they've sped up." He crossed his arms and watched her, smiling just a little.

"Oh, well, that's great." She tapped her fingers against her thighs. Oh, for God's sake. Just ask! "Is he coming back soon?"

Nick quirked a brow at her. "You haven't talked to him?"

Now he was toying with her and enjoying it a little too much, the ass. She shot him a glare. "I've been busy training and working for you. Plus, we got into an argument." She sighed. "It was my fault. And I don't want to go over there and force myself on him. But if he ever comes to work, I could apologize. So just tell me when he's coming back."

"He's at the office right now."

"You are an evil human being." Her fingernails itched to scratch that smug smile off his handsome face. Letting her suffer through the confession part of their conversation was typical Nick. Well, typical for the last few days when she'd dubbed him Semi-Good-Mood Nick.

He threw an arm around her shoulders and squeezed good-naturedly for a moment before releasing her. "Forgive me if I tell you a secret?"

She raised an eyebrow, determined to make him suffer a moment. "Maybe. If the secret's good enough." But probably not.

Nick cracked his knuckles and glanced over her shoulder with a smile that would make all the ladies in Maple Falls swoon. "He just pulled up, firebug."

She whirled around, and sure enough, Jay was parking his truck next to Charlie's cruiser. Her heart lub-dubbed against her ribs. She turned back to face Nick, her mood brightened. "How is that a secret?"

"Did you know it before I told you?" He shot her a wink, then turned when Charlie and Jay approached.

An unseasonable warmth along with the strenuous physical activity she'd just put herself and Havoc through accounted for the sweat rolling down her back. Ack. Penelope wished she could do a quick mirror check. Instead, she settled for smoothing her hair with her hand and wiping the sweat from her forehead, her stomach fluttering as if a swarm of butterflies had just taken up residence.

Charlie sidled up next to her and bumped her shoulder. "So, how'd the training go?"

Penelope glanced at Jay, trying to gauge his mood. "Nick thinks I'm ready for my evaluation."

Jay twisted his head to glare at Nick. "Oh, he does?"

"Yeah." She ignored his narrowed eyes and the tick of his jaw. "Havoc and I have been working really hard. We even found Brent today."

Jay shook his head, folding his arms over his chest, his fingers thrumming against his tense forearm. "Penelope, you trained on yet another sunny day. I haven't seen you train under any bad weather conditions. Did you tell Brent where to hide or was it a double-blind exercise?"

She narrowed her eyes and breathed in through her nose as her stomach churned. Why was he raining on her parade? Was this his way of getting back at her for posting the photo of his sculpture? Ridiculous. Especially after she'd apologized. Even Gramps appeared to side with her. "Nick thinks I'm ready, and so do I.

Havoc's trained in bad weather before and not to mention, I don't control whether or not it rains. And as you know, it hasn't rained lately." Sweat continued to trickle down her spine.

"You think you know everything, don't you?" The challenge in his voice went straight to her red button of death center. He raked a hand through his hair. "I trained Zip for three years before I even considered certifying as a canine team. We trained in every type of condition possible. Do you think people only get lost on nice, sunny days? And let's not forget how someone who has their land searcher certification had such a lapse in judgment she started a fire that burnt down a building."

Low-fucking-blow.

She stepped closer to him, ready to challenge him. Surely he'd made mistakes. But she snapped her mouth shut because there would only be one mistake he'd focus on. One that was still so raw.

Zip.

Of course this was about Zip. Havoc and her training must be a constant reminder for him. After all, it was only a little over a year he'd lost his beloved partner. So she kept quiet, hoping a few minutes of silence would allow his tension to dissipate.

Nick led Charlie toward the path to the parking lot, giving her and Jay some privacy. Which she wasn't sure she wanted right now. Until she noticed how wet his eyes were, how red they were. Then there was the slight tremble in his lips. When he began to pace back and forth, she knew something was wrong. Very wrong.

"Jay, what's going on?"

He took a deep breath and exhaled slowly, the vein

in his forehead thumping visibly. He shoved his hands into his pockets and looked off into the trees. "I actually need to talk to you about something else."

"What is it?"

He paused. For a long time. Then he rocked back onto his heels and looked up at the sky. "Is that buyer still interested in the sculpture of Zip?"

Of all the things she'd expected, that wasn't one of them. "I, um, I deleted the post after I talked to your grandpa. I thought you didn't want to sell it?"

Jay blew out a breath, his shoulders and head slumping toward the ground. "I don't have a choice. I need to sell it now."

Penelope's heart ached at the pain etched into Jay's features. Something big had happened to change his mind. "Why?"

"My situation has changed."

She waited, but he didn't elaborate. She couldn't let him sell that statue. Not with knowing how much it meant to him. How much it represented his love for his deceased companion. "Maybe you could sell one of the others."

He shook his head. "I need the money now if the buyer is still interested."

Their project was coming to an end, and they didn't have enough money to start the safety program. It was her fault, and she'd have to live with the knowledge that he'd gotten rid of his memento to finance the program she'd destroyed. But he made it sound like he might use the money to finance something other than the project.

She scratched her head, trying to understand what was going on without outright asking him. It'd probably just piss him off. "Jay, I called a bunch of contractors I worked with who're hunters. I know we'll get the money in time. Don't sell the statue." God knew she couldn't match the bid any more than she had the words to convince him not to part with the sculpture.

He laced his fingers at the back of his head and stared up at the sky and sighed. He seemed so far away. Not the man she'd touched the stars with in ecstasy. How did they get here? And why were things always so complicated?

*You're just unlucky in love.*

She stared at the ground, feeling exhausted suddenly. Yeah, she wasn't falling for the ranger, she was already in love with him. And he was shutting her out.

"Penelope, can you get ahold of the buyer or not?"

Yes, she could, but she'd always regret it. On the other hand, it was his sculpture. His decision. "The address should be on the page I framed for you. I folded the paper, so you just have to take it out and unfold it," she said quietly.

"I have some things I need to take care of. But thank you." He dropped his hands to his side, turned on his heel, and went to Nick's truck. Nick climbed in the driver's side and off they went.

Her lungs deflated as he walked away. Every breath was laborious, as if the air was too thick to breath in. She fought to swallow past the lump in her throat, the action taking way too much effort.

Penelope glanced at Charlie and the police cruiser she'd brought out to the park. "Good thing you showed up. I've watched too many horror shows where the hitchhiker gets slashed. Can I get a lift?"

"Of course." Charlie opened the back door and Havoc ran and leapt into the backseat.

Penelope closed the door, then stood with her arms on the top of the car and looked at Charlie, who paused before climbing in. She copied Penelope's pose so they faced each other. "We need to talk."

When they got into the car, Penelope dropped her head back against the headrest and closed her eyes. Charlie started the engine and drove toward the main road. Jay'd been so disheveled in appearance. Had she caused him that much stress? Hurt him that bad? Maybe there was too much water under the bridge for her and Jay to ever work out. Maybe it was time to give up and go back home. "I can't wait to get out of here."

Charlie pursed her lips. "You always run when things get hard?"

Penelope jerked her head sideways to face her friend. "No, why would you say that?"

Charlie shrugged and pressed her lips together. "Just seems you're running because Jay's upset. Man has a lot going on. Though, maybe it's better if you do go home."

Penelope's mouth opened and closed, no words coming out. What the hell? Since when did Charlie side with Jay—to the point where she insinuated Penelope was no good for the ranger. "Look, whatever is going on he can talk to me, not snap my head off."

Charlie quirked a brow at her. "He criticized your training. Or more like questioned it, and now you're looking to run home. Not someone I'd say is ready to get certified in anything to save lives. Certainly wouldn't have wanted a person like that in my unit when I was deployed."

Penelope crossed her arms in front of her chest. "And what sort of person would you want? Someone who was a doormat?"

"Hell no. I'd want someone who stood their ground but also found a way to solve the problem and make it work." Charlie took in an audible breath. "Jay's always been a private person. Even avoided talking about his divorce. If it wasn't for Karen, no one would've known for sure what happened. Which is why I'm going to share a bit of information I probably shouldn't."

Penelope straightened, her pulse picking up its pace. "What happened?"

Charlie chewed her lip, hesitant. "Couple days ago, Gramps ended up in the hospital. He fell, got a nasty gash on his head, and became disoriented, leaving the house in his bathrobe, carrying one of those old-time coffeepots. He didn't know where he was going. His Parkinson's is advancing, and Jay won't put him in a nursing home. So he's taking care of everything, and you saw him. He's not sleeping. Not taking care of himself."

Penelope blanched when she connected the dots. The way Gramps stumbled so easily that night. The reason Jay reconsidered selling the statue. Oh, God. And she knew memory loss was often a progression of Parkinson's. Perhaps that was the real reason the safety program meant so much to Jay. It was personal. A way to keep Gramps safe.

Penelope's gaze fell to the floor. She had still been mad about his response to her training, and she was also sensitive to how upset he'd been with her about the sculpture, so she didn't bother to press him to open up. And for someone who claimed to care about him, she certainly failed at making an effort to show him. And she needed to rectify that. "Can you drop me out at his place?"

Charlie cleared her throat. “I could, but he’s selling the place.”

“Can we swing by Gramps’s at least?”

Charlie nodded, and they pulled into the driveway fifteen minutes later. Wherever he’d gone, Jay hadn’t come back, but Penelope waved Charlie away and knocked on the door. If there was no one home, she’d wait until he returned. Havoc roamed the lawn, sniffing and investigating, before he settled on chasing a butterfly.

The door opened and an older woman in blue scrubs pushed open the screen. “Can I help you?”

Penelope took a respectful step back and smiled at the woman. “I’m Penelope. Is Jay home?”

The woman shook her head. “Not yet. Did you want to come in and wait?”

Last thing she wanted was to go inside and be a problem. “No. I’ll catch him tomorrow. Would you mind telling him I came by?”

“Sure.”

The woman closed the door and Penelope grabbed Havoc’s leash and headed toward the road. For all the walking she’d done in the last few days—through the park, from the office to the ravine, from the duplex to Clover’s—she would have thought her legs would have been strong enough for a four-mile walk back, but by the time she arrived in the yard, she had aching calves and sore soles. She opened the door, fed Havoc, then ran a bath. She wanted nothing more than to wash this day off and try again tomorrow.

# *Chapter Twenty*

*Jay*

Another sleepless night didn't make Jay a happy man. Part of it was worry for Gramps. Part for his finances. And part because he missed Penelope. A month ago, he would have never thought he would say it, but it was true. He missed every passionate, frustrating, and optimistic part of her.

Selling the statue of Zip hadn't been as hard as he'd thought it would be. Not in theory, anyway. Of course, he hadn't packaged it yet. Or arranged delivery, but the idea of parting with it hadn't been as bad as he'd thought. Zip had been a hero in life, and now his statue would not only allow Jay to keep Gramps at home, but he wouldn't have to sell his house just yet. Maybe selling more of his sculptures would allow him to keep his house.

Maybe Penelope had been right all along.

He checked the clock. Only five, but not much point to lying in bed pretending to sleep when he could just as easily sit at the kitchen table with a cup of coffee and worry. When he walked into the kitchen, Gramps sat with the picture frame and the copy of the email. Jay popped in a filter and three scoops of coffee grounds. He needed it strong this morning.

"You sure you want to sell it?"

Jay stared at Gramps. This was the man who'd taught him everything from fishing to cooking to how to be a man. Even if Jay hadn't owed him everything he was and would ever be, he wouldn't let his grandfather be put into a nursing home. If Gramps wanted to be in his own house, sleep in his own bed, eat when he wanted—in front of the TV, even—then Jay would make it happen. "It's just some wood."

"I think we both know it's more than that."

And maybe it was, but not more important than his grandfather. "I'm ready to let go."

"It's about time. Your girl was here yesterday." When Jay raised his eyebrows, Gramps chuckled. "The brunette."

As if Gramps needed to clarify. There was only Penelope. *His girl.*

Had he not been a jerk to her—again—he would have liked the possessive sound of that. He actually *did* like the sound, anyway, just knew it wasn't true. He slid a mug to his grandfather, then waited while Gramps set the frame aside as if it were made of precious jewels. When the picture was perfectly perpendicular to the edge of the table, Jay poured Gramps a cup. "What did she say?"

"She talked to the nurse, but I think the gist was to tell you she'd stopped by." Gramps wrapped both hands around his mug as if trying to absorb his warmth. "Cute dog, too."

He sipped his coffee. Why in God's name had Nick told her she was ready when she wasn't? She had something…instincts and a way with her dog that reminded him of how Zip reacted to him. But the broader knowledge just wasn't there yet. She'd probably never even seen a rescue. It was one thing to prepare and test under perfect conditions—sunshine, warm or even semi-warm breezes—but not a lot of rescues happened without something treacherous causing the need for a rescue—floods, natural disasters, man-made tragedy. Confidence, in this case, just wasn't enough, and if he was still her evaluator, he would have chosen the rainiest, most awful day for her testing. Let her see what she'd endure during a real callout.

If she wasn't ready, she wouldn't be safe, and that's what had his craw bent.

"What are you thinking about?"

Jay shot his grandfather a blank stare. "Nothing."

"Mmm-hmm. That's why one minute you're wide-eyed and starstruck and the next you have a frown so deep it looks like it's painted on." Gramps pushed his cup toward Jay. "You make horrible coffee."

Jay chuckled. "I make horrible coffee because you taught me how."

"Well, I didn't teach you how to be bad with women. Where did all that come from?"

"Must've been from the other side of the family."

Gramps nodded. "Well, are you going to call her?"

"I work with her. I'm sure I'll see her later."

Gramps rolled his eyes, sighed, then shook his head. "If she wanted to talk to you at work, she wouldn't have hauled her cookies all the way out here, now would she?"

On a normal day, Jay loved and respected the words of imparted wisdom. God knew, on more than one occasion, he'd benefited from Gramps's knowledge. But today, he could do without it. All of it. "Gramps, I don't want to get into anything with her. She's going back to New York City soon. She has a dog."

Gramps grabbed his robe where it lay over his chest. "A dog, you say? Oh, dear. Well, that makes all the difference. She must be a horrible person."

"Go ahead. Make fun." Jay clicked his tongue against his teeth. His grandfather had seen the emotional toll losing Zip had taken on Jay. It wasn't as easy as just bouncing back from something like that. This pain was too big to just walk off. And while Jay couldn't control much else in his life, he could protect himself and his heart from suffering so deeply in his soul. "But I'm not getting attached to another animal. No dogs. No cats. No goldfish."

Gramps shrugged. "Shame. She's a sweet girl. Pretty, too. With your ugly mug, not much chance you'll get another pretty one."

"I should date her because she's beautiful?" He pictured her standing in the sun, the way she'd been last week, smiling, her hand on his chest and her body nestled close to his.

Gramps's lips twitched and his forehead creased—his laughing-on-the-inside look. "I'm just saying, one of these days, you're going to have to stop using me as an excuse and settle down."

How much more settled could he possibly be? He worked. Moved back into his childhood home. And he couldn't remember the last time he'd had more than two beers. "Yeah. I'll work on that."

"Don't sass me, boy. I'm telling you that when you talk about that girl, your face gets younger. Your smile is real. And I haven't seen that in a long time. You let her go and you're going to regret it."

"I don't even know her that well."

Gramps shook his head. "I hear excuses. I hear you hiding your heart away because you're scared." He stood and leaned heavily on his new cane as he took his cup to the sink and poured it out. "What I don't hear is a man who deserves a woman like that. If I was fifty years younger, she wouldn't even be looking at you. And there are other men out there. How long you think she's going to let you behave like a moron before she takes her business elsewhere?"

"She can take her business anywhere she wants." The words tasted sour, sounded bitter. Another day, another lifetime maybe, he would have stayed and argued his grandfather into submission. Their verbal sparring kept them sharp, but this particular argument felt too close, too pertinent. He cleared his throat and poured himself another cup of coffee. "Do you like Trisha?"

The home health aide had spent half a day yesterday with Gramps without Jay as a buffer. Leaving him with a stranger yesterday had almost killed Jay, but he'd used all his paid time off setting everything up, painting and repairing his own house for sale, and moving into his old room, so going back to work wasn't a choice as much as a necessity.

Gramps stared out the window. "She's a babysitter." He glanced back at his grandson. "You know she even set out my clothes this morning? Next thing she'll wanna do is wipe my ass. I'm not an invalid. Yet."

Jay hadn't told Gramps his options—nursing home or home health aide—he'd just hired home health. But if Gramps didn't like Trisha Kittredge, there were other aides out there. "Do you like her? If not, I can find someone else."

"Well, she makes better coffee than you do." He glanced down into his cup. "This tastes like motor oil."

Jay laughed as Gramps drained his mug and held it out for another serving. Jay cocked an eyebrow. "Look at it like she's a new friend. Teach her to play cards. Make her sit through the ninety-nine John Wayne DVDs you have. Tell her about your glory days. I interviewed her for an hour and a half. I really think if you give her a chance, you'll like her."

And if anyone could out-chat Gramps, he'd learned it would be his home health aide, Trisha.

Driving into work, Jay thought of Penelope. Which was nothing new. He thought about her when he showered, when he put on his uniform, when he walked to the truck. Aside from her determination, aside from her beauty, aside from the way she talked to him, he couldn't think of one damned reason why he couldn't get her out of his head.

Okay, that was a lie. There were a million reasons why she was like crack to his brain. And yeah, there was that. Crack was horseshit for your health.

He pulled into the lot and shut the truck off. He'd arrived before her on purpose. He wanted to get in, get his assignments for the day, and get out before she showed up. Seeing her wouldn't help. Wouldn't make not seeing her socially any easier.

In fact, he was determined not to see her outside of the office again.

Nick sat at his desk like he never left. When Jay walked in and sat in the chair in front of him, Nick looked up. "Need you at the check station today. Governor is doing a photo op and I can't stomach another one of those."

"All right." He stared at Nick for a minute, picturing the absolute joy on Penelope's face when she told him Nick thought she was ready for her evaluation. Setting her up to fail. "About Penelope." No segue needed in Jay's head since he'd developed the uncanny ability to connect everything in life to her. "She isn't ready, and you shouldn't be pushing her to test."

Nick scrunched his brows together. "What?"

"She isn't ready." His voice, hard and angrier than the situation called for, boomed through the room. Probably through the walls, too.

"Were you ready when you went out the first time?"

"You're damned right I was." He'd trained for three years. Spent every waking minute on the trails. In the rain. The snow. Winds strong enough to carry both him and Zip to the far corners of the earth. He'd trained in rivers, flooded and rushing. And so far, Penelope had only trained in the Vermont on sunny days. God only knew what her training was like in New York. From studying maps, the terrain was pretty tame in and around the city. Nothing like up here.

Nick chuckled. "I was on that first rescue with you. Remember?"

They'd been called to a town in Iowa, ravaged by a tornado. He'd made mistakes. Newbie mistakes. Working Zip too hard, too long. And he almost walked away from it all when he stumbled on the bodies of a woman and her child who hadn't survived. But he'd learned from it. Painfully. The face of that woman had haunted him so many nights after. "Yeah. I remember."

"Then you know that you can't be prepared for a scene like that. She's trained hard and she deserves a chance to show her stuff." He cocked an eyebrow at Jay. "I would think you would be happy for her."

Jay grunted.

Nick shook his head. "You are so arrogant, so holier than thou. She's ready, and you know it. You saw her out there. You saw the connection between her and her dog. And her training logs show she's trained in inclement weather. Maybe not recently, but she has. Did you even bother to look them over?"

Jay hadn't thumbed through her training log. There was no need. Her team leader back in New York had to sign off that she was ready when the application was sent into the national organization. But there was no mandate on how many days or how inclement the weather had to be.

Jay shook his head and stood. When he reached the door, he turned for one last parting shot. "She isn't ready, Nick. If you do this, you're putting lives in danger. Hers and everyone she's called out to rescue."

He slammed out of the office, spun tires on rocks as he left. Penelope Ramos had no business taking her test yet. She was still unsure, still lacked the confidence in herself to be able to deploy to a real emergency. Still needed to experience a variety of environmental conditions.

She needed *time*.

Fuck. He paused at a stoplight, not even sure where he needed to go.

*I need time.* It was slipping through his fingers as he made all the wrong moves with Penelope. If Nick thought she and Havoc were ready, she was another step closer to leaving Maple Falls.

And there was not one damned thing he could do to stop the test.

# *Chapter Twenty-One*

*Penelope*

Maple Falls, Vermont, took Halloween as seriously as Santa Claus, Indiana, took Christmas. The whole town had already started decorating. Pumpkins lined sidewalks. White plastic bag ghosts hung from tree branches. Hay bales and corn stalks lit with white twinkle lights graced all the front porches in town. Literally.

The crowning glory to the celebration of fall was the Halloween Festival. Rides, games, trick-or-treating, a haunted house—six square blocks of carnival and the whole town pitched in. The town divided the revenue among the various committees and commissions, and that was why Maple Falls remained in shipshape condition.

Right now, Penelope couldn't think about the festival or the evaluation. Right now, she had to make things right with Jay. Had he not taken avoidance to new heights of expertise, she could have done it at work, but he'd somehow managed to take away every single opportunity for them to have a moment together. He'd even gone so far as to volunteer to take the governor to lunch—a man he despised and blamed almost as much as he blamed Penelope for setting the safety program back by more than a year.

She'd waited for him to come back, but by six that evening, she knew he wouldn't be returning to the office. So, with no choice left, she asked Charlie to watch Havoc and she drove out to the farmhouse. She knocked. Would wait all night for him to come home if she had to.

Gramps answered the door. "Can I help you?"

Nick had warned her not to go, that Jay was in a mood, so she'd prepared for that, but she found herself unaccountably flustered running into Gramps. "Hi, Larry. Is Jay around?"

Trisha, the home health aide, appeared behind him and smiled. "Hi. Just me and Larry right now. But Jay should be home soon. He went into town to get dinner." She pushed open the screen door. "Did you want to come in and wait?"

Penelope cast a worried glance at Gramps. "Is it okay?"

"Well, of course it's okay. I may be falling apart, but it's not contagious. Get on in here." He turned and went to his recliner. The TV was set on some game show and he stared at the screen, ignoring Penelope and the nurse.

Trisha led her to the kitchen. "Larry has been pretty grumpy and unsteady this afternoon, and Jay wasn't taking it very well. So, he offered to go pick up dinner. I think he just needed some time away to process. Parkinson's is a mean disease." She filled a pitcher with water, then stirred in some lemonade crystals. She couldn't have been more than fifty. A blond ponytail swung to the middle of her back, and her slender body shook as she put her whole arm into stirring the liquid. “Jay didn’t mention you would be coming over.”

Of course not. Why would he? She’d been terribly insensitive to the family crisis he’d been facing. “I need to go over some things for work with him.” Ugh. That sounded lamer coming out.

“I tried to impress upon Jay that staying positive is key for Larry.” She turned, holding the stirring spoon. “If it’s stressful, probably best if you and Jay do your work things at work.”

“Oh.” She hadn’t considered she would be disturbing Gramps. “I’m sorry.”

“This is a time of adjustment for everyone,” Trisha said, keeping her voice down. “Imagine if you started losing your independence. Needed someone to help you bathe. To dress. And then you start to project what’s in store down the road. Not being able to control your bladder or bowels, not being able to walk, to feed yourself. And if you live long enough, you’ll start to lose your memories. That’s the cruel forecast Parkinson’s hands you. That’s why they lash out at their loved ones. They’re scared and angry.”

Heat crawled up Penelope’s face. She should’ve called. But she hadn’t because she was afraid Jay would tell her not to come. Or worse, not answer at all. She stood. “I’ll go and call Jay later.”

The nurse shook her head. “No. No. Jay will be back soon. Larry doesn’t mind having you wait. I just wanted you to know what Jay is up against.”

She shouldn’t have come. She was being selfish, wanting only to ease her conscience. Jay had enough to deal with without her adding to his worries. Right now, he needed to concentrate on his grandfather. "I'm going to go. Just tell Jay I'll catch him tomorrow at work."

The nurse closed her eyes and sighed. "Sometimes my mouth runs away with me, and I forget that I'm here to help, not run the show."

Penelope appreciated her candor and smiled. But when the back door swung open, and Jay walked in with two carryout bags from Clover's, her pulse jacked sky-high. Seeing him so close made her want to run into his arms. She wanted to smell his shampoo, feel the warmth of his body and the strength of his arms wrapped around her.

She wanted him to tell her he forgave her, that everything would be okay.

Instead, he raised his eyebrows at her, but didn't speak. She blew a breath out and smoothed the papers she'd been rolling and unrolling as she spoke with the nurse. "I brought the, um, Halloween fundraiser ideas from Nick."

He nodded and pulled foam containers from the bag. "All right."

She waited, but he didn't say anything more. Didn't even look at her. "Well, guess I'll be going now."

He finally turned and considered her for a minute. "I'll walk you out."

This wasn't what she'd played out in her head. She'd pictured them talking, really talking, enough to work out whatever was wrong between them. But at this point, she'd take whatever time with him that she could get. Her heart thrummed. When she reached her SUV, he leaned against the front fender and crossed his arms. He'd changed out of his uniform into a pair of basketball shorts and a T-shirt, and he smelled so good. "Thanks for bringing those out here."

"Nick said you left in kind of a hurry." She had a thousand things she wanted to say and no ability to form the words. The only way to handle the awkwardness of this situation was to get the hell out of there before she made anything worse. She opened the door and slid behind the steering wheel. "Your food's probably getting cold."

"Yeah. And I need to let Trisha get home." He nodded toward the house but didn't move away from her car. He rubbed his palms together as if he needed the friction to rub away something sticky. "Nick said you're going to test this weekend."

She nodded.

"Well, good luck, then." He cleared his throat and pushed off the fender. "I should get back in there."

When he turned and walked back toward the house, Penelope reversed down the driveway and drove straight to the duplex. It seemed like one or the other of them was always walking—or running—away. Was it a sign they were terrible for each other? That they didn't care enough to try to walk through the fire?

And the longer they went without addressing these questions, the harder it would be to finally open the topic. To delve into the wounds they each had.

When she pulled up to the duplex, Charlie was outside. Penelope climbed out of the Audi and waved. She needed to do something to burn off the anxious energy coursing through her veins. "Want to go hiking?"

Charlie nodded. "Sure. Let me change, and I'll meet you back here in ten."

They drove to the park and climbed out. After they'd

walked for a few minutes, Penelope filled her in on her brief encounter with Jay. "It was like talking to a zombie. Like Night of the Barely Living Park Ranger."

Havoc bounded ahead, sniffing leaves and marking random tree trunks along the way while Charlie trudged along the dirt path. "He's going through a lot right now. Give him some time."

Time wasn't something she had. The building was almost finished, and then it was back to Manhattan, her job, and her life.

They passed under a canopy of trees to a clearing that led to a little babbling brook. Charlie sat down at the edge of the stream's bed and dangled her feet over the edge. Havoc splashed into the water and Penelope stood watching the water trickle over rocks and limbs. Charlie chucked a stone in the water near her feet. "Nick said you're testing this weekend. You nervous?"

"More anxious. I keep going over everything in my head, running scenarios and thinking about what I need to do to keep Havoc focused. It's the variables that scare me more than the test, the things I can't control." This was one test that required her to figure out how to manage the uncontrollable, and she hadn't formulated a plan for that just yet. Nick would be watching everything, taking points off for her mistakes, for Havoc's behavior. And while she'd been working with the dog, he still had moments of rebellion.

"I'm sure you'll do great. Just be confident. If you make a mistake, roll with it."

"Roll with it? That's your big advice?"

"That and *stay alive, don't text and drive*." Charlie smiled and wiggled her eyebrows. "That's probably all cops, though. And it's more motto than advice."

"What about *know when to say when*?"

"I think that's a beer commercial." Charlie chuckled and slapped at a mosquito on her arm. She stood and dusted off the back of her jeans. "You ready to head back? I'm starving."

"Food sounds good."

They headed back down the trail to the parking lot. Havoc, wet and muddy, jumped into the rear of the SUV and Penelope tied his leash to a carabiner she had installed to keep him from crawling into the front and dirtying the rest of the car. After, she climbed into the driver's side and started the engine.

A few minutes later they arrived at the bar, which was dark and loud. The food came pretty quickly along with lime margaritas. Penelope downed the first margarita more from thirst while ignoring the nachos. Then, when another drink magically appeared, she guzzled it, too.

Charlie matched her drink for drink.

"Don't you dare drunk text, Penelope. Give me your phone." Charlie reached across the table and knocked over an empty margarita glass. The slice of lime still hanging off the rim stopped it from crashing to the floor.

Penelope held her arm out to the far side. She turned her back to Charlie and hit the message icon. She was just going to send a short message and apologize to Jay. Nothing long or stupid or embarrassing.

*Penelope:* I know you're mad at me, and I'm sorry.

Oh, yeah. She could do this. Could do this so well she might never have to talk to people in person again.

*Penelope:* I miss being your friend.

She stared at the screen and saw two sets of texts, so she closed one eye and tried again.

*Penelope:* You looked HOT in those shorts tonight.

Nothing wrong with flattery. Apparently, he didn't respond to it, either, though.

*Penelope:* If you were here with me right now, I would take your clothes off with my teeth and lick your body from your earlobe to your kneecap and every inch in between.

"Oh, hell no," Charlie said from over Penelope's shoulder, reading her pathetic texts. What ensued next was likely very entertaining to the bar patrons at the next table. "Give me your damn phone!" It was really no contest. Charlie was a trained officer of the law after all, and Penelope had no practical idea how to escape from a rear wristlock.

Penelope squawked loudly as Charlie grabbed the phone with her free hand and dropped it into the margarita pitcher on the table. "Oh, come on!"

When Charlie released her, Penelope whirled around, ready to read her the riot act, but the off-duty sheriff cut her off with a pointed finger right between her eyes. "You've groveled enough for one night, sister. Get yourself together, or I'll do it for you."

Fine. She'd get herself together all right. Tomorrow, she'd march right into the office and confront Jay, then let the chips fall where they may.

# *Chapter Twenty-Two*

## *Jay*

Jay hadn't exchanged much more than inscrutable eye contact with Penelope since her text messages had blown up his phone a few days ago. Honestly, those few texts had destroyed any resolve to keep his distance from her. She'd let herself be vulnerable and that got under his skin faster than anything. But yeah, she'd made it very hard to pursue what her honesty might mean because every time he walked into a room, she walked out. His phone had been blessedly or damnably—depending on his mood—silent. And when she did have to speak to him—which was seldom—she barely looked at him.

But as he waited in Nick's office for a call from the governor, she strolled in and shut the door behind her. "We need to talk." She didn't wait for him to look at her or speak before she continued. "I know I should have told you I was posting your statue online. It was wrong and I've apologized. I thought that since you sold the statue anyway, we could move past it, but I guess not." She paced a line in front of the desk, even shoving the visitor chair out of the way for more room. "I thought we were friends. I mean, I actually thought we were more than friends, since…" Her skin turned an adorable shade of pink. "Since we had sex, but okay. I was wrong."

Shame washed over him. He wanted them to be more than friends, cared about her in a way that was beyond friendship. But whenever he thought about her as more, or whenever a moment would occur, he'd remember she was leaving. And his heart couldn't take Penelope abandoning him. The same way it couldn't take something bad happening to her while out searching for a missing person. "I'm sorry, Penelope."

"I know we started off badly." Her long sigh hit him in the gut, and he admired her determination to get through this. Her eyes widened and even with a desk between them, he could see every fleck of gray in her beautiful green eyes. "I'm a big enough person to admit. Plus, it's a matter of public record. It was my fault. But I miss my friend. And I have a really big evaluation coming up. I need you."

*Don't say it. Don't say it. Don't say it. Last chance, dumb ass. Don't. Say. It.* "About your evaluation… you're not ready. You're not ready, and even if you convince Nick into passing you, you won't be prepared for a real rescue."

Her head jerked back as if he'd slapped her—which probably would have been kinder. "Excuse me?"

He sighed. In for a penny, in for a pound. His gut wrenched as he witnessed the surprise in her eyes. How could he make her understand? Make her aware of everything that could go wrong? Make her realize he didn't want her to leave? "Penelope, you have good instincts, but a real search is dangerous for you and for

Havoc." If anyone knew that, it was Jay. "You need more time, more training. Or something bad might happen."

"Nick thinks otherwise." Defiance shined in her eyes. "And I'm sorry for what happened with Zip, but that doesn't mean it's going to happen to me or Havoc."

"What, you think you're immune? That you're some kind of superhero that can't get hurt?" The moment the words left his mouth, he cringed. He only wanted to keep her safe, not insult her by sounding like an arrogant and condescending jackass. He clamped his trap shut, to stop the verbal barbs he was throwing at her. If only she hadn't mentioned Zip.

"*Oye, cabron.* I full well understand the dangers and worked my ass off to train Havoc to do this job. How dare you imply I don't know what's on the line. And if I decide to put my life on the line to help someone, that's my call, my decision. Not yours." She wheeled toward the door, then turned to stomp back and lean over the desk. "And another thing, *friend*, when someone texts you, it is common courtesy to reply." Her glare faltered for a moment. "You didn't reply to that last one, did you? Because I actually don't know since Charlie—oh, never mind!"

He stood and walked around the desk, desperate not to leave things between them like this. "I like you, Penelope. A lot. And I didn't reply to those texts because I didn't want to beg you to come over." And how close he'd come, but he'd never tell her. "But if you take that test, if you pass… I won't be able to be…anything to you." Saying that out loud was like a giant fist squeezing the life from his heart. But there was no other way. He couldn't face the possibility of something happening to her on a mission, the way it had to Zip. He gazed at her helplessly. Wouldn't a man try to do everything he could to prevent that from happening to the woman he loved? Why couldn't he make her see?

She stared for just a second, then scoffed loudly and threw both hands up in the air. "Do you guys all read from the same handbook? What's it called? *My Way or the Highway for Dummies*? *Ridiculous Ultimatums for the Man's Soul*?"

"What?"

"You sound just like my ex-boyfriend. Let me tell you something. I trained for two years to become a land searcher. Then when I decided to specialize in K-9, I trained even harder. Complete with blood, sweat, and tears. This certification is important to me, and if you truly cared about me, it would be important to you, too." She walked back to the door and stomped through.

He lurched up from the chair to go after her, to catch up to her and apologize, to explain, but the damn phone rang, and he knew it was going to be their patronizing governor so he had to sit back and listen to him ramble on about the quick work of the rebuild.

Nick strolled through the door five minutes later, his tie askew and his jacket hanging over his arm. "You look like crap."

It took everything Jay had to keep himself together. He didn't appreciate Nick's witty repartee nor did he want commentary from the man who would potentially be responsible for Penelope's death. Rage burned inside him, a rage he needed to let loose. He inhaled and pinned Nick with a glare. "Not funny."

His boss held up both hands and walked into his office, probably expecting Jay to follow, but he remained at the desk out front. Nick turned and looked over his shoulder. "Oh, come on. It was a little funny. You might be losing your sense of humor."

"Fuck you."

"Excuse me?" Had there not been real confusion clouding Nick's features, Jay might have jumped out of his chair and slugged him.

"She's not ready to test and you know it. What are you thinking?"

Nick walked over, each step measured, and leaned over, bracing his fists onto the top of Jay's desk. "What makes you think you know better? That you're the be-all, end-all of search and rescue training? Human error happens. Canine error happens. Tragedy happens. But everyone in the world except you, except poor, sad Jay Gosling, bounces back or figures out a way to learn from it. You wallow in it. And you expect everyone else to wallow with you. She's got skills, skills that could benefit the program, but you can't see it because you can't see past the fact that she has her dog and you don't have yours."

Jay jumped to his feet, his face mere inches from his boss's. "You think this is about jealousy?"

"No, I think it's about you. You lost your dog and it was horrible and we all felt really bad for you." The sentiment was there but the harsh tone lessened its sincerity. "You could have come back, at least used your skills to train others for the program, but no. Instead, you sit on your pedestal, all alone, trying to knock everyone else off theirs. Because you're hurt. And when you lost Zip, you lost a lot, but now, you're going to let losing the dog make you lose everything else. And that's stupid." Nick stood tall, glowering at Jay until the scowl morphed into something else that made Jay even more uneasy. "I think I know what this is really about."

Jay's palms started to sweat. "Oh, yeah? Why don't you enlighten me since you seem to think I don't know my own mind."

"Everyone you've loved has left—whether it was their choice or not." Nick's voice softened. "Your grandmother, Zip, Karen, and now you have to deal with Gramps's illness." Nick paused, blinking at him, considering, while Jay scrambled to find some appropriate rebuttal. *"And,"* Nick continued relentlessly, "now we add Penelope."

"She has nothing to do with this!" Jay finally barked.

"Oh, but she does. More than you're obviously willing to admit. You're in love with her." He shook his head. "As much as you dislike it, as much as you try to deny it, you are. And"—his voice dropped even further—" she's going to leave, too."

Jay slammed his fist on his desk, pulse racing feverishly. "You know nothing!"

Nick's eyes reflected pity, which pissed Jay off even more. "You can't fix a problem until you're honest with yourself. I'm here if you want to talk. But in the meantime, Penelope will be taking the test because she's ready. If you let that come between you, that's on you. I'm going home. Lock up before you leave."

Nick quietly walked out of the office without a backward glance. Jay exhaled and sank back into his chair and stared at the black of his computer screen. Nick wasn't wrong. Jay was upset because he wanted to keep Penelope safe, and he wanted to protect himself because she was leaving. That wasn't a secret. She lived in New York. But abandonment? Ridiculous. The fuck was that about? He was a grown man. Only children had abandonment issues. Besides, he—

Hadn't thought about his biological parents in ages. His *mother* dumped him and moved away after his birth, so he'd never even known her. His *father* went AWOL a short time later. He'd never heard from either of them. But they were a nonissue because all he'd ever known was Gran and Gramps.

Jay rolled his eyes, running his hands through his hair. This psychobabble was absurd. Delving into his past like this when everything was perfectly fine was enough to make a sane person go bonkers.

No, this wasn't about *abandonment.* And it definitely wasn't about Penelope.

It was about *grief.*

What did they expect him to do? Just go get another dog. Replace Zip. No dog would replace Zip.

He sat there for who knew how long, Nick's words whipping around his mind.

Sit on a pedestal. He didn't do that, did he? That was annoying as fuck. He cared a lot about Penelope, and even if he loved her, that would only further justify worrying about if she was ready. This wasn't a joke. It could mean life or death.

*Oh, fuck.*

He rubbed his hands over his face. He was out of line. He might have lost Zip, but Nick and his family had lost so much more when Nick's sister died. And he knew the grief the Karalis family went through. Jay cracked his knuckles. He needed to apologize to his friend.

But as far as wallowing, he'd never wallowed a day in his life. And he didn't give two shits if anyone thought he did. Zip had been his best friend. It was reasonable to grieve over the death of a best friend. Wasn't Jay's fault he'd preferred the company of his canine companion to any human.

Until Penelope anyway. He liked her, sure. But if she'd come to him and said he had to choose between her and Zip, Zip would have…or maybe…no. Zip would have won. He would never want to be with someone who made him choose between their romance and his dog. So expecting her to choose him over certifying Havoc was enough to make him want to kick his own ass. Something about this woman had him all tangled up, unsure of himself, of anything really. And fuck if he knew what to do about it.

Okay, so yeah, maybe he really liked her.

Hell, he *was* in love with her.

Christ.

He'd have to apologize to Nick, but first he needed to try to fix the discord with Gramps.

He pulled his cell phone from his pocket and dialed Trisha. He swallowed past the lump in his throat as the phone rang. He'd already lost so much. He couldn't lose his relationship with Gramps, too.

"Hello?"

Jay shook his head, rubbing between his eyes. "Uh, hi, Trisha. How is he?" Gramps's long life had turned on a dime so many times, and he'd bounced back. But this time he wasn't going to get better. Parkinson's was so unfair.

"He's in his room watching TV."

Jay glanced over his computer at the door and sighed. "Good day or bad?"

"Good for the most part. Did the doctor explain how this disease behaves?" He'd tried, but Jay hadn't wanted to hear. "Your grandfather's disease is what is called progressive. The symptoms worsen over time. You're going to need a support system, someone you can talk to and lean on."

Jay leaned back in his chair and cleared his throat. "I have friends." Half of whom were not likely to rush to his aid even if he would manage to swallow his pride and call for them.

"You have another if you need."

"Thank you. I'll keep that in mind. I'll see you when I get home." Jay hit the end button and tucked his phone back into his pocket.

His chest was heavy as if it were filled with lead and the lump in his throat developed into a knot. His lungs screamed for oxygen. He started gasping over and over, yelling "get ahold of yourself" in his head. A tear involuntarily slid down his cheek. He couldn't take it anymore.

The swell of his sobs filling the air and shaking his body uncontrollably was the sound of him, finally, hitting rock bottom.

# *Chapter Twenty-Three*

### *Penelope*

Two grueling hours, a backpack that weighed almost as much as she did, ninety-degree temps, and eighty acres of wilderness with Havoc leading the way did not make for a pleasant flowery scent. She would've killed for a shower, but first she had to get back to civilization. Her legs ached, her spine had to have twisted itself into some sort of distorted pretzel shape, and her head throbbed with the lack of sleep. It would take every ounce of energy she could summon to get back to the check station. She promised herself the reward of a long, soothing bubble bath as soon as they got home.

She'd trudged through weeds and brush, around fallen branches and limbs, over terrain so rocky and rough there were minutes she'd considered taking a lower certification standard. But Havoc pulled her through, helped her remember the greater good, their goal, and the purpose of this whole thing.

Nick clapped a hand on Penelope's shoulder. "Excellent job, Penelope. Excellent."

Normally, his praise would have delighted her into

some sort of celebration, but fatigue set in with its typical vengeance, and she only managed a nod. "Thanks."

Penelope turned to look over her shoulder. Mrs. Clover pushed a branch out of the way and continued to hike down the path. Penelope hoped she'd be in as great shape when she reached Mrs. Clover's age. "Thank you again for hiding for Havoc's test. I really appreciate it."

The woman looked up and smiled. "Anytime, dear. The two of you work so hard and I am proud to be a part of something so special."

Penelope put one foot in front of the other and repeated the process until finally, the new three-story check station loomed on the horizon. Glass and metal with a stone foundation and landscaping all the way around. The old one might have looked a bit ragged and in need of repair, but this new one singlehandedly destroyed the aesthetic pleasure of the forest. She had to hand it to Jay. He'd called that one. Too bad every single other word that came out of his mouth was ridiculous and uninformed. Because she would delight in rubbing his nose in her certification.

"I'll get your paperwork sent in and your name listed in the database and the registry." Nick grinned. "Hell, I might even call in the newspaper, maybe some local TV. It's been a long time since we had so much to celebrate. And I'm sick of the governor getting all the headlines."

Again, she nodded, and this time, threw in a yawn for good measure. "Thanks."

Mrs. Clover stood at the rear edge of his truck. "Come to the diner. I've got a little something special for you and for Havoc." She nodded to Havoc and reached down to give him a nice long scratch under his jaw. He nuzzled her leg.

Penelope turned to Nick. She didn't want to ask, couldn't stand that she'd even had the thought, but her powers of discretion had apparently faded sometime this morning. "Have you talked to him?"

Nick sighed. Her question had obviously put a damper on his good mood. His frown said it all. "He's not talking to me, either. Makes working with him all day a real pleasure. Not that he was a rainbow-farting unicorn before, but now, he's one grimace away from becoming a grumpy old man."

A smart girl, one who protected her heart, would have shrugged it off, would have said, *oh, well*, but Penelope's heart had its own mind and apparently a willingness to forgive where her mind didn't. "He's going through a lot with Gramps."

"And with the town's favorite fire starter."

"I thought we said we would come up with a different nickname. I'm not a big fan of that one." She smiled. The joke didn't bother her as much anymore, but she could have gone light-years without being reminded of her stupidity.

"You know it's because we all love you so much." Nick slung an arm around her, then backed away. "Listen, Penelope, Jay has a lot of baggage."

She wasn't sure she was ready to open this can of worms with him. She quickly put her hand up. "I know, I know. Trust me. I may not know everything about his past, but what I do know tells me he's been through a lot. I appreciate you trying to smooth things out between us, but it's not fair for Jay or myself to put you in that role. Especially because you are both of our bosses, not to mention my evaluator. So please, can we just…not?"

Nick looked like he wanted to say something more, but then he nodded. "You should probably get cleaned up." He wrinkled his nose and wagged his finger toward her shirt and pants.

She sighed in quiet relief. "Yeah. No telling what I carried out of the woods. Especially ticks." She shuddered. "Which I should really get home to check."

Nick nodded. "Shower up while I go drop Mrs. Clover off. Charlie will be waiting for all of us. She is dying to hear the trials and tribulations of a search and rescue."

And Penelope was dying for a bed, but these were her friends, friends she would miss when she went back home. So, she would shower until she sparkled, down a couple cups of coffee so she wouldn't fall asleep in her undoubtedly large meal, and then she would go home and collapse. It was a plan and one she was really looking forward to.

And she was damn well not going to think about Jay's baggage.

One problem at a time was plenty for her.

Almost human was about the best description she could find for herself in the rearview mirror as she smoothed her wet hair back into a ponytail. Havoc, from the backseat, groaned when she climbed out and opened his door. "*Ojo*, Havoc. Don't give me that. If I have to go in and regale the crowd with our glory days, so do you." She snapped her fingers and pointed to the ground beside her, and he dragged himself out of the SUV. "And tomorrow, you're going to the groomer."

He walked beside her into the restaurant, stopped short at his bowl, and dropped to his belly like someone had pulled his legs out from under him. Nick, Charlie, and Mrs. Clover stood at the counter with noisemakers and those triangle hats kids wore at birthday parties. “There she is! My little superstar!” Mrs. Clover rushed around the counter and threw her arms around Penelope.

Nick stood back. “You look a hundred times better than the last time I saw you.”

He’d changed clothes, too, so she smiled. “Back at you.”

Charlie still wore her uniform because she was only half through a long evening shift. She joined in on the bout of hugging that seemed to have affected Penelope’s friends. “I heard you rocked that evaluation.”

And she hadn’t had to bat an eyelash at Nick, either. Nary had a feminine wile been used. *So, eat that, Mr. Judgmental Park Ranger.*

“You know, for a gal who traveled all the way here to get certified, then *got* certified today, you look like you ate a pickle dipped in lemon.” Mrs. Clover’s observation was probably correct since the description mirrored Penelope’s exact emotion. Sour and bitter shared a familial connection, right?

Where Nick would normally have smirked or acted smug when he replied for her, this time he looked equally miserable. “Jay’s pissed at us.”

“At both of you?” Mrs. Clover wiped the counter without looking anywhere but at Nick. He, like Jay, had that effect on women young and old.

Rather than relate the story, Penelope shrugged. With her second wind came another round of anger at Jay’s attitude. “He’s an equal-opportunity idiot.”

Mrs. Clover nodded. “He carries his sadness in his

shoulders. I thought he was coming around, though. I really thought when he started falling for you, he'd bounce back, but..." She nodded to Havoc.

Whoa. Whoa. Whoa. Rewind. Back up. Reverse. "Falling for me?" She scoffed. Then scoffed again. "Pfft." And because two scoffs weren't nearly enough, she added another. "No. He's...no."

Nick smiled as if he believed Mrs. Clover's deduction to be one of the Sherlock Holmes variety. "You know, now that you mention it, since the fire at the check station I haven't heard many sentences out of his mouth that didn't have a certain brunette's name in it. A name that curiously rhymes with Skenelope."

"And Frenelope."

Penelope glared from Nick to Charlie as they continued rhyming her name with words they made up. "Are you two about finished?"

"Helenelope?" Charlie sobered. "Sorry. You were saying?"

"Denying. She was de-ny-ing." Nick laughed, then held up both hands as she curled her lip at him. He held up both hands. "I'm sorry, too. Go on."

"I was saying it doesn't matter if he likes me or not. Or did like me and hates me now or hated me, then liked me and hates me again." She cocked an eyebrow, daring them to continue with this conversation. Fiery brunette was one thing. Fiery brunette on zero hours of sleep and a growling belly endangered everyone and everything around her.

Charlie pursed her lips but remained silent. Nick shrugged and took a drink of what looked like Clover's Kitchen's signature sparkling iced tea. And Mrs. Clover disappeared through the swinging door that led from the dining room to where all the magic happened. Mrs. Clover brought her plate and a special rhinestone-studded bowl for Havoc. Penelope's stomach wasn't ready for food, so she sat and listened to the conversations around her, the soothing sounds of clinking silverware against china plates, the murmurs of conversation while the other patrons enjoyed their dinner.

She really liked Maple Falls. Could see herself buying a place here to visit, like Lori had. The people were friendly, cared about one another like communities of old. Nothing like the city. Even her friendship with Charlie was more authentic than any of those she had back in the city. Come to think of it, no one from there bothered calling or texting to see how she was.

There were also the trees, the fresh air that didn't smell of car exhaust, the numerous places that called to be photographed. Plus, the open space for Havoc to run. In the city, all she had were dog parks. And she certainly wasn't a fan of those. Not when owners refused to acknowledge their dogs' bad habits. Bites and fights were quite common. But here she could have a yard for him to run in. Not to mention the numerous hiking trails.

Yeah. The more she thought about it, the more Penelope could see herself here. In Maple Falls. Maybe for good.

An hour later, she'd picked at her food enough to satisfy Mrs. Clover and accepted a to-go box full of goodies for breakfast, then brought Havoc home, where they curled into her bed and slept until noon. At some point she would have to log into her work computer. She should probably call Nick, too, but still exhausted—

which added to her despair over Jay—she lounged in her pajamas until sunset.

When Charlie showed up after her shift, Penelope let her in, but remained under a blanket on the sofa. Charlie sat on the arm of the sofa. "You are really taking this moping to Olympic heights."

"I'm not moping, but as you may have noticed, I do everything at gold medal levels, so if I was at least I would be doing it better than anyone else." She clicked the remote on the TV to silence the flat screen, then flung off her cashmere throw and sat up. "You know, he's being so unfair. I get how tough Gramps's disease progressing must be on him, but that doesn't mean it's okay to take his frustration out on me." She didn't—couldn't—consider what she would do if something happened to Havoc. "And I'm all for constructive criticism, but unsolicited opinions that don't have a basis in reality? No. And who made him the be-all, end-all of search and rescue?"

Charlie nodded. "Yep. Good thing you're not moping."

Penelope scoffed. "Ranting is different than moping. Worlds apart." She stood and paced in front of the TV. "You know what else? He was obviously wrong. Because Havoc performed like a seasoned pro this morning. And I controlled that. Me."

"Have you ever stopped to think that he believes in you, but he's just scared for you after what he went through? Makes sense that he wouldn't want anyone else he cares for to go through something like that." Charlie picked up the empty to-go box and carried it to the kitchen while Penelope sat there, not really wanting to see it from her perspective. Which was a terrible flaw, but so hard to get over.

Charlie returned with two glasses and a bottle of wine. “Or maybe Jay’s acting this way because he’s scared for *him*.” She poured and gave Penelope a soft, but plaintive look. “Let’s try to look at it from his side. He got Zip after he lost his grandmother. Trained that dog from the time Zip stopped chewing shoes all the way until they started working together. And when he lost the dog, his wife, Karen, picked that opportune time to leave him, the selfish bitch. So in one fell swoop, Jay lost his best friend, his woman, and a job he loved. Now, he’s got front-row seats to watch his grandfather deteriorate. Seeing you go into that same field *and* having such strong feelings for you is probably igniting and magnifying a bunch of emotions stemming from fear.”

Penelope clenched her fists, torn between hope and fear. Hope that maybe Charlie was right and Jay really did have feelings for her. And fear that even entertaining the idea was setting herself up for yet another heartbreak. The more she thought about it, though, the more her friend’s words made sense. Oh, God. Her stomach clenched and she tasted something sour. Poor Jay. With everything he’d gone through—and was now dealing with—she should have been more understanding. Tried harder to see past her anger and understand the motivation behind his protests about her and Havoc testing.

Maybe she was hoping for too much at a time when he wasn’t in the right place to pursue something more than casual. God, what was the right way to respond—to react—in a situation like this? She closed her eyes and shook her head. “He said I wasn’t ready.”

“Ready for what? To face a situation where you

might lose your dog? To get caught in a scenario where you could be hurt or killed? Penelope, the guy was one of the best in the world, and a tragedy caught him off guard. He doesn't want that to happen to someone he's falling in love with." She cocked an eyebrow as if daring Penelope to argue.

"But—"

"No." Charlie held up one finger.

"He isn't—"

"No." She added a finger wave.

"Charlie—"

"Penelope, if he isn't in love with you, or at least damned close, I'll eat my shoe." She sat back on the sofa and kicked her bare feet onto the table.

Falling in love with her was about as believable as pigs dancing the cotton-eyed Joe. "Are we talking flip-flops or something with a steel toe?"

Charlie rolled her eyes, but Penelope continued with levity because this conversation was making her uncomfortable. "Hey, I don't want to end up on the wrong side of a lawsuit over your dental work."

"Okay, smart-ass. I get it. You think he's gruff with you, and he's judgmental, and more than a little rigid, but you should've seen him before you got here." Charlie made claws out of both her hands. "Picture Meryl Streep's character in *Devil Wears Prada*. Except Jay didn't have thousand-dollar dresses to hide the stick up his ass." She had a way with words that made Penelope smile despite her bad mood. "And you did kind of set his pet project on fire." When Penelope glared, Charlie held up her hands. "Just saying."

"So being hurt gives him the right to say whatever he wants." She shook her head at the ridiculous notion.

"I better get a pen and write that down. Wouldn't want to forget all the concessions the world makes for his broken heart."

Charlie blew a low whistle. She cocked her head, one of those knowing smiles tilted on her lips. "Maybe we should talk about that for a minute. I mean, if you know you're ready to be out there with Havoc doing the job, why does what he says matter?"

"It doesn't." A weak rebuttal and not preemptive enough to stop Charlie venturing where Penelope knew her friend planned on firing the next shot.

"Oh, but I think it does. I think you care very much what Jay says. Why do *you* think that is?" Smug. Know-it-all. Satisfied with her own deduction, even if she wasn't speaking it aloud. She downed her glass of wine and stood. "And while we're at it, why would you guess he felt comfortable enough to say it?"

Before Penelope could reply—because throwing the wine cork at Charlie wouldn't have been at all neighborly—Charlie's pager went off. She looked down at the device and swore. "Well, shit. I can't assist because of the wine, but I have to at least call in. Later, chica." She walked to the door, gave a little wave and a wink, then left.

Penelope clicked the remote and tried to immerse herself in this week's edition of Must-See TV, but her thoughts floated away from the sitcom to the same place even when she tried to draw it back in—to a grumpy park ranger with the nicest smile this side of the Atlantic Ocean.

# *Chapter Twenty-Four*

*Jay*

Jay didn't care about crown molding or whether or not the laminate plank floor was waterproof, whether the windows were specially tinted, or how many chairs fit into the small theater the governor felt necessary to invite the public to learn about the state of Vermont. Not that the governor would look at this building again once he squeezed all the good press he could out of it.

Still, the tour continued with the contractor oozing his charm all over Penelope. He'd liked Daniel as a worker but seeing him standing so close to Penelope caused his stomach to knot. Honesty, how many times did he have to smile at her like that? Jay was sure Daniel had never smiled at *him* like that.

Jay stopped listening right around the time Penelope smiled at *Daniel* for about the hundredth time. He turned and walked toward the elevator. In a check station. The eye roll was implied.

He had to wait around for the building inspector, but he didn't have to watch Penelope and *Daniel* jive like they'd known each other for years. Which they had, but that didn't mean he had to like it. Didn't mean he had to listen to her compliment Daniel, or watch the contractor take her arm to guide her around the remaining construction areas.

For being a new building, the elevator was certainly slow enough. He stabbed the button again and tapped his foot, then glanced at the stairwell. Maybe he could walk off some of this unsettled sensation that seeing Penelope with Daniel triggered. Not that there was anything wrong with Daniel chatting and joking around with Penelope. More, Jay desperately wished he was the recipient of her radiant smile. Which was stupid, seeing as how she'd be heading home soon.

He took the stairs and tuned out everything—his own thoughts included—favoring the echo of his boots against the metal treads. The stairwell opened to a lobby that included a small gurgling fountain of water that trickled over rocks, a semicircular reception desk with a marble top and multiline phone system and a new computer, the elevator bay with *Welcome to Vermont* etched on the mirrored doors, and a plaque to the governor. The tile floor had been painted with a map of Vermont.

The old check station was better. A stop-through. A check-in sheet, some pamphlets, and complimentary maps of the park and its trails and hunting areas. It had, for years, served the exact purpose of a check station. This monstrosity was a grandiose gesture by a self-serving governor afraid he wouldn't be reelected.

He pushed through the glass—tinted with reflective glaze, no doubt—doors and stood on a freshly dried and stamped concrete pad surrounded by flowers and mulch. The whole thing made his stomach turn.

Penelope's dog sat in the shade, his leash wrapped around a concrete pole in the dog care station to the left of the building. He had to admit, that was a good idea. While the humans rested and got their information, their canine friends could enjoy a drink from a slow-running spigot, nap in the shade, or find relief among the many trees planted there. They'd even installed a gumball machine filled with dog treats. He would've guessed the area to be at least half an acre, maybe more. Had to have been one of *her* contributions to the planning.

He reached down to give Havoc a rub between the ears. Havoc's big brown eyes blinked a couple times, but he continued staring at Jay. "Don't look at me like that. I was trying—am trying to protect her."

"What are you doing?"

Ah, shit. Busted. Why couldn't Nick have been the one to catch him talking to the dog instead of Penelope? Jay cleared his throat and stood. Havoc moved away to push his snout, then edge his body between Penelope and Daniel. "He looked lonely." Jay looked at the building. "I have to wait around here for the building inspector to sign off, but you don't need to stay." God, he wanted to touch her, wanted to pull her against him and hold her, wanted to apologize, at least, but his feet didn't move, his arms hung limp at his sides, and the words didn't come.

A stab of hurt—damnit—pierced her expression. She thought he'd dismissed her, and he did, but he also just didn't want to witness any more of those smiles bestowed upon someone else. Not when they served as a painful reminder of the times she'd smiled up at him, her eyes all aglow. "Or you can stay? It's up to you." The shrug at the end was more for show since it mattered very much to him whether or not he got the chance to talk to her.

She nodded. "I should probably get to the duplex and start packing."

The air knocked out of him. Of course he knew she'd be heading back to New York, to her life there. He just hadn't realized how quickly that would happen. "Right."

He hadn't meant it as an agreement with her, but a recognition of his own realization. But before he could clear it up, she turned to Daniel, gave him a hug, and told him to give her a call next time he was in New York.

Jay's eyes narrowed when she walked past him to Havoc without speaking. She gripped the dog's leash and they sped-walked to her SUV. Jay's opportunity to talk to her was driving out of the parking lot just as the building inspector pulled up.

He had to give Daniel and his crew credit. The building, for being a rush job, stood up to Inspector Joe McGurn's scrutiny without incurring a single checkmark to lower its overall perfect score. And Joe had checked everything—plumbing, wiring, HVAC, cables, the foundation. If he'd missed a single detail, Jay couldn't imagine what it would have been.

His nostrils engulfed the delicate hint of coconut lingering in the air, and with it, Jay's brain flooded with pictures of Penelope. The twinkle in her eyes when he showed her his art, the color on her cheeks after they'd made love. Even the frustrated glower when he corrected her search and rescue technique. His chest ached at the thought of not seeing her every day. But why bother? What was she going to do? Give up her life in New York to stay here with him and help take care of Gramps?

Better for both of them that he let her drive away without putting up a fight.

After all the paperwork had been signed and turned over to Nick, Jay headed home. He pulled into his driveway and parked the truck to the left of Trisha's car. She'd been great with Gramps, but since the building inspector finished early and Jay had a random afternoon off and no one to spend it with, he decided to take Gramps fishing like they used to when he was younger.

When he walked into the house, Gramps and Trisha were in the kitchen. Gramps was washing dishes while Trisha dried and put them away. She smiled. "Hi. Short day today?"

Jay nodded. "Yeah. Thought I'd see if Gramps wants to go fishing this afternoon."

Gramps turned around without a wobble, dried his hands, and tossed the dish towel into the air. "It's about damned time." He nodded to Trisha and grabbed his cane. "I'll finish these later. Right now, I've got some worms to hook and some lines to cast."

Jay smiled. Today was one of those good days. He followed Gramps out to the garage, close enough to reach out if he stumbled, but far enough not to annoy him or make him feel coddled. "Are we picking up that pretty brunette you're so sweet on?"

"I thought today it should be just you and me." He ignored Gramps's stare.

"You're a damned fool. Prideful." Larry shook his head. "You're gonna mess around and lose that little lady, then it'll be another year of wallowing in your own stupidity."

"I *don't* wallow." What was it with these people?

"Oh, you wallow. Better than anyone I ever saw."

Gramps leaned his cane against the workbench, then pulled the rods and reels down from the shelf where Jay stored them, bouncing a bit on his heels, as excited as a youngster and scaring the hell out of Jay. "Not that she isn't worth a little wallowing…cute as a button, that one. Kind eyes, too. The kind of girl a man should snap up and make a wife." He shot Jay one of those meaningful glances. "I'm not gonna be around forever to take care of you, you know."

"Gramps—"

His grandfather sighed. "I haven't been feeling real right these days, you know?"

Soft, because his broken heart wouldn't allow for much volume, he answered, "I know."

"All I ever wanted for you was happiness. I'd sure like to see it before my meeting with the undertaker." Gramps crossed his arms and stared at Jay. There was strength in this man. If Jay ended up half the man his grandfather was, he'd still be a better man than most. With the sun behind him, Gramps looked bigger and stronger than Jay had seen him in a while.

But he hated when Gramps spoke as though death was imminent. "I'm happy."

"And a liar." Gramps handed him the tackle box and the bowl of bait they always kept in the fridge. "What happened between you two anyway?"

Jay shrugged. Being an ass and admitting he'd been an ass were entirely different matters. Especially after a day with Gramps that promised to bring him back to happier times. "It just didn't work out. She's going back to New York soon anyway."

Gramps walked beside him to the truck. "Damned fool."

"Gramps." But what could he say? He put the gear in the back, then drove around to the side of the garage to hook up the boat trailer. They'd had this same johnboat since Jay was a kid, but Gramps had modified the motor—he loved power—and the seats—what was power without comfort?

When he climbed back into the driver's seat, Gramps was using his hanky to wipe perspiration from his brow. Damn, he should have helped him get in the truck. But how to do it without making him feel like an invalid? Jay groaned and put the keys in the ignition.

"Well, are you gonna call and invite her along?" Gramps said, irritably.

"No."

"Why not?"

"I want to spend the day with you. That okay?" A day in the sun with Gramps was just what he needed. Penelope Ramos was not.

"Damned fool." Gramps shook his head and looked out the window. Jay knew he hadn't heard the end of it. Maybe inviting Penelope along would have given Gramps something other than Jay to focus on. Instead, he had to listen to Gramps rail about what he should do and hadn't done. He should've called her. Should've gotten down on his knees and begged her forgiveness. At least, that was the mantra Gramps stuck with all afternoon. Every few minutes on the lake he'd come up with a new reason Jay was a fool. And every reason had Penelope all over it. But they'd hauled in twenty or so bass, some crappie, and a few bluegill.

Jay did the cleaning while Gramps supervised and continued his running commentary about Jay's bullheaded foolishness. “You know, maybe I didn’t do quite right by you.”

Jay jerked his head up. The last thing he wanted was Gramps to regret anything about the way he’d raised him. He couldn’t have asked for a better role model, a better man to lead him into adulthood. “What are you talking about?” But even as he spoke the words, and probably because he’d heard it all day long, he knew where this was headed.

“Sometimes being strong means you say ‘I’m sorry’ and take the lumps that go with it.”

Jay sighed. “I say it plenty.”

“To her? When it counts?” The old man shook his head. “You’re everything I hoped you’d be as a man. But we both know I’m fading away. Right now, not so bad. A few weak days here and there, but soon, likely I’ll be in a wheelchair. After that, I probably won’t even know my own name. So you listen to me right now.”

Jay swallowed a boulder in his throat.

“I have loved you your whole life, and all I’ve ever wanted is to see you happy. No matter what you decided, I didn’t care as long as it made you happy.” Gramps waited for Jay to nod before he continued. “When you have a chance for it, you can’t let it go. You gotta grab it with both hands and hang on. I saw you with that girl. I saw the way you looked at her and the way she looked at you. She’s your happiness, and if you let her haul herself back to New York without telling her, you’re going to regret it for the rest of your life.” Gramps sighed. “You take it from someone who knows. Regret isn’t something you wanna take with you when it’s your time.”

The situation with Penelope was too complicated to explain while he was elbow deep in fish guts and gills. But he nodded again. He didn't need to burden Gramps with it, anyway. Gramps had enough to deal with. "I hear you."

"So I'll expect her at dinner this week."

And that was the period at the end of their conversation. Gramps walked slowly—more unsteadily now—to the truck, and with a lot of effort, climbed in, tipped his cap forward with a hand that shook with tremors, and napped.

Jay watched the clock tick past three a.m. to three-oh-one just as he'd watched every minute flip to the next since midnight. And as much as he wanted to blame Penelope, he couldn't. This was his fault. His mistake. His idiocy.

He picked up his phone. An apology text would help him sleep.

*Idiot. You can't apologize with a text. Gramps will kill you.*

But he could wish her goodnight.

At three a.m.

He put the phone on the nightstand next to the alarm clock. They might as well mock him together.

He shoved the blanket toward the end of the bed with his foot and let the fan-swirled air blow over his skin. When his eyes finally fluttered shut, his mind tortured him with pictures of Penelope…in his bed…wearing his shirt…eyes burning with desire then shining with ecstasy. He felt her hand gliding down his chest and around to cup his ass, her thighs squeezing his hips, her mouth on his skin. His body tightened, his focus narrowed, and he groaned.

Plain and simple, he wanted her. Not just for sex, although at the moment, he would have been powerless to turn her down. He wanted her sass and her determination. Every smile and glare. Every idea in her head and word from her mouth. The entirety of who she was.

Tomorrow he would make it right. He would tell her he was wrong. Apologize. Tell her he loved her.

Loved her?

Yeah. He certainly did. Jay Gosling loved Penelope Ramos.

A weight lifted off him as he gave words to the thoughts that had been plaguing him. Tomorrow and every day after, he would make sure she knew. He turned away from the clock, closed his eyes, and fell right to sleep.

# *Chapter Twenty-Five*

*Penelope*

Charlie sat on the sofa stroking Havoc's head, wineglass in her free hand, while Penelope tried smooshing her clothes and the mementos she'd collected since she'd been in Vermont into the suitcase. "You should at least stay until the Halloween Festival."

"I need to get home." Sadly, she had only a job and an empty apartment to get back to. No circle of friends who would come over and watch TV on Sunday nights. No homey diner where she got a hug every time she walked through the door. No fully furnished rental complete with best friend next door and a big fenced-in backyard in a town with a damaged but dreamy park ranger who spoke out of turn, but still made her heart do a jig when he came around. And in New York, no way would a judge drop in at her place to release her from her sentence.

"You've been working remotely since you got here. I don't see why you would have to go back."

"That was only temporary. No way my uncle will allow it to be a permanent opportunity. Not to mention, I need to check up on my dad. Make sure he's okay. We haven't had our weekly dinners since I've been here. I'm worried about him."

Not to mention staying in Maple Falls, having Jay so close, yet so far away, was more than she'd be able to take. She could understand his reasons, but that didn't excuse the ultimatum and constant yo-yoing with his emotions. Did he want her or not? One minute she thought so, and the next, she thought he'd be happiest if she took a flying leap off the highest Vermont cliff.

She wanted him to own up to his mistakes like she had. She'd tried to anyway.

Maybe he didn't think it had been enough. She paused her packing, her shoulders slumping. She wanted someone who wouldn't constantly run hot and then cold.

Someone who'd *fight* for her.

She flipped open the flap on her luggage when it wouldn't zip shut, staring at the assorted Vermont memorabilia that would host lots of memories—seven shirts, a pair of flip-flops with the state motto *Freedom & Unity* emblazoned on the toe straps, a coffee mug with a map of the state park, a dozen postcards with pictures of scenic Maple Falls, her travel journal, a framed picture of Clover's Kitchen she'd snapped as she drove through town to the park on that first day, the guidebook she'd picked up from the park's main office, and a *Got Vermont?* coaster.

She didn't want to leave any of it behind.

"That is quite the collection." Charlie cocked an eyebrow at the teetering tower of stuff.

"I want to remember my time here." Well, most of it anyway.

Charlie shrugged. "Not like you can't come back." She took a sip of her wine. "Or stay."

“Maybe I’ll come up with Lori next time. Then the three of us girls can hang out.” She continued tugging on the zipper, which steadfastly refused to close.

Charlie chuckled. “I think it’s a sign. Even your luggage doesn’t want to go back.” When Havoc stood and walked to the back door, Charlie followed. “I’m getting more wine. You want anything?”

Yes, she did, but what she wanted wouldn’t be found in the kitchen. Or the apartment. He was in a house a few miles out of town. “No. I’m fine.”

When Charlie returned, she leaned against the doorframe. “You guys could be really good together if you both let go of the past instead of allowing it to get in the way.”

Penelope threw her hands up in the air in frustration. “I don’t have anything to get over. I made mistakes and I made amends.”

“Oh, really? Then why do you get so upset anytime he tries to correct you about search and rescue?”

Penelope huffed. “Because he’s trying to interfere, just like Trevor. Do you know I gave up photography because of that jerk? It wasn’t uppity or whatever. All my friends were mutual friends, and ask if any of them bothered to call while I was here? None!”

Charlie swirled the wine in her glass. “So, what you’re saying is you have issues just as much as Jay.”

Penelope forced out a rough breath and refocused her attention on the luggage at her feet. “Doesn’t matter. I’m going back to New York, and he’s staying here. So”—she shrugged—” it doesn’t matter.”

“How does it *not* matter?”

When Charlie widened her eyes and cocked her head, Penelope waved her off. “He won’t talk to me. He won’t let me in. How can I even think about telling someone like him that I love—I mean—you know what I mean."

Last thing she needed was Charlie to take some off-handed remark and blow it completely out of proportion. When Charlie smiled and opened her mouth, Penelope pointed and glared. Charlie remained silent.

There were a thousand reasons Penelope couldn't love Jay Gosling. She'd gone over them so many times in her head, hoping her heart would get with the program, even before she realized what she felt might be stronger than like. But in the light of her own almost-admission, not a single reason was too big to overcome. Would she regret it if she didn't say anything?

"You should tell him."

Her chest hurt from the thought of being that vulnerable. "I'm not telling him anything." She didn't need to add rejection to her memories of him. She didn't need to heap any more heartache on top of the pile. "And you're not, either."

"You know I'm not going to tell him. But Penelope, you should. I've known him for most of my life. And I've seen everything he's been through. Knowing you love him…knowing would make a difference."

"I doubt it." At least, that was what she told herself, because this game of speculation over whether or not Jay loved her was too painful. Better to go on believing that he didn't and remind herself of all the ways they were incompatible.

"What if he loves you? What if he's just scared to say it or feel it or admit it to himself?" Charlie sat forward, her voice rising a little higher in volume with each word. Obviously, her friendship with Jay inspired loyalty, and

Penelope wondered if Charlie spoke as fiercely on Penelope's behalf when she talked to Jay.

"What if he doesn't?"

Charlie shook her head, scoffed, then stood. "If he doesn't, you lose nothing because it wasn't yours to have. But if he does and you walk away from him, you might end up regretting it." And like one of those always-gets-the-last-word characters on drama TV shows, Charlie walked out the front door.

Penelope stared at the closed door until Havoc barked from the backyard. She walked through the kitchen and let him in, then went back to the sofa. Well, this had turned out to be quite the day.

She'd gone and fallen in love with Jay Gosling.

What a stupid-ass, sorry thing to do.

She closed her eyes and pictured him—the way his eyes closed just before their lips touched, the way one hand always bunched the hem of her shirt where it rested over the small of her back when he pulled her close, the way his five-o'clock shadow remained no matter what time of day. And when she added in the things that weren't physical—his devotion to his grandfather, a work ethic that made the hardest worker she'd ever met seem like a slacker, the kindness with Mrs. Clover, the way he'd helped her train even when he didn't believe he could.

Yeah. She loved him.

If only she knew what to do about it.

# *Chapter Twenty-Six*

## *Jay*

The people of Maple Falls, Vermont, loved their town, took pride in its minuscule crime rate, its homey, everybody-knows-everybody feel. Even Jay had pictured a life here with a wife, a couple kids, Zip, and the requisite white picket fence. But that was a lifetime ago.

Now as he drove through town, passing the decorated storefronts, the lampposts wrapped in corn stalks, the hay bales on the porches, the sticky webs in window corners and in trees, his heart just wasn't in it anymore. When he woke this morning, he'd found that his courage to tell Penelope about his true feelings had abandoned him.

Damn himself for being such a chickenshit.

He pulled in front of Clover's. The lunch crowd had dwindled to stragglers, and the old-timers who usually played chess in the park got rained out again today. Jay took a booth by the window. Nothing like a gloomy day to match his mood. Sad thing was, he had no one to blame but himself.

"Afternoon, Jay." Mrs. Clover set her coffeepot on the table when he shook his head. "Lemonade today?"

"That would be great. Thank you."

She smiled. "You hiding from the rain, or you hungry?"

"The rain for now." And his boss. And the woman he loved.

"All right." She stopped at the table beside him. "How about you boys? You ready for those chocolate sundaes for dessert?"

The little boy—maybe ten—grinned. "Yes, ma'am." When she walked away, he looked at the man sitting with the boy, whose baseball cap and chair angle had made him hard to recognize when Jay had first arrived.

"Mornin', Judge Carter," Jay said. "This the grandson from California we've been hearing so much about?"

Judge Carter swiveled around to face Jay. "Well, hello, Jay. Yes, this is Matthew." Carter's face showed just how thrilled he was to have the boy in town. "We've got a fun, busy week together planned, haven't we?"

Carter rustled the boy's hair, and the three talked for a few more minutes until Mrs. Clover reappeared at the side of Jay's table.

"I have the donations ready for the festival," she announced. Mrs. Clover always donated pies that went for far more money than someone could walk into the restaurant and buy one for. This year she'd added certificates for dinners for two, a "romantic" celebration of love—whatever that meant—and a year's worth of coffee and desserts. And any other day Jay would've been excited for such sought-after additions to the auction items, but he was consumed with thoughts of a young, red-haired boy of his own someday.

Jay nodded, pretending like he'd heard everything she'd said. "I can pick it up tomorrow morning."

"I was surprised to hear you were selling sculptures. Your grandfather always grumbles about how private you are about your art." Lurlene cocked her head, her eyes shining.

"It's just a hobby."

Mrs. Clover smiled. "You're too modest. That dog didn't look like 'just a hobby.' The details were so intricate anyone from town could identify it was Zip." Her eyes lit up even more, and she paused a moment, her smile going full-watt as she pointed to a spot by the door where a coat tree stood. "It's going to look so smashing right in that corner."

Jay's eyebrows shot to his hairline, his whole body on alert. Now she had his undivided attention. "*You* bought it?"

"Of course I bought it." She patted his shoulder. "I couldn't let that beautiful piece leave town. Not when I know how much it means to you. How much Zip meant to all of us."

Gratitude swelled in his chest. "I don't know what to say." Especially since he knew exactly how much she'd paid—an amount that allowed him to keep his home and get Gramps the help he needed.

"You don't have to say anything. I've been looking forward to the surprise. Had my granddaughter use her Gram account thing. You know me, no idea how to use all those applications or whatever you call them. Gave her a check so she could pay through the internet pal thing. Had it shipped to her so you wouldn't put any clues together. Think you might've met her once or twice years ago. Crossed my darn fingers you wouldn't recognize the name."

He hadn't, and part of him felt bad. Everyone in town

was family, and while he could place the girl's face—she had to be in her twenties now—he certainly didn't recognize the surname. His chest squeezed tighter. Mrs. Clover must've spent her entire nest egg. He had to say something and *thank you* just wasn't adequate. "I'm—"

She nodded and shot him a wink. A bell in the little window that separated the kitchen from the dining room tinkled. "I better get that."

She scuttled away, and Jay turned the sweaty glass of lemonade in his hands, watching the ice twist and the lemon slices in his glass spin. He wouldn't have imagined someone from Maple Falls would have bought the sculpture. Hadn't known how much Zip meant to others. And if it wasn't for Penelope, he would never had known.

He pictured her as she'd been that day she'd seen the sculptures—cheeks flushed, fingers brushing over each piece, gaze lingering until she had taken in every detail. Her excitement. His insecurity. Her gushing. His pride.

He downed the lemonade. Screw fear.

So what if she rejected him? It's not like he'd be out anything besides his pride. Which was considerable, but rewards required risk.

Jay Gosling loved Penelope Ramos.

And he needed to tell her.

Stomach somersaulting, he turned again to Carter. "So, what time does this shindig start tomorrow?"

*I love Penelope.*

Jay sat in his truck in the driveway at home and let his mind wander with fanciful thoughts of them together, walking hand in hand through the park, sipping hot chocolate and cuddling in a sleigh at the Christmas

Carnival, dancing on Valentine's Day at the Two by Two dance, wearing matching green hats and hunting for the pot of gold at the Shamrock Scavenger Hunt.

He could see it all. They would hold hands, and every once in a while, he would pull her close and press soft kisses against her full, lush lips. She would wrap her arms around him, lay her head against his chest, and maybe tilt her chin up so she could look into his eyes. Most importantly, she would love him back.

Of course, none of it would happen unless he got over his issues and figured out a way to grovel and profess himself to her. And fast. She was probably packing her bags to get the hell back to New York right now.

Jay shook his head and climbed out of the truck. After she'd put up with all his bullshit, he needed some grand, sweeping gesture. But how to do it?

A light mist of rain coated his clothes and a chilly wind swirled, knocking the orange and red leaves to the ground. Maybe he'd stay home, rake the yard, straighten up the barn, and maybe even paint a new picture as he brainstormed. He could capture her the way he saw her—full of light and life.

Light and life she'd be taking back to New York.

He stopped midway to the house on the driveway, thunderstruck.

What if she *wanted* to go back?

The thought made his gut hurt. And his chest. And his head. He walked inside to find Gramps at the table reading the newspaper. He glanced at Trisha, who'd walked into the room when the door opened. "How are things today?"

Gramps looked up scowling, hiding his hand tremors under the table. "You don't always have to ask her. I haven't lost my marbles yet."

Trisha smiled. "Judge Carter came by today, and they played some cards. Had their heads bent together most of the afternoon like they were making a plan for world domination."

Jay tried to smile. "So, a good day?"

Gramps shoved his chair back clumsily. "I'm going for a walk."

When Trisha moved toward the door, Jay stood and shook his head at her. "I'll go with you, Gramps." Anything beat sitting in the house trying to figure out what to do about Penelope.

He handed Gramps a coat, then slipped his arms into his own. When they got outside, Gramps turned up his collar. Jay had always cherished his time with Gramps. Maybe not as much as he should have, but now, no telling how much time they had together. He closed his eyes and pushed the thought away.

Gramps leaned heavily on his cane as he led the way toward the barn. "I wanna see those carvings. You got any new projects started?"

Currently the barn only held a pottery wheel, paintings, and sculptures—some of which would be leaving this afternoon to be sold at the festival. Others he'd planned on selling online, hopefully with Penelope's help.

"Not yet, but I was thinking—" Jay cut himself off when, instead of turning toward the barn, Gramps headed toward the split rail fence that bordered the pasture. If he could've walked the entire property line, Gramps would have seen the new sections and the ones still needing to be replaced. Once upon a time, he would have insisted on fixing it himself. Immediately.

Today, he hitched one foot up on the bottom rail and rested his arms on the top. "Was a time when a man's head wasn't so clouded by love." He shook his head. "She was supposed to marry that Army guy from up in Nashua." Gramps looked at Jay.

Jay had heard the story a hundred times. Gramps had met Gran just after she graduated high school, after her summer in Connecticut when she'd been promised in marriage to some oil tycoon's son.

Gramps stared off into the pasture. "He was some bigwig rich boy. Could've given her the kind of life she deserved. All I had to offer was a run-down farmhouse and a few acres of corn and wheat." His smile was sweetly reminiscent.

"You loved her," Jay stated softly.

Gramps nodded. "More than I ever loved myself."

"Did you tell her straight out?"

Gramps nodded. "You damn right I did. Woman needs to be informed. I got in my truck and wasted no time getting to her even though I knew she could do better than me." Gramps shook his head. "I couldn't imagine life without her."

And now Jay couldn't be sure who the story was about anymore.

He had a bit of his own staring out at the pasture to do, some deciding, some contemplating the life he could give Penelope and whether or not it was reasonable to think she would uproot her life if their relationship advanced beyond a long-distance thing.

He shook his head. Relationship. Hardly. If he'd gotten over himself, figured out his love for the woman was stronger than his aversion to getting attached to her dog, realized how much he wanted to be with her, she wouldn't be leaving Maple Falls now that she was done with her sentence.

He had to stop her.

# *Chapter Twenty-Seven*

*Penelope*

Since Lori's duplex was still furnished, there was no sign other than the suitcase on the sofa that Penelope was leaving, but it felt like she was leaving her own home. A real home. Her stomach ached at the thought of not coming back to this place every night, not having Charlie next door to drink wine and bond with. Of going back to New York, where she had no one to talk to.

Charlie stared at the suitcase, her nose scrunched up and her eyes narrowed. "So this is it, huh?"

Penelope pointed to the duffel sitting in the chair. The black nylon sides bulged and the zipper threatened mutiny, but so far it had held together. "And that."

"You know, if it's a place you're worried about, I have a spare room." She shrugged. "Couldn't you talk to your uncle and at least see if he'll let you work remotely? At least until you find a new job, if that's something you want to do."

"It's not so simple. Family business and all. But I'm good at what I do. Worked hard to get where I am. And I do actually enjoy it. Plus, like I told you before, my family is there." Yet her throat hitched at the thought of leaving Maple Falls. She hadn't been here much more than a month, yet it had been long enough to fall in love. With the vibrant autumn colors. With the homey atmosphere. With the no-nonsense, maddening park ranger. And even though she brought plenty of nonsense of her own into any relationship, she still spent the better part of the afternoon imagining what life would be like if Jay remained in hers. And even as frustrated as he made her, she couldn't get the picture of their imaginary life out of her mind.

"I think there's a certain park ranger who might say you could have a life here." Charlie handed Penelope a pair of blue rhinestone earrings that matched the faded denim color of her top. As Penelope poked the small studs into her ears, Charlie pulled a makeup bag from her purse and applied a few swipes of mascara to her long lashes.

"If he cared that much, he would've already been here trying to convince me to stay."

"He just needs more encouragement." Another swipe of mascara before she turned to Penelope. "You could go talk to him. Ask him flat out if he wants to carry you off to his castle and fill it with little squawking kids and barking puppies." She eyed Havoc, who stood in the door watching them get ready for the festival. "Why is he staring at me?" She smoothed a wrinkle from her shirt, then looked back to Havoc. "Better?"

Havoc crouched into downward dog to stretch, then yawned before lying down. Penelope chuckled. "He's pretty indifferent about fashion."

"What about the men in your life? Does he have opinions on them?" Charlie reached into her bag and pulled out a tube of lipstick as Penelope considered how best to answer.

Havoc had never really bonded with her ex-boyfriend, even though it took him a full five minutes to warm up to Jay. That fact wouldn't really support the go-back-to-New York plan she'd been working on. Although right now, Charlie's encouragement to stay made her like the plan even less. And she didn't *want* to like the plan less. She wanted to love it. Wanted it to make her feel as warm as thinking of Jay did. Damnit.

"Havoc likes Jay." Which was a bit of an exaggeration, but that was all she planned to say about it.

"You should trust Havoc's instincts." Charlie capped her lipstick, then nodded, smug and certain.

"True." Again, her mouth overrode brain. Besides, not much point denying what she'd admitted already. She shook her head despite its ache. "But it's more than that. I have no one up here but you."

Charlie snorted. "Hello, you have Nick. Wait, strike that. He's so grumpy, he makes Jay look like a fluffy bunny. But you have Mrs. Clover and Brent. Everyone who's spent time with you adores you. People in this town care for one another. You'll make friends faster than you know."

Penelope's shoulders dropped as she sighed. Every fear she had Charlie countered with a sound argument. The only thing truly holding her to New York was her family and her job. She was tired of thinking right now. "We're going to miss the apple bob if we don't hurry up." A lie. And a lame one. Charlie's eye roll said she saw right through it.

"Now who's running away from the subject?"

"I'm not running. We simply have to hurry." That was her story, and for now, she was sticking to it.

Fifteen minutes later, she and Charlie walked around the town square after she dropped off Havoc for the pet parade. People milled in the shutdown street, on the sidewalks, by the food stands and exhibits. The sweet smell of funnel cake and cotton candy blew on a slight breeze that kissed Penelope's cheeks. Everyone had a smile or a wave, and once again, her stomach clenched at the thought of leaving.

"Wow, Pen, you look beautiful."

Penelope turned around to find Brent, the younger ranger she'd worked with to clear the old check station. She returned his smile. "Well, skinny jeans and a chunky knit sweater do not beauty make." Not when she had a closet full of designer clothes that lifted and tightened, enhanced and highlighted. Maple Falls wasn't a Prada-in-the-town-square kind of place. "But I do thank you for the complimen—" The words died on her lips when her gaze snagged on Jay selling some of his sculptures at the fundraiser booth a half dozen yards away. She forced her eyes back to Brent. "Ah, I mean, thanks."

"Haunted hayride is starting soon. You and Charlie want to join me and Eric?" Brent asked.

She would have probably agreed, but Jay spun in a small circle, then turned back. She followed his gaze to where his grandfather stood talking to Judge Carter and a young boy. The tightness in his face and the rigidity of his shoulders relaxed. He might have even smiled when he caught her watching.

Now was her chance. She'd either say goodbye forever or confess her undying love. It could go either way. She glanced at Brent and Charlie. "I'll be back in a minute."

She navigated through the crowd until she finally stood just inches away. Her heart hammered and she looked down to make sure her chest wasn't flapping with her heartbeat. Satisfied Jay wouldn't know unless he pulled her close—the thought of which did nothing to slow it down—she looked up. "Hi."

"Hi." Jay handed his latest customer a wrapped sculpture and placed the money in the cash box before turning his attention back to her. "You look incredible."

From Jay, she believed it, because this was a man who didn't have an insincere bone in his body. Her cheeks heated and probably turned redder than the apples in the water barrel. "Thanks. You do, too." Such an understatement. In his jeans and T-shirt, which made his legs look even longer and his chest broader, he could have been a *GQ* model.

He ducked his head, then smiled. "Having a good time?"

There was something different about him today.

She motioned to Charlie, who watched them with a smile on her face—an "I told you so" smile. "We just got here." But Charlie was still standing with Brent.

Jay frowned momentarily. "So, did you sign up for the pumpkin carving contest? First prize is a couple tickets to the monster truck jam next week."

She wouldn't be here next week. "Um, I probably won't. I'm supposed to be at work on Monday morning."

He nodded slowly, his eyes becoming guarded.

*Tell me you want me to stay. Please, Jay.*

"Pie throw, then? Nick is getting in the booth. I already bought my tickets." Instead of pulling them out, he shoved his hands into his pockets and her heart went dark.

He wasn't ready to fight for what could be between them. And if he wasn't going to, why should she? She wanted to run back to her car, crawl in the backseat, and bawl her eyes out.

"I might get in on that," she murmured. She should've walked away. Stopped torturing herself, but she wanted one last look at his beautiful features.

"I'll share my tickets. That line is gonna be a long one." Probably an exaggeration. Far as she could tell, everyone loved Nick. Assholes who sat in the pie-in-the-face hot seat sold way more tickets.

"Sure." Nothing like saying yes to more heartache, more unrequited love, more misery. Who knew she was such a masochist? Then again, it was just one more day.

And there it was—the smile, genuine, beautiful, heart-stopping. Easy to return. And easy to lose herself in. Too easy. He looked down again. "Let's talk later."

She was about to ask him about what when Charlie walked up. "You ready for the dead walk?"

"What's a dead walk?" It didn't sound like something fit for a child.

Charlie laughed. "The dead walk is our Halloween answer to a cake walk. All our beautiful senior citizens are this year's zombies, manning the tables, taking the bids. You should see Mrs. Collett. If she didn't have someone professionally make her up, she should be working in Hollywood." Charlie made a claw of her hand and slashed it at Jay.

"I should get back to fundraising." Jay turned and walked to the other end of the booth to talk to a customer.

It took less than an hour for Penelope to fail at the dead walk—hello, distraction in the form of a hunky park ranger—and bid on ten gorgeous cakes. She would've stopped at three, but the line at the sandwich booth was too long to stand in, so naturally, she'd broken the cardinal rule about shopping while hungry. Now she sat in front of a crystal ball with Madame Maxine while the woman in the tie-dyed maxi-skirt and neon pink bat-wing shirt dealt from a deck of tarot cards.

"You have decision to make." The accent was fake but part of the gimmick, so Penelope rolled with it. "Stay or go, yes?"

"Yes." Penelope didn't give much credence to the validity of fortune telling as a profession or even a carnival trick. But she'd paid her five dollars and now she'd let her curiosity keep her butt in the chair.

"Your heart is full. And love is within your reach. You need only grab it." Madame Maxine shot Penelope a meaningful glance before she flipped another card. "There is much change coming for you." Maxine flipped another card. "What is lost will be found."

Did that mean her car keys? Love? The dog leash Havoc must have hidden? What loss would be found?

This was why she'd never bought into this kind of thing. Why she'd always looked for the little card with all the pat phrases and generic lines. These people never gave specific details, just vague guesses that could have fit anyone depending on how they listened to the words.

Why, then, was her heart beating so fast?

She stood. "Anything else?" She wasn't being flippant, she just knew when she walked in, the line had been long, and she didn't want to eat up more than her fair share of time.

"Love is a part of your journey. Don't walk away from it." Madame Maxine nodded as if dismissing Penelope, who walked out more unnerved than she cared to admit.

# *Chapter Twenty-Eight*

*Jay*

Jay was watching for Penelope. Might as well admit it.

But only to himself.

She'd lost two dollars at Three Card Monty, spent five bucks in the psychic's tent, and won three cakes and a full body massage in the silent auction tent. Yep, full-on stalker mode. But he hadn't seen her in at least twenty minutes.

"Jay!"

He glanced over to his right where Mrs. Carter was scuttling between slower-moving fairgoers, her face flushed and sweaty. His gut dropped and he moved swiftly from behind his display table to meet her. "Marylou, what's wrong?"

She bent at the waist, putting her hand to her chest. "Golly, am I out of shape! Have you seen the judge?"

Jay frowned. "No, is everything all right?"

Finally catching her breath, Mrs. Carter pushed herself upright and gave a sheepish smile. "Yes, sorry to have worried you. Just wanted to make sure my grandson is with Carter. Last I saw the young boy he was waiting in line for the hayride. Now I can't seem to find either of them."

"Let me help you look. They must be around somewhere." Jay asked the jewelry artist in the booth next to his to watch his table, then looked to the table where Trisha had been sitting with Gramps earlier. She still sat, plate in front of her, lemon-shake-up glass sweating but empty in front of Gramps's empty chair.

Jay told Marylou to wait, then hurried over to Trisha. "Hey, where's my grandfather?"

Trisha smiled. "Don't worry, he's in good hands. He and Judge Carter went off together about twenty minutes ago."

"Any idea where they were going? Did you see a young boy with them?"

Trisha shook her head. "No, sorry. Gramps is having a good day, so I didn't fuss much when Carter wanted to 'take him for a spin' as he called it. Wasn't paying close enough attention to notice if there was a child in the area. Too concentrated on your grandfather looking for small signs that might indicate I should've gone with them."

"Okay, thanks." He went back to Marylou and explained what he knew, glancing through the crowd. No way Carter would leave his grandson unsupervised. Maybe someone else offered to keep an eye on the child. People in Maple Falls were like that.

His gaze landed on Penelope. It was like a punch in the gut. Her effect on him was growing, not weakening. It must have shone in his eyes because she started moving toward him.

He forced his attention back to Mrs. Carter. "Check the lines for some of the rides. Maybe Judge Carter asked someone else to keep an eye on Matthew while he and my grandfather go off to do who knows what."

Marylou fidgeted with her purse. "Matthew is such a shy boy. He wouldn't feel comfortable around people he doesn't know well. If the Andersons were here, I wouldn't be so nervous. He likes their children. But little Dougie is home sick."

Penelope waited a discreet distance away as he finished talking to Marylou. When Mrs. Carter walked away toward some of the more popular rides, Penelope edged closer. "Is everything okay with the Carters?"

He nodded. "Appears to be. Though we should find the judge and make sure his grandson is with him. Marylou is a bit worried."

Penelope's smile made his heart melt. "Can I help?"

"If you have time, it would be appreciated."

Most every resident of Maple Falls along with those from the neighboring towns seemed to have picked this moment to stop and congratulate Jay for raising enough money to save the safety program, for the beauty of his art, even for organizing the festival, for which he had no part, but he didn't have the patience for more than a few hurried thank-yous. Penelope, on the other hand, managed the crowd like a champ. Gracious and efficient. Even asked if any of them had spotted Carter or his grandson.

She was a marvel in so many ways.

Jay hustled across the street and down a block away from the festival. It was easier to talk when he was in motion. "You're good at handling people."

"Thanks," she replied, as he led her through the alley behind Ferrar's Formal Wear, the tuxedo shop. The alley was dark, and when Penelope reached for his hand, his heart squeezed. "Supposedly, Lurlene spotted the little boy almost an hour and a half ago by the hayride. She said he was by himself."

Jay grimaced. Not good. Especially for a shy kid. He prayed to himself Matthew was with his grandfather and hadn't somehow gotten lost.

He stopped short at the back door, where Jacob Ferrar's family accepted their weekly deliveries. The heavy metal door was open and cigar smoke wafted out. Gramps, Judge Carter, Malcolm Ferrar, Fred Clover, Scottie, and Levi Colletti sat around a green-felt-covered table, cards and chips littering the center along with a plate of funnel cake, a few empty beer bottles, one of Mrs. Clover's pies, and heaping plates of fried mushrooms, green beans, and French fries.

Jay unintentionally squeezed Penelope's hand. No Matthew. Shit.

Carter looked up to nod at Jay as Gramps regaled the group with an old war story. His cigar hung out of his mouth as he threw a stack of his chips into the pot.

Jay let go of Penelope's hand and walked into the room. "Looks like you two have been busy. Marylou was looking for Matthew. Hoped he was with you."

Carter's bushy brows knit together. "Gave the boy the tickets to the hayride. Was supposed to go on it with my wife. Damn ride had a reservation time on it. Marylou knew that."

Jay's chest tightened. Not good. Definitely not good.

Gramps waved a hand in the air. "Carter, boy's probably hanging out with those his own age. Doesn't want to be a fuddy-duddy like us old folk."

Jay pulled out his phone and called Trisha, giving her a quick update on his grandfather and asking her to help Mrs. Carter look for Matthew. The kid had to be around the festival somewhere. Then he and Penelope stepped back out into the fresh evening air to head back toward the rides. "Where's Havoc tonight?"

He shouldn't care, but he found that he did.

"I dropped him at the doggie costume booth when we got here. He's going as a sunflower in the pet parade."

"A sunflower?" Jay smiled, heart squeezing, but not as bad as he thought it would. Zip had gone as a ghost the last time.

"Fierce flower. Can stand up to wind, rain, and the most severe elements of nature." She grinned. "Plus, I like yellow." They walked in silence for a few steps before she stopped.

He turned to her and closed the distance between them, taking her hand in his, and pulled her around the corner to the steps of Colletti's Bicycle Shop. They huddled, standing close enough that he could smell her perfume, see every freckle on her nose and every eyelash. "We need to go and make sure Mrs. Carter has found Matthew. But before we get back to the crowd I need to tell you something."

He wanted to tell her he loved her, that he needed her, but those words didn't come. Neither would the things he wanted to say so she at least understood. Starting at the beginning made sense, because if anyone would understand, she would. "I got Zip when he was a puppy right after my grandma died. Gramps and I needed something to take our minds off the loss. Zip was rescued from one of those puppy mills. He was malnourished, caged for all of his life. He didn't take well to people, but I saw him and as soon as I brought him home, I knew I made the right decision."

When he closed his eyes, Jay could still see Zip as he'd been on that first day—running along the fence line, zipping toward his freedom, ears back, little legs eating as much space as they could. "But he was a handful. Had so much energy that needed focusing. He took to training right away. And he worked hard." His voice caught, cracked, and he cleared his throat. "We got certified for search and rescue. He didn't mind the bad weather, working through long nights and hot days. He did his job. Whenever we went out, he led. I followed."

She covered his hands with one of hers, and he closed his eyes, savoring her touch. "Jay, you don't have to—"

"I do. I don't want you to go back thinking…whatever you think." He turned his hand over and laced his fingers with hers. "When we got the call to go to West Virginia, I thought we would do the job and come home, but the flooding was so bad. It was utter devastation. There were so many people stranded and lost and…" The memories assaulted him, and he swallowed hard, but the lump in his throat wouldn't dislodge. "As soon as we'd save one person, we'd find someone we didn't get to in time. Homes were floating down the river. It was one of those thousand-year events. There were so many people stranded and desperate. We were the ones people were waiting for to save them."

"Jay—"

He shook his head, didn't deserve her kindness. "I pushed Zip when I should've let him rest. If we took longer breaks, maybe took a day off, he might still be alive." He couldn't look at her, didn't want to see the pity he didn't deserve.

"Bloat isn't something you could control."

"It is. We got back to the control station, and I let him eat. He was so hungry, but a call came in about a little boy lost by the river. So we went back out. If we stayed in for the day, his stomach wouldn't have twisted." A tear slipped down his cheek and he swiped it away. He hadn't told anyone this story, not all of it. Not even Gramps knew what happened that day. "We got to the boy too late. It was too late. I'd pushed Zip for nothing." His shoulders shook with the strain of holding his emotion in.

For a month straight after Zip died, Jay had cried every day, until he thought he couldn't produce another tear. But now they came faster than he could wipe them away. Penelope laid her head on his shoulder and wrapped her free arm around his waist. He kissed the top of her head, then laid his cheek there. He never wanted to let her go. "I'm sorry for the things I said, the way they might have sounded. It's not that I don't like Havoc or that I don't think you're qualified to do the job. I just can't stand the thought of something happening to you. Or him."

She nodded and when she lifted her head to kiss his cheek, her eyes glistened with tears, and her cheeks were wet. "When I decided to do this, I knew the risks, I knew things could happen that were beyond what I could do anything about. And I talked myself out of it plenty of times." Her eyes cleared, and she used her thumb at his waist to caress the skin over his ribs. Though only his cotton shirt actually touched his skin, he imagined her touch and let it soothe him.

Penelope cupped the side of his face. "I've seen dogs bloat at the shelter. Even getting Havoc, I knew he was at risk just because of his breed. There is no explanation for why it happens, no real preventative outside of gastropexy surgery."

He inhaled deeply, but before he could go on, she brought her hand up to his cheek and guided him around to look at her. She pressed her lips against his and his body reacted. God, he'd missed her. Missed kissing her and holding her against him, missed the little whimpers when he kissed her and the soft sighs when they pulled apart. "Don't go back," he whispered, shaking with his vulnerability.

She opened her mouth to answer, but Charlie rushed toward them, calling her name. Havoc ran on one side and Brent on the other. "Penelope! Jay!"

She jerked away as if they'd been caught doing something much naughtier than kissing. She smoothed her shirt, then brushed the seat of her pants just as Charlie reached them.

"What's up?" Penelope's voice came an octave higher than its normal melodic tone.

"Matt's missing. Mrs. Carter and Trisha checked all the rides, all the tents. He's nowhere. I even ran down a couple of the streets close by and couldn't find him." Charlie shook her head.

Penelope turned to Jay. "What do we do?"

As they rushed back toward the festival, Jay calculated the amount of time the boy had been missing. The last time someone saw him was in line for the hayride. "Maybe he went on the hayride by himself. We should check the trail. The ride through the timber lasts about fifteen minutes."

When they arrived back, they found Mrs. Carter with

Trisha sitting at a small table, dabbing the tears from her eyes. Jay's stomach turned. While he never had someone in his family get lost, it was a constant worry lately this same thing would happen to his grandfather.

Brent and Eric were next to them along with Scottie, most likely collecting information. Jay pointed at the two young rangers. "Go do a hasty search along the trail the ride follows. The boy could have possibly went on the ride himself. Maybe he fell off or something."

The two nodded and hustled off. He then turned toward Mrs. Carter. "Do you have a recent picture of your grandson?"

"Yes, on my phone." She pulled it up and showed him.

"Can you send it to Penelope, Charlie, and myself?"

The woman nodded and after they shared their phone numbers, she sent them the image. Jay opened his text message app, then forwarded the image to everyone in his contacts who would have been at the festival asking if anyone had eyes on the boy or for any information. He glanced at Charlie. "Let's circulate and show people the picture. Lots of the attendees are from neighboring towns tonight. They wouldn't be familiar with who Matthew is. Also, what else has been searched?"

"All the rides and tents have been searched. The bathrooms, the food prep stations."

Jay nodded. "Recheck the bathrooms. Maybe ask for a volunteer to stand there. Matthew may show up eventually. Don't think he's the type of kid to pee on a tree."

Penelope tapped him on the shoulder. "What about lights? The police lights may draw him out. Like someone safe to speak to if he's lost. Or the fire engines. Firefighters might be viewed as more friendly, especially if he feels he might be in trouble for wandering off."

Jay sucked in a sharp breath. He definitely underestimated this beautiful woman. "Great idea."

Charlie directed Scottie to spread the word to any officer on duty and to the firefighters before racing toward the bandstand, then up the stairs to the stage and grabbing the mic from the singer mid-song and pulling out a notebook. "Sorry for the interruption, but a little boy is missing. His name is Matthew Gray. He's four feet six inches tall, blond hair, red shirt and jeans. He was last seen waiting in line for the haunted hayride over two hours ago now. If you've seen the boy, please come to the action tent or speak to any deputy. If you are unsure, we do have a picture of the boy."

Jay glanced at Penelope retrieving Havoc from the pet parade and then removing his costume. His breath caught in his chest, mouth running dry.

It didn't take a genius to know what she wanted to do. A sense of déjà vu slammed into Jay. His brain fired off a million unhelpful thoughts at once, complete with visuals from past searches he'd been on. No matter how hard he tried to push them away, they kept coming. And the more he looked at Havoc, the more Jay questioned if he should remain at base instead of going out with Penelope. Questioning if he could handle being in the field with a dog that wasn't Zip.

But Jay had been on this kind of rescue. She hadn't. He knew the terrain. She didn't.

Time wasn't on their side. Darkness was closing in. The temperature was dropping. It wouldn't take much for a kid Matthew's size to suffer from hypothermia. They had to find the boy soon.

Jay had no other choice. He and Penelope had to work as a team because they had to find Matthew and find him now.

# *Chapter Twenty-Nine*

## *Penelope*

Penelope shivered. The temperature was definitely dropping. Her breath even fogged in the air. This was not an ideal situation to be lost in. Not that being lost was ever an ideal situation. But there were certain things a person could control, and other things, like Mother Nature, that no one could.

This was what she'd been training for. Though, at this moment, she didn't want to be needed. Not that she wasn't ready. She just didn't want a little boy to be lost.

Jay was tense, his body rigid. Whether over the situation or the fact she'd grabbed Havoc in case they were needed, she didn't know. This must be painful for him. "Please, God, let Brent and Eric find the poor boy."

The whispered plea was fruitless when the two rangers arrived back twenty minutes later alone. Their faces etched with concern. "We found nothing. Not even a missing shoe. Even asked the guy steering the horses, showed him the picture, and he doesn't remember the boy."

Penelope's grip on Havoc's leash tightened. More time had gone by without anyone spotting the boy. Not to mention her teeth now clattered. She really needed to grab a jacket. But first she pulled out her phone to check the temperature to make sure this wasn't some symptom from adrenaline.

"Shit. Jay." When he turned to her, she held up her phone, hands shaking. "Not only is the temperature supposed to drop close to freezing, but it's going to rain."

This couldn't be happening. Not in a town she'd been part of. To people she knew. Her breaths came in rapid bursts. It was too surreal. The couple of searches she'd been on in the past had been for strangers. While there was tension in the air, it was nothing like this.

Maybe Jay had been right. There was still a lot she needed to learn. To experience.

Mrs. Carter burst into tears and then looked at the two of them. "I swear to you, my damn husband is going to be put on trial himself. Where is he anyway?"

Her mouth opened and closed, but no words came out. Judge Carter was not a person she wanted to throw under the bus. Jay could handle that. Yes, she could let the sexy-as-hell ranger deal with this situation.

Jay turned bright red and cleared his throat. "Let me call him."

He stepped away, out of earshot, and put the phone to his ear. Penelope was glad not to be staying in the Carter household. There certainly would be hell to pay. But right now, she needed to concentrate on Matthew. Time was working against them.

"Mrs. Carter, is anyone at your house? Do you think maybe Matthew tried going home, especially if he got scared?"

"Maybe. But no one is home."

Charlie placed a hand on the woman's shoulder. "I'll

take a ride by there, even check the local roads. I have to head to the station to grab some supplies and change anyway."

With that, the sheriff took off, leaving Penelope waiting on Jay. They needed Havoc. If Matthew had wandered off into the woods, her dog would be able to catch his scent. Especially with the growing humidity. This was one of the better situations for her dog to work in, though not the best. Damp air made skin rafts easier to detect.

She walked over to Jay, shoulder back and spine straight. No matter what the ranger threw at her, Penelope wasn't taking no for an answer.

Jay stared at her, eyes downcast. "Charlie hasn't gotten back yet."

"Time's against us, as is the weather." She pulled out her phone and punched in her team leader's number. There were still protocols and procedures to follow. Jay needed to call her team back in New York to have her activated in an official search capacity. That way, she was covered no matter what happened. Not that she believed anything bad would happen, but just in case, she needed to be officially put onto the roster. "You need to ask them to activate me."

He stayed mute, looking at her like she was a stranger.

She wanted to shake him, to help him snap out of this strange trance. "Jay, I don't want to have to go to Nick."

She glanced over her shoulder toward Nick, who was in the process of taking over a tent, as a few rangers came bringing equipment and a large map. Yeah, this was definitely becoming a serious situation.

Penelope faced forward once again. How could he

be so reluctant? What if it was Gramps who was out there? She huffed and stepped closer to him. "It's a little boy, and every minute you waste being stubborn is another minute we aren't out there searching for him."

After his self-disclosure in the alley, she thought he was coming around. Maybe even thought there was a chance between them, but his refusal here was going to drive a wedge between them. "Please, Jay."

Penelope understood how hard this was for him, the memories it must bring up. But he needed to learn to trust her. To guide her to become better. She just hoped his wounds didn't run so deep he'd never allow her the opportunity to succeed.

He sighed, ran his hands through his hair, and closed his eyes. "I'll make the call, but I'm your flanker. We do this together, or we don't do it. And we wait for Nick to give us the go-ahead."

She would have agreed to anything to get him to dial the phone. She handed him her cell and they headed back toward her SUV. Like most SAR personnel, she carried some gear in her car all the time. She pulled off her shoes and stuck her feet into her work boots. She grabbed a jacket.

She loaded Havoc into the car. He'd have to wait until Nick gave them clear directions. No sense in having teams doubling over the same areas. Would be counterproductive. Plus, she had to wait until Jay confirmed she'd been activated.

Jay was off to the side of the tent, her phone still to his ear. A few meters away someone was screaming. Then a high-pitched sound cut through the air. She turned to find Judge Carter's head slightly angled, hand to his cheek. Mrs. Carter stood right in front of him. "Oh, my."

"She just smacked him, in front of all those people. Woman is definitely a force to be reckoned with." Jay stood next to her and handed the phone back. "Your team leader confirmed your activation. Now, where is my grandfather? You see him?"

She held out an arm and pointed. "Over there, next to the cotton candy machine. Trisha is with him, along with the rest of the poker-playing crew. Guess no one else wanted to be in the way of Mrs. Carter's wrath."

"We should get inside the tent and find out what Nick has set up."

She nodded and they walked in. At a folding table were a couple of people taking names of others who were willing to help. She signed in and wrote down her information, including that she had a canine on-site.

Nick was just hanging up the phone and turning back to the large map laid out on the table, Brent and Eric to his right. He looked at them. "Charlie said she hasn't found anything. Matthew wasn't at the house, either."

Penelope clenched and unclenched her fists. This was becoming direr by the second. She looked at the map, which had already been broken down into quadrants. Her eyes flew to the creek, fear tightening her throat.

She'd been on a search late January of last year where a drunken teenager had fallen into the water and ended up drowning. Granted, Matthew wasn't drunk, but could the boy swim? She clutched her stomach.

Jay stepped closer to the table. "We need to ask everyone in the residential areas if they have video doorbells. Could get eyes and a point last scene."

Penelope sucked in a breath. How'd he even think

of that? The thought certainly didn't cross her mind. The more this night went on the more she was starting to believe Jay had been right. That she wasn't ready for this. Especially since being the canine handler meant she'd be in charge of a small team.

"Brent, you and Eric get on that now. Make the announcement on the mic if you have to," Nick said.

Brent nodded and the two took off. Jay pointed toward the creek. "Has anyone run the beds yet?"

Nick nodded. "Charlie's got some people on it now. Got fire trucks posted along the road near it with the lights on, too."

"Penelope's got Havoc. Cleared it with her team. Where do you want us to check?"

Nick jerked upright, eyes wide. His head swiveled between the two of them and she almost wanted to laugh. But this wasn't the time to discuss his shock. Or explain it. There was a job to do. After a few minutes, he returned his attention to the map. "According to Marylou, her grandson had what you might call an obsession with the hayride. Maybe he tried to walk the trail."

Jay shook his head. "Brent and Eric already pulled a hasty down the trail."

"But if he accidentally followed a deer trail instead and headed into the woods, they wouldn't have seen him. And Matthew wouldn't have heard them calling out if he'd been walking it. Four hours have already passed."

Penelope glanced down. The area had to be at least a hundred and twenty acres. Even if Nick had broken it up into a couple of quadrants, that would still take time. The level one canine test gave five hours to complete an area that big. Five hours wasn't an option tonight. "Nick, what about the ride appealed to him?"

The man knit his brows together and pulled out his notepad. After a few minutes of scanning his notes, he looked up. "The horses."

Jay bent over the large area, his fingers running along the map. "What if we take Havoc and concentrate here. The barn isn't too far away."

While the concept made sense, Matthew was a young boy. "Could he have really walked that far?"

Both Nick and Jay looked at her, both quirking a brow. Ugh, yeah. She was still green. Not to mention, she already learned the answer back when she studied for her land searcher certification. She swallowed hard. Maybe she should stay back and help look around town.

But neither ranger mentioned the faux pas. Instead, Jay gently squeezed her shoulder before turning his attention back to the map to help Nick strategize.

Penelope stepped out, needing some air and space to calm her frayed nerves. Mrs. Carter sobbed nearby, dabbing her eyes with a napkin. Sucking in a deep breath, she walked over to the judge's wife and sat beside the woman. "I'm sure Jay and Nick will find Matthew. He'll be safe and sound."

The woman patted her hand. "Is your Havoc going to help?"

"Yes."

Or at least her dog was going to try.

Mrs. Clover stepped in and led Mrs. Carter across the street to the restaurant just as Charlie arrived in her squad car. "What's going on?"

"Jay's just putting together some finishing touches on a plan, then we are taking Havoc out."

Charlie spun around, almost colliding into the car. "Wait, Jay is going out? With Havoc?"

"And me."

Her friend blinked rapidly, but before she could continue, Jay stepped out of the tent. "Go get Havoc ready."

Penelope didn't speak, just turned and headed to her car as directed. Her heart was in her throat. Ready or not she was about to go on her first search as a canine handler.

Methodically, her mind focused on getting Havoc ready. She double-checked his gear. Slipped on his vest. Attached his leash. Then he hopped out and she closed the truck door, her focus turning to Jay.

Even though she'd asked a stupid question, even though Jay was against her certifying and believed she wasn't ready, he'd still activated her. He still chose to be her flanker. And while she wanted to take a few moments to think about what that all meant, she didn't have the time.

A boy's life was at stake. And it was Penelope's and Havoc's job to find him before it was too late.

# *Chapter Thirty*

## *Jay*

Jay grabbed his boots and put them on before hoisting his pack onto a shoulder. At least Nick remembered to grab his gear before heading down to the festival. How could this have happened? In all the years he'd been alive, Jay had never heard of a person getting lost during the festival.

A deep, weighted sigh escaped his lips as he shoved his hands into a pair of gloves. Penelope appeared determined, but he caught the tension in her shoulders, how she went quiet after asking a question a more experienced person would have known the answer to. As much as he'd like to argue she wasn't ready, what handler ever was.

That's why he was going out with her. The last thing he wanted was for Penelope to get hurt out there. She didn't know the woods like he did. Especially not at night.

Speaking of. "Scottie, grab your rifle. You're coming with Penelope and me."

"Sure thing."

Jay headed into the tent and grabbed a radio and map

of the section they were going to cover. When he exited, Penelope was standing there waiting. She held out her hand. “Mind if I take a look at the map?”

Jay sidled up next to her. “We have this area right here.”

Penelope angled her head, finger running along the contour lines on the paper. “This area is very steep.”

“Wouldn’t let Havoc get too close. Especially if the ground is muddy. But I think we’d better run along this direction, check the drainage. If Matthew slipped into there, he’s small enough it might be difficult for him to get out.”

Penelope lifted her head and turned around in a slow three sixty before looking at the map once more. “Wind here seems to be coming from the northeast. What if we head in off this road here.”

“Wind might be changing a bit. Let’s get closer to the area first. Plus, I think if he might have headed toward the stables, better to enter off of Hallows Road.”

Just then Scottie walked over. “Ready.”

Penelope’s brows furrowed. “Oh, didn’t know you were joining us.”

Jay cleared his throat. Some dangers she wasn’t aware of, not being from the area, and another reason he was skeptical about activating her. “We have moose and bear in the area. Both are a danger. Havoc better have a spot-on recall. A bear might flee, but a moose will fight back.”

“His GPS collar also has an electrical and sound component, so if I need to get his attention, I’m equipped.”

Jay tucked the map into his pocket, and they all headed toward Penelope’s SUV. They climbed in just as it started to drizzle. Jay clenched his fingers into a tight fist. No, no, no. The situation was getting worse. Cold was one thing, but being wet and cold was quite another. They needed to find Matthew.

"Lots of volunteers to help search. The party supply store donated whistles and another handed out water bottles. Got some for the hike," Scottie said.

"Oh, crap." Penelope tapped her steering wheel. "I should've made sure you had gear and supplies before we left."

Jay smirked. He'd forgotten to do the same thing on his very first search. Told the two officers with him they were on their own, his water was for Zip and himself. Luckily, the search was over pretty quick. Another team had located the missing hunter. "Think he was going to have most of them do a grid search of the close-by areas. Maybe have Eric and Brent lead a team on the east end in the wooded areas along the hayride trail."

He pulled out his phone and typed a quick message to Nick. A few seconds later, a response came through. "No update on point last seen. Matthew didn't appear on anyone's doorbell camera."

A stressful silence filled the SUV until they pulled up along the shoulder near the intersection of the road leading to the stables. It was the perfect area to enter the woods at—two defined borders and the brush wasn't too extensive. Penelope exited the Audi and walked ahead a few feet before pulling out the bottle of powder and spraying it into the air. Sure enough, the wind had shifted. Not that there was much of a breeze anyway. Havoc would have his work cut out for him.

Jay and Scottie stepped out into the cascading rain. Shit. The hills, while ominous at night, could become close to deadly with the wet ground. One slip and, depending how a person fell, could end up with someone's head hitting a rock or tree trunk.

Jay grabbed his pack, pulled out his headlamp, and placed it on his head. Scottie did the same. Even with an insulated coat that was both wind and waterproof, Jay began to shiver. The air was already several degrees cooler from when they left. "Penelope, is Havoc ready? We need to move and fast."

She opened the rear door and let Havoc out, the dog already outfitted with his GPS collar and search vest. Penelope took a moment to attach two blue chemical light sticks to the D-rings on either side of the vest. Then she put on her own headlamp, grabbed her pack, then closed and locked the vehicle. "Ready."

Jay nodded and the three of them walked up to the corner of the intersection and stepped into the forest. Being in the woods at night was disorienting for an adult, much less a child. Jay couldn't imagine where Matthew might actually be. They could end up in a completely wrong area, especially since the boy wasn't familiar with the area.

He groaned, the sound covered by the heavy rain hitting the canopy of leaves above them. While the sense of sight was pretty much useless except for the areas illuminated by their headlamps, hearing also became less effective because of the rain. This was one of the worst scenarios for Penelope to be out on for the first time.

For him to be out on the first time.

He steeled himself before the train of thought progressed any further.

Penelope stopped and looked over her shoulder at Jay. "Hopefully, this won't turn into a full-out downpour, otherwise Havoc won't be able to work."

Scottie looked between the two of them. "Why? Dog have an injury or something?"

Jay chuckled when he caught Penelope roll her eyes. "No, when the rain is too heavy, they can't pick up a scent."

Penelope leaned over, grabbed her dog's harness, and unhooked his lead. She swatted his flank and released as she commanded, "Go find."

The dog took off like a bullet, moments later circling back. After five minutes or so, he seemed to fall into a steady pace. Jay would've slowed the dog down at the beginning, made sure Havoc didn't miss catching scent.

Fifteen minutes passed with no signs or clues the boy had been in the area. Their pace was slow due to the hazards the weather created. Jay clicked on the radio to check in and turned just as Scottie tripped. He reached out to help the deputy regain his footing. The narrow deer path they were on was riddled with knotted roots and large stones. He glanced up toward Penelope, who was carefully picking her way through thicker brush up ahead. "Watch your footing."

She nodded in acknowledgement. Penelope walked on the skinny path while he and Scottie flanked twenty-five meters to the right and left of her. The thumping of his heart grew louder in his ears the more he noticed about Penelope's behavior while actually on a search. He'd never seen her so focused, nor so willing to take directives from *him*. Even keeping control when he knew she was nervous.

He cleared his throat. "You're doing great. Just keep making sure to check for clues at all angles."

She turned over her shoulder, offering a forced smile. "Okay."

"First time is nerve-racking. Between the adrenaline and being in a real situation where it counts makes it easy for self-doubt to creep in. But Scottie and I have your back."

Penelope stopped and turned to him, then to Scottie. "Oh, thank God. I'm a ball of anxiety right now."

Scottie snorted. "You're not the only one. Think I like being out here?"

Jay shook his head. Scottie was never one for going camping or hiking. He preferred staying close to civilization. He turned his attention back to Penelope. "Just take a deep breath and let your dog do his job. He's smart. You both are."

Jay noticed how Penelope stood taller as she spun around and started walking once again. If only he could chase his own fears away. At least he was able to keep them at bay.

For the next half hour, the only noise heard came from the rain and the radio as different teams checked in with base. No one had found Matthew yet.

Havoc weaved from side to side, coming and going out of sight as they called out the boy's name. When he checked with Penelope, Havoc was ranging about two hundred and fifty meters from them.

Jay was impressed.

Zip ranged farther but ran in a circular pattern rather than weaving to look for a scent cone. He knew better than to compare the two dogs. Just because they worked differently didn't mean one way was more or less effective. Hell, he even knew some dogs that didn't range very far until they came into scent.

But he still worried, for Havoc. And for Penelope. The dog wasn't familiar with the area and Jay wasn't sure how much experience the dog had with running in steep terrain at night while it was raining. Havoc could easily get injured to the point he'd need to retire. Or worse. His stomach flipped, bile crawling up the back of his throat. No. He didn't want to go there. Not now. Not ever. He never wanted Penelope to experience the pain of loss the way he had when Zip died.

He stopped in his tracks, his breath coming in shallow spurts, the bile crawling farther up his throat as his chest tightened to the point he bent over and placed his hands on his knees. Fuck his idea that Penelope wasn't ready. Maybe he wasn't.

"Jay, you all right?" Scottie's voice made its way through the pounding in his ears.

When he stood back up, everyone was looking at him. He forced in a deep exhale and let it out slowly. "Yeah, let's go."

"Actually, I have to break Havoc." Penelope held a whistle to her lips and blew. Moments later the shepherd came bounding over.

Under the canopy of a nearby tree, the group took a break. The dog lay down and drank some water while Jay checked in with base to let them know everything was okay. He pulled out the map and compared it to the GPS.

Penelope leaned in. "We could cut across more instead of being on the trail or to each side. What's the brush like?"

"Pretty thick in some areas. But Havoc seems to be covering the area pretty well. Maybe we can spread out more, increase to one hundred meters from each other."

Both Penelope and Scottie nodded.

He took the few remaining minutes to get his emotions in check. It wouldn't help anyone if he fell apart. But the longer the search went on, the larger the knot in his stomach grew.

When their ten-minute break was up, Penelope cast Havoc off and they continued on their search. They continued in the same pattern for the next two hours, and as the time passed, Jay began to feel more comfortable being out in the woods, realizing how much he missed being on a search.

Only one issue.

The temperature had dipped below forty degrees and Matthew was still lost.

Time and Mother Nature were working against them. If the boy wasn't found soon, the probability of him being discovered alive was shrinking.

# *Chapter Thirty-One*

*Penelope*

Penelope could feel the darkness drawing closer, pressing down and suffocating her slowly as she stepped carefully through the thick maze of densely packed trees. Dark didn't cover the inky blackness of the woods. Beyond where her headlamp illuminated appeared to be a wall covered in black paint. Only as she walked closer to it, nothing solid was there. The lack of light made the darkness appear solid. "Never realized how accurate the setting was for *The Blair Witch Project*."

No one commented, so she looked sideways to make sure both men were still there. They were. Maybe they hadn't heard her, or maybe they thought her comment was stupid. Just like her comment back at base.

Her hands began to tremble from the cold. And the fear creeping in. Fear she would fail, that she was too new and wouldn't be able to find the boy, that Jay would realize his belief in her had been misguided. That his previous concerns were spot-on.

She refocused her attention back to the GPS, knowing she had to snap out of it. After making sure Havoc wasn't near any cliffs or steep terrain, she tucked the device back into her pocket and scanned the area looking for any clues Matthew might have been in the area. But the more they pressed on, the more her heart raced.

The ground was sopping wet and Penelope's boots sank in the mud. Both Jay and Scottie called out for Matt, while she tried to listen for an answer. But all she could hear was the squish of each footstep, the rain, and her own heartbeat.

She tried not to imagine Matt alone, huddled in fear of the darkness and the dangers of what could have been lurking in the woods around them. Yeah, she hadn't thought about moose or bears until Jay mentioned it. Why not add lions?

Penelope swallowed hard. In some areas, mountain lions were a threat. Luckily, not in Vermont. Or could they be here? She was completely out of her element. A fish out of water trying to save a life. What was she even thinking?

Havoc yipped as he crossed in front of her and snapped her focus back to the present. She admired her dog's nose-to-the-air determination, his changes in direction, and the way he worked. If only she could be as confident as Havoc was.

But when he disappeared back into the woods, Penelope's mind focused on how she was soaked from thigh to toe, her boots weighing her down. Then on Jay and his request for her to stay followed by his hesitation to allow her to help as a canine handler.

And once they started searching for Matthew, Jay supported her. Helped settle her nerves a bit.

She glanced over her shoulder toward him. She'd been concerned when he doubled over earlier. But nothing physical had been wrong. And by his distant behavior afterward, she could only assume thoughts of Zip had invaded his mind.

How could they not?

Havoc whizzed past her again, startling her. Damn darkness. It made things so much scarier. And why didn't she think about how much her dog resembled a darker-colored wolf. She shook her head.

And that's when she saw it.

Nearly missed it except for the white stripe across the side.

A sneaker.

"Jay!" Her voice cracked, hands shaking.

Both men hurried to her side to see what she'd found. Jay walked around the area, head angled down as he combed through the brush as Deputy Mason pulled out a notepad and started jotting something down. Penelope pulled out her GPS and got the coordinates as she knew both men would need them, then used the tone button to signal Havoc to head back to her.

After Jay called in the information, they combed the general area hoping for another clue to tell them what direction to head in. The sneaker had been off the deer path; it looked as if maybe Matt had stumbled or slipped.

If only the rain hadn't been so heavy, they might have been able to find a footprint or two.

Jay turned her way. "Penelope, is Havoc focusing in any particular area?"

She looked at the tracks on the GPS, Havoc now resting at her feet. Her dog was following a tighter path that angled toward the east by a couple of degrees. "He's definitely changed his search pattern."

She handed the device over to Jay and they came up with a new direction to head. Unfortunately, the terrain was steeper. And it was closer to the drainage. There would be a scent pool if Matt was down there, which meant she'd have to approach the problem differently.

But what if he wasn't? What if she made the wrong call?

Jay placed a hand on her shoulder. "How do you want to approach this?"

She took a deep breath and placed her finger on the map. "I'm going to cast Havoc off from here. When we get closer to the hill and the drainage, you take the ridgeline."

Jay tensed.

Her turn to reassure him. "I'll be fine. Look"—she pointed at the map once again—" I plan to walk the line here. Terrain isn't too steep."

Jay nodded, but the rigid expression on his face could only mean he was still uncomfortable. She clapped her hands and turned to Scottie. "Let's get going."

The group gathered up their belongings once again. The moment she cast Havoc off, he stopped, sniffing the base of a nearby tree, before moving on. The three of them came off the deer path and headed deeper into the brush and trees. A branch whipped her across the cheek, and her skin burned, but she followed. They had to be close.

*Come on, boy, let's bring Matt safely out of the woods.*

"Easy," Jay said when she slipped going up a hill. Footing wasn't the best between the sudden incline, saturated dirt, and the fact there wasn't much to grab onto.

To her right, she could make out the ChemLights on

her dog's vest. Havoc stopped near the saddle two hundred feet away. Then he took off like a bullet, running in a straight line. Penelope froze, heart in her throat. "I think he found something."

*Please don't be crittering. Please don't be crittering.*

Moments later, her dog's high-pitched bark cut through the inky blackness. "Oh, thank—"

Her temporary relief washed away at the realization of what the bark meant. He hadn't been crittering. He'd…he'd found his subject. He found Matt.

Penelope took off at a brisk walk, GPS in hand as she followed the track toward her dog, Jay and Scottie behind her. She wanted to run, to race over and make sure the boy was okay. But if she tripped and got hurt, she'd become a liability.

Seven minutes later, they came upon Matt curled up against the roots of a tree with his eyes squeezed shut and hands over his ears as Havoc continuously barked. Penelope leashed Havoc and he went silent. Deputy Mason knelt and placed a hand onto Matt's shoulder. "You're okay. We've got you."

Jay radioed the information back to Nick as Deputy Mason checked Matt for injury. Penelope turned toward Havoc and gave him a hug, then pulled some treats she had in her backpack. While Havoc preferred a different reward, the circumstances weren't ideal for it. But by the licking of her face, Penelope figured her dog understood he'd done a good job.

"I got lost. I couldn't find Grandma or Grandpa. I walked around looking for them. Then I saw the hayride leaving, but the horses were too fast. Then I couldn't see them anymore." Matt started crying and wrapped himself around Penelope. Maybe from the relief of being found, but more likely in anticipation of how his grandparents might react.

"It's okay, buddy. No one's going to be mad at you. We're just all so glad you're okay." As she spoke gently, her hands soothed his back and his tears soaked her shoulder. Havoc inched forward and pressed his snout against Matt's head.

"Let's get you back to your grandparents." Jay hoisted Matt up into his arms.

Penelope pulled out a bottle of water, taking a swig. She needed a minute to let her emotions settle, to tamp down the feelings bubbling inside of her, and to will her hands to stop trembling. She'd done it. Completed her first search with Havoc.

All the time, the years, she'd trained paid off. They'd found Matthew. They saved a child. A member of the small town she'd grown to love.

Trevor can suck it.

She laughed at the thought, tears starting to flow down her cheeks. Mrs. Carter believed in Havoc. Believed in her. As did the town.

And now she believed in herself.

But she was also glad Jay was along. His support, his guidance meant more than she could ever express.

For a moment, she watched him with the boy, the way he soothed Matt with gently spoken words until the boy actually smiled up at him. "You know what else? I'm really good friends with twenty-five letters of the alphabet. I don't know why."

It took a second, but Matt threw his head back and laughed. He looked up at Jay. "My dad said if it keeps raining, he's going to build an ark. I told him I Noah a guy. Get it?"

Deputy Mason looked at her and whispered, "Don't know that one. What's the answer?"

She shrugged, not knowing herself.

Penelope watched the two as everyone headed back to the main road, listening to their punny jokes. Jay kept his voice jovial, and for the first time in a while, Penelope saw him completely at ease. No tension in his neck or shoulders, his one hand remained unclenched at his side.

Red and blue police lights cut through the tree line. They were close to the main road. When they finally stepped into the clearing, the Carters raced over and grabbed their grandson, hugged Matt ferociously. Mrs. Carter let go of the boy and threw her arms around Penelope, pinning hers at her side. "Thank you so much, young lady!"

Penelope's eyes were misty by the time Mrs. Carter released her death grip and returned to her grandson. Penelope turned back to Havoc, leaned down, and squeezed him. "Good boy. Let's get going so we can get you home and get us both cleaned up."

But for every step she took toward her car, someone stopped her with congratulations for finding Matt, to pat her back, or to pat Havoc and tell him what a good boy he was. All she wanted to do was clean up and curl into bed. The search was both physically and mentally exhausting. And she still needed to head back to the festival base to debrief and fill out a report.

Charlie fell into step beside her. "So, you're a real-life hero now."

Penelope smiled and shook her head. "Havoc did all the work."

When they got to the Audi, Charlie groaned, complete with an overexaggerated frown. "Do you really have to go? Can't you just stay here and live happily ever after as my best friend?"

Penelope opened the rear door to her vehicle and loaded Havoc up, then tossed in her coat and pack. "Would love to give it a shot…but Maple Falls doesn't have a search and rescue team. And what if Jay interferes with me trying to join one? I know how those relationships go. A team won't want drama with a park ranger. There won't be any of that back home. My team won't put up a fight or hesitate to activate me, either. Do you even know what that felt like? To have to convince Jay?"

Charlie rubbed her temples. "Staying doesn't mean you have to have anything to do with him. And I get it. Jackass move on his part. Just look at what you did in the end. You and Havoc found the boy."

"You know as well as I do, it was also luck. If we hadn't been given the area, if no one searched this particular area, Matt wouldn't have been found. Us being here had to do with finding out he liked horses and Jay suggesting the idea." Penelope folded her arms in front of her chest, clenching her jaw. "Plus, I made mistakes. But I need to learn, not be held back."

"Did he criticize you?"

"No. But this was the judge's grandson. It was more personal. What happens if the next person is a visitor? If there is no connection?" Penelope shot her friend a stern glare. "What happens if other teams are readily available?"

"I just keep hoping you'll change your mind." Charlie frowned, then turned to look at her. "I'm gonna miss you."

"New York isn't that far. We can get together and shop or hang out." People always said it and never did it, but she promised herself to make the effort.

Charlie leaned in to give Penelope a hug. "I have to get back and fill out the reports for tonight, but don't leave without saying goodbye, okay? Unless you change your mind, of course."

"I probably won't leave until late tomorrow night. Too tired to do much of anything right now."

The two hugged before Penelope hopped into the driver's seat. Her heart twisted. She'd hoped that the successful search might have prompted Jay to have a change of heart, but no. He hadn't even bothered to find her again once Matt had been handed back to his grandparents. Instead, she watched him hop into a squad car with Scottie and take off as Mrs. Carter was busy squeezing her. While she figured he was heading back to the same place she was, it still hurt.

And it made her fears about him interfering in her being activated resurface.

However, Charlie was right. A relationship shouldn't be a factor in deciding whether to remain in Maple Falls. She loved it here, felt like she belonged, like the community cared about her. And cared about Havoc.

The town offered everything she could ever want.

Come to think of it, Nick was on her side. And he was Jay's boss. So maybe she didn't need to be concerned about being part of search and rescue up here. Nick could probably even help her find a good team to join.

Though, if she did decide to stay, she'd still need to go back to New York and get her affairs in order. Talk to her father and uncle face-to-face to tell them about her decision. She wasn't a person to drop that information over the phone. So many thoughts continued to swirl around her head as she drove toward the festival. Thoughts that would have to be sorted out tomorrow because she was way too tired to make any decision right now. And certainly shouldn't be making one after such an emotional situation.

Staying or leaving would have to wait for the morning.

# *Chapter Thirty-Two*

## *Jay*

The Sunday morning sunlight slanted in through Jay's truck window, warming his forearms as he sat staring up at the front door of Penelope's condo, trying to think of the best words to grovel. He hadn't seen or even caught a glimpse of her in the past few days. After they'd finally found Matthew he'd been busy in the aftermath with reports.

He spent most of last night mapping the route to her hometown. Three hours, fifty-one minutes.

Did he want to do a long-distance thing? *Could* he? The idea made him nervous. He'd known plenty of couples whose relationship fizzled when put to the test by miles. But Penelope had a life in New York, while his was in Maple Falls. And, of course, he couldn't leave Gramps.

He put his hand on the truck door handle and remembered the softness in his grandfather's eyes as he talked about Gran. He wanted a love like that.

A love like that was worth a little hardship.

*Penelope* would be worth it.

He slammed the terrible thought shut in sync with

his truck door. He raced up to the door and knocked, skin nearly feverish. No answer, no dog barking. *Shit.* A bad feeling moved through his chest. He flashed back to when he'd asked her to join him in the pumpkin carving contest. He wanted to win tickets to take her to the monster truck jam next week.

But she'd turned him down. Said she had to go to work on Monday morning.

That was less than twenty-four hours from now.

He rang the doorbell this time.

Nothing. He banged on the door. "Penelope?" He continued knocking a few more times but she never answered.

Fuck. If she'd gone back to New York, he was too late.

He ran next door to Charlie's place, but she wasn't home, either. He jumped in his truck and sped to the sheriff's office. When he charged inside, Scottie was at the copy machine and Charlie was sitting at her desk frowning at a mountain of paperwork.

"She's gone, isn't she?" he choked out, a knot in his throat, a knife twisting in his heart.

Charlie slowly lowered the paper she was holding, refusing to look at him. That alone told him everything he needed to know.

"She didn't even say goodbye."

Charlie finally looked up from her papers, raised an eyebrow, and pursed her lips. "Did you give her a reason to think you'd care?"

"Well…she…*fuck*! I may have been an ass, but I thought when I asked her to stay, before the whole Matthew situation—"

"You should've had your butt over there last night

after you guys found the kid. Actually no, you should've told her how you felt even *before* that. Asking her to stay without opening up wasn't going to do much. Communication is central to all healthy relationships. She *tried* with you. More than once. You couldn't even meet her halfway, you idiot!"

All the air seemed to go out of his lungs.

He was *not* too late. God damnit.

He couldn't even respond to Charlie—what could he say, she was right—so he turned around and walked out of the office like a zombie not even sure where he was going or what he was doing. Just feeling so *lost*.

The day passed by in a blur. It hurt to breathe. He couldn't eat. Couldn't think. Didn't even know what *time* it was. Gramps was worse than usual—bumping into furniture, knocking over a lamp, slicing his fingers open when he tried to cut an orange, and grouching at everything and everyone under the sun. Jay felt like they were both moving through the twilight zone.

Like everything was wrong. Nothing was right.

And he felt so alone. Even though he and Penelope hadn't lived together, just knowing she was in the same town and he could drive over to her place at any time had given him a peace he hadn't realized.

He looked at the clock, desperate with the need to fly to wherever Penelope was, sweep her into his arms, and meld her into this body so she'd never be gone from him again.

But he couldn't leave Gramps unattended overnight.

Less than an hour later, he helped his grandfather get ready for bed and then settled in himself for a long, sleepless night.

* * *

The next morning, he was in his car—a large thermos of coffee in the seat next to him for the caffeine rescue he needed after not sleeping last night—the moment Trisha drove up to relieve him.

"Don't come back without her!" Gramps hollered from the porch.

"I won't," he yelled back and fastened his seat belt.

The hours passed slowly with him rehearsing over and over in his mind what he wanted to say. He was going to beg if he had to. Ask for her forgiveness. Tell her he loved her.

Why had he been so afraid of loving her, of sharing how he felt with her? Penelope was nothing like Karen. She'd never done anything but comfort him, be vulnerable with him, help him. She was goodness personified, sweet, sexy, honest, hardworking, loyal, and dedicated.

She was everything he never knew he needed.

He navigated the insane New York traffic and eventually pulled up to her uncle's place of business. He felt almost light-headed as he stepped into the bright, modern office filled with stainless steel and gray leather furniture and lush green plants in seagrass pots. A young woman looked up from the front desk. "May I help you?"

"I'm here to see Penelope Ramos?" The uptick in his voice was unfortunate. He hoped his face didn't look as desperate as he felt.

"Oh, I'm sorry, she doesn't work here anymore."

He froze, every muscle locking down like those lions stalking their prey he'd watched on a nature show with Gramps last month. "What? She—are you sure? I must have the wrong place."

"No, you're at the right place. We're definitely going to miss her around here, but she decided to move to someplace in Vermont. Manville, maybe?"

Jay's eyes widened. "Maple Falls?"

"Yeah, yeah, that's the one. Maple Falls." The receptionist smiled.

Jay's stomach somersaulted as he tore out of the building without even thanking her. Could it really be true? Why hadn't she told him?

On the drive home, he tried to call her three or four times, but each call went straight to voicemail. Where had she been yesterday when he'd stopped over? He bet Charlie had known all along that she wasn't leaving.

But then he smiled, joy bubbling up through his chest. He deserved to be put through the wringer after what he'd put her through. Oh, hell yeah, he deserved the insecurity because he'd made her feel the same way.

When he rolled into Maple Falls, he drove straight to Lori's duplex, but Penelope wasn't there. He banged his palm against the steering wheel, but he wasn't really mad. She was here somewhere, and he was damn well going to find her and drop to his knees to beg for forgiveness whenever he found her.

He drove everywhere. Clover's Kitchen, the ranger office, the park where she liked to run Havoc, the sheriff's office—where Charlie just smirked at him and wouldn't give him any other information—until finally, he drove back to his place on the off chance she'd be there.

Well, she wasn't, and he wasn't about to get out of the truck and go tell Gramps he still hadn't found her. Gramps would run him off the damn property. Probably with a butcher knife. So he drove back to the office.

He'd never be able to concentrate, but it would give him a little more time to perfect his I'm-sorry-I've-been-an-asshole-I-love-you speech.

Nick was there, sitting behind his desk with a file folder open and a pen in his hand. He launched the pen across the room, narrowly missing Jay's forehead. "Fuck him."

"Good afternoon to you, too. Governor again?"

Nick grunted his reply, then slammed the folder shut. "The building with its no-frost windows and electric sliding doors. And for the love of God, who the hell needs a voice-activated elevator? We went eighty grand over budget. Where the hell am I supposed to get a spare eighty grand?"

Jay's stomach sank. "Tell me we don't have to take it from the safety program."

Nick sighed. "I don't see any other way."

Normally, Jay would have thought Nick's anger an overreaction, but the fundraising booth had nothing to do with the new building. Or Jay would've added the money from his sculptures to the total raised.

"I do." Penelope, like a ray of light, stood in the doorway.

Jay spun around and stared at her, drinking in the sight of her glossy curls, the soft curve of her hips, the sweet smile he'd come to love. She moved into the office like a panther, every step fluid and smooth. Here was his chance, one he wouldn't let slip by. If he had to, he'd say it here in front of Nick and anyone else who walked in, but he'd rather bare his soul without witnesses. Mostly because he wanted to seal his devotion with a kiss.

A very office-inappropriate kiss.

She had a slow secret smile on her lips. His heart thudded against his ribs in response.

Nick nodded at Penelope. "Nothing about you surprises me anymore. So tell me. What is this idea you have?"

She cocked her head, her smile broader, more radiant than only a second ago. "Well, I could tell you. But then you wouldn't be surprised. And I'm all about the surprises today."

Nick sighed. "I would love to sit here and play twenty questions with you, but if your top-secret plan fizzles out"—the doubt was implied if not spoken—" I think I better have something else in place for the governor to steal." Penelope's smile widened farther. "You go do your witchcraft, woman. I'll try to get lover boy to quit mooning long enough to revise his safety program so we can afford it, and we will meet back here in what? An hour?"

"You have so little faith. You should work on that." She wiggled her eyebrows and sashayed out of the room.

Jay was right behind her.

Penelope went toward her desk, pulling her cell phone from her purse. Her eyes sparkled at him, making his throat parch. God, she was so beautiful. "If you're out here to eavesdrop or spy for Nick, you're too late. Plan already in motion."

Self-satisfied on Penelope looked almost as good as Jay-satisfied had looked on her. "Not here to spy," he said, hoarsely, leaning against the wall, weak as a newborn calf. Now that she was standing before him, everything he wanted to say got tied up on his tongue like it all wanted to come out at the same time.

What actually came out was, "I wanted to tell you again you did great finding Matt the other night."

She cocked her head and pulled her lips between her teeth. "Again? I don't really remember you telling me the first time."

He cleared his throat and ducked his head. He hadn't told her. It went on the list with the other thousand things he needed to say to her. "You saved that kid's life."

She grinned but her skin turned a light shade of pink. "Thank you."

His stomach churned as he pushed off the wall and made his way toward her. Since he didn't want to scare her off, he stopped and shook his shoulders.

She chuckled. "Practicing your dance moves?"

His skin heated from his ankles to his eyelids. "No." When he reached the desk, he held out his hands. "Take a walk with me?"

She curled her fingers around his palm and stood. Her fresh floral coconut scent wove around him. "I have to tell you something."

His gut bottomed out. "Can I go first?"

She nodded as they passed through to the porch outside the office. He led her down the steps and to the trail that wound around beside the offices. His heart hammered and his stomach clenched, but if he didn't do this, he would lose her. The trail itself was only one person wide, but Jay walked in the grass beside her.

"I love you, Penelope." Oh, God. He'd just blurted it out like some freak show who needed the zipper over his mouth until his brain caught up.

She stopped. Fast. Tugged him back toward her when he kept walking. "Did you just say…?" Her hand slipped out of his and up his arm to his throat, then into his hair. Okay. He could work with this.

"Um, I said..." Yeah. He'd said it. And he meant it.

She curled her fingers in and out of his hair. "You said it."

He had so much explaining to do. "Yeah, and I'll get right back to it. But first... I know that there's a lot you've left behind in New York, but..." Oh, good Lord. How badly could a man bungle such an important talk? "I needed you to know..." He sighed. "I was scared to death to go out into the woods with you and Havoc." Truth poured out of him like he'd left the fucking faucet on, and it didn't come in the order he wanted. Damnit. "I thought all the old memories and the old heartache would come back. But as soon as we were out there..." He shook his head. "I'm a walking cliché."

Her gaze remained locked into his. "Go on."

"As soon as we were out there, I felt so alive, and so useful. I haven't felt that for a while." With her thumb, she caressed the side of his throat and he fought to control the urge to kiss her. Not because he didn't want to, but because he didn't want to yet. "I think I forgot how good it felt."

"Jay." She didn't add anything except a tilt to her chin and a soft smile.

"If I was going to tell the whole truth, I would say that I haven't ever felt more alive than since you first came to town. And when I thought you'd left..." The words choked inside of him.

"I'm sorry about that. I left late Saturday night to visit with my dad and get a few more of my things." She cocked her head, her eyes soft. "I heard you came looking for me. That means a lot, Jay. That tells me a lot. So, what was it you braved New York traffic to say?"

He squeezed her tighter in his arms. "I don't want you to ever leave. I hope you'll stay." In for a penny, in for a pound. "And give me another chance. You need someone who understands how important what you do with Havoc is, how the training and the rescues could leave you broken inside or so elated that you can't contain yourself. You need someone who's been in the trenches, and who can understand the emotion that comes with every search and every rescue."

She pursed her lips and nodded. "And you know of someone?"

Most important moment of his life to date, and she'd turned it into fun. "Well, I'm not really Match.com, but I might have someone in mind."

"Someone who loves me."

His lips twitched, and he finally felt like he could take a full breath. "Yeah. Someone who wants to be with you through the good times and bad times"—he blew out another heavy breath—" all the time."

"Will he mind that I'm kind of high-maintenance? I mean, who doesn't love a bag of ramen every once in a while, but I like a good grilling out. And I like sleeping in on Saturdays. Of course, he would have to know me and Havoc are a package deal. And..." She let her hand glide over his chest, and he couldn't hide the excited thump of his heart under her palm. "My womanly needs—sometimes they're powerful. Can your guy handle all that?"

Oh, yeah. He could handle her womanly needs. "Yeah. I *know* he can."

"Well, then I'd love to meet him." He caught a

glimpse of her smile just before she pulled his head down for a kiss. He'd never kissed a woman he loved so completely and though they'd even made love, something about brushing his lips over hers felt different, more intense, more perfect than before.

When they pulled apart, she stepped back. "When could I meet him?"

God, he loved this woman—the light shining in her eyes, every grin and frown, the personality that could be fiery one minute and soft and sweet the next. He held out his hand. "Jay Gosling."

She slipped her hand into his and shook it gently. "Penelope Ramos. And I love you, too."

The weight on his shoulders lifted. This woman, this incredible woman, loved him. And never in his life had he thought he could feel so much again. Now he wanted more, to hold her against him, to whisper her name as he plunged inside of her.

He nuzzled her neck, loving the tremors that ran through her body from his touch. "I think we should take the day off."

"We take a lot of days off." Her voice was low, aroused. "Let's wait it out. See how long we can go before we just can't stand it anymore."

He pulled back to look down into her eyes. "Torture ourselves?"

"The reward, though." She traced a nail over his lips. "It's going to be so worth it."

They lasted until noon, unless he counted the ten minutes they'd spent kissing and touching in Nick's office when he went out to meet the governor. Or when she pulled him into the supply closet and pushed him against the wall, then ground her body against his until he thought he would explode. Or the ride to the duplex when she'd left her hand in his lap and used one finger to stroke his cock through his pants.

To their credit, they didn't race up the walk or break down the door when she fumbled with the keys. She also took a minute to let Havoc out into the backyard before she came back through the kitchen, shedding clothes as she walked. Her shirt landed on the countertop, one shoe ended up under the dining table, the other in the doorway. Her jeans made it to the sofa arm. Until finally she stood in front of him wearing the most transparent bra and panty set he'd ever seen.

With a flick of her wrist, she unhooked the bra and let the straps slide down her arms. Jay's mouth went dry and his dick was hard enough to mine for diamonds. But when she hooked her fingers into her panties and dragged them down, her eyes on him, her tongue wetting her lower lip, he couldn't wait any longer. He hauled her against him, then lifted her. They didn't have time for a teasing, leisurely stroll to the bedroom.

As he walked, her lips latched onto his throat and his hands attacked the buttons on his shirt. When she shoved the shirt away and her skin was pressed against his, he laid her in the center of the bed and stood over her. There wasn't a single square inch of her that he didn't want to kiss, to feel, to lick. But first, he wanted to look his fill. See every curve and plain, every dip and valley of the perfection that was her body. And she let him. Didn't shy away or cover herself.

Jay needed to slow this down or he wouldn't last long enough to get the condom on. He leaned over her for a kiss before he slipped out of the circle of her arms and used his mouth on her throat, her collarbone, the swell of her breast. But when he took an already pebbled nipple into his mouth, she moaned, low and deep, and he almost lost it. Almost came in his pants without ever having been touched.

She arched her back and his greedy little minx guided his other hand to toy with the ignored nipple. Her nails raked his shoulders, and her hips swirled as she twisted trying to find friction.

"Oh, God, Jay."

He slipped down her body, hands working her breasts as he tasted her. Her skin, smooth as silk under his hand, quivered with every graze, and her eyelids fluttered as he continued down to the warm, wet center. Oh, God. He wanted her. Wanted to slip inside and lose himself in the heat of her. Desire pulsed through him as he slid a finger inside. She moaned, lifted her hips, then cried out as he withdrew. He'd never seen anything so erotic as Penelope driven by desire.

When he kissed the inside of her thigh and swirled his tongue against the soft skin, she tangled her fingers in his hair and tugged until he turned his head just the fraction it took to taste her. Penelope bucked and twisted but he clamped a hand down on her hip and held her there, held her to his tongue.

"You taste so good," he groaned, lifting his head briefly. Need and longing mingled in his gut as he lapped at the absolute sweetness of her. Her body shook and her hands clenched the sheet as she cried out and rocked against his mouth.

When her cries subsided and her shudders calmed, Jay couldn't wait any longer. He shed his pants and rolled on a condom. He notched himself at her entrance, desire forking up his spine like a streak of lightning. “Are you sure?”

“Yes,” she whimpered, her hands gripping his biceps as she wrapped her legs around his waist, easing his first deep thrust.

His mouth was pressed to her neck, the rhythm of him taking over, rocking hard into her center. Everything dissolved as he reared over her until they were both lost in a storm of pleasure, one pounding and the other clinging as they worked in tandem, stroke for stroke until they orgasmed and collapsed on the bed. Making love with Penelope consumed him, mind, body, and soul.

Penelope snuggled in with her head against his chest, her hand stroking lazy circles around his belly button. At some point, they would have to go back to work, but not yet. Not until he etched every moment and every detail into his memory.

Penelope was back. In his life.

And there was no way he’d ever let her go again.

He woke to the sound of humming. He smiled before he even opened his eyes. If this was going to be his life from now on, he’d never ask for anything else.

“Hey, sleepyhead.”

He turned on his side to find her fully dressed and refreshing her makeup at the dresser. “Don’t wear such complicated clothing from now on.”

She giggled. “You don’t have a problem getting *anything* off me.”

Well, that was true. He yawned and indulged in a luxuriant stretch. “How long was I out?”

“Over two hours.”

"What?" He shot out of bed, sweeping his clothing into his arms. He was low on sleep but that was ridiculous. "I've got to relieve Trisha. She has to get her nephew to a basketball game tonight."

Penelope put a hand on his arm. "Relax. I called Judge Carter about an hour ago and asked if he could go over and hang with Gramps for a few hours. It's all taken care of."

He swept her into his arms, gratitude and love for this woman almost overwhelming him. "Thank you for thinking of him. You have one of the most generous hearts I've ever known."

She squeezed him back, and they stayed that way, breathing each other in for a long time until they made their way to the kitchen, where they scrounged around for supper.

"I'm impressed with what you can do with a chicken breast, a can of black beans, sour cream, and some salsa," he managed between ravenous bites of a tomato-basil wrap.

When she didn't reply, he glanced over to where she sat with her meal largely untouched. He set his wrap down and wiped his mouth with a napkin, trying not to worry. "What's wrong, Pen?"

"Do you think you'll ever go back to search and rescue?" Her voice came in a tentative whisper, as if she didn't want to break the mood of their contentment.

He smiled, relaxing. "I was thinking about that on my way to New York. And I was actually going to bring it up earlier…" He winked at her across the table. "But some little seductress lured me back to her place so she could ravage my body."

"Lured? I didn't see you putting up much of a fight."

He ran his hand up the inside of her thigh under the table. “No sane man would.”

The companionable silence stretched for a few moments before she got up and went over to him. He scooted his chair back and pulled her onto his lap. She had something more on her mind. He wrapped his arms around her and waited for her to spill it.

“Nick mentioned starting a search team here,” she said. When she swiveled to straddle him, she could have told him Nick turned into a search and rescue dog himself, and Jay wouldn’t have had the blood left in his brain to doubt her. She met his gaze. “That something you might be interested in?”

He stood with Penelope in his arms and headed for her bedroom, kissing a line from her earlobe to her throat and up to her mouth as he walked. “Right now, I’m interested in starting round two.”

She giggled. “Well, then. Ding. Ding.”

# *Chapter Thirty-Three*

## *Penelope*

Jay reclined against the pillows on her bed. They'd spent the night at his place so he could keep an eye on Gramps, but when she'd insisted on going home this morning, he'd volunteered to drive. She'd let him because a night like theirs wasn't one she wanted to end.

"You spend the nights at my place anyway. You could just stay with me."

Penelope loved when he asked—which he did every day—but it was way too soon for him to see her in her weekly charcoal mask or see her laundry-day underwear or make room in a cabinet for her year's supply of tampons.

"Lori is having hip surgery, so she won't be visiting for a while. She said I could just rent the place from her. And since my uncle"—the darling man that he was—"made my telecommuting job permanent, I kind of want to give living on my own a try."

Jay twisted his lips to the side. "How often do you have to travel?"

She shrugged. They hadn't worked everything out with her new position. "The big trade shows are three times a year. He might send me to a couple small ones, but those would just be the ones on the East Coast." There would be times she had to travel to a couple job sites if the job was big enough to merit an on-site consultation, but she would have plenty of time to get to know Maple Falls.

Jay tossed a rubber ball against the wall and caught it while Penelope unpacked the bag she'd spent almost two hours packing to head home to New York that Saturday with Charlie. It felt like forever ago. Since she'd decided to stay, she'd spent so much time at his house, she'd been living out of the damned thing and now, all her shirts were wrinkled.

"Just saying, it would be more convenient. Havoc has room to run. Gramps likes you." He caught her around the waist and pulled her onto his lap. "I more than like you." His eyes flickered with desire and sitting on his lap was not the place to be if she had any hope of getting her clothes hung in the closet.

She kissed his cheek. "I have to unpack, and you are screwing with my progress." His fingers slithered under the hem of her shirt and inched up her stomach. Every touch was a tingle, every tingle a spark, every spark a fire under her skin.

No way could she concentrate on unpacking with his lips teasing, then soothing the back of her neck. "I would rather screw with something else." To emphasize his point, he slid his hand up her ribs to cup her breast. In a move swift and confident, he pulled her back onto the bed and kissed her belly just above her waistband.

She'd planned to tell him about the safety program's new sponsor on Tuesday when they went back to work, since Nick didn't even know about it yet, but if she didn't do something they would end up back in bed and—not that she minded more than what merited a token protest—she needed to get things done.

"Jay..." And that was as much as she could manage.

He slid her shorts and panties down. Her hand trailed down the dusty line of hair arrowing from his belly to his cock. She fisted it and moved her hand back and forth. Penelope could do that all day without getting bored. Admiring his body. Learning what gave him pleasure.

"Penelope," he groaned, pulling her hand away and rolling on a condom before sliding on top of her.

Jay entered her in one smooth stroke and Penelope moaned at the sensation of being so full, both physically and emotionally. Something in their lovemaking had changed. He held her gaze with his own when he entered her. She felt claimed. Cherished. Whole. It was more than sex. It was true connection.

A forever-I've-got-you kind of sharing. It gave their lovemaking a whole new dimension.

Her back arched when Jay started thrusting. This was everything she wanted. And when his movements became jerky, she quivered around him.

"Pen, I'm gonna come. Come with me."

She nodded and let go. They came in each other's arms, with him moaning her name and Penelope whimpering when his cock drilled into her one last time.

God, she loved this man. And she was never gonna let go.

"Haven't we gotten enough exercise for the week?" Jay grumbled as he pulled his truck into a spot at the park. "Now you want to go for a run?"

"We have, but Havoc has been cooped up in the

house a lot lately. He needs to expend his pent-up energy, too."

Jay leaned in and tangled his fingers in her hair to draw her close enough for a kiss. Something about this man made her want to forget the run and crawl onto his lap. Again. "Fine. But I'm probably already dehydrated from our earlier...exertions. If I keel over because you made me come out here to run, just know I loved you."

"Oh, my goodness, you big baby. We won't run. We'll just walk." To be honest, she was plenty tired herself with all their late-night lovemaking. Walking would be okay. And they could talk—one of her two favorite things to do with him.

They hopped out of the truck and when they met at the front, Jay laced his fingers with hers. "Have I told you how glad I am you decided to stay?"

Several times. But she never tired of hearing it. "You might have mentioned it."

"I should probably send your uncle a big bottle of whatever he likes to drink."

Oh, if only he knew. "Maybe."

It was right there on the tip of her tongue. She wanted to tell him her big secret, but something like this deserved a big reveal, maybe even balloons or a parade. And this was a secret that definitely wouldn't blow up in her face like the last time.

She watched Havoc run ahead, stopping to sniff flowers and leaves that lined the trail. Anything to keep from spilling her guts. Plus this was the kind of thing she'd always dreamed of doing with a man. A leisurely stroll while Havoc did his version of frolicking through nature.

This was such a perfect day, with her perfect dog and

the perfect boyfriend. A slight breeze whipped around them, and she adjusted her cap to shield her eyes from the bright, shining sun. "New York might have some five-star restaurants, but it sure doesn't have a view like this." The canopy of trees overhead, the wildflowers, and natural landscape only reinforced what she'd already decided. She loved Maple Falls, Vermont.

"Nick is going to let me work the check station for the turkey hunt." Apparently, every year, the state sponsored a turkey hunt in time for Thanksgiving. As soon as Nick told her about it, she volunteered to work it. Not only did she want to be a part of Jay's world, she wanted to become a full-fledged member of the Maple Falls townsfolk.

"Oh, yeah?" He used their clasped hands to direct her away from a rock sticking through the dirt on her side of the path. "Well, I, too, am working the check station for the turkey hunt." He wiggled his eyebrows and brought her hand to his mouth to press a soft kiss against her knuckles.

"Quality time." Nothing she liked better these days.

Jay nodded. "And Mrs. Clover always delivers food for whoever works the turkey hunt." They came to a split in the trail. Left went up and around while the right side went down in a curve toward the office. "Let's go toward the river."

Penelope grinned. He thought he could stump her, but she'd show him. She pulled him left. "You got a fishing pole in your back pocket?"

She whistled for Havoc, who loped back toward them. Jay reached his free hand to scratch Havoc between the ears. "Don't be talking dirty to me in front of the d-o-g." He widened his eyes and pointed to Havoc.

When she cocked an eyebrow, he chuckled. "You're the one asking about the pole in my pants."

"Fishing pole. For the *river*." She loved his sense of humor. His smile. The way he seemed to be falling as much in love with Havoc as he was with her. So far, she hadn't found anything about Jay not to love.

"There's a little waterfall about a half mile down from the low crossing."

A waterfall. The state of Vermont was full of natural wonders. And seeing this place with Jay would make it all the more wonderful.

"Penelope, you're dripping all over the lawn." Charlie looked out her front door, laughing.

"I fell in the river." Jay followed behind, probably laughing quietly, smirking, at least.

"Tell her why you fell in the river."

She shot him a glare. Telling the story wouldn't make her feel more adequate or coordinated. "Shut up."

"She was all bent over trying to show me how a real woman could catch fish with her bare hands. But she leaned a little too far and went in head over booted heels." He waved his arms in a windmill motion. "Took a couple minutes of splashing and flailing before she figured out she could stand."

Charlie hid her smirk behind a twitching mouth and furrowed forehead. "Did you get the fish?"

"Shut up, both of you." She stomped into the foyer and stood on the small tile cutout to strip down. Before she could even grab the throw from the back of the sofa, Jay popped open the screen door and wrapped his arms around her from behind. "I'm covered in river water."

Jay laughed and the sound tickled Penelope's stomach. “I wouldn’t care if you were covered in swamp water. If you’re getting naked, I’m all over it.”

His tone, his hands on her stomach, his warm breath on her skin stoked all the feelings she’d been experiencing for the last week, all the desire, the love, the need. “If you wouldn’t have laughed at me, I would have invited you to join me in the shower. But…you had a little bit too much fun at my expense.”

He turned her in his arms so that her chest bumped against his. Nowhere else she would have preferred to be than wrapped up in Jay.

“What if I apologize?” His eyes darkened, made promises his body would keep, if she let him. Which, of course, she would. She hadn’t quite figured out how to say no to him yet.

“It’s going to have to be a really good apology.” Her voice came in husky breaths. “I mean, I could have died.” If she didn’t know how to swim. And if he hadn’t been there to pull her out. And if she hadn’t been able to stand on the bottom and have everything from the knee up out of the water. “The current could have carried me away.” The slow current would have been lucky to carry a fallen leaf downstream. But such things happened. She’d seen pictures.

He kissed her, a soft, toe-curling touch she took a second to savor before she opened her eyes.

“The best apologies are the slow, soapy ones.”

“It better be if I let you in my shower, big boy.”

Jay picked her up and kicked the door shut in the same motion. And for the tenth time in the last week, carried her through the house. This was one ride she could get very used to.

# *Chapter Thirty-Four*

*Jay*

Even if long weekends were the only thing he had to look forward to for the rest of his life, so long as they were with Penelope, he'd gladly sign up. They'd spent an equal amount of the weekend in bed as doing regular couple things—long walks, reading together, watching TV. Hell, somehow she'd even convinced him to go dancing.

Of course, leaving her at the crack of dawn to come into work the next Monday morning wasn't high on his list of favorite things to do, but in the interest of keeping his job, he'd managed. Grumbling, but there.

He missed working with her every day, her unique spin on the small things. Like deer season. She called it deer pruning, no matter how many times he or Nick corrected her. But she refused to even discuss rabbit and squirrel seasons, even when Nick spent an hour explaining the importance of population control. She'd even designed some picket signs they would undoubtedly have to call Deputy Mason to pry from her hands at some point.

He'd been called back to the check station—the one

now housed in the new building—and he strolled into Nick's office. "What's up?"

"You have visitors," Nick said, gesturing to Penelope, who stood behind him and next to a man who could only have been her father and another shorter, stockier man.

She made her way around Nick and crossed the floor to stand beside him and thread her arm through his. "Papá, this is Jay." He couldn't have felt more like a sideshow at the fair if he'd been wearing a blue ribbon and a leash. "Jay, this is my dad, Pedro, and my uncle, Enrique."

He stepped forward and shook hands. "Good to meet you both."

They sure as hell had better not be here to drag Penelope back to New York. Because they'd have to go through him to do it.

But Enrique stepped forward and held out an envelope. "Well, son, Penelope told us about your safety program, and I just want to say, damned fine idea." Jay took the envelope and glanced at Penelope. Was this the secret she'd been keeping? The reason she would start a sentence and not finish it? Granted, some of those times had been his fault, when he'd kissed the words away, but the bulk of the instances had recently started bugging him.

He lifted the flap and looked inside. Oh, wow. Enough money to start the program and to keep it going for a good year, at least. He looked at Penelope. "This was you?"

"Uncle Enrique knows a good cause when he hears about it." Her skin had a lovely pink glow as she ducked her head.

"And how did he hear about it?"

She shrugged. "Might have been me." She chuckled once, then sobered. "Are you mad?"

Mad? If he couldn't tell how much she meant to him, how much this meant to him, he was definitely doing this boyfriend thing all wrong. He wanted to swing her around in the air, kiss the embarrassment off of and then back onto her face. "Oh, God, Penelope. This is the best thing anyone has ever done."

Enrique stepped up. "Son, a while back I had a heart attack on a hunting trip. Thank the good Lord I had one of those fancy cellular phones with the GPS coordinates I could relay to a park ranger who had me airlifted out. If not, I wouldn't be here today. This is a good program, one every county needs. I'm hoping with the success in Vermont, New York will pony up some funding and get one started." He clapped a hand on Jay's shoulder. "Aside from stealing the best job quote person on my staff, from everything I hear, you're a man to be trusted."

Heat crept up Jay's neck to his cheeks, but he nodded. "Thank you, sir. So much. You have no idea what this means."

Nick chuckled and chimed in. "It means, after I tell you the rest of it, drinks at the Rusty Nail are on you."

Even Penelope's head jerked up. "The rest of it?"

Oh, so there was something she didn't know? He smiled. "Yeah. What's the rest of it?"

There were things Nick was an expert at, things he was just okay at doing, and things he shouldn't have even bothered trying. Drawing out suspense was on the latter. "The SAR program is a go and I thought, why not keep it all in the family, you know. So I did a little digging, made a few calls, and it just so happens, two of Havoc's siblings were still in a shelter. And when I explained what we were doing and why it was so important and how fabulously their brother worked out, the woman at the shelter donated both dogs to the program. I'm driving tonight to pick them up."

Penelope's mouth hadn't stopped hanging open since he started talking. "Wow, Nick."

"That's right, girlie. You and Havoc are part of a team now." He beamed a grin as she threw her arms around his neck. "Now all we have to do is convince Captain Stubborn to get to work training these dogs, fill out some paperwork, get everyone registered under the nonprofit seal, and we're ready to save lives."

Enrique frowned at Penelope. "Still able to do your job, though, right?"

Her father answered for her. "Of course she can. My little girl can do anything she sets her mind to."

The resemblance between father and daughter—same bright eyes and dark brown hair, same glowing smiles and tallish, lanky builds—struck Jay. If they ever had kids, he hoped they looked just like her.

It took a full second for him to realize he'd just contemplated kids with a woman. He waited for fear and panic, but it never came. He smiled. Kids with Penelope would be a goal now. Further down the line, of course.

Jay couldn't think of a better partner to have, both in life and in the field. She was strong, determined, and a great problem-solver. With Penelope by his side, there was nothing to be anxious about anymore because she always managed to find a way to fix things. And that's why he could see a future he wanted to reach out and grab.

Jay watched Penelope dancing the Cupid something or other with her uncle. She laughed and clutched his shoulder as he tried to show her the steps. Watching her happy made him smile.

Her father sat to his left with a grim look on his face. "I know you and my daughter have been spending time together."

Uh-oh. This didn't sound like it was headed anywhere good. If this guy tried to warn him away from Penelope, he didn't know what he would do. "Yes, sir."

"She's a handful. Has been since she was this high." He reached to his side and held his hand a couple feet from the floor. "But what you've done for her—the confidence she has now—"

"I don't know how to thank you. She was floundering. Not that she isn't sharp, but sometimes when I looked at her, I could see something missing. Something I couldn't give her." He took a long drink from his gin and tonic. "Today, I didn't see it. All I saw was my girl beaming. She carries herself different."

Jay couldn't take the credit. "She did it all herself, sir. She trained and worked hard. She made a mistake, but she owned it and picked herself up and fixed it. All of it." He shrugged and stared at her for a moment longer before he met her father's intense gaze. "I'd like to take credit, but it was all her."

"I think she might see it differently, but I couldn't go back to New York without telling you how grateful I am." He held out his hand for Jay to shake.

"Thank you, sir. I just want you to know I love her, and I'm going to do everything I can to make her happy." Oh, Lord. Where had all that come from? Even as he had the thought, he realized the truth behind the words. He truly wanted to do everything for her, be by her side, love her until the day he died. Although, rather than scare her back to New York with his intensity, he planned to keep those bits of information to himself for a while.

From the dance floor, Penelope crooked her finger at him as her uncle weaved his way back to the table. “Careful, son. That girl doesn’t have an ounce of rhythm in her entire body. Must get that from her mother’s side.”

Penelope’s uncle and her father laughed as Jay made his way to the dance floor. “Give a girl a spin around the dance floor?” She could have asked him to walk on his hands over a bed of hot coals and he would’ve been powerless to refuse.

He pulled her in close. “You bet.” She laced her fingers around his neck, and he lowered his head for one of those chaste kisses she turned into something a little less sweet.

“My uncle likes you.” She stepped on his toe. “Sorry.”

He didn’t mind. “I like them, too.”

“I saw you and my dad with your heads all bent together. What was that about?” She tilted her head and licked her lips.

“Vixen.”

“Tell me.” Nothing in the world made his heart beat in quite the same way her smile affected him.

Jay groaned and chewed the corner of his lip. “He told me I wasn’t good enough for you.”

Her eyes flashed and she stopped swaying in his arms, which was probably a good thing since his toes were already aching. “He did what?” She tried to pull away, but he held on tight.

“Settle down, Rocky. I’m teasing.” She relaxed in his

arms. "He just told me how happy you look." No point in telling her the rest.

"I am happy. Thanks to you and this town and all these people who just opened their doors and let me in." She ran her hand over the back of his neck. "Mostly you."

"Yeah?" Hearing she felt the same way made his heart hammer. "I didn't think I would ever be ready to go back out on a call or feel so content again. It was like I was… I don't know. Lost, I think. I mean I made it through every day, but you make everything easier."

"You were kind of grumpy when I met you." She nodded.

"I met you less than a minute after you set fire to the check station and all the GPS equipment." That day seemed like years ago rather than the six weeks that had passed since then.

"You hugged me that day. You remember?"

Of course he did. He'd committed every minute of their time together to memory. "I do."

"And you hated me."

"Disapproved. I didn't hate you." Her laugh, a little loud, a little long, rang through his chest straight to his gut.

"You hated me. It's okay. You love me now." She pulled him down for another kiss and he could have lingered there all night had she not pulled away.

When the song ended, they walked back to the table. "Where's Gramps tonight?"

"Poker with Carter and the guys down at the grocery store." Jay chuckled. "When it's Ray's turn to host, they set up the table in the produce section."

Uncle Enrique's head turned, and Penelope's dad took

new interest. “Poker?” Enrique nudged his brother’s shoulder. “You hear that? Poker game in town.” He pushed his chair back at the exact moment Penelope’s father stood. “Tell me. How does a guy get to this grocery store?”

Jay smiled at Penelope and she shrugged. “They play for real money, Tio.”

He held up his hands and laughed. “What am I, a pauper? Lead on, young man, and I’ll tell you the story of the time Penelope got caught sneaking out in high school.”

Penelope sighed. “So, that’s how it is?” She turned to Jay. “I didn’t get caught sneaking out. It was the sneaking back in that got me in trouble.”

“Funny story.”

Penelope’s dad shook his head. “I like the one where she ran your front-end loader through the shed wall.”

“Papá! Whose side are you on?”

They could tell all the stories they wanted, and he hoped they did. There was nothing about Penelope Ramos that he didn’t want to know and nothing they could say that would rattle his feelings for her.

Jay Gosling loved Penelope Ramos and that was all there was to it.

# *Epilogue*

Penelope clicked the remote control and the TV went off, plunging her and Jay into darkness. They'd been dating for almost six months and every day was better than the one before. She snuggled into his side.

"Are you ready to move in with me yet?" Jay nudged her with his chin.

She stared at the curtain billowing in front of her open window and the sliver of moonlight that cast a triangle onto the floor next to the bed. Move in with Jay? "Yeah."

He sat up, levering her away from his chest and bending her back at an unnatural angle. "Really?"

She'd turned him down so many times, needing the time to get herself settled into her new life. Of course, having a job and a place to stay made it easy, especially after Lori offered her a yearlong lease. Her former coworker planned on using the extra income to book a European vacation.

Penelope also hadn't wanted to rush into living with a new man. And after rejecting Jay's offer so many times, she figured eventually Jay would quit asking. But he hadn't.

She straightened and rested her head on her fists

next to him. The heat from his body warmed her and she wanted nothing more than to touch him, but she kept her fists on top of one another. "I think so. Unless you're just teasing me with asking." She smiled in the darkness until he flipped on the bedside lamp. She snapped her eyes shut and waited for them to adjust to the light before she looked up at him.

"You're serious." She nodded, waiting for the moment he believed her, the hug that would follow. "Not that I'm complaining, but what changed your mind?"

"I don't know. Today, saying yes felt right."

"But yesterday it didn't?" He chewed the corner of his mouth. It was a tell that he honestly found this situation befuddling. He had a lot of tells that clued her into his feelings, and she'd learned and memorized every single one.

"Nope."

"All we did was watch TV. We haven't even had sex. I don't understand."

The old Penelope would have gotten huffy, maybe chewed him out for questioning something he'd apparently waited a long time to hear. But tonight, she would let him have his doubts because the end reward would be so worth it. "Jay, I love you. I love the nights when we're all cuddles and happy times, and I love the ones when we fall asleep watching *The Tonight Show.* I don't love the ones where we're apart. There's just no good reason I can think of anymore. I want to spend every night with you. From now on."

"Yeah?" His smile said everything she wanted to hear.

"If you still want me there." She pulled her lips between her teeth. Even though he'd asked, she wanted to hear the words because maybe he'd asked out of habit, never thinking she would say yes. Dear God, she hoped that wasn't true. She hoped he wanted her with him as badly as she wanted to be there.

He turned on his side to run his finger from her shoulder blade to her tailbone through the tank top she'd been hoping he would get around to peeling off her. "Penelope, I want nothing more in my life than for you to live with me. I want to wake up with *you* every morning and sleep with *you* every night. I've never wanted anything more."

He kissed her shoulder, then her neck until she turned to face him, and he dropped a kiss on her nose. "Good."

And as if he'd been summoned to the room, Havoc nosed the door open and jumped on the bed between them. "Bud, we gotta work on your timing." But Jay patted Havoc's head without shoving him onto the floor, laughing when Havoc put his head down on the pillow and closed his eyes.

Penelope chuckled. Charlie mentioned Mayhem did the same thing. Her best friend was the handler to the most stubborn of the siblings. But according to Nick, Mayhem was the best suited for human-remains detection, a job suited for both SAR and the police department.

Havoc had begun to snore, and as much as Penelope loved that dog, she was seriously considering sending him out of the room. Nick complained Havoc's sister, Calamity, snored so much that the ranger had to keep the dog at the other end of his house at night.

Before she had the chance to move Havoc, Jay's cell rang.

"Hello...yeah...all right. We'll be right there." He

swiped the screen and turned to Penelope. “We’re being called out. You ready?”

With Jay by her side, there was absolutely nothing Penelope couldn’t do. “Let’s go.”

Hand in hand, they walked out the door with Havoc.

* * * * *

*Reviews are an invaluable tool when it comes to spreading the word about great reads. Please consider leaving an honest review for this or any of Carina Press’s other titles that you’ve read on your favorite retailer or review site.*

*To find out about other books by Paris Wynters or to be alerted to new releases, sign up for her monthly newsletter at t.co/LY85lqtaLK?amp=1.*

# *Acknowledgements*

First and foremost, thank you to my Heavenly Father for blessing me beyond all measure.

Thank you to my family for your support and encouragement. Thank you to my amazing agent, Tricia Skinner, for always believing in me. Thank you to John Jacobson for believing in this book and for pushing me with your edits and guidance to make this story the best it could possibly be.

A huge thank-you to Tricia Lynne, Emily Hornburg, Gwynne Jackson, and my fellow Long Island Romance Writers group who helped me revise this novel over and over again.

And most importantly, thank you to my search and rescue team, to Gwen and Heidi, who push me daily to become a better handler. And to K-9 Vader. You are gone but will never be forgotten. You and Gwen set the standard I hold myself and my dogs to. You are missed every day by all of us.

## *About the Author*

Paris Wynters writes steamy and sweet love stories that celebrate our diverse world. She is the author of the Navy Seals of Little Creek and Three Keys Ranch series. She is represented by Tricia Skinner at Fuse Literary.

When she's not dreaming up stories, Paris can be found assisting with disasters and helping to find missing people as a Search and Rescue K-9 handler. Paris resides on Long Island in New York along with her family. For fun, Paris enjoys video games, hockey, and diving into new experiences like flying planes and taking trapeze lessons. Paris is also a graduate of Loyola University Chicago.

You can find Paris at her website, www.pariswynters.com, on Twitter at www.Twitter.com/pariswynters, and on Instagram at www.Instagram.com/pariswynters.

SPECIAL EXCERPT FROM

*Navy SEAL Jack Daniels is back home after a bomb left him scarred with only his dog, Dakota, for company. Nichole Masters is on a losing streak with men and her rescue puppy won't get in line. Jack offers to help her with her dog, but when Nichole feels like she's being watched, he's the only person she can turn to.*

*Read on for a sneak preview of* Operation K-9 Brothers *by Sandra Owens, available now from Carina Press.*

"The first rule to remember is that you're the pack leader."

"Okay. How do I do that?" Nichole asked. Jack was standing next to her in her backyard, and his masculine, woodsy scent was a distraction to the point it was hard to pay attention.

He'd followed her home, and they had ordered a pizza. While eating, she'd told him what Trevor had done, and she had the feeling Jack regretted letting Trevor off so easily. She'd never expected to have a real-life warrior on her side, but here one was in the flesh. And what nice flesh it was.

What impressed her the most was that Jack hadn't used his fists to get his point across to Trevor. If it had been Lane there today, her ex-boyfriend wouldn't have been

CAREXPSOOK9B0621

satisfied until Trevor was bleeding and begging for mercy. Because of Lane's violent tendencies, she had grown to despise any kind of fighting. But Lane was history that she had no wish to revisit, so she pushed thoughts of him away. If only the man himself would stay away.

"I'll teach you that as we go along."

"Teach me?" What were they talking about?

A smile curved his lips and amusement lit his blue eyes. "Where's your mind, Nichole?"

*On how good you smell. Those blue eyes of yours. Kind of wondering just what things you could teach me.* She gave herself a mental shake. "Um, my mind wandered a bit. Sorry."

"Mmm-hmm," he murmured, his smile morphing into a sexy smirk.

"Ah, you were saying?" She was sure she was blushing, which only confirmed that he was right as to where her thoughts had wandered to.

"Since my mama taught me it's impolite to embarrass a lady, I won't ask what's going on in that beautiful head of yours."

Oh boy. Another sexy smirk like that and her panties were going to melt off without any help from her. Jack Daniels was lady-parts lethal, something she'd best remember.